A MOTHER'S SIN

Also by Lynda Page and available from Headline

Evie
Annie
Josie
Peggie
And One For Luck
Just By Chance
At The Toss Of A Sixpence
Any Old Iron
Now Or Never
In For A Penny
All Or Nothing
A Cut Above
Out With The Old
Against The Odds
No Going Back
Whatever It Takes
A Lucky Break
For What It's Worth
Onwards And Upwards
The Sooner The Better

A MOTHER'S SIN

Lynda Page

headline

First published in 2007 by
HEADLINE PUBLISHING GROUP

1

Cataloguing in Publication Data is available from the British Library

978 0 7553 2834 5

Typeset in StempelGaramond by Palimpsest Book Production Limited,
Grangemouth, Stirlingshire

Printed and bound in Great Britain by
Clays Ltd, St Ives plc

Headline's policy is to use papers that are natural, renewable and
recyclable products and made from wood grown in sustainable forests.
The logging and manufacturing processes are expected to conform
to the environmental regulations of the country of origin.

HEADLINE PUBLISHING GROUP
A division of Hachette Livre UK Ltd
338 Euston Road
London NW1 3BH

www.headline.co.uk

For my Great-Aunty Madge (Marjorie Pearson)

I did not realise until I had nearly finished this book that my character Madge is just like you are, warm, caring, funny, loyal, would go to the ends of the earth for the ones you love, and that's why I subconsciously named her after you. The only difference between you both is how you earned your money.

This book is for you with all my love.

Your great-niece

Lynda

Acknowledgements

With very special thanks to Graham Corneila.

Sometimes a misspent youth can be invaluable for a researching writer and I am grateful you agreed to dilvulge yours to me, enabling me to bring to life the area and characters in this book.

CHAPTER ONE

The ferocious and unexpected blow across her face had Diane Kirby shrieking out in pain and shock, reeling back to land hard against an unyielding brick wall.

'I'll ask you once more, and if yer don't come clean, I'll beat it out of yer. Now, is the woman me dad was going on about anything to do with you or not?' her assailant demanded savagely.

Dee stared back at him. Her background could not have remained a secret forever, and she'd had every intention of telling him, only not yet, she'd thought. Maybe sometime in the future when their relationship was more settled, she'd told herself, and hopefully by then he'd feel enough for her that it wouldn't matter to him.

She realised now she'd made a mistake. Kevin Coombs was a well-made man of twenty-four, fashionably dressed in tight blue denims, white tee-shirt and a leather jacket. He wore long pointed winkle-pickers on his feet, and his hair was stiffly Brylcremed into a DA. He was not over tall at five foot nine, but his muscles were toned from working as a labourer in a builder's yard. If the force of the slap he'd just delivered was anything to go by, she had a good idea what she'd be in for when she responded to his question. But Kevin did not frighten Dee. She belonged to a world where violence in all its guises was part of everyday life. She had faced far more intimidating situations at the hands of worse bullyboys than Kevin, and lived to tell the tale. Sticking her chin in the air defiantly, she gave him his answer.

'Yes, I am. She's my mother.'

His handsome face twisting in disgust, Kevin spat incredulously, 'Your mother? *You're* the daughter of a filthy whore called

1

Back Alley Sal!' Slapping one hand to his forehead, he exclaimed furiously, 'Jesus Christ, I can't believe I've been associating with the daughter of a prossie. Me dad said she's the lowest of the low, the sort that'd do 'ote with any bloke, anywhere, for a couple of coppers.' A momentary expression of regret crossed his face. 'You're a good-looking bird, Dee, I can't deny that. You're different from the others I've been out with. I thought me luck was in when you agreed to go out with me, thought I'd found someone special in you. But if I'd have known who you really were, I wouldn't have touched you with a barge pole.' His eyes darkened then. 'I just hope, for your sake, that none of me friends have found out what yer mam does for a living. You'll be sorry if they have, believe me. Anyone at work either. I'd never live this down . . . never!'

Pacing back and forth, he continued, 'I just thank God it was only me dad we bumped into the night before last, on his way to the Crow's Nest. He talks a load of cobblers at the best of times, and pure bollocks when he's had a skinful, but when I got home that night and he mentioned that you looked like a well-known prossie . . . well, at first I laughed at the very idea of it. Then later, in bed, it struck me that in the two weeks I've been seeing yer as me girlfriend, I've never heard you mention yer family in any way whatsoever. And you never let me see you home either, always insisted you caught the bus even though I've got me motorbike. That got me wondering if me dad was talking drivel as usual or not.' Kevin's lip curled. 'Well, seems for once he wasn't.'

He paused and stared at her for several long moments then blurted out, 'Follow in Mummy's footsteps, do yer, Dee? Have yer been seeing me on yer nights off, or do you go to work after we say goodnight? Or maybe you thought I was the sort who wouldn't turn a hair at having a prossie for a girlfriend . . . or a wife even, did yer?' A sudden thought struck him. 'Oh, was that yer plan then, Dee? Hoping I'd make an honest woman of you and then yer could give up selling yer body for a living.' Shaking his fist at her, he hissed, 'Well, yer plan failed, you dirty slag. Now you'd just better hope I never see you around these

2

parts again 'cos if I do, I'll make it me business to make you very sorry.'

He turned to storm off then but stopped abruptly and spun back to look at her, a lustful glint sparkling in his eyes. 'How far do you go for a handful of coppers?' Flashing a look up and down the alley they were in to make sure it was still deserted, Kevin shoved his hand into his pocket, pulling out a handful of loose change which he held towards her. 'Seems a shame to waste the opportunity. This is the sort of place your sort do business in, ain't it? What sort of a good time will you give me for this much?'

Then, before Dee knew what was happening, he'd replaced the money and launched himself on her. One hand was inside her coat, groping hard for her breast, the other wrenching up her skirt. And all the time he was making disgusting suggestions in her ear.

Dee fought with all her might to push him from her but was no match for a strong man intent on having his way. There was only one avenue of escape open to her and she prayed it would work. Raising her knee, she thrust it as hard as she could into his groin.

He yelped in excruciating pain. Doubling over and clutching at his crotch, he screamed, 'You fucking bitch!' His face was tight with fury and pain. 'Think you can make a monkey out of me, do yer? Well . . .'

But before he could launch himself back at her, Dee had spun on her heel and sped off into the night.

CHAPTER TWO

Forty-year-old Magdalene Feeny's heavily made-up eyes had been on the look out for a potential client since she'd ventured out at six o'clock. It was well past eight-thirty by now and she feared this evening would prove as disappointing as most since the end of the festive season three weeks ago. Thankfully Christmas and New Year's Eve had both turned out more lucratively for her. On those two nights Madge hadn't even managed to slip off to the local for a reviving rum and black before she was being commandeered for her services again by yet another drunken punter. Most of them were so far gone by then it was questionable if they'd even remember the next morning they'd been with the likes of her the night before, let alone manage to perform the deed they'd been paying for.

Despite the urge to share her seasonal good fortune by treating her colleagues to a drink down the local, as a veteran in her line of work, well aware that for herself lean times far outweighed profitable ones, Madge had wisely resisted. Now her seasonal gains were keeping the rent paid on her miserable lodgings. But if things didn't pick up soon . . .

She began to wonder whether she was wasting her time being out tonight at all. Anyone with any sense would be huddled inside around the fire, even the types she was on the look out for. It was certainly well below freezing, or felt like it was. She could hardly feel her own feet. Every breath she exhaled was hanging on the icy air like clouds of thick smoke. She had a sudden vision of some poor sod on his way to work in the morning, finding her lifeless body frozen to the lamp-post she was leaning against. But, regardless, going back to her miserable

5

lodgings – the state of which was so dire even the most desperate of punters would turn up his nose at doing business there – and possibly losing out on earnings was not an option. Moving to a place that was always busy, regardless of the weather, was. She should try outside the railway station, despite risking verbal and possibly physical abuse from the regulars there who felt they had sole rights over that patch. She knew they wouldn't think twice about invading hers if the need arose, though. All was fair in love and war, as the saying went.

Taking a last drag on her Park Drive cigarette, she flicked it away and was preparing to make a move when her keen eyes spotted a figure emerging from the icy mist further down the street. Hope surged that her luck was about to change.

Quickly giving her mane of newly henna-ed hair a tease out with her fingers, she moistened her pillar-box-red lips with her tongue while simultaneously adjusting her full breasts inside her shabby bra. They bulged enticingly out of the top of the cheap, low-cut blouse she wore under the only decent item of clothing she possessed, her fur coat, albeit it was showing signs of age now. Madge hitched up her tight black skirt to above her knees and prepared to approach her potential client, only to have her hopes dashed as it registered with her that the figure advancing towards her was female. Sighing despondently, she was about to head off in the opposite direction when recognition struck.

A broad beam of delight splitting her face, she waved and called out, 'Hiya, lovey.' When she received no response her smile faded to be replaced by a frown. The newcomer seemed to be deeply distressed. As quickly as her down-trodden red patent stilettos would allow, Madge hurried over to join her.

'Oi, gel, what on earth is ailing you?' she asked in a voice roughened by years of chain-smoking.

A deeply distracted Dee jumped in alarm. Fear flooded her face at the thought that Kevin had caught up with her and was going to resume his attack. Fists clenched, she began wildly flailing her arms, shouting, 'Stay away from me . . .'

'Oi, Dee, it's me – Madge,' the older woman cried, catching hold of the girl's arms to calm her and stop her hitting out.

Dee stared blindly at her for a long moment before recognition dawned and she sagged in mortal relief. 'Oh, thank God it's you, Aunty Madge.'

'Who did yer think it was?' the older woman demanded, releasing her grip on Dee's arms. Then she added, 'More to the point, who was yer worried it was?'

'Eh? Oh . . . no one. No one, Aunty Madge,' came the dismissive reply.

Madge looked knowingly at her and snapped, 'Do I look like I came up the Clyde in a banana boat? Someone's got you in a right state. Is it them louts that hang round the chip shop? Have they been . . .'

'No, no, Aunty Madge,' Dee cut in. 'I haven't passed by the chip shop tonight.' She plastered a smile on her lips and said lightly, 'Honestly, there's nothing wrong. It's just this weather. It's eerie out tonight, isn't it? All this mist.'

'Stop taking me for a bleeding idiot, Dee. Something's upset you. It's as plain as a pikestaff you've bin crying. I might not be yer real aunty by blood but I care as much about you as if I was. As if you was me own daughter, in fact. I was at yer birth and I was the first to hold yer, don't forget.' She looked thoughtful. 'Oh, you was off to see that new young man of yours tonight, wasn't yer? This isn't summat to do with him, is it? What's he done then? Yer'd better tell me, Dee, or we'll stand here all night until you do. And if I miss out on a punter meantime, be warned, I'll be looking to you to stump up the money I missed out on.'

Dee knew Madge's threat to be an idle one but was also aware that the older woman could not afford to lose out on a possible earner, however small the amount she'd make off him. Sighing in resignation, she began, 'Kevin . . . that's my new boyfriend's name . . . well, he *was* my boyfriend, he's not any more. He'd probably spit on me if we crossed paths now. Well, he . . .'

'Gave you a good wallop, by the looks of it,' Madge cut in, suddenly noticing the angry red mark on her cheek. Pulling Dee to her, she hugged her protectively. 'Yer don't need to tell me, honey. By the state of yer, I can guess. This new fella of yours found out who yer mother is and wasn't a happy chappy, was he?'

'It was awful, Aunty Madge,' Dee sobbed.

Madge's expression was grim. 'Mmm, I expect it was. It's 1959 and the powers-that-be keep telling us we live in a modern world. We've machines now that do our washing, contraptions that suck muck up off our floors, cars to save our legs . . . yet how people see yer mam's and my occupation hasn't changed since time began. Prostitutes were seen as the scum of the earth then, and they still are.' She said harshly, 'Thieves and murderers are treated with more respect than us, though when all's said and done we're only providing a service.'

Her heart went out to this pretty young girl in her arms. Dee was trying to make a life for herself beyond the one she had been born into, but it seemed her background was always going to be a barrier to that.

Madge flashed a quick look up and down the street, glad for once to see it deserted so she could justify to herself making this suggestion.

'I could do with a thaw out, ducky, so how about you inviting me to yours for a quick snifter, if yer mam's got any dregs of medicinal left in her bottles. Or I'll settle for a cuppa.'

Dee knew the reason behind this suggestion. Pulling away from her embrace, and despite her need for company, she smiled appreciatively and replied, 'You're welcome any time, Aunty Madge, but I know you're only after an invite because you're worried about me. But I'll be fine. It's not like this is the first time something like this has happened to me, and I suspect it won't be the last. I'll get over it, like I usually do.'

But before she could stop herself Dee's face puckered and tears started to roll down it. 'I really liked Kevin, though. I hoped he would like me enough not to be bothered about what me mam does for a living, once I finally plucked up the courage to tell him.' Wiping away her tears with her hand, she shook her head sadly. 'I was stupid to hope that, wasn't I?' She took a deep breath and with forced brightness said, 'Look, I don't want you to risk losing the chance to earn some money so I'll leave you to it. See you soon.'

Before Madge could stop her, Dee had given her an affectionate peck on her thickly rouged cheek and hurried off.

Feeling deeply concerned, Madge stared after her. This latest incident was just another in the long line of setbacks she knew Dee had suffered throughout her life. People behaved so harshly to her once they discovered her mother's profession. Although it grieved her to know how hurt Dee had been on each occasion, it grieved her even more to realise there was absolutely nothing to be done to end her suffering, unless people's attitudes towards prostitutes suddenly changed and Dee was spared the stigma of being the daughter of one. Madge doubted that would ever happen, though, or not in her own lifetime, at any rate. It worried her to think that Dee was returning to an empty house tonight. At times like this a woman needed the company of another sympathetic female, and if nothing else Madge could have offered her that. And she really could do with a warm. Hopefully by the time she ventured back out on her beat, trade would have improved. She could live in hope, at any rate.

Thrusting her hands deep into the pockets of her shabby fur coat, she tottered after Dee.

After shouldering open the swollen, flaking back door, Dee let herself inside the dilapidated two-up, two-down terrace house she shared with her mother on grimy Lower Hastings Street. It stood a stone's throw from the busy thoroughfare of the London Road with its mainline railway station, and a fifteen-minute walk away from the centre of Leicester. For a hundred years this area had housed a mixture of the lower working class and those with criminal tendencies.

Shoving the door shut behind her, she shuddered violently. It seemed to be colder inside the house than out, if that were possible. Still in her coat, Dee walked through into the small back room and immediately saw the reason why. Her mother had not banked up the fire before leaving. Her eyes settled then on the tatty oak gate-legged table. Dee herself had tidied up the remains of their meal before going out on her ill-fated date that evening. Now it was littered with numerous items her mother had used to tart herself up with, as well as a used glass and a tin holding the stubs of the cigarettes she had consumed during the process.

The houses in Lower Hastings Street were still waiting to have electricity installed – it was generally agreed by the locals that they'd be demolished before that ever happened – and lighting was provided by smelly old gas mantles. Dee had just lit the ones in the back room when she heard the door open and shut. Before she could wonder if it was her mother returning home early for some reason, Madge burst in.

'Bloody hell, gel, you can't half shift when you want to. You should see about representing Britain in the next Olympic Games, I'm sure you'd get a medal. Move yerself and let me see the fire, lovey.' Her eyes settled on the dying embers in the old-fashioned grate and she exclaimed in disappointment, 'Oh, there ain't no fire! Well, not what I'd call one.'

Dee might have known Madge would never leave her on her own in an emotional crisis. The older woman was the closest person she had to a friend. In the past any potential friendships with her peers had soon been nipped in the bud by parents forbidding their children to be in any way associated with the daughter of a known prostitute. The couple of friends Dee socialised with now, whom she'd met through work, were not aware of her background. She dreaded to think what the outcome would be if they found out. It would most likely be a re-run of what had happened this evening with Kevin, and then once again she'd be ostracised, cast out from society like a leper. Despite that, though, and the fact that even thinking of charging men for the use of her own body totally appalled Dee, she did not condemn her mother or Madge or any other prostitute for what they did. In her opinion they were earning their living the best way they knew, and she admired them for that. Having lived amongst them all her life, she knew what a harsh and brutal occupation it could be. Few of the women escaped unscathed, mentally or physically, by the experiences they suffered in the trade.

'I'll have it stoked up in a jiffy,' Dee reassured Madge, going over to pick up the coal bucket which thankfully she had filled herself before going out that evening. She'd known her mother wouldn't, not while she had her daughter on hand to see to such chores.

As Dee busied herself, Madge poured herself a very generous measure of sherry from a three-quarter-full bottle she had been delighted to find on the dining table. It was a half-pint beer glass, purloined from the local pub and with a Guinness transfer on the side of it. Della herself had already used it for her own drink earlier while readying herself for the night ahead, but Madge wasn't fussy. She settled herself in a threadbare armchair by the side of the fireplace. Setting the glass down on the hearth, she unbuttoned her coat and then leaned over to ease off her tight-fitting shoes and give her frozen feet a vigorous rub to coax life back into them. Happy she wasn't going to lose her toes from frost bite, she retrieved her drink and took a large gulp from it while casting a glance around the room.

The expensive paper, bought in more affluent times, on the walls was now dingy with age and peeling off in places to reveal cracked plaster beneath. Damp patches were steadily creeping across it too. What furniture there was had seen far better days, but apart from the cluttered table it was neat and tidy enough. Madge knew that was all down to Dee as Della Kirby was no housekeeper. Now the girl was struggling to restart the fire in the grate. Madge saw the flickering flames dancing behind the sheet of newspaper Dee was holding up across the front of the grate, to create an updraught. As the fire flickered back into life, her own face lit up. 'On a night like this, that's a sight for sore eyes, Dee, me darlin'. Can't beat a real fire, can yer? I hardly get any heat out of the gas one in my lodgings, and it costs me a fortune to run. The way things are business-wise at the moment, I can't afford to have it on as much as I'd like. Now that's done, you are going to join me in a drink, ain't yer?'

Dee glanced across at the bottle of sherry on the table. She wasn't averse to a tipple now and again, had in fact been tiddly on quite a few occasions in the past, but she wasn't overly fond of sherry, especially not the cheap out-of-a-barrel type her mother bought from the local off licence. It definitely wasn't the best Cyprus that the licensee proclaimed it to be and had a tendency to upset her stomach the next day. But, regardless, it was all that was on offer and maybe just a drop would help to raise her spirits.

'Just a little one,' she agreed. Folding up the sheet of scorched newspaper for later use, she straightened up. Knowing the only glass they possessed was in Madge's clutches, she added, 'I'll fetch a cup.'

A few minutes later they had both taken off their coats as the fire was now throwing out a decent amount of heat. Madge stretched out her stockinged feet comfortably on the hearth and studied her young friend. Dee was looking lovely tonight in black figure-hugging pants and a bright yellow thick-knit sweater that covered her shapely backside. A wide black belt encircled her trim waist and she wore flat black pumps on her feet. Her long dark hair was swept up in a fashionable pony tail with a fringe across her proud brow. She had on just a trace of make-up, which Madge felt she didn't really need to enhance her looks as she was pretty enough without it. Pity all her efforts to look her best had been wasted on a man who'd bullied her because he didn't agree with the way her mother earned a living.

'Sherry doing the trick, is it?' Madge commented, with a smile for the girl.

Dee managed to smile back. 'Yes, it certainly is. I feel tons better now.'

Madge knew that was not true. Dee might be smiling but her eyes held the look of someone who had resigned themselves to the fact that their life was never going to get any better than it was right now. Despite still wanting the full low-down on what had transpired that night, she didn't feel that reliving it would help Dee. Taking another draft of her drink, she said, 'I wonder if yer mam's faring any better than me tonight? I noticed when I was on me way to my patch that she wasn't working her own. Did she tell you where she was off to?'

'Mam never discusses her work with me on principle, you know that, Aunty Madge. She'll never forgive me for refusing to follow in her footsteps, like she did her mam and her gran.'

Madge looked at her thoughtfully. If the child she herself had once carried had turned out to be female, then having experienced what she had over her years in this line, she would have encouraged that girl to do anything but, by way of earning her livelihood. 'Well, I think she must have got the message by now that yer going to follow yer own path,' Madge said reassuringly.

Dee gave a heavy sigh. 'Whether she has or hasn't, she won't let up. Every chance she gets, she has a go at me. She makes me feel I'm a traitor to the family business.'

'You can't do what you can't do, and that's all there is to say, Dee,' Madge told her with conviction.

How Dee wished her mother could share these views!

With her voice heavy with regret, Madge added, 'If I had my time over again, I'd do anything but what I do now.'

Dee eyed her quizzically. She had known this woman all her life, spending a lot of time in her company at first until a few years back Madge's visits to their house began to grow less frequent. Now she only called by occasionally for a quick chat with Dee when she knew for certain Della was not at home. Unlike others in her line whose experiences had embittered them, like they had Della, Madge still managed to retain her kind and caring nature. As she looked at her it suddenly surprised Dee to realise just how little she knew about Madge's background. She found herself wanting to learn it now. 'What made you go on the game in the first place, Aunty Madge?'

What indeed? Madge's thoughts drifted back to the moment the Kirbys had first come into her life . . .

Madge had just turned fifteen. The night was a bitter one, similar to tonight, but at the time the weather was the last thing on her mind. Sitting distraught on a park bench, she'd been contemplating how best to kill herself, running through all the scenarios she was aware of for a quick and painless demise. She'd been so consumed by misery she hadn't noticed the clack of high heels approaching or the presence of someone sitting down next to her. It was only a light punch delivered to her arm that had alerted her to the fact that she had company.

'I said, have yer got a light?'

'Oh . . . no, I don't smoke,' she'd said to the young, gaudily dressed woman sitting beside her.

Her companion's face fell in disappointment. 'Don't yer? Oh, blast. I've just dropped me box of Vestas in a puddle and I'm gasping for a fag.' She spotted a man hurrying by and jumped up, running across to him while calling out, 'Oi, mister, got a light?' The man having obliged and also been charmed out of his box of matches, she returned to sit down again, dragging deeply on her cigarette. 'Oh, that's better,' she said, taking the smoke down into her lungs. Then she looked searchingly at Madge. 'What's up with you then, 'cos yer've a face like a corpse? Boyfriend chucked yer, I take it?'

Madge wished it was that simple.

Before she could make any response, her companion knowingly added, 'Let me guess. Yer pregnant and the father don't want to know? Well, you ain't on yer own 'cos so am I.'

Madge gawped at her. 'You are?'

The other woman nodded. 'Not quite sure how long. Coming up for two months, I think. No idea who the father is . . . could be anyone. You keeping yours?' she asked matter-of-factly.

How could Madge possibly do that? Her staunchly Catholic family had disowned her, calling her a liar and a blasphemous one at that when she had finally broken down under great duress and admitted to them who the father of her child was. Her mother had guessed her condition when she hadn't had the task of boiling clean her daughter's sanitary cloths for over a month. But it couldn't be the priest! They'd all refused to believe he had lured her into his vestry while she'd been helping to clean the church brasses, and then raped her. He was a man of the cloth, pledged to abstain from bodily desires in the service of God. Father O'Flannagan was an upstanding member of the community, well respected by all his congregation. Madge had to be hiding the real truth about the culprit. It was more than likely a youth she'd met through work at the local Co-op. Ashamed to admit she had given herself to him, she was obviously seeking instead to put the blame on an innocent man, in an effort to redeem herself in the eyes of others.

Madge's reward for sticking to the truth was to be thrown out on the streets without a by your leave, with only the clothes on her back and a few shillings in her pocket. How many other innocent young women Father O'Flannagan had abused in such a way she didn't know. All she was sure of was that he had done it to her, leaving her feeling dirty and defiled and carrying the results of his inability to honour his vow to God. And after his rape of her, he hadn't even bothered to warn her to keep her mouth shut, supremely confident in the knowledge that she wouldn't be believed if she did dare to denounce him.

It wasn't the baby's fault how it had been conceived, and Madge bore it no malice because she'd always wanted to be a mother . . . but not like this, with no husband to give the child his name or provide for it. As matters stood this child would be subjected to a life of direst poverty, worse even than she had been raised in herself. Her own mother had aged before her time trying to house, feed and clothe her seven children, husband and herself on the paltry wage her spouse brought home from his job as a farmhand. And how would Madge's child fare when people discovered who its father was?

'I take it yer not?' said her companion.

'Sorry?'

'Keeping the baby. I ain't either. Got an appointment to get rid of it tomorrow. Me mam ain't none too happy about the money we're having to stump up, though. She reckons the rubber johnnie company should foot the bill, for selling faulty goods.' She saw the confused expression on Madge's face then. 'Yer know, French letters . . . Durex? Don't you know nothing?' She took a long drag from her cigarette. 'What's yer name anyroad?'

'Magdalene Feeny. People call me Madge.'

'Feeny . . . That's Irish, ain't it? Catholic too, I bet. You lot don't believe in contraception, do yer? I can never understand meself how that Pope of yours thinks he's got the right to decide that a woman's duty is to give birth to as many sprogs as she can, whether she can feed and clothe the little blighters or not.

Don't believe in God meself. Think someone made him up by way of conning money out of poor people, to fund their own rich lifestyle. Well, you go to any church and before you've sung a word a collection plate is being stuck under yer nose – and it's silver they're after, not coppers. Not that I've ever bin inside one, it's just what I've heard. So, when's your abortion then?'

Madge gawped at her, totally shocked by the very idea she would contemplate such a thing. 'Oh, I couldn't even consider it. God would punish me! I'd end up in hell for ending a life.'

Her companion gave a sardonic chuckle. 'And hell's not where you are now then? I take it yer family chucked you out when they found out you was up the duff. I suppose I'm lucky me mam didn't me, when she found out. But then, I'm worth too much money to her. She never stops telling me that the only reason she kept me and didn't put me up for adoption as a baby was 'cos I was a girl and had the earning potential to keep her in her old age. Me mam had three abortions before she fell with me. She didn't get rid of me 'cos apparently me dad was high up in the Council in them days. She used her pregnancy to get money out of him, threatening she'd tell his wife and his bosses, and we all know what that means – even ignorant Irish like you! So she was on a nice little earner for a while, 'til just before I was born he died of a heart attack. If I'd been a boy, I'd have been handed over to the authorities straight away, but as me gran pointed out, gels are an insurance policy for your old age in our line of work. I don't need to think about planning for me own old age, though, not for a few years yet. Anyway, it's my guess you was sitting here thinking of ways to kill yourself. Isn't that just as punishable by God in your eyes, then?'

'Well . . . yes, it is.'

'Seems to me you're going to end up in hell either way so you'd better prepare yerself.' Flicking her cigarette butt on to the wet grass, she said, 'Best way to top yerself is using the gas oven. If you can stand the smell, you just fall asleep and don't wake up.'

The way Madge was feeling at the moment, ending her life that way sounded a reasonable prospect. All she had thought of doing so far was throwing herself in the canal and hoping that death by drowning was quick. 'I haven't got the use of a gas oven,' she stated miserably.

'Well, me mam might let you use ours. For a price.'

Madge look at her hopefully. 'Would she? Oh, but I haven't got whatever your mam would charge me. I used the last of my money on me bus fare over here.'

'Over here from where?'

'Earl Shilton.'

'Never heard of the place.'

'It's near Hinckley.'

'Never heard of that place neither.'

'Shilton's a small market town about fifteen miles from Leicester. I didn't know the bus was headed here, I just got on it. I've been walking round since I got off at the bus station this morning, and I landed up here.'

'Seems to me you've got yerself in a right pickle.' Her companion suddenly looked thoughtful. 'I wonder if old Ma Tiler would do a cheaper price for two abortions instead of one? I bet she would, she's a money-grabbing old cow. She could do us one after the other. It's me first time and I wasn't looking forward to it, but having someone to go with . . . well, we'll be company for each other, won't we?' She then said knowledgeably, 'It's not really a baby, yer know, not 'til yer've been carrying it much longer.'

'Isn't it?'

'No. They ain't had long enough inside us to turn into babies. They're just things at the moment, so yer don't need to feel bad about getting rid of yours. It's the same as an egg ain't a chicken until its mam's sat on it for a while, while it forms proper inside the shell. Look, like I said, you're going to hell anyway so wouldn't you rather it be later than sooner?'

Her companion had a point, Madge supposed. Hell sounded such a horrible place from all she'd heard of it. Burning in damnation for eternity didn't appeal to her one iota. The longer she could put it off, the better. She gave a miserable sigh. 'Well, yes, I would. But anyway, I've told you, I haven't got the money to pay for an abortion even if you did strike a bargain with the woman who's doing yours.'

The other young woman gave a secretive smile. 'Oh, getting the money for it ain't a problem.'

'Isn't it? Does that mean you can get me a job?'

'I can tell you how to earn the easiest money you'll ever get, and lots of it. 'Cos you ain't bad-looking. Not as good as me, of course, but passable.' She glanced Madge over. ''Course, you ain't really dressed right for it, but you'll do for now. I'll show you how to dress and make up properly next time. And I'm sure me mam will let you stay with us 'til yer can afford to get a place of yer own, 'cos she don't turn down nothing that means a profit for her. Well, let's be off then. Time is money as me mam's always telling me. Oh, I suppose I'd better introduce meself. I'm Del – Della Kirby.'

With that she jumped up from her seat and headed off, disappearing around a bend in the shrubbery, leaving Madge staring after her, bemused. They were going to work now? The job must be in a factory working night shift then. Her spirits lifted. A few moments ago she'd been contemplating ending her life, sure it was her only answer. Now like a miracle a stranger had offered her the life-line of a well-paid job and a roof over her head. Madge glanced down at her belly. By what had just been said, the girl did seem to know what she was talking about and she said what Madge was carrying inside her hadn't been in there long enough to turn into a baby, so she wouldn't actually be killing another human being . . . Still without a clue what she was getting into, she jumped up off her seat and hurried to catch up with her mysterious benefactor.

At first Madge couldn't see hide nor hair of Della and panic reared up in her. Her saviour must have thought she wasn't going to take up the kind offer of help. Then, thankfully, Madge spotted her over by a clump of bushes, deep in conversation with two men, middle-aged by the look of them. Not wanting to interrupt, she hung back.

Della looked around then, saw her and beckoned her over. When she joined them Della was saying to the men, 'This is me friend. So, as I said, ten bob each.'

Madge felt confused. 'Ten bob . . . for what?'

Della grabbed her by the arm and yanked her out of earshot of the two men. 'What do yer think?'

She looked mystified. 'I don't know.'

'To be nice to 'em, yer thick sod.' Della gave a meaningful glance at her belly. 'Like yer was to the chap that gave yer that.'

The truth dawned on Madge then about just what this well-paid job entailed. She gawped at Della in utter shock, but before she could make her feelings known one of the men was slapping ten shillings into her hand and pulling her into the bushes. Before she knew it, he had shoved her up against a tree, her skirt was around her waist, knickers off, and he was taking from her what he'd paid for.

Della found her a while later, hunched against the tree, sobbing hysterically. She'd been sick. Della stared down at her, bemused. 'What's up with you? You ain't done n'ote you ain't done before, but you was paid for it this time. Told yer, didn't I? Easy money. And there's plenty more where that came from. Now, put yer knickers back on, for Christ's sake, before yer catch a chill. Ma Tiler charges five pounds for her services. Hopefully she's gonna knock a bit off for doing both of us at once, but you're still way short of her price. And there's your lodging money for stopping with us . . .'

'I can't!' Madge blubbered.

'Can't what?'

'Do that again. It's wrong.'

'Wrong! What's wrong about charging for summat if it gives you a living? It ain't like yer thieving it off them, is it? Oh, well, it's up to you. Yer'd better start praying to your God then, see if he'll grant you any mercy, 'cos you'll need every bit you can get where you're going. See yer then.'

As Della left her, a vision of what faced her in Purgatory danced before Madge. The priest who had got her into this dire predicament, along with her deeply religious parents, had taught her all about it. Then there was the pain she'd suffer by way of getting there. Della had presented her with a way out which a while ago she hadn't thought possible. Despite the fact it totally repelled her, it *was* good money she had just earned for not much more than ten minutes' work. What if she could bring herself to continue just long enough to get herself out of her current situation? Then she could go somewhere where no one knew her and start again. And maybe she could do some good works as well, to redeem herself in the eyes of God before her natural time came to face him.

Hurriedly pulling on her knickers, she grabbed her handbag and raced after Della.

At just after one o'clock that night, she followed her new friend through the back door of a crumbling back-to-back terrace house.

'Well, this is home sweet home,' Della said to her as she shut the door behind them.

Madge was still having trouble with her conscience, trying to convince herself that what she had been doing for the last few hours was as reasonable a course as Della had said, because people were willingly paying for something they wanted and she could give them.

Just then the door opened and a woman came in. Her hair was dyed platinum blonde and she was good-looking. Della's resemblance to her was strong enough for Madge to be in no doubt that this was her mother. She was dressed well, if flashily. She took one look at Madge and demanded of Della, 'Who's yer friend?'

'This is Madge. She's new to the game, I've bin showing her the ropes.'

'Oh, I see. Well, so long as that doesn't mean she was taking custom off you,' her mother said, giving Madge a meaningful glare.

'There was plenty to go round, Mam.'

'Glad to hear it. I've not had a bad night either,' she said, moving through into the back room.

Della followed her, motioning Madge to come along too.

Nora Kirby was by now stripping off her coat and easing off her tight shoes to ease her swollen feet.

'D'yer mind if Madge stops for a bit, Mam? Only she ain't

got nowhere to go. She's new to the town, see, and she doesn't know anyone. Besides, she's in the same way I am so I thought Ma Tiler might do us a deal.'

Nora stopped what she was doing and looked at her daughter knowingly. 'Company for you, yer mean?'

'Well . . . yeah. You won't come with me, will yer?'

'Yer big enough to sort yer own mess out. No one held my hand the first time I saw the likes of Ma Tiler. Besides, I've a regular tomorrow afternoon. No point in me losing money when you're going to be out of action for a couple of days and not bringing anything in.' She flashed a glance over at Madge who saw a look in her eye then that she was quickly to learn was a hint Nora was seeing another way to make some money. 'She can bunk in with you, I suppose.'

Despite the fact she had money in her pocket, Madge was worried she'd not get anywhere else to stay this late at night. It was back to the park bench for her if Della's mother refused her shelter. Having come from a background where if you had decent quality second-hand furniture you were considered well off, on entering this room it had surprised her what good furniture she saw. It was definitely not second-hand, although it was most apparent that neither Della nor her mother saw tidiness as a priority. The place was littered with discarded personal items, the table still holding the remains of an earlier meal. 'Oh, thank you, Mrs Kirby. I really appreciate your offer,' she enthused.

'It's Miss,' she corrected Madge. 'I have enough of men at work without coming home to one, and all his washing and dirty habits to deal with.' She looked at her daughter expectantly. 'Tip up then,' she ordered, holding out her hand.

Madge watched in bemusement as Della emptied her purse of the money she had earned that night and gave it all to her mother.

Nora counted it. 'Four quid. Not bad, but ten bob light on last night,' she said disapprovingly. Then she looked at Madge, and again held her hand out. 'Now you. Well, while yer stopping under my roof the same rules apply to you. And you can do your share of the housework, too. Take it or leave it.'

As matters stood, Madge didn't feel she had much choice.

Counting Madge's money, Nora looked impressed. 'Not bad for a first-timer, I suppose. Well, neither of you can expect any back as pocket money tonight, considering what I need to fork out tomorrow to Ma Tiler on your behalf. Just present yerselves at her address at two o'clock, I'll see to all the rest. And, remember, when I had my three abortions my mother gave me two days to get meself right then I was off out earning again. I shall expect the same of you two. You get n'ote for n'ote in this world.'

Madge was eternally grateful for the shelter she was being given but didn't plan to stay under it for long, nor did she plan on continuing to earn money the way she had tonight. But it appeared she wasn't going to be leaving here with much in her hand – not if Nora Kirby was taking most of it from her.

The next evening Madge had never felt such pain. It was as though someone was sticking a knife into her insides and twisting it around. The whole experience was something she never, ever wanted to repeat.

They had presented themselves at the appointed time at the back door of a downstairs flat several streets away from where the Kirbys lived. Aggie Tiler, an elderly rotund woman with an abrupt manner, ushered them inside her dismal abode, saying, 'Right, let's get on with it. I've got someone else coming in an hour.' She took Della first into the kitchen, leaving Madge to wait her turn in her parlour.

Twenty minutes later Della came back in, looking to all outward appearances as if nothing had happened to her. 'Piece of cake,' she told Madge, lighting a cigarette and dragging deeply on it. 'Didn't feel a thing. Baby came away right there and then, the old cow told me. Said it was the easiest one she'd ever done. I might not have a monthly for a while, while me body settles back, but that'll suit me. She told me to send you through.'

Madge had been shocked upon arriving in the kitchen to be requested by Mrs Tiler to take off her knickers, pull her clothes up around her waist and lie on the table with knees bent, legs splayed out, exposing her backside. What followed was a living nightmare for Madge as the old woman proceeded to induce her womb to reject what it contained. After much prodding and poking with something that felt very sharp to Madge, the older woman told her it was all done and the baby would come away in due course. Handing her a thick wad of padding to put inside her knickers to catch anything meantime, she sent Madge on her way.

The pains started almost immediately they left the house and quickly heightened to an excruciating level. Four hours later they had still not subsided and she was writhing in agony in Della's bed.

Nora put in a brief appearance and said harshly to her daughter, 'For God's sake, can't you put a gag in her mouth? I can't hear meself thinking downstairs.'

'Well, I can't understand it, Mam, I didn't feel a thing. Should we fetch the doctor to give her summat for the pain?'

''Course she's in pain. What do you expect?' her mother snapped. 'It's only the baby coming away. She'll start getting better when it has.' She gave her daughter a disparaging look. 'Trust you not to suffer anything! Must have the insides of an ox, that's all I can say.'

'Well, I did suffer,' Della said defensively. 'Mrs Tiler said I lost a lot of blood when the baby came away.'

'Are you still losing?'

'Not a sign of any since she cleaned me up.'

'Then there's no excuse for you not to be out working tonight, is there?'

Madge's baby finally came away in the early hours of the morning, she knew by the feeling of something jelly-like on the wadding between her legs, but the painful cramps still persisted. They lasted for the next six days along with the bleeding and she was left with a terrible dull ache in her belly and a sense of dreadful remorse for what she had done. Della also was none too happy that she now had to sleep on the floor while Madge recovered.

When she finally arrived downstairs, still feeling so weak she could barely stand, Nora slapped a packet of condoms into her hand and advised her to keep herself well supplied in order to protect herself from facing that again – not that she need have worried on that score. Whether Mrs Tiler's method of dealing with the problem was responsible or the condoms did the trick, Madge never fell pregnant again. She was back on the streets within a week, her landlady being most insistent that she was owed for six nights' lodging.

Three months later it was most apparent why Della had suffered no ill effects after Mrs Tiler's ministrations. She was still pregnant! It transpired that Mrs Tiler had not actually performed an abortion, only fiddled a bit to make Della believe that she was. It was done for revenge on Nora Kirby for blatantly stealing one of her own daughter's clients from her a few years before and, as if that wasn't enough, flaunting the fact. A furious Nora had no choice but to accept this payback for her own past misdemeanour, but not for a moment during the rest of her daughter's pregnancy did she let Della forget how stupid she had been not to realise what had been going on – or not going on, as it turned out.

Nora informed her that if she delivered a boy the authorities could take care of it. A girl they would keep as by the time she was of age to work, Nora herself would be ready to take a back seat and Della and her daughter could then provide for her. Little did she realise she would be long dead by that time; she was already in the early stages of the sexually transmitted disease that would eventually kill her.

Madge's stay with the Kirbys stretched to over six months due to Nora's conviction that she was entitled to help herself to whatever she wanted from Madge's earnings. The girl had to save what she could out of what Nora gave her back as pocket money. After laying out for her food and personal needs, she hadn't much left over and it took a while for her to save enough to move on.

To say Nora was not pleased when Madge announced to her that she was leaving for other lodgings she had found herself with a nice elderly woman, herself an ex-prostitute who kept clean, comfortable rooms, was putting it mildly. Despite the fact she had been rewarded handsomely for her so-called generosity towards Madge, she accused the girl of being ungrateful.

Several weeks after leaving the Kirby household, Madge was back in the room she had shared with Della, assisting at her baby's birth. Nora was out occupying herself with clients, and the birth of her grandchild wasn't going to stop her earning money. After a long labour, during which Della did not hold back from letting the others know how painful it was proving to be, Madge was the first to hold the new arrival and instantly fell in love with her. Whether she was bestowing on Dee the maternal love she would have showered on her own child had she not terminated her pregnancy was debatable, but at least Della's baby was shown some maternal love as neither Nora nor Della gave her any. They both saw the new arrival as purely a money-making commodity, her childhood needs for clothes and food to be met only until she was of an age to make herself useful around the house and earn them. Later on she would join the family 'business', in the same way as Della and Nora had done.

Only two weeks after her birth, Dee was left with what was to become a succession of babysitters while Della went out to work. At five it was felt she was old enough to be left alone in the house after being put to bed. The minders were all old widow women, desperate for extra income, uninterested in the child herself or her wants and needs. Many times, worried for Dee's welfare, Madge would cut short her working hours to take the baby off the minder's hands. She'd take Dee back to her own home, putting her down in her cot and staying with her until Della returned in the early hours of the morning, or sometimes not until well into the next day. Not that she ever thanked her friend, just thought she was an idiot for giving up her own valuable earning time.

Initially Madge had thought she would stay in her new lodgings only as long as it took her to amass enough to set herself up in a proper place of her own, and secure a legitimate job. As time passed, though, she found she was starting to view her work in the same light as Della did: it was just a job that paid good money, and Madge could not deny she was enjoying the benefits it was bringing her. Now she could regularly update her wardrobe with good quality clothes and shoes, eat decent food, buy expensive bits and pieces for her room, and all when she saw them without having to save up for weeks. The prospect of returning to her old life with its penny-pinching became less and less appealing until the time came when she knew there was no going back for her now.

She did only stay a year in her new lodgings before moving out to a two-bedroomed, bay-fronted rented house of her own in a good part of Highfields, furnishing it in accordance with the excellent money she was earning by then. Like most young women in her line of work, she saw old age as being unimaginably far away. Madge, same as others, thought there was time enough to start building a nest egg for her retirement, and meanwhile she spent what she earned in the belief that there was plenty more where that came from. Fifteen years later she realised she had been badly mistaken when her earnings went into a gradual decline as advancing age and its effects mounted.

When Nora's illness took its toll and rendered her bedridden and awaiting death, it was readily apparent to Madge that Della was intent on doing only the bare minimum towards caring for her mother, and then only when she felt like it. Consequently the dying woman was left alone for hours on end, in her own filth, often thirsty and hungry. Madge did appreciate that Nora was only reaping the rewards of the way she had raised Della. If their roles had been reversed, Madge knew she would be acting towards her daughter in exactly the way Della was acting towards her now. Madge, though, could not forget that Nora had taken her in at a dreadful stage in her life, regardless of the fact that she herself had paid heavily for it. Despite not receiving a single word of appreciation from Nora, Madge did her best as often as she could to ensure the dying woman's last weeks were as comfortable as possible.

Madge knew that had Della not helped her out that fateful night, admittedly from selfish reasons, she would not be alive now. Though she had sacrificed her own child she had grown to love Dee as her own, and had lost count of the number of times she wished she could scoop her out of this dreadful environment and raise her herself in a place where the child felt loved and wanted for the right reasons. Dee sensed all this without its ever being expressed and loved her for it in a way she could never love her mother.

Now Madge flashed her a smile and patted her hand. 'Oh, I wouldn't want to bore you with all that ancient history, ducky.' She took another swig of her drink and added matter-of-factly, 'Anyway, it's too late now for me to change me occupation, I must just get on with it.' Draining her glass, she rose and went over to fetch the bottle from the table. She poured herself another generous measure and stowed the steadily depleting bottle by the side of her chair. 'How's your job going?' she asked.

It was obvious that what had led Madge into taking up the oldest profession in the world was too painful for her to discuss, and Dee was far too respectful of her to keep badgering her just to satisfy her own idle curiosity. 'My job's going fine, thank you. I heard a rumour yesterday that Miss Gibson is retiring soon, so that means the manager's job will become vacant. I was thinking of applying for it.'

'Oh, and they'll jump at you, lovey, you mark my words.'

Dee smiled appreciatively at this encouragement. 'Well, there are a couple of older women to consider who've been working there longer than me. I might not get a look in.'

Thinking of her own life, Madge said, 'Experience isn't always what people are after, Dee. Youth's the thing.' Her face clouded over then. 'With a better wage, you could think of getting a place of your own. A little flat or summat?' That way, she thought, at least Dee would have a fighting chance to live her life the way *she* wanted. But Madge would miss her if she moved far away.

Dee gave a wistful sigh. A place of her own was just a pipe dream as far as she was concerned. She'd be hard pressed to fund decent accommodation on her wages, even with a pay rise.

But besides that she couldn't leave her mother to fend for herself when Dee knew she was not earning the amount she claimed to. It was obvious from the way she was always cadging off her daughter for drink and cigarettes, something she'd never needed to do in the past. 'Mam's only got me. She'd struggle to keep this place on without what I stump up each week, then before I knew it she'd be moving in with me. I might as well stay put.'

'Della could always get a lodger in to help with the bills,' Madge suggested.

If only it were that simple. Dee looked knowingly at her. 'Apart from the fact there's not too many people would live with a prostitute for a landlady, unless they were prostitutes themselves, this place is hardly a palace and offers few home comforts.'

Madge pursed her lips. Dee had a point, but regardless it was better accommodation than she herself was living in at present. An idea began to form in her mind. Relations between herself and Della weren't exactly amicable, but if her moving in would resolve Dee's problem it would be worth it to Madge.

Dee was reading the expression on her face. 'Don't even think about it, Aunty Madge. Don't get me wrong. I really appreciate what I know you're about to suggest, but you and I both know you'd soon be pleading with your old landlady to give you your room back.'

Madge heaved a sigh. 'Yes, I suppose yer right. I did suggest we should pool resources when things started getting tough for us both a few years back, but Del wouldn't entertain the idea. It's a pity she's like she is towards me, I'd jump at the chance of being her lodger. As you know, I ain't always lived in the awful place I do now, with a doo-lally landlady who puts out stale bread for the family of mice that lives in her kitchen, like they were pets. I'm exaggerating a bit but you get me drift. I had me own house once,' she added wistfully.

'I remember it,' said Dee. 'Mam used to bring me round to visit you. You had it done up lovely. This place was all right too, wasn't it, before me mam started selling stuff off and replacing it with what we have now? You'd be hard pressed to get tuppence for this lot,' she said, glancing sadly round. 'All it's fit for is burning now. Still, it's better than nothing, isn't it?'

'It certainly is,' Madge agreed. 'And when all's said and done, I've still got me fur coat and so has yer mam. So life ain't all bad, is it?' She gave a laugh. 'I remember when we bought those coats . . . about twenty-five we were at the time, and with money to fritter. Like royalty we felt, going into the furrier's on Market Street. Right posh place it was too. Right snotty assistants. 'Course, they knew what we was, but our money was as good as anyone else's and we made sure they knew that. We made 'em model everything in the shop before we made our choices.'

A quizzical expression crossed Dee's face. 'You and Mam used to be really good friends at one time but she treats you like an enemy now, Aunty Madge.'

The older woman gave a snort. 'That's because, to yer mam, I *am* the enemy, lovey. Not having our pick of the punters any more, we're fighting between us for what we can get. And not just me and yer mam but the other prossies of our age and older who ply their trade around these parts.'

The wistful expression returned to her face then as she looked down to study the contents of her glass. 'I loved my little house. I was so proud that what was in it was all mine, bought with money I'd earned myself. I never took any of me punters back there. It was my sanctuary, that little house was. It broke me heart when I was turfed out because I couldn't keep up the rent.' She raised her head and glanced across at Dee. 'When me trade started slowly petering off a few years back, it took me a while to realise it was because the sort of punters I was used to getting had started to look towards younger women. My days of getting the type who would pay well for what they wanted, taking a room so we could do it in comfort, were over. The sort I'd got to look to in the future was more yer Average Joe. When it came to paying for a room as well . . . that was out of the question. It was a shock to me, Dee, hurt like hell, I can tell yer. Letting go of me dream to retire comfortably to a little house in the country with roses around the door, and where all the neighbours hadn't a clue about me past, treating me with respect . . . that was what hurt the most.'

Madge gave a heavy sigh. 'No woman likes to admit that age is catching up with her. When I was starting out on the game, I used to see the old brasses dragging themselves about and made a promise to meself that I'd never be in such an embarrassing position, flogging me wares at a time when I should be hiding them from the world, 'cos they ain't such a pretty sight any more. But life seems to run away with you. Before yer know it, middle age is on yer and it's the younger girls looking at me now, promising themselves they won't end up like me.'

Dee looked sadly at her. Although her body was thickening, Madge still possessed a good figure. Under the layer of make-up she always wore, and despite the lines and the weathering, it was still evident that as a younger woman she had been blessed with the sort of looks to turn men's heads. The same went for Dee's mother, too. She had childhood memories of them both sitting at the table, both dressed in quality underclothes underneath expensive silk dressing-gowns, readying themselves for the night of work ahead, albeit at the time Dee hadn't understood quite what that work entailed. All dressed up and ready for the off, both of them had looked like film stars to Dee, with all the right credentials to literally charm the pants off any man they set their sights on. Which was hardly the case now. Those quality underclothes had been replaced by cheap market ones; silk dressing-gowns had been traded for well-worn candlewick. Madge seemed to be resigning herself to the ways in which advancing age was affecting her, whereas Della never held back from expressing her resentment at the way her life had panned out.

Dee knew that deep down her mother, Madge, and all the other women who worked the streets, still secretly hoped a decent man would materialise for them, an open-minded one who liked them for the person they were, not the way they earned their money. Then, like a knight in shining armour, he'd release them from it. For some women that did happen but it certainly hadn't up to now for Madge or Della. In the past several men had come to stay with them, and Della had pinned her hopes on being saved by them. For Dee these had been more turbulent times than normal as after a short honeymoon period Della always began to see the men for the wasters they really were, soon finding she was supporting them and not the other way round. No one had been more relieved than Dee when her mother finally turfed the last one out. Thankfully advancing age had wised her up to men's flattery and it had been a few years now since Della had introduced any 'uncles' to the house. Not liking to see her mother being used, Dee hoped it would stay that way. She did though, harbour a forlorn hope that saviours might still be out there for both Della and Madge. Dee knew that most of her mother's problems stemmed from worry over money, how to keep it coming in. With that burden lifted from her she wouldn't be half so volatile as she was now. As for Madge, well, having experienced for herself the caring side of her that her clients probably didn't, Dee knew that given half a chance she would make a special man a wonderful wife.

'Summat's bugging me,' Madge piped up unexpectedly, breaking into Dee's thoughts.

'Oh, what's that, Aunty Madge?'

'Well, I know I'm trying to get you to forget what happened to you tonight, but if you never told that fella you was seeing about yer background, then how did he find out about yer mother?'

Dee took a deep breath. 'Oh, we met Kevin's dad on the way to his local last night . . . the Crow's Nest on Hinckley Road. He told Kevin when he got home later that he thought I resembled a prostitute they called Back Alley Sal, and closely enough that I must be related to her in some way.' With a pained expression on her face she added softly, 'I didn't know that was what they called my mam behind her back.'

Better than Dirty Gertie, Leper Lil or Syphilis Phyllis, to recall just a few of the nicknames Madge knew for local prostitutes. She dreaded to think what her own was. 'Well, yer know what they say, me darlin', sticks and stones, et cetera. She could be called worse, believe me. Anyway, yer mam doesn't operate anywhere near Hinckley Road and never has. Which has got me wondering just how Kevin's dad knows what she looks like?' Madge was staring at Dee meaningfully.

She looked back at her for a long moment before she said, 'You mean, Kevin's dad must be quite well acquainted with me mam, to have noticed the resemblance between us. Is that what you're getting at?'

Madge nodded. 'Which can only mean he's been a visitor to these parts – and there's only one reason I can think of why a man who lives the other side of town would come to our district.'

'You mean . . .'

'Certainly do,' Madge cut in. 'Our part of town is the place to come when yer want a bit of *how's yer father* behind the wife's back, ain't it? Well, talk about the pot calling the kettle black!' Her face screwed up angrily. 'People like that make me sick,' she hissed. 'Ain't averse to using the likes of us to give 'em what their wives can't or ain't willing to, but otherwise we're scum to 'em. Well, it's *them* that's the scum with their lousy double standards, and you deserve better, lovey.' Downing the rest of her sherry, Madge said with reluctance, 'Well, I'm warmed up a treat. Suppose I'd better get back on the street. Time is money, so to speak.' She eyed Dee searchingly. 'But . . .'

'I'm going to be fine,' the girl cut in, smiling at her reassuringly. 'As I said before, I'll get over this like I have all the other times.'

They both jumped at an unexpected knock on the back door. They heard it open, quickly followed by a voice calling out, 'Oi, Dee, you there?'

Before she could rise to answer, a mop of red hair appeared around the door and the heavily painted face under it looked relieved to see Dee. 'Oh, there you are, ducky. Thought I'd better let yer know that I was just passing the Admiral Beatty and there was a rumpus going on inside. Heard the word *police* mentioned. Thought I'd better tell yer 'cos the loudest voice I could hear was yer mother's. Oh, hello, Madge. You not working tonight?' Before she could answer the visitor added, 'Gotta rush 'cos I've got a gentleman friend waiting outside for me and I don't wanna risk anyone else nabbing him, not with business being as it is just now. Toodaloo then.' With that she was gone.

'Oh, God,' Dee groaned. 'What's Mam gone and got herself

into now? She was in quite a good mood for a change when I left her tonight so something must have rattled her meantime.' She jumped up from her seat. 'I'd better go. The police warned her the last time they were called to deal with her that the next they'd lock her up and throw away the key.'

Madge really needed to get back to work herself, especially after Ava – which wasn't her real name, that being Elsie, just her working one, used because she felt she resembled the film star Ava Gardner, which she might have, once . . . to the very short-sighted – had mentioned she had a client, which meant there could be some trade going on Elsie's deserted beat close to Madge's own. But then, if Della was in a fighting mood, which it sounded as if she was, it could need the two of them to drag the stubborn cuss out of it. 'I'll come with you,' Madge offered, sighing.

Dee was already coated for the off, keen to pluck her mother out of possible trouble before it got serious. She could not waste any time arguing.

CHAPTER THREE

Arriving ahead of Madge, the sound of her mother's voice greeted Dee as she pushed open the saloon bar door of the Admiral Beatty, a rundown public house frequented mostly by low-class working types and members of the criminal fraternity. She cringed in embarrassment at the sight that met her eyes. A jeering crowd standing around her, her mother was standing barefoot on a table in the centre of the room, skirt pulled up around her thighs displaying stocking tops held up by fraying suspenders. She was shouting out furiously, 'Satisfied now that I ain't hidden that fucking ten-bob note in me nylon tops?' She then proceeded to unbutton her blouse to reveal a shabby brassiere out of which bulged ample breasts. 'Now, who wants to have a ferret around in here to check I ain't hidden it in me bra?' she challenged her audience.

'No, thanks, Del,' a sneering member of the congregation shouted back. 'I've got a pair of sagging tits like yours at me disposal back home – and I don't have to pay for them.'

The audience erupted into laughter.

'Okay, that's enough, Del, you've made yer point,' said the thick-set, bearded landlord behind the bar. 'Now get down and get yerself off, there's a good gel.'

On the other side of the bar, a tall, thin, balding, middle-aged man, dressed in an iron-shiny blue suit and well-worn grey overcoat, obviously a representative for a second-rate company, looked at the landlord incredulously. In a thick Birmingham accent he moaned, 'You're not going to take that slapper's word for it, are you? She's nicked me ten bob, I'm telling you. I don't care if she's emptied her handbag, pockets, practically stripped herself naked, she's got it on her somewhere. Now if you don't have the police fetched, I will.'

The landlord glanced worriedly over at several shifty-looking characters sitting around a table in a gloomy corner. He knew the police would take a great interest in them and he himself relied heavily on their trade. He also knew they wouldn't take kindly to its coming to official notice just where they conducted their business. 'Not advisable, mate, if you value your life,' he quietly warned the man, then focused his attention back on Della who was still egging on the crowd. 'Del, I said, that's enough. Now get down and get yerself off.'

Dee pushed through the crowd and stood before the table where her mother was standing. Despite being used to finding herself in embarrassing situations caused by her, Dee was nevertheless mortified by this one. 'Mam, you're making a public spectacle of yourself. Please do as the landlord asks you before you end up spending the night in a cell. Remember what the police warned. They said they'd throw away the key the next time they found you mixed up in any trouble.'

Madge arrived then. 'Yeah, come on, Del, think of the money you could miss out on if yer get yerself locked up. And don't forget the fine you'd have to pay.'

Completely ignoring her daughter and Madge, an indignant Della glared across at her accuser. 'I could have you for slander, you cretin! You wanna mek sure you have proof before yer accuse anyone else of stealing. And as for you...' She was wagging a warning finger at a smug-looking young woman, tartily dressed, hanging on his arm. 'Think yer clever, don't yer? Well, blatantly entice a punter off me again and you'd better watch yer back.'

Clambering off the table, she pulled down her skirt and buttoned up her blouse while loudly proclaiming, 'I ain't going nowhere 'til I've finished me drink.' Grabbing her ageing beaver coat from the back of a chair, she pulled it on and sat down, picking her handbag up off the table to set it squarely on her knees. Then she peered around on the floor and, not seeing what she was looking for, shouted accusingly, 'Some arsehole's nicked me fucking shoes!'

'No one has nicked your shoes, Mam,' Dee told her sharply, bending down to scoop up the scuffed and down at-heel stilettos from where they had slid when Della had thrown them down earlier. Dee held them out to her.

'No one's that desperate, Del, even in here,' Madge jocularly commented. 'Now get that drink down yer neck and let's get off,' she coaxed.

Snatching her shoes off Dee, Della glared up at her former friend. 'What the hell are you doing in this pub? I'm working this one tonight, and if yer think yer gonna nab any of my potentials, like that slut over there, then be prepared for a long stay in hospital, lady. Like that trollop needs to, 'cos if I see her around on a dark night she'll be sorry for what she's done to me. And anyway, who the hell are *you* to be bossing *me* about? I'll leave when I'm good and ready.'

The landlord arrived then and in no uncertain terms ordered, 'You'll leave now, Del. You're in the mood for a fight and I don't want no trouble.'

'Oh, so I'm not supposed to retaliate when someone accuses me of stealing, am I?'

'There's ways and ways, Del, as you very well know, and the way you did ain't on, not in my pub. If I wanted a strip show, I'd hire a proper stripper. Now, are you going peacefully or what?'

Even volatile, stubborn Della knew when to call it quits. Grabbing up her glass of barley wine, she drained the contents at a gulp while slipping her feet into her shoes. Then she stood up and held her chin in the air, pushing her way through the crowd and on outside.

Dee glanced apologetically at the landlord. 'I'm sorry about this.'

He patted her arm. 'You can't help having an argumentative old sod for a mother, gel. In fairness to her, though, before that chap accused her of stealing his ten bob, the young woman with him did steal his custom from her. Del didn't take that kindly, and I can't say as I blame her. Best get her off home to stay put for the night,' he advised, then added jocularly, 'hopefully she'll get out of the right side of the bed tomorrow.'

Sound advice, Dee thought, but not so easy to carry out when dealing with someone with Della's personality. She turned to Madge. 'Thanks for coming with me.'

'Well, thankfully I wasn't needed as much as I thought I would be.'

'Yes, thankfully. And thanks again for earlier.' She smiled warmly at her friend. 'I really appreciated your company after . . . Well, anyway, I'd best get off after Mam and see if I can make her go home, or the mood she's in, she's likely to pick a fight with the first person she meets.'

Madge gave a shudder as a blast of icy air whipped through her. 'I feel like going home meself but work beckons. No rest for the wicked they say, don't they? Keep yer fingers crossed, lovey, that Elsie didn't nab the only punter out tonight.'

'I'll keep everything crossed for you.'

Dee caught up with Della several streets away and it was obvious from the direction she was taking that she was on her way to the Jolly Miller on Conduit Street, another seedy public house.

Falling into step beside her, Dee said to her in a coaxing manner, 'Why don't you call it a night, Mam, and come home?'

Della stopped and eyed her sharply. In an equally sharp manner she snapped, 'If you were out earning proper money then I might have bin able to consider having a night off. But as it is, I have no choice, have I?'

Dee sighed. 'Let's not start that, Mam. Look, we're managing . . .'

'Managing! Is that what you call it? That's not what I call the way we're living. I call it being on the breadline. And it's all *your* fault! We could be living the life of Riley if you'd just get off yer high horse and do the job you was born to do. With your looks and figure you could be down those posh hotels now, creaming it in like I was at your age, and I could be at home putting me feet up, having done more than my bit towards the family coffers, like my mam was at my age. You should have bin born a boy . . . As it's turned out, pity for me yer wasn't!'

The last thing Dee wanted was a slanging match in the street, which was just what Della was hankering after to vent her pent-up anger against the events of tonight. Sighing in resignation, she shook her head. 'All right, Mam, if you want to risk catching pneumonia and being laid up for weeks, it's your decision.'

Hunching her shoulders against the biting wind, she abruptly turned and headed off home, just as the wind heightened and a blizzard of snow swirled at them.

Dee had hardly shouldered shut the back door behind her when it burst open again and Della charged in, covered in a thick coating of snow which she shook on to the kitchen floor, heed-less of the puddles her actions created.

'Bleeding Arctic weather! It's coming down that thick, yer can't see in front of yer face. I've popped home for me brolly but I might as well have a quick warm and a snifter while I'm here,' she grumbled, pushing past Dee and on into the back room where she stripped off her wet coat. She threw it over a dining chair, plonked her handbag on the table, then kicked off her shoes. Staring at the table, she exclaimed, 'What have yer done with me bottle of sherry? And . . . whose is that handbag?'

'Mine,' answered Madge, entering with Dee following close behind her. 'I forgot it when I left in a hurry to get down the Admiral with Dee, see what rumpus you were in the thick of. In case yer wondering, it was Elsie who popped in to tell us what was going on.'

Della was glaring at her suspiciously. 'What I'm wondering is what you were doing in my house in the first place?'

'I was paying Dee a visit.'

'Why?'

Not knowing whether Dee wanted her mother to know what had happened to her earlier or not, Madge answered, ''Cos it was cold and I fancied a warm.'

'Oh, use our coal and save on yer own, yer mean?'

'Gas in my case, but no, that's not why, Della. I wanted to see how Dee was 'cos I hadn't seen her for a while. You haven't got a problem with that, have yer?'

Turning away to look at the fire, Della gave a nonchalant shrug. 'I suppose I can't stop her seeing who she wants.' Then she spun her head back, face stony. 'But I have got a big problem with you helping yerself to my sherry.' She pointed to the half-full bottle sitting on the hearth along with the empty glass.

Madge shook her head in disbelief. 'Begrudge an old friend a drink, Della, what are you coming to? I'll replace what I drank, if it means that much to yer.'

'Soon as yer can then 'cos I ain't got no spare at the moment to buy any more, what with having punters stole off me and this bleeding weather hampering business. 'Course, if Dee was bringing decent money into this house, I wouldn't have to be so stingy. Bleddy pity she wasn't born a boy . . .'

'Now, Del, yer don't mean that,' Madge shot back at her.

Della glared at her. 'I do. For a start, I wouldn't have had the trouble of . . .'

'Now, Del,' Madge cut in, a worried expression on her face. 'Don't let yer tongue run away with yer, just because yer angry.'

'No, let Mam finish, Madge,' erupted Dee. 'She's always telling me she wishes I'd been born a boy because she then wouldn't have had the trouble of raising me, only to have me turn out like I did. What do you mean by that exactly, Mam?'

Della made to open her mouth but was stopped in what she was about to say by Madge's warning, 'Del!'

Della stared at her daughter for a long moment before she made a grab for her handbag to find her cigarettes. She misjudged it and knocked it over instead, revealing the underside.

What she saw there stuck to the bottom with chewing gum made Dee gawp in shock. Della might be some things but Dee had never known her be a thief before. 'So you *did* steal that man's ten shillings after all, Mam?' she gasped.

Della's face darkened thunderously. 'I did not steal it,' she hissed, insulted.

'Oh, it stuck itself to the bottom of yer handbag, did it then, Del?' asked Madge.

'Don't be bleddy sarky, you,' Della spat at her. 'It was me dues.'

'What dues, Mam? I thought that other woman took the man's custom from you?'

'Yeah, the floozy did. But he was talking to me for at least ten minutes before that, discussing terms, and my time is money. He wasn't going to give it me voluntarily so I helped meself from his pocket when he got up to go off with that young madam, after she'd lured him off me.'

Madge laughed. 'Well, I admire yer, gel. Gotta say, though, your time is rather expensive. Ten bob for a ten-minute chat? I shall have to up me rates.'

'Ain't you got to be off somewhere?' Della snapped at her.

'Ah, Mam, don't be mean to Madge. It's blowing a blizzard out there. You wouldn't send a dog out in that. She is your friend.'

'Friends like her I don't need,' Del barked, flashing Madge a derisive look. 'Warming herself on my coal, drinking me booze behind me back, and I ain't convinced she wasn't eyeing up the potential in the Admiral tonight while claiming to be there 'cos she cared about me. And as for you . . .' she hissed, glaring at her daughter, 'well, seems you mind poor old Madge working in this weather, but where's yer concern for me, eh?'

Dee gave a heavy sigh. Her mother was hungry for a fight to quell her anger about what had gone wrong for her tonight. The dreadful weather having driven her inside was unfortunate for Dee herself and Madge, who were now bearing the brunt of it. She supposed, though, that Della had a right to be angry. She would be herself if someone undermined her in such a callous way as the woman in the pub had her mother. She just wished Della didn't have such an aggressive way of venting her feelings. After her experience of earlier, it was the last thing Dee needed tonight. 'Mam, I've already asked you to call it a night, and you gave me your answer.'

Della stepped over to the hearth, picked up the bottle of sherry and the used glass, and poured herself a generous measure. After downing a good portion of it, she responded gruffly, 'No other answer I could give yer, is there? Not with things the way they are with you.'

Madge, knowing that Dee was heartily sick of this topic of conversation, came to her rescue. 'Ah, now, Del, leave the gel alone. She ain't cut out for a life like ours. Why can't you accept . . .'

Before she could finish, Della blurted, 'Apart from the fact this ain't no business of yours, how does she bleddy well know she ain't cut out for it when she ain't even gave it a go? Did yer know she was still a virgin?' She announced this as if it was a cardinal sin.

'Mother!' Dee cried, humiliated.

'Well, you are, ain't yer? How do you know you wouldn't take to it like a duck to water if yer gave it a try, that's all I'm asking? The day I officially left school, my mother handed me a packet of johnnies and told me I was to accompany her out to work that night, so she could show me the ropes. I did my duty like I was expected to. Yet when the day came for *me* to show *you* the ropes, you cowered in yer room, wailing like a baby, begging me not to.'

Dee remembered that day vividly. From the moment it became apparent that her mother was expecting her to follow on in the family business, she had dreaded that confrontation. She had never found the courage to speak up first and tell her mother that the thought of selling her body for money totally repelled her, and was something she would never be able to bring herself to do. This turn of events had never even occurred to Della. The packet of contraceptives she had ceremoniously presented to Dee, as a mechanic would a toolbox to his son on his first morning at work in a garage, had been flatly refused. Dee had then flown up the stairs, locked herself in her room and refused to come out, despite Della's threats to break down the door and drag her along with her. Della thought at first it was merely stage fright. Wasn't she terrified her first time, like anyone would be terrified on their first day at any job? Dee had lost count of the number of times she had tried to make her mother understand her feelings, but all her efforts had fallen on deaf ears and still the battle raged on. This was one battle, though, that Dee was not prepared to lose. She just couldn't bring herself to perform the duties her mother's job called for, and that was that.

'Come on, Del,' Madge coaxed now. 'Yer just annoyed that youngster took yer punter off yer, so yer taking it out on Dee.'

Pouring herself another generous drink, Della took a large swallow. 'Yes, I am fucking annoyed! You'd be too if some young trollop muscled in on you and made yer look stupid in front of a roomful of people. But if Dee would just get on with what she's supposed to, I'd be able to live in a decent place and have special clients visit me at home. Then I wouldn't have been put in the situation I was tonight, would I?'

She gave Dee a look of disgust. 'Yer don't tek after my side of the family, that's for sure. And before yer start, no, I don't know who yer bleddy father was and I'm sick of hearing you ask me. He could have been anyone. I was very much in demand at the time – like *you* should be now. We Kirby women are loyal to the family tradition.' She stuck her chin in the air. 'I come from a long line of prostitutes and I'm proud of it. So should you be. My grandmother, your great-gran, entertained royalty. Okay, he might only have been a Duke who was passing through the city but, still, royalty when all's said and done. I hope you're happy that you personally are responsible for bringing an end to the good name of Kirby in this profession.'

She fixed her eyes on Madge then. 'And some friend *you're* turning out to be, backing my daughter instead of me.'

Madge's face darkened. 'Eh, you listen here, lady. After the way you've treated me over recent years, you're lucky I'm even speaking to you.'

Della knocked back her drink before responding. 'Well, how d'yer expect me to treat yer? You was in a right hole when I first met you and took you under my wing. Me and me mother helped sort you out. And look how you repay us.'

Madge looked taken aback. 'What do you mean by that?'

'Well, when things started to get tough a few years back, the least you could have done was find another patch of yer own. After all, the one we work was originally my gran's turf, then my mother's. I inherited it and was kind enough to let you in on it, when I was busy. I'm not now.'

Madge gawped at her. 'I've worked that patch with you for

over twenty-odd years, and to my mind that gives me some rights to it an' all. You can't just expect me to move to another 'cos you want it all to yourself when times are hard. And what about the girls working the other patches round these parts? They'd hardly welcome me into theirs with open arms, would they, Del? You know as well as I do, I'd be lucky not to be lynched. Are you seriously expecting me to do to them what that youngster did to you tonight?'

Del gave a nonchalant shrug. 'Just saying, it's the least you can do, after all I've done for you.'

'God, you take the biscuit, Del! In case you ain't noticed, I do try and keep out of yer way when I know what particular street or pub yer working that night, but I ain't a bloody mind-reader and sometimes we're bound to clash. We used to work together, Del, have you forgotten? We kept an eye on each other, we was company for each other when we was idle . . . until you got it into your bloody head you'd fare better working solo. If you hadn't been so bloody daft a few years back and listened to my suggestion that we should pool resources during these difficult times, I could be living here with you now. We'd have this place looking good again, and use the spare room upstairs as a place to do business in, instead of paying a backhander to the likes of Nell Baker and Winnie Watson when we get a client who'll stump up the extra.

'By now we could have had a nest egg put by for our old age, Del, instead of both being terrified of what's in store for us once we're really too old for this game. And, more to the point, your Dee could be living her own life instead of you constantly badgering her to help you fund yours.

'But you wouldn't even listen to my idea, would yer, Del? Well, why would yer, when you was conceited enough to believe I was only grabbing some of your action for meself when I had to leave me house for lodgings?' Madge's face was wreathed in hurt. 'After all our years of friendship, you should have known me better than that, Del. I could see the writing on the wall, for both of us. If you hadn't been so blinkered, you'd have seen I was trying to help the both of us, not just myself.'

Madge shook her head at Del then, her lips tight. 'I never realised yer befriending me all those years ago came with conditions. I thought you was a good woman offering the hand of friendship to another in need. Your current attitude is making me seriously regret I chose that particular bench, in that particular park. Now, I'm off back to work.' She eyed Del meaningfully.

'I know you're making a stand against them two bastards and *not* paying up. I wish I had your gumption, Della, but I haven't and I don't fancy the consequences if I can't pay them their dues this week.' Snatching up her handbag, Madge flashed Dee a smile. 'Tarra, me duck. See yer soon, eh? And keep yer pecker up. Don't let the buggers grind you down, that's my motto.'

At the sound of the back door slamming shut behind her, Della downed the dregs of her drink, pulled her coat and her shoes back on, and while Dee watched silently, she left also.

As the back door slammed behind her mother, Dee gave a heavy sigh. Madge had obviously been telling the truth or Della would without doubt have vocally retaliated. It was a pity she hadn't thought more about Madge's suggestion a few years back, then they might not both be in such a precarious financial position now. She wondered if it was too late for the plan to work. It made sense financially. But getting her mother to admit she'd been wrong not to take up Madge's suggestion in the first place, and to mellow enough for Madge to be able to live with her, was another matter. Della had a stubborn streak and would sooner die than admit she was wrong.

Still, at least now she knew how her mother and Madge had first met, though the full facts of Madge's situation at the time remained a mystery. And then another thing struck Dee. Who were the '*two bastards*' Madge had just mentioned, whose weekly dues she was in danger of not being able to pay if she didn't get back out to work? Apparently her mother was making a stand against paying them, but what consequences exactly would there be if she didn't? Dee herself had always been of the opinion that men paid the women for their services, not the other way round. It was puzzling.

She walked across to the window, pulled aside the worn

curtains and looked outside. Snow was still floating down, settling thickly in the tiny yard outside. In her mind's eye she pictured her mother battling her way through it to wherever her destination might be, in the hope of securing a last bit of business for herself tonight. A surge of guilt swept over Dee then for not being able to bring herself to do what her mother expected of her. She prayed that the manager's position would be given to her when Miss Gibson retired, and then the extra money she earned might offer her mother a way out.

Then she remembered the confrontation with Kevin and her hand went to her smarting cheek. She could still feel the effects of his attack on her, still vividly see his look of disgust when she had admitted whose daughter she was. She had made a bad choice so far as he was concerned. He was good-looking, fun to be with, had shown her consideration on their nights out together – up until tonight, but he was most definitely not the understanding sort she had thought him to be.

Dee was no different from most women of her age who were not already attached. She dreamed of a nice man sweeping her off her feet, falling for her enough to propose marriage, and then they'd live happily ever after. She'd had her fair share of boyfriends in the past, not all strong contenders for a husband's role, though a couple had shown great potential. Regardless, all of them had reacted badly to hearing about her mother's occupation when she could no longer keep it to herself, and, like Kevin, had wanted nothing more to do with her after that. Now, faced with yet another rejection, Dee was beginning to doubt there really was a man who would want her purely for herself. Her romantic vision of gliding up the aisle in a flowing white dress to unite herself for life with a husband she loved was beginning to fade. But she knew from experience that wallowing in misery over her latest loss would not achieve anything but to prolong her own pain. Her only course of action was to store it away at the back of her mind, along with all the other memories of hurt caused by the very same topic.

Letting the curtain fall back into place, she made her way over to the dining table to tidy up the mess her mother had created readying herself for work earlier that evening.

Della meanwhile was struggling her way towards the Jolly Miller in the hope that some potential clients were still lingering there. They risked having to camp down in the pub for the night if this blizzard continued.

She nearly jumped out of her skin when a voice unexpectedly said, 'Nice to see you out and about, Del.'

She stopped abruptly, jerking round her head to see two men sheltering in a shop doorway. A look of utter contempt filled her face. 'Well, fancy seeing you pair of clowns out on a night like this,' she snapped. Then, sarcastically, she added, 'Come to offer to take me for a drink, have yer?'

The slighter, more handsome of the two men glared darkly at her. 'We wouldn't be seen dead out with scum like you. Now you know why we're here. You owe us money and we've come to collect.'

'Business that bad, eh, it brings you out collecting in this weather?' She looked at the huge man accompanying him. 'See yer've got yer puppet with yer as usual. I never see one without the other. I'm beginning to wonder if you ain't a pair of poofs.' Then she fixed her attention on the spokesman. 'Or it's my guess you're scared to go out without Frankenstein here to protect you and do your dirty work for you, 'cos really you're just a fucking coward!'

The huge man's face contorted. Clenching his fists, he made to launch himself on Della but was stopped by a warning gesture from the man beside him. Meaningfully, he told Della, 'This is your last warning. Pay what you owe us now and keep up the regular payments, or we'll make sure you do.'

She gave a scoffing laugh. 'I ain't scared of you, or him with yer, or anyone else. I've dealt with far harder men in me time than you pair of fairies. I owe you n'ote. I ain't paying you my hard-earned money. When will you get that through yer thick fucking skulls?'

The handsome man smiled at her. 'Your choice, Della.' Then

he said to the other man, 'Show this slapper just how we make people pay up.' Face screwed up, the ugly brute started to advance on her, but then a man and woman approached them, arm-in-arm. Spotting them, the spokesman said, 'Maybe this isn't the right time. Come on.'

As they walked off Della shouted after them, 'Yeah, that's right, go and crawl back into the hole you just crawled out of.'

She had only gone a short distance when a voice said, 'Are you looking for company?'

She turned her head to see a middle-aged, balding man addressing her. Her sharp eyes took in the quality of his clothes and excitement rose within her. Unlike the majority of her clientele these days, this man clearly had money. Without further ado Della hooked her arm through his and smiled winningly at him. 'I certainly am if you are, ducky.'

CHAPTER FOUR

The blizzard raged on into the early hours and Dee, like thousands of other workers, had to struggle through deep drifts the next morning to get to work as no buses were running. Since she hadn't heard her mother return during the night, Dee had not been surprised to find her bed empty. This was nothing unusual, considering her mother's line of work, and she automatically assumed that Della had spent the night with a client. On retiring to bed herself, anticipating the worst, she had set her alarm for an hour earlier than normal to leave herself time to set a fire for her mother to get up to – or as it turned out come home to – and also to allow herself plenty of time to get to work. Thanks to her astuteness, she arrived just before her usual starting time of eight o'clock. Her manager at Cleanrite Laundry and Dry Cleaning Company, Olive Gibson, was a stickler for time-keeping and no excuses for lateness were accepted.

Having hurriedly discarded her outer wear and pulled on her white overall, Dee went to join her colleague behind the shop counter.

Nina Baylis was just opening the outer door ready for business. She was an attractive woman who was prevented from being classed as pretty due to her protruding tombstone-like top teeth. Some of the women in the back room unkindly referred to her as Bugs Bunny behind her back. A couple of months older than Dee, for the last year she'd been courting a man called Len, a tall, lanky, reserved sort who worked for the Council's parks department. Nina was doing her utmost to marry him as she had decided he was the one for her.

Dee had worked for Cleanrite since leaving school, working her way up from laundry assistant to her present position, in charge of the customer counter. The management had been only too glad to secure her labour at a time when most girls leaving school wanted more prestigious jobs than a laundry company could offer. They hadn't taken the time to probe her background and had readily accepted her not exactly truthful version of it. Working with several other women of various ages, at times it had been difficult keeping her background secret due to the other women's natural nosiness, but up to now, thankfully, she had managed. As far as everyone at Cleanrite was concerned, Dee's mother was a factory worker.

On hearing her enter, Nina turned and gave her a welcoming smile. 'I was worried you wouldn't make it on time today. I don't envy you that trek you must have had, right across town then out the other side here to Westbridge. When I got up this morning and saw the fall of snow, I was so grateful I only lived a few streets away. My journey was bad enough, so I can imagine what yours must have been like. Anyway, I don't suppose we'll get many customers in today, but at least we're both here to serve 'em if we do.' Her face suddenly lit up as a memory struck her. 'Oh, how did last night with Kevin go? I hope the blizzard didn't cut short yer night with him.'

Dee was checking Miss Gibson had given them the correct float for the till because shortages at the end of the day came out of their pay packet. 'Er . . . no the blizzard didn't, but Kevin did.'

As she flicked the Closed sign to Open and made her way back around the counter, Nina stared at her non-plussed. Eh?'

The float was correct. Shutting the till drawer, Dee said, 'Seems I wasn't his type after all.'

'Eh? What do you mean? Bloody hell, Dee, they don't come much prettier than you, and you're a lovely person too.' Nina looked utterly bewildered. 'This doesn't make sense to me. I mean, I saw what he was like with you when he used to come in here and chat you up before you agreed to go out with him. He was smitten, I've no doubt about it. What reason did he give for not wanting to see you again?'

'Look, Nina, would you mind if we didn't talk about it?'

Of course she minded! She wanted to know every detail. Reluctantly, though, Nina answered, 'Oh! No, right, 'course I don't. It's just, I know you liked him a lot and you must be hurting . . . If you ever want to get it off yer chest, I'm here for yer. Anyway, plenty more where he came from.'

Another young woman arrived behind the counter then, her arms filled with hangered garments covered in clear cellophane wrappers, the company name printed in bold lettering across the front. Laying the pile over the counter, she said, 'This is the first lot of readies for today, though I can't see many coming in to collect 'em meself, not unless they're absolutely desperate. I just took a quick look outside and it seems like it's going to snow again. I'll bring the next lot through in a minute. Sally's only just arrived and Ada's not turned up yet so you can imagine Old Gibbo isn't very happy. If the world blew up one night, I still don't think she'd excuse us being late for work the next day. Anyway, we still on for a girly night at yours tonight, Nina, or will this snow put the damper on it?'

'Why is it always my house we have our girly nights in?' Nina responded. 'What about we all come to yours for a change, Sue?'

'Well . . . er . . . you could. Of course yer could but . . . well, me dad's in the middle of decorating at the moment and the house stinks of paint.'

Nina looked at Dee. 'What about yours then?'

'Mine? Oh . . . er . . . yes, of course, that would be fine.' Fingers crossed behind her back Dee then added, 'Only I've just remembered, Mam's got her Bible class coming round tonight and they'll rope us into joining them.'

Nina pulled a face. 'Oh, I don't fancy that. Looks like it's mine again then. Bring your new Elvis LP round, Susan, and we can have a bit of a dance. Our Dee here needs cheering up. Kevin dumped her last night.'

Susan Johnson's pleasant, plump face dropped in shock. 'Oh, he never, the rotter? Why?'

Before Dee could answer, Nina said, 'She don't wanna talk about it. Too painful.'

Susan laid a hand sympathetically on Dee's arm. 'Well, that's understandable. You liked him, didn't yer? Well, I know yer don't fancy him . . . but there's always my Owen's friend Mick. He's crazy for you, makes no bones about it, Dee, and yer never know, you might get to like him too if yer gave him a chance. Another bloke always makes you get over the last one quicker, everyone knows that. Shall I arrange a foursome?'

Dee didn't like to tell her that however good-looking a man was, she could never fancy one who picked his nose in public which she had seen Mick do, and he had a habit of sniffing back snot instead of blowing his nose. She just smiled appreciatively. 'I'll think about it and let you know.'

Just then Olive Gibson, a tiny, thin, prim-looking woman in her sixties, her greying hair cut into a short bob and gripped back behind her ears, round tortoiseshell glasses perched on the bridge of her long straight nose, appeared in the doorway to the workroom and in a brisk tone said, 'Miss Kirby, could I have a word in my office, please?' With that she disappeared.

Nina frowned. 'Gibbo's got summat on her mind. Important it must be, 'cos she never told us off for standing about yakking.'

Susan pursed her lips. 'Mmm, must have 'cos she never misses an opportunity to let us know who's boss. Wonder what she wants you for, Dee?'

She shrugged, perplexed. 'I don't know. I wasn't late in this morning, and I've done nothing wrong so far as I know.'

'Oh, I know what she wants you for!' exclaimed Nina. 'She's going to tell you she's finally retiring and putting you forward for her job. That's got to be it, Dee. What else could it be?'

'Oh, pray that's what it is!' cried Susan. 'You'd make a great manager, Dee. I'll let you make me your second-in-command, if yer want. I love bossing people about.'

'Eh, that job's earmarked for me, I've been here longer than you,' said Nina. Then she elbowed Dee in her ribs. 'Well, go on then, 'cos sooner you do, sooner we can celebrate your promotion and seeing the back of old Gibbo.'

A surge of excitement rose in Dee. Hopefully Nina and Susan were right and promotion was coming her way. It would mean she'd be able to give her mother extra money each week, help ease her financial situation, and then her battle to get Dee to join her on the game might ease up. What was she waiting for?

Olive Gibson was seated behind her desk, bony hands clasped tightly together, looking very pensive when Dee entered her office.

'Ah, Miss Kirby, er . . . please close the door and sit down,' she requested in an anxious tone.

Her manner confused Dee. It seemed to her that her boss was worried about something. What, though? Then it struck her that it probably wasn't worry she was suffering, more likely she was upset that after all her years of service she had to offer someone else her position.

When Dee had done her bidding, Olive took a deep breath and said, 'Well, this is very awkward, but I have to ask you a question, Miss Kirby, and I'd like a truthful answer, please.' She took another deep breath. 'What is . . .' She stopped and cleared her throat before continuing. 'What is your mother's occupation?'

This was the last question Dee had been expecting. She stared at her boss in shock. 'My mother's occupation?'

'Yes. It's a simple enough question. What does your mother do for a job?'

Dee felt beads of perspiration appear on her brow. 'Why are you asking me this, Miss Gibson?'

'Well, you see, I have to confirm there is no substance behind the lie before I take this matter any further.'

Dee looked bemused. 'What lie?'

'I found this pushed through the letter-box when I arrived for work this morning,' she said, pushing a piece of paper towards her.

Dee picked it up and an icy current of fear ripped through her when she saw what was written on it: '*Did you know Diane Kirby's mother is a prostitute? Like mother, like daughter?*'

Olive Gibson was continuing to speak. 'It's a lie obviously, a despicable lie, I can tell by the look on your face how horrified you are by it. Have you any idea who would want to slander you and your mother like this, Miss Kirby?'

This could only be Kevin's retaliation for last night. 'Er . . . no. No, I haven't.'

'I can't think of anyone who would want to bring grief to you in such an awful way either. I've always found you to be a lovely girl. A pleasure to have working here at Cleanrite.' Olive's face looked grim. 'People who have nothing better to do than write such filth are criminals, in my book.' She picked up the telephone receiver and began dialling. 'Hopefully the police can get to the bottom of who sent this and punish them accordingly.'

Dee's thoughts were still with Kevin. It was such a callous way of getting back at her. But when she heard the mention of the word 'police' she exclaimed, 'The police! Do we really need to get them involved, Miss Gibson?'

The older woman stopped dialling and looked at her hard for several long moments before saying, 'Why are you against my getting them involved in such a serious matter?'

'Well . . . there's no harm done.'

'No harm? Apart from the fact I can see how badly this has affected you, surely you want the person who tried to spread such a vicious rumour stopped from doing it to anyone else?'

'Yes, there's that, but really I'd just like to drop the matter, if you don't mind, Miss Gibson?'

Replacing the handset in its cradle, Olive Gibson stared at Dee again. Finally the truth dawned on her and with a look of horror on her face, she said, 'This letter isn't a poison pen at all. What it says is the truth, isn't it?'

A mortified Dee gulped, 'Er . . . yes. Well, no . . . only in part.'

Looking totally shocked, Olive Gibson demanded, 'Which part, Miss Kirby?'

She gulped again and whispered, 'About my mother.' Then she blurted out, 'But what she does doesn't affect my job with Cleanrite.'

Olive Gibson was staring at her, appalled. 'I beg to differ, Miss Kirby. I can't imagine what our customers would think of us for employing people with such . . . well . . . dubious backgrounds. And I have to think of the firm's good name. Then there's the fact that you lied about your mother's occupation when we first employed you. Worked in a factory, you told me. How do I know you aren't lying about yourself? Maybe you do the same work as your mother in your spare time.'

'But I don't, Miss Gibson!'

The older woman gave a heavy sigh. 'I want to believe you, Miss Kirby. I've grown fond of you over the years you've worked for me. I was considering putting you forward as my replacement when I retire, but how can I trust you after this?'

'Oh, Miss Gibson, I was wrong to lie about my mother's job when I first started, but I was frightened you wouldn't give me the job if I came clean.'

'And you were right, we wouldn't have. The fact is, though, you still lied and I have no idea how many other lies you've told since. I have to consider the firm's good name and also the rest of the staff, how they might feel about working alongside you now this has come to light.'

Dee's jaw dropped. 'You're going to ask me to leave, aren't you?'

'I have no choice. How your mother earns her money ... well ... it's immoral and Cleanrite won't be associated in any way with anything of such a nature. I have never had any problems with your work and will give you a good reference. And because I like you, Miss Kirby, I'll put an addendum that the parting of our ways was your decision, due to a personal matter.'

Dee desperately wanted to point out to Miss Gibson that when she was at school the word 'immoral' was defined as 'dishonest' – and there was nothing dishonest about using your personal assets in order to feed and clothe yourself and put a roof over your own head. But there was no point. 'That's very good of you, Miss Gibson,' she said through gritted teeth.

'If you collect your things and wait in the locker room, I'll have your pay made up and cards brought up to date, along with your reference.' Miss Gibson gave a sad sigh. 'I'm deeply sorry that we're parting under these circumstances, and I do wish you the best for your future.'

While people continued to judge others by their parents Dee

felt she didn't have much of a future to look forward to. She rose and made her way over to the office door. There she stopped and turned to face her former boss. 'May I ask if your mother worked, Miss Gibson?'

The older woman frowned, puzzled as to why she was being asked this question. 'Yes, actually, she did. She was widowed young with three children to look after. She took in washing and did cleaning jobs, when she could get them.'

'I see. So your mother provided a service for those wishing to pay for it?' Dee paused before adding, 'Just like mine.'

As she made her way through the main laundry room towards the staff locker room to await her dues, Dee was conscious that work there had come to a standstill. All eyes were riveted on her, and by the expressions she could see they all knew her secret now and no longer saw her as socially acceptable, to be included in their circle, but someone to shy away from, as if she carried a contagious disease. She wanted desperately to chide them for their ignorance, but saw little point. Better people than she had tried to change public opinion towards prostitution. All she would achieve was to make a spectacle of herself.

As she ran the gauntlet, it struck her there was only one way that word could have spread so quickly. Someone must have had their ear to Miss Gibson's door during her interview. Whatever the rights and wrongs of eavesdropping were, she felt deeply hurt by that person's actions in repeating all they had overheard. Until moments ago she had been on friendly terms with everyone here, had laughed and joked with them, shared intimacies – yet one person hadn't spared a thought for the humiliation she would suffer because of their loose tongue.

Once she had felt welcome and secure working alongside these people. Now all she wanted to do was get far away from their accusing eyes as soon as possible.

She was emptying her locker of her personal belongings when the door opened and Nina entered. She looked awkwardly at Dee as she opened her own adjacent locker. 'Er . . . I need me hankie out of me handbag. Got a runny nose, must have a cold coming.' Then she blurted out: 'Look, Dee, I think it's best to cancel tonight, what with this snow, and it looks like we're set for more so . . . well . . .'

It was all credit to Dee that she managed to stem the flood of tears that threatened her then and plant a smile on her face instead. 'It's all right, Nina. I was going to tell you I couldn't come tonight anyway. I suddenly remembered I had another engagement.'

The young woman looked mortally relieved as she shut the locker, her need for a handkerchief apparently forgotten. 'Oh, well, that's all right then. Er . . . I'd better get back behind the counter. See yer.'

Dee knew from experience that should their paths cross in future, Nina would look straight through her, pretend she hadn't noticed her.

A short while later she began her trudge home through the drifts of deep-frozen snow, the thick blanket of clouds above threatening more. She wondered what the future held for her now. Despite yet another devastating disruption to her life, she still couldn't bring herself to attach any blame to her mother for her role in this. It wasn't Della's fault how others viewed her occupation. The only option open to Dee now was the one that had always been open to her: accept what had to happen and prepare herself to deal with what lay ahead.

The sensible thing would be for her to make her way imme-diately to the Labour Exchange to check what was on offer and hope to secure herself a start for Monday. But tomorrow would be soon enough for that. Thanks to her reference, she was confi-dent she would get something, most likely in the shop assistant line. Although prospective employers wanted details of school leavers' backgrounds, she was now twenty-two and her previous work experience and ability would be their prime concern. Well, hopefully. She would count the rest of the day as an unexpected holiday.

CHAPTER FIVE

Feeling as though her whole body was one big icicle, Dee was mortally glad to arrive home but most surprised to find no sign of her mother. But then, in the past, visiting businessmen to the city with company expenses at their disposal had commandeered Della's company for several days at a time, so Dee wasn't too perturbed by this. It looked like her mother's luck could be turning, and if she returned with a decent amount of cash in her purse, she would be in a rare good mood.

Thankfully the fire was still in, just, so Dee soon had it roaring back into life. With no untidy Della at home, the room was as she had left it a few hours before so there were no household chores to be done except to prepare the dinner for the evening. As it was Wednesday it was egg and chips so there were only potatoes to peel. Having tackled a few personal chores usually done at the weekend, Dee picked up a book she was reading. After lighting one of the gas mantles to afford her enough light, she settled herself comfortably in an armchair.

The book was an historical romance, set on a farm in the middle of the last century; the heroine was beautiful and spirited, the hero tall, dark and ruggedly handsome. Dee was soon lost in its pages, the harshness of her own life forgotten as the relationship between the two main characters gripped her. How she wished she was the heroine, and the strong, charming man she was reading about was labouring hard to make her his own.

By mid-afternoon she had reluctantly dragged herself away from her book three times. The first time was to replenish the fire, the second to make herself some tea and a sandwich, and brave the cold to visit the outside privy. She refilled the coal

59

bucket while she was out, noting that their supply was running low due to the cold snap and hoping that what remained could be eked out until the coalman called again. The third time she got up it was to answer a loud summons on the back door.

Winnie Watson, a shrivelled, toothless, shabby old soul wrapped in a moth-eaten Army greatcoat, worn-down zipper boots on her feet, did not look very happy. 'You all right, Mrs Watson?' Dee asked her. 'Only, you look upset.'

'I bloody well am,' she snapped. 'Yer mam in?'

Dee shook her head. ''Fraid not.'

'Well, you tell her when she comes back, we have a long-standing agreement for the use of me spare bedroom every Wednesday af'noon, and whether she uses it or not I still expect me money. I don't appreciate either being disturbed by her *gentleman friend*. He woke me up from me af'noon snooze, enquiring where she was when he got fed up waiting for her at their usual rendezvous. He didn't look too happy when I sent him away disappointed. I have to say, I've known Del a long time and it ain't like her to miss the chance of earning a bob or two. Summat important musta kept her from doing so.'

'Oh, er . . . well . . . I can only apologise on Mam's behalf, Mrs Watson.'

She gave a disdainful sniff. 'Well, like I said, I'm put out.'

'I'll tell her you called when she comes home, Mrs Watson.'

The old woman stood staring at her and Dee wondered why she wasn't making any effort to depart. Then it dawned on her that Winnie Watson was expecting her to pay for the unused room on her mother's behalf. It was quite likely she relied on the bit of income she made from Della every Wednesday to buy her own dinner that evening. Dee went off to fetch her purse.

Having settled up with Winnie Watson, she returned to her book, eager to pick up where she had left off. She had just reached the final chapter and was about to discover whether the heroine was going to leave her brute of a rich husband, whom she had been forced to marry to save her family from ruin, or find the courage to run away with the penniless man she truly loved, just when another loud knock on the back door made her jump and had her exclaiming in annoyance, 'Oh, bugger!'

Her displeasure soon evaporated when she saw who the caller was. 'Come on in,' she said warmly to Madge.

'I won't lovey, ta. I don't want to risk antagonising yer mam so soon after our words yesterday. I just popped by as I was passing on me way to the Hind to check you're bearing up all right after what happened to yer yesterday? It seems to have got bloody colder, if that's possible, and threatening snow again. I've decided I ain't working outside tonight, I'm going to try me luck inside. Hopefully yer mam doesn't choose the Hind or the White Swan, but if she does . . . tough! After her attitude towards me yesterday, I ain't going to pussyfoot around her any more. I've got a right to work wherever I want on our patch. Anyway, how are things with you?'

'Just come in, Aunty Madge,' Dee urged, mindful that precious heat was escaping. 'Mam ain't in,' she assured her. As she shouldered shut the swollen door after Madge had entered, she continued, 'She hasn't been home since last night, in fact. She left just after you did and I haven't seen her since.'

Madge didn't looked too surprised by this news and said matter-of-factly, 'Oh, she's obviously landed herself the type with plenty of brass in his pocket and is holed up with him in a hotel somewhere. If I know Della, she'll be abusing room service.' Madge gave a heavy sigh. 'I can't remember the last time I landed the sort to show me a real good time while I gave him one. I'm jealous, I ain't ashamed to admit. But good luck to her, I hope she does well out of it. I might be annoyed with her at the moment but she's still me friend.' She was following Dee into the back room. Once there she stood with her back towards the fire, inching up her tight skirt to warm her cold legs. 'So how are you then?'

'Oh, I'm fine, thanks.'

Dee's response was just a little too glib for Madge's liking. Then the warmth of the room struck her and she noticed the empty plate on the hearth, the mug beside it, the open book on the arm of the chair. These were clear signs of someone who had been home a while. She looked quizzically at the girl. 'Were you sent home from work for some reason? Oh, Dee, did last night affect you more than you're saying and you haven't been in at all?'

Dee looked uncomfortable. 'No, I went in to work today but . . .' Suddenly she felt a desperate need to unburden herself of recent events to someone who would lend her a sympathetic ear. The only person she felt comfortable with and trusted enough was standing right in front of her. 'Aunty Madge, have you got time for a cuppa? But if you're in a rush, I understand.'

Madge hadn't, she needed to be off out earning money and she knew Dee knew this, but it was obvious something had happened to her at work today, something that had sent Dee home early and was upsetting her now. Unhooking her handbag from her arm and flinging it on to the seat of the vacant armchair, Madge began taking off her coat. 'I've always got time for a cuppa with you, lovey. I'd sooner have summat stronger but I don't think yer mother would appreciate me helping meself to her bottle again so soon. Put plenty of sugar in, darlin', I'm hoping I'll need the energy tonight. Maybe some of yer mother's luck will rub off on me, eh?'

A while later an angry Madge exclaimed, 'Excuse my French, but fucking ignorant imbeciles some folks are! I feel like going round there and sorting the lot of them out. Who do they think they are, turfing you out just because of what yer mother does? Call her immoral . . . what's immoral is their attitude towards *you*. You've done 'em a good job all these years, and *this* is how they repay you? Well, if that's how their small minds think yer best out of there, gel, in my opinion.'

Dee looked guilty. 'Well, I did lie when they asked me what my mother did when I first applied for the job.'

'You had no choice, did yer? Your old boss told you herself they'd never have taken you on in the first place if you'd been honest with 'em. Anyway, getting rid of you is their loss. You said you was being considered for the manager's position? Well, they've just lost themselves the best one they could ever have had. When you're asked why you left yer last job, just tell them you was needed to nurse a sick relative. You've done nothing wrong, Dee, so no need to act as if you have. And as for those so-called friends you socialised with there . . . well, let me tell yer, they ain't real friends, lovey. Friends never judge, and they never turn their back on yer, no matter what.'

'Like you don't my mam,' Dee put in.

Madge smiled. 'It's hard sometimes to be a proper friend to someone like Del, but I hope I have been to her.' A distant look glazed her eyes as she said distractedly, 'At a time when I once thought I had no one and nothing to live for, Del made me see I could still have a future if I wanted it. Not everyone would have seen it as a good one, mind, but it was better than the one I was contemplating at the time. For that reason I'll be eternally grateful to her, and it's why I stick by her through thick and thin.' She realised she was thinking out loud and mentally shook herself. 'You'll make more friends in your new job, lovey,' she said to Dee with conviction.

'Yes, I hope so, but then sooner or later the same thing will happen again.'

Madge knew that the only way Dee was ever going to prevent situations such as this and the encounter with Kevin last night was to take the drastic action of packing up and leaving this area, or better still town for one where no one knew her. She could change her name, invent a new background for herself. But she knew Dee would never even consider it. Della hadn't exactly been the perfect mother, and was becoming more and more cantankerous as she struggled to make ends meet and come to terms with her own wasted life. It wasn't easy to live with her sometimes, near impossible in fact, but Madge knew Dee loved her mother and was deeply loyal to her, so there was no point in even suggesting she should move away.

'Well, it might, it might not. That's a chance you'll have to take. There are people out there who won't give a toss what yer mother is because they'll like you enough not to. Believe me, lovey, I know there's a future for a lovely gel like you. You just have to play the patience game. Anyway, what's yer plan of action now?'

Dee shrugged. 'I haven't got one. I'm going to start looking for a job tomorrow, hopefully get a Monday start.'

'Well, that's a plan in my book. Look, sod yer mother! Go and get the sherry. We'll drink a toast to yer new future.'

Dee stepped over to Madge, bent down to give her a hug and an affectionate peck on her cheek. 'I know you really haven't got the time to listen to my woes, Aunty Madge, but I appreciate the fact that you did. I do love you, you know.'

Madge blinked back a tear. She had forgotten the last time someone had said this to her and meant it, and found she was having difficulty handling it. Flapping one hand dismissively, she said, 'Go and get that sherry before it goes off and is undrinkable!'

Dee laughed at that. 'Coming up!'

CHAPTER SIX

The next morning at just before nine o'clock Dee gave her appearance a final check in the mottled mirror hanging above the fireplace. She wanted to look her best for the interviews she hoped to have today. Her long hair was pinned tidily into a flattering French pleat, face scrubbed clean of make-up. After careful consideration she had chosen to wear a white blouse and plain straight black skirt. She hoped her ageing winter coat, which she had no choice but to wear in this appalling weather, did not spoil the effect. She had been saving up to buy a new coat, bit by bit as money allowed, but those savings had had to be handed over to her mother after she had suffered a particularly bad couple of weeks. Dee was still waiting for the return of her loan and was of the opinion now she'd be lucky to see it. Della had a short memory so far as money loaned by her daughter was concerned, viewing it more as a gift.

A fresh fall of snow had been added overnight to the earlier blanket and there was still no sign of a thaw. Dee dearly hoped the Council, who had proved very slow to react in the past, had cleared the main roads by now and that the buses were back running as she didn't fancy another trudge like yesterday's.

She was just about to pull on her coat when she heard the back door thrown open and just as loudly banged shut. Her mother burst in. She looked dishevelled to say the least but with an expression on her face like a cat who'd just polished off a saucer of cream. Dumping two carrier bags on the dining table, and not seeming to notice that Dee would not normally be home at this hour, she commanded, 'Get the bottle of sherry, gel.'

Dee gawped at her. 'At this hour, Mam?'

65

'Don't care what hour it is,' said Della, stripping off her coat and flinging it over the back of a chair, not caring when it slipped off onto the floor. 'I've got summat to celebrate!'

'You've had the luck to get a well-off client, Mam?' said Dee, eyeing the bags on the table.

Della had parked herself on a wobbling dining chair and was easing off her shoes. 'That's about the size of it. From Doncaster, in Leicester on business for his firm, and I spent the last two nights with him in the Highfields Hotel! I really enjoyed making sure the room-service staff earned their money. Me gentleman friend didn't seem to be worried, though, said his expenses would take care of it and to have what I wanted. So I did. Generous firm he works for, eh?' She pulled a wry face. 'Pity his visit here was just a one-off, it woulda been just great having his sort as a regular, but at least landing him tells me I've still got it in me to get that type.'

Dee was pleased for her mother. It was about time she had some good luck. Della didn't usually discuss business with her on principle but it was obvious she was desperate to relate her good fortune today and didn't care to whom.

'While he was working yesterday he gave me some cash to go shopping with, retaining me services while he was gone,' Della crowed. 'Long time since I've had a decent enough amount to buy meself some new clobber. I got a dress and a pair of shoes.' She flung her old ones scornfully over by the kitchen door. 'Won't be sorry to see the back of those! Cripple me ain't the half of it. Sling them in the dustbin when yer passing, gel.'

Della seemed to have forgotten she owed her daughter money but Dee didn't begrudge her the pleasure her shopping was giving her. 'Mrs Watson called in yesterday afternoon to ask where you'd got to. I gave her the money for the room you didn't use. Half a crown it was.'

Ignoring her, Della stood up, giving a loud yawn and a stretch. 'Forget the sherry. I'm off up to bed for a bit of shut eye to refresh meself for tonight. I'm hoping I'm on a lucky streak and there's more where he came from, beating a path to me door.'

She made her way upstairs, leaving Dee staring after her. She was relieved Della had not noticed the way her sherry had dwindled, though. Dee hoped she'd time to replace it before her mother found out. Her well set up client had certainly put her in a good mood, good enough for her to pass up on an opportunity to have a go at her daughter for her refusal to be out there earning big money too. She said a silent thank you to her mother's new punter for unwittingly saving her from that.

As she set off for the Labour Exchange Dee prayed her mother's luck would rub off on her too.

Just after twelve o'clock she smoothed back her hair to tidy any loose strands, tapped her feet to free them of caked snow that had built up during her journey, took a deep calming breath and entered the premises of Pringle's hardware shop on the Green Lane Road. As the buses were still not running, the journey to the Labour Exchange had seemed to take forever as Dee slipped and slid her way over the packed slippery snow on the pavements. Now, on the other side of town, she was feeling quite tired but hoped it did not show as she wanted her prospective employer to see her as the enthusiastic sort, ready to tackle any job given her.

The job of counter assistant at Pringle's was one of three she had spotted on the Vacant Positions board. She dearly hoped she was successful here so she could safely go home and not face another trek today.

Before she entered the shop, Dee took a moment to gaze through the glass door and get a feel for the place. The shop appeared larger than she'd thought it would be and looked to contain anything anyone could ever want in the hardware line. Behind the counter, up to ceiling height, were rows of small drawers, containing she assumed small items such as nuts, bolts, screws, bath plugs, fuses, et cetera. Rows of gardening tools were stacked against one wall, along with a couple of lawn mowers, watering cans and such like. On the opposite wall hung several different-sized tin baths, and jostling for space on the floor below were dustbins, stacks of galvanised buckets, plastic washing-up bowls, sink plungers, dolly pegs, and lots of other items Dee couldn't make out from here. A couple of rows of shelving in the middle of the shop floor appeared to hold such items as packets of seeds, rat poison, slug pellets and the like. It looked an interesting sort of place to work, she thought. More to sell and ways to help the customers than Cleanrite had afforded her.

Several seconds after the shop bell had clanged, announcing her presence, a harassed-looking middle-aged man dressed in a brown shop coat appeared through a curtained doorway at the back of the counter.

Placing his hands flat on the counter top, he gave her a smile and asked, 'What can I do for you, me dear?'

Dee smiled back. 'Mr Pringle?'

He looked askance at her. 'I am he, yes.'

'Diane Kirby. I saw your vacancy for a counter assistant advertised in the Labour Exchange and I've come to apply for it.'

The harassed expression on his face vanished, to be replaced by one of sheer delight. 'Have yer really? Oh, I am glad! You must be keen, I'd say, traipsing from the Labour Exchange all the way here in this snow. I know the buses still aren't running . . . Well, come on through the back and we'll have a chat.' He lifted the flap at the end of the counter to allow her to pass through and led her into a small back room, old fashioned in appearance but with a welcoming feel to it. There was a fire burning in the leaded grate. He indicated a comfortable-looking armchair to one side of the fireplace, and when she had seated herself sat down in the matching chair opposite and looked at her keenly.

'Well, you look presentable enough. Done shop work before?'

'I worked for Cleanrite, the laundry service, as their senior counter assistant. I've got a reference from them.' She took it out of her handbag and held it out for him to take.

He took it and laid it on the arm of his chair to read later. 'I'll tell you what I can about the job. We get rather busy . . .' He was interrupted here by the clanging of the shop bell and jumped up. 'As you can see. I'll be as quick as I can,' he said, rushing off to answer the summons. He came back five minutes later and resumed his seat. 'Sorry about that. Customer after a light fitting and some disinfectant. Anyway, where was I?' He was looking to Dee for guidance.

She obliged. 'You were telling me about the duties.'

'Ah, yes.' He scratched his head. 'Well, it's to serve the customers really. Up until very recently my wife and I ran the business together.' He paused and swallowed hard, his voice faltering for a moment as he added, 'She died a couple of months ago. Very sudden it was. I miss her dreadfully. It's taken me until a couple of days ago to bring myself to start looking for someone to replace her. Not that I *can* replace her, you understand.' He paused, an embarrassed expression flooding his face, and awkwardly cleared his throat. 'Forgive me, I got carried away, you're here to learn about the job. Of course, there are a lot of different stock items to become familiar with, but you look intelligent enough to cope with that. I'd want you to keep an eye on stocking levels so we didn't run short of anything and have to turn customers away disappointed. I go out to the wholesaler's a couple of times a week, and I do deliveries for customers who telephone with an order and want that service. I don't suppose you drive, do you?'

Dee shook her head. 'Afraid not.'

'Oh, well, if you'd be interested we could see about getting you lessons and then maybe you could do some of the deliveries.'

Dee's eyes lit up. She would like that. She liked the sound of working here, in fact. Mr Pringle seemed like a nice man. Cleanrite had paid the going rate and she presumed Mr Pringle would either match that or, with a bit of luck, be offering a little more. A surge of anticipation rose within her. She hoped she was going to be offered the position.

'I wouldn't mind learning to drive,' she told him keenly.

He looked pleased. 'Oh, good. Well, the hours are eight until six on weekdays, an hour for dinner, and on Saturday we close at one-thirty. I pay three pounds five shillings a week.' He looked at her hopefully. 'Does the job sound interesting to you? If so, how soon can you start?'

Same wage as Cleanrite, and same hours of work, but her job

here would be far more rewarding in respect of the variety of stock that was sold and helping the customers with their purchases. Of course she wanted it! She'd start as soon as he wanted her to. She opened her mouth to give him her answer but was stopped by the clanging of the shop doorbell. Before Mr Pringle could apologise to her again and rise to answer the summons, a tall, thin, stern-looking woman entered. Her greying hair was scraped back into a severe bun at the base of her neck. She wore a black coat and hat, black zipper boots on her feet, dusted with snow, and was clutching a large black bag before her. A young man, several inches shorter than the woman, studious-looking and spotty, his mousy hair cut into a short back and sides and plastered flat to his head, was hovering by her side.

The woman flashed a suspicious glance at Dee before fixing her eyes on Mr Pringle.

'What's going on, Neville?' she asked abruptly.

'Oh, Clarice, this young lady has come to apply for the job,' he told her delightedly.

'Well, she isn't suitable,' the woman sharply responded. She fixed her eyes on Dee. 'I'm sorry if my brother has wasted your time.'

Neville Pringle looked at her aghast. 'Clarice, what on earth do you mean, saying Miss Kirby isn't suitable? Of course she's suitable. She's most presentable, as you can see for yourself, and has done shop work before. She's got a reference . . .'

'Oh, for goodness' sake, Neville! She's a young woman.'

He flashed a look at Dee then back at his sister. 'That's obvious. And a very pretty one too.'

'Don't be flippant, Neville,' she snapped crossly. 'You take this young woman on and you'll be the talk of the street, not to mention at church. The gossips would have a field day. Your wife, God rest her soul, is barely cold in her grave and you want to take on a young woman? You two on your own here together . . . Have you thought how your business could suffer if you went ahead with this folly? *You* might not mind the gossip, but I'm your sister and my own good name is at risk too. Not to mention how the business could suffer, with people taking their custom elsewhere.'

Neville tutted. 'I'm sure you're exaggerating, Clarice.'

She glared at him. 'Need I remind you of Mr Hubbard, and what happened to him when he employed that young lady as his clerk after his wife died?'

Neville looked worried. 'Oh, I'd forgotten all about him.'

Clarice Pringle grabbed the arm of the young man by her side and yanked him forward. 'This is Mrs Riddle's son, Alfred. You know her, she does the flowers at church. Alfred left school at Christmas and so far has had no luck in getting set on. But that's fortunate for you as he will suit you admirably and can start at once.' She looked at Dee. 'I apologise on my brother's behalf for wasting your time.'

Neville Pringle picked up the reference and handed it back to Dee. 'I'm sorry about this, but my sister's right. It wouldn't look good if I took you on.'

Deeply disappointed, she smiled politely at him as she retrieved her reference and made her way out. As she retraced her steps towards town, Dee couldn't believe she had just lost the chance of a good job, purely through being an attractive woman. She did wonder, though, how the gossip-conscious Miss Pringle would have reacted if she had discovered her brother had been on the verge of employing the daughter of a prostitute?

Well, that job was not meant to be. She hoped the one at her next port of call had her name on it.

Arriving at the premises of Kitchen's, a builder's supplier situated off the Abbey Lane with a vacancy for a clerk, she again checked her hair for loose strands, gave her snowy shoes a quick tap to rid them of what she could, then took a deep breath before walking purposefully through the entrance gates.

The yard was cluttered with all manner of building materials. As she glanced around for the offices, a donkey-jacketed man in the process of clearing drifts of snow piled up against the materials spotted her. He chopped the spade he was using into the snow to hold it upright and sauntered across to her.

He was a stocky man, podgy-faced, and his overt scrutiny of

her made Dee shift uncomfortably on her feet. 'Well, ain't you a sight to brighten a red-blooded male's day? What can I do for you?' His tone was suggestive.

If she was going to work here, she needed to let this odious man know she expected him to respect her. She hoped all the other workers weren't like him. Fixing him with her eyes, Dee said firmly, 'I'm looking for the manager. I've come to apply for the job of stock-control clerk.'

His face split into a grin. 'And don't I hope you get it! We could do with someone like you working here to liven the place up. The old bag that's just left was a right prude. Got a fella, have yer? He then looked at her more closely. 'Have we met before, only you look kinda familiar?'

Come to think of it, he looked familiar to her too but she couldn't at that moment place him. 'You were going to tell me where I could find the manager,' she said briskly.

His grin widened. 'Vixen type, eh? Oh, we're in for some fun, we are.'

'Coombs!' a stern voice shouted. 'Get back to work.' Dee automatically turned her head in that direction to see a pleasant-looking man of about thirty heading towards her. As he came level with them he glared at the stocky man, who had still taken no notice of his order, and reiterated: 'Coombs, I said, get back to work. You should have had all that snow cleared by now. You've been at it all morning and I can't see too much progress.'

Coombs cast him a scornful look. As he sauntered away to resume his task he muttered under his breath, 'Fucking upstart.'

The new arrival turned his attention to Dee then and smiled at her welcomingly. 'I'm Mr Lamb, Mr Kitchen's second-in-command. He's out on business at the moment. How may I help you?'

He seemed nice, not at all like Coombs. Hopefully he was the only man like that here and all the rest were more like the man currently addressing her. She made to respond, then something struck her. Coombs . . . Why did that name ring a bell? Then she froze as she remembered. Kevin's surname had been Coombs. Oh, God, and he worked alongside his father for a

72

builder's merchant. Surely it wasn't this one? As if on cue, out of the corner of her eye she saw Kevin himself over at the other side of the yard, driving a fork-lift truck, a pallet of bricks on its forks. And he was heading this way!

Her heart thudded painfully. She dreaded what Kevin's reaction would be if he spotted her. She had no concrete proof that he was responsible for the anonymous letter that had got her the sack from Cleanrite but it had to have been him. And besides that, he'd hurt and humiliated her. She couldn't risk meeting him here. To her horror Coombs Senior's voice boomed across the yard. 'I've just realised who you are. You're . . .'

Knowing what he was about to divulge, she blurted to Mr Lamb, 'I'm sorry, I have to go.'

With that she spun on her heel and, as quick as the slippery surface would allow, rushed out of the yard. Outside on the pavement she heaved a sigh of relief that she had escaped unscathed. The job at Kitchen's definitely did *not* have her name on it. One thing she did know, though, judging by Kevin's father's behaviour – he had to have had dealings with her mother to have spotted the resemblance between them. Traumatic for her as it had proved, Dee was glad now that her relationship with Kevin was over. She'd clearly had a very lucky escape from becoming embroiled with a family like that.

The time was getting on for three o'clock. The thick grey clouds above looked to be threatening to shed another load of snow. Dee faced a dilemma. Her job search today had proved a total disaster and she felt like going straight home in the hope that tomorrow would prove more fruitful. But unless a new batch of vacancies had come in at the Labour Exchange, only one suitable vacancy remained on her list. If she didn't try for it now then she risked it being filled by tomorrow. She had no choice but to press on. There was one consolation. The job was a counter assistant's position in the babywear department of Lea's department store on Humberstone Gate. Although it was a good walk from where she stood now, it was at least in the direction she would take to go home.

* * *

An hour and a half later, a jubilant Dee had secured herself the job, to start next Monday. Mrs Stafford, the manageress of the department, had assured Dee she liked to run a tight but fair ship and her staff to get on. She thought Dee would fit in nicely. She took her explanation for leaving Cleanrite at face value and seemed impressed by her reference. The hours were the same as at Cleanrite but the pay was half a crown a week more, which pleased Dee. The staff she had come across seemed nice and she had a feeling she was going to enjoy working there. Her prayer for some of her mother's luck to rub off on her had indeed been granted.

Thankfully the imminent snowstorm had held off. Light flurries only began to fall as she arrived home, just a little later than she normally would have had the buses been running. She found her mother in dressing-gown and rollers, about to brave the icy yard and replenish the coal bucket.

Della looked relieved to see her daughter. 'Good, yer home,' she said, handing Dee the bucket which she automatically took. 'While yer've got yer coat on, fill that up and stock the fire. It's burning low. Hurry up and get the dinner on too, I'm starving. Eh, yer don't know where me bottle of sherry is, do yer? Only I can't find it.'

Dee knew where it was. She had hidden it right at the back of the pantry so she could replenish it before her mother saw how low the contents were. With all that was on her mind today, and in her need to get home before the snow started falling again, she had completely forgotten about calling in at the off licence, though.

She gave a shrug. 'I've no idea,' she fibbed. 'I'll have a look for it.'

A while later Dee was clearing the table of the remains of a hurriedly assembled meal of mashed potatoes and slices of tinned Spam, and her mother was putting the finishing touches to her appearance.

'You'll do,' Della said to the reflection in her Max Factor compact mirror, an expensive item purchased quite a few years back when she'd had money to fritter away. She chucked it into her handbag along with her lipstick, clicked the bag shut, stood up and pulled her coat from the back of the chair next to her. She put it on over her new red dress, courtesy of that generous benefactor, along with her new bright green patent stilettos, and hooked the bag over her arm.

'Well, I'm off. Hopefully you won't see me back tonight, if me luck's holding.'

Snow was falling steadily now, adding another thick layer to the deep covering that, thanks to the below-zero temperature, had not yet had a chance to thaw out. Della would find conditions far more hazardous to journey through than Dee had earlier. She feared her mother was in grave danger of breaking her neck, tramping down badly lit interconnecting jetties at the back of the terraces, particularly in her most unsuitable footwear, but she knew she would be wasting her breath pointing this out or asking her to stay home in the warm tonight. And, besides, staying at home would only be an opening for her mother to have her usual go at Dee for not being out there herself, bringing in a substantial amount more than she did from her day job.

Her hands filled with plates from the table, Dee smiled at her. 'I'll see you when I see you then, Mam.'

After completing the chores that needed to be done, she switched on the radio to a popular station for background music then settled down to finish off her novel. The story had a very satisfactory ending. The heroine did pluck up the courage to leave her brutish husband for the penniless man she loved, and together they walked off into the sunset to begin their new life together. Putting that book away, Dee fetched another from the store of second-hand ones she kept in her bedroom. Again her book had a romantic theme, the blurb on the back informing her this story was set in a Northern town and told the tale of a girl born in poverty who took the fancy of the local squire's son when she went to work for his family. Again the hero was ruggedly handsome and Dee was soon lost in the book's pages, vehemently wishing she was the heroine who was being pursued.

It seemed strange to her to be going to bed that night without having to set her alarm. Stretching ahead of her was a whole weekday plus the weekend to do whatever she liked in. She must be careful she didn't wake her mother, as usually Della slept most of the day, but otherwise it would be time to herself and she meant to savour every minute of it. Hopefully she wouldn't have any more for a while, if the new job worked out.

Out of habit, though, she woke at the usual time in the morning. Unable to get back off to sleep, she got up, hurriedly pulled on her faded dressing-gown then took a peek out of the window to see what the world outside looked like. Through a veil of icicles hanging from the window-frame, all she could see was a sea of white, broken here and there by the blurred outlines of things the snow had not yet covered completely. The sky was still masked by a thick blanket of cloud and it didn't take an expert weatherman to predict that the snow was not yet finished with them. Not exactly the sort of weather for venturing out in if you really didn't have to, but Dee did as there was nothing in for dinner.

When she arrived downstairs it was apparent she needn't have crept as there was no sign of her mother having returned. It was obvious Della's run of luck had not ended yet and Dee hoped this meant she had secured herself another regular client, hopefully with plenty of money at his disposal, just like the last one.

The five-minute trip to the shops took half an hour today. Thankfully, early workers had forged a narrow track through the banked-up snow in the couple of alleys she needed to use. Subsequent pedestrians had kept the track clear although under-foot the compacted snow was slippery so care needed to be taken. As Dee concentrated on keeping from falling to left or right against the mounds of snow that had drifted against the alley walls, she kept guessing what lay hidden beneath them. It was impossible to tell exactly. Could be anything as people were prone to dump in the street any old items such as boiling coppers, mangles or prams that they couldn't be bothered to take to the tips themselves for the Council to take care of.

She returned from her shopping trip, thankfully without any mishap, and set down the ingredients for their dinner of tinned Frey Bentos steak pie and potatoes, to be cooked as chips later.

With the household chores done, radio turned low as background music, gas mantle on the wall nearest her chair turned just high enough to read by, Dee settled down with her book.

It was with surprise that she lifted her head and realised night had fallen. The book had held her attention and she hadn't noticed time passing. Dee glanced at the tin clock on the mantle. Six o'clock and still no sign of her mother. Matters looked good for her then. She was obviously being kept fed and watered by her new benefactor. But Dee wasn't. The pie she had planned to cook was for two and wasn't as palatable when reheated. She settled for a plate of chips instead, accompanied by a dollop of HP sauce and slice of bread and margarine. The rest of the night passed pleasantly enough for her with her book and the radio for company. She retired to bed at just after eleven.

Next morning Dee rose and peeked out of the window, thankful to see that the icicles on her window-frame were dripping water, heralding a thaw.

It was still cold, though. As she arrived downstairs and set about making the fire, it surprised Dee to realise that although she had enjoyed her own company, she was beginning to miss her mother, no matter how untidy, loud and domineering she could be. Dee hoped she wasn't being selfish by wishing that Della's time with her new client was now at an end and she'd return today. When she did come home she would expect to find food in the pantry and Dee was expected to provide it as her mother didn't do food shopping, not while she had her daughter round to do it for her. As it was Saturday, two days' worth needed fetching. Oh, and she mustn't forget to call by the off licence for half a pint of sherry to replace what Madge and she had drunk from her mother's bottle.

Her trip this time was not so precarious thanks to the thaw having well and truly established itself, but filthy slush and rivers of water had resulted. By the time Dee returned home her feet were sopping, as were the bottoms of her slacks and the shoulders of her coat where falling drips from the guttering had caught her as she passed underneath.

Wet clothes hanging up to dry, shopping put away, beds

stripped and remade, the week's washing hanging in the outside washhouse and on a clothes horse around the fire, Dee prepared herself to relax for the rest of the afternoon. She had barely started her book when a loud knock resounded on the back door. She couldn't think who would be calling now. The milkman had caught her for his dues just as she was leaving for her shopping trip that morning; the coalman she had encountered on her way to the shops and settled his bill, so it wasn't him. The rentman called on a Monday evening, and if it was him she couldn't afford to pay him anyway, considering what she had already laid out of her last wage from Cleanrite.

Handling the household finances was something Dee had done for a long while now. She couldn't remember when or just how her mother had passed on the responsibility to her. On a Friday evening the understanding was that Dee would tell her mother roughly how much she needed to get through that coming week. With many a grudging comment Della handed it over, provided she had it on her, or was honest enough to admit she had it on her. If not, Dee had to cope on what she did hand over. Dee had long ago learned that to get out of her mother the amount she really required, she should say she needed at least ten shillings more. That way she usually broke even. It was a game of bluff, but a game that worked. Della thought she was getting one over on Dee, while Dee knew she was getting one over on her mother.

Upon opening the door to her caller, Dee's heart sank and she sighed aloud.

'How much?' she demanded of the fresh-faced constable who looked fifteen if he was a day to her.

He seemed taken aback. 'Sorry?'

'For my mam's fine. You've come to tell me you've arrested her for soliciting, haven't you? Well, whatever the amount is, I can't pay it. God knows how I'll raise it. Unless I can perform a miracle, you'll have to keep her in instead.' Then a thought struck her. Why hadn't her mother paid her own fine? After all, she must have earned a decent amount by now and she hadn't had time to spend it, had given Dee none, so she had to have

78

money on her. Della was obviously just being awkward, choosing to do her time, keeping her hard-earned cash for herself.

'I'll come and see what she's playing at,' Dee said with an air of resignation. 'What station is she in? Charles Street?'

Nineteen-year-old Brian Purcell, a novice at this job, was desperate to be in at the thick of real police work, such as chasing down criminals and making arrests. It was all he'd dreamed of from a young boy when he'd decided he wanted to follow his father into the force. His father, like many other policemen, had no sympathy whatsoever with women who sold their bodies for money; he thought them the dregs of society who deserved all they got, and that opinion had rubbed off on his son. Brian hadn't wanted this assignment. Really it should have been given to a more seasoned officer who was used to dealing with such matters, but they were otherwise engaged with what Brian deemed to be real police work.

A robbery had taken place earlier that afternoon in the centre of town, involving a bank and sawn-off shotguns. The culprits were still at large, or had been when Brian had reluctantly left the station a short while ago to bike the half-mile or so here. He was desperate to get this meeting over with and hotfoot it back to the station where hopefully he would be called upon to help in the big case. He had to admit, though, the woman who'd answered the door to him didn't look like the usual sort, dressed tartily and brash of character. This one actually looked quite presentable. Regardless, he assumed she shared the same occupation as her mother and therefore felt no respect for her at all. 'Look, your mother isn't in the cells,' he said matter-of-factly.

Before he could continue, a puzzled Dee demanded, 'Well, where have you taken her then?'

'To the morgue. Look, Miss . . .'

'Morgue!' she erupted. 'That's where dead people go, isn't it? Why have you taken her there?' At the expression on his face a cold shiver ran down her spine. She pressed her hands to her face and uttered, 'Are you here to tell me my mother's dead?'

He took off his helmet, placed it under his arm and asked, 'Look, can I come in?'

Della had a deep distrust of policemen after years of being harassed by them: moved on from her pitch, arrested for soliciting, losing precious earnings through the fines she'd had to fork out for. She had warned Dee in no uncertain terms never to let a policeman into the house because if they didn't find any evidence to convict you with, they'd only plant it. Respecting her mother's wishes she told him now, 'You don't need to come in to answer my question.'

It might have warmed up enough to thaw the snow but it was still extremely cold and the last thing Brian wanted was to catch a chill. He was meeting Trisha's parents tomorrow for the first time, over Sunday lunch, and wasn't going to impress them much if he was sneezing all over the roast. He gave an irritated sigh. 'As you wish. Well, I'm very sorry but, yes, she is dead.' He said he was sorry, but really he wasn't. A dead prostitute was one less for the force to waste their time on, in his opinion.

Dee was staring at him in shock. 'But . . . but she can't be! She's out with a . . . er . . . friend. Been with him . . . her . . . for a couple of days.'

'She's possibly been dead that long,' he told her bluntly. 'It's hard to determine the actual time of death in this weather, as you can appreciate. Kids discovered her body this afternoon when they were playing in the last of the snow behind the Admiral Beatty. Scooping it up with buckets and throwing it at each other, that's how they found her. She was wearing high heels . . .' He refrained from voicing the opinion that such footwear was ridiculous in these weather conditions, and no wonder she'd had an accident. 'It's obvious she slipped, fell over and knocked herself out. The snow that fell afterwards covered her. The police surgeon believes she froze to death.'

Her face a deathly white now, Dee stood leaning against the doorframe for support. 'You're . . . you're sure the body you have in the morgue is my mother's? Della Kirby?'

He nodded. 'The landlord of the Admiral identified her, along with a couple of his regulars. They said they knew her well. We need you to identify her officially, of course. I'll escort you down there now, if you feel up to it? If not, tomorrow morning will do.' The lure of proper crime was calling to him now. He would hate to miss out on this chance to be in at the thick of it because there was no telling when a bank robbery would come his way again. 'Look, I really need to get back to the station, Miss.' He should have asked her if there was anyone he could fetch to be with her for support, but that would take more precious time. 'So, are you coming with me to identify the body or leaving it till tomorrow?' he urged.

Dee's thoughts were all over the place. Her mother wasn't dead . . . she couldn't be. Stupid accidents like that woman in the morgue had suffered didn't happen to street-wise women like Della. Dee needed to see for herself that it was indeed her mother before she would believe it. The thought of viewing a dead body made her feel physically sick, but how could this matter be resolved if she didn't?

'I'll fetch my coat,' she whispered.

CHAPTER SEVEN

A frantic Madge only had to glance at Dee, huddled in a chair with a look of utter desolation on her face as she clutched Della's handbag to her chest, to know that what she had just been told was indeed true.

'Oh, me darlin',' she uttered, crouching down at the side of Dee's chair and laying one hand gently on her arm. 'I don't know what to say. I was praying a mistake had been made somehow.'

Dee slowly turned her head. 'Who told you, Aunty Madge?'

'I was on me way to Connaught Street to start work when I bumped into Beattie Knight. She'd just come from the Admiral, she cleans for them, it was all they were talking about.'

Dee swallowed hard in an effort to rid herself of the lump that was constricting her throat. 'I imagine the landlord's relieved my mam's no longer around to cause him grief. And the other prostitutes in there this evening will be glad there's one less to fight for business with in these parts.'

'Oh, Dee, yer wrong,' Madge assured her. 'Della was a character all right, she didn't shy away from trouble and is . . . was . . . downright annoying at times, but people liked her deep down.'

'I'd like to think so, Aunty Madge. The policeman who called to tell me . . . well, I could tell he was frightened that if he came too close to me he might catch a dreadful disease or something.'

Madge looked horrified. 'Oh, Dee, I'm so sorry you were treated like that. It's a fact of life, I'm afraid, that the police see us sort as scum. Why didn't you have him fetch me to be with you? Believe me, I'd have made sure he showed respect towards yer.'

'He never asked if I wanted anyone fetching.'

The bastard! Madge thought. 'And you've been sitting here all on your own since he told you? Oh, Dee, if only I'd known. You shouldn't have been on your own at a time like this. Anyway, yer not anymore, I'm here now. When you've arranged to go and identify Della officially, I'll come with you, it goes without saying.'

The girl gave a shudder. 'I already have. I had to, you see. I couldn't believe it until I saw her for meself.' A lone tear rolled down her face and she clutched Della's handbag tighter to her chest. 'It was awful, Aunty Madge,' she sobbed. 'The woman lying on the slab was my mother but she wasn't, if you understand me. She had bruises all over her face. They told me she got them when she fell over and knocked herself out. Oh, Aunty Madge, I can't bear to think that she lay unconscious in that jetty, slowly freezing to death. I went to the shops this morning, I walked down the jetty they found her in. I must have passed her and didn't realise it. Maybe she wasn't dead by then, and if I'd been more observant . . .'

'Stop torturing yerself, Dee,' ordered Madge. 'Della was under a lot of snow by all accounts.'

'Kids found her when they were playing. Oh, those poor children, it must have been awful for them.'

'Yes, it must have,' Madge admitted, but it was Dee's welfare she cared about now. Let the children's own parents deal with them. 'Look, have you had a cuppa?' Without waiting for an answer, she stood up. 'I'll make you one. Best thing for shock is sweet tea.'

A short while later, having forced a reluctant Dee to drink the tea she had made, Madge was cradling her protectively on the sofa. A spring was digging painfully into her backside but she had too much on her mind to pay attention. Dee was still having difficulty accepting what had happened to her mother, and so was Madge herself.

'Oh, Aunty Madge, you don't think she suffered, do you?' blubbered Dee.

Madge hoped she hadn't. 'I'm sure not, lovey. Didn't the

person who was with you at the morgue put yer mind at rest on that score?'

'He never gave me the chance to ask. He was looking at his watch, like he was in a hurry to be somewhere else, and just kept asking me if the body was my mother's or not.'

Anger against the officials who had dealt with Dee so shoddily rose within Madge. No matter what their own feelings were in respect of Della's profession, the least they could have done was treat Dee respectfully in her bereavement.

'No, I'm sure she didn't suffer,' was all Madge said to her.

There was silence for several long seconds before Dee unexpectedly asked, 'Do you think she loved me?'

'What! Of course she did, lovey.'

'She never told me. Not once, she never.'

'Well . . . some people find it hard to say words like "I love you". Your mother wasn't one for sentiment. It don't play any part in the line of work we do, and you learn to toughen up, to save yerself from getting hurt. Wouldn't do to fall for a client, would it? The chances of them falling for you ain't exactly high. It does happen, of course, but very, very rarely. I know Della never openly showed affection for you, Dee, but she did show me she felt it. She was so proud of you when you played the Angel Gabriel in your junior school nativity play. Not that she said as much to me, but I know she was.'

Dee looked astonished. 'How could she have been when she never came to see me in the play? I was the only one whose mother never showed up. You came, though, didn't you?'

'Oh, yes, I wouldn't have missed it for the world. But yer mam was there too, lovely. She snuck in just after the play started and stood by the door. She didn't know I'd seen her. How I wish you could have seen the expression on her face, then you'd be in no doubt that in her way Del did care for you very much. Yer mam wasn't shown any affection by her own mother, Dee, so she didn't know how to show it herself. I don't suppose you remember yer gran. She died when you was about four, if I remember right.'

Madge didn't wish to point out that it had been due to syphilis.

Nora Kirby must have known she was suffering from it long before its effects on her stopped her from working. But Madge didn't know whether Dee knew the exact details and this was hardly the time.

'I don't remember much about her,' Dee confessed. 'What I remember most is her lying in bed just before she died. I don't remember her ever cuddling me or anything like that. I do have one memory of her, though, before she took to her bed. She was dragging my mother out of hers and shouting at her to get to work. Mam was ill at the time, all sweaty and hot. I realise now she had 'flu, a really bad dose of it. I'd been doing my best to look after her, taking her up drinks of water and trying to get her to drink them.'

That was Nora Kirby all over, Madge thought. Nothing got in the way of her earning money. She hadn't allowed Della's pregnancy to stop her either, forcing her to continue right up to going into labour with her grandchild. She had been a hard woman, and her daughter Della had developed into almost a mirror image of her.

'I don't know whether we should entirely blame Nora for being like she was, and how she made Della. Although Nora never spoke much about her own mother during the time I knew her, I gathered she wasn't the kindest of women and Nora herself had a very hard upbringing . . . well, from what I deduce she practically raised herself from a very early age. Yer great-gran was not only an alcoholic who would disappear for days on end on benders, she also shacked up with any bloke she got her hands on then, leaving Nora on her own meantime, to fend for herself until the bloke got fed up with her mam and chucked her out. I think Nora spent most of her childhood living with a sucession of other prostitutes who took pity on her during her mother's absences and gave her a roof over her head.'

Dee hadn't been aware of any of this before. It made her feel unexpectedly sorry for her grandmother and gave her some understanding of why she had been like she had. No wonder Della had been tough also.

Dee sighed heavily. 'I was a huge disappointment to me mam,

though, wasn't I? Because I couldn't bring myself to follow her into the business.'

'Well . . . you have to understand that Del only expected of you what was expected of her by yer gran.'

Dee gave another heavy sigh. 'Yes, I suppose. My mother was always telling me it was a shame I wasn't born a boy, when I stood up to her about not wanting to earn my living the way she did. Why did she keep saying that, Aunty Madge? What difference would my being born a boy have made to her?'

Madge stared at her blankly. Dee's memories of Della would never be the fond ones a daughter should have of a nurturing mother. Della hadn't had it within her to show love, as her own mother hadn't towards her, and consequently Dee had been starved of maternal affection. Madge felt she didn't need the added burden now of learning what had been planned for her had she been born a boy, or the fact that Della only kept her daughter to ensure a prosperous old age for herself, just as Nora did with her.

She gave a nonchalant shrug. 'Oh, I suppose what she meant by that was that with a lad she wouldn't have had the same worries as raising a girl brought her. Lads can't get pregnant or anything, can they?' Madge hoped her explanation would be enough to satisfy Dee.

Silence prevailed again for several long moments before the girl whispered, 'I keep thinking Mam'll walk in and throw her coat down on the chair, expecting her dinner to be on the table.'

Madge glanced at her sympathetically. 'Well, it's not had time to sink in yet. They do say yer don't start to accept things until after the funeral.'

'Did you lose either of your parents, Aunty Madge?'

'Er . . . I don't know, lovey.'

'Oh! Does that mean you don't see them?'

Oh, Madge had seen them all right, not in the flesh but every day in her mind's eye, along with her brothers and sisters, and often in her dreams. She missed her family dreadfully, constantly wondering how they all were, or even if they were alive still.

Had her parents ever learned of their mistaken belief in the priest and regretted their rejection of her, or had the holy man been left at liberty to continue to abuse his position of trust? She had often thought of returning to find out, praying the truth had been discovered and she'd be welcomed back into the bosom of her family. She could always lie about how she'd earned her living since. But thought was one thing, action another. She had never found the courage, fearing that the priest was still managing to hide his wickedness and she would once again witness revulsion for her in her family's eyes. She couldn't go through that again.

'Er . . . yes, it does,' Madge said dismissively. 'We had a falling out. Do you want another cuppa?'

By her abrupt changing of the subject, Dee was left in no doubt Madge did not want, for whatever reason, to pursue the subject of her family. Obviously the parting of the ways had been traumatic for her. Dee wondered what had caused it but was too respectful of Madge's feelings to probe further. 'No, thanks. I feel sick, if you want the truth.'

'A slice of toast would help settle your stomach. Have you any bread, I'll make you one,' Madge offered.

Oh, why couldn't her mother have been more like Madge? Dee thought now. It had always been Madge who'd shown concern for her welfare, her own mother never had. It struck her then how over the years, whenever she'd had a problem or needed comfort, knowing her mother's shortcomings, it had been Madge she had sought out to help her, and Madge had never failed her. In truth, the woman whose arms were now protectively cradling her had proved far more of a mother figure than her own ever had. She loved Madge as a proper daughter should love a mother, unlike the way she'd felt for Della which had stemmed chiefly from duty. She just hoped that one day she would be able to show Madge how much she appreciated her.

'I really couldn't eat anything at the moment, thanks, Aunty Madge. Maybe later.' Dee paused and looked her in the eye before adding, 'I do love you, you know, and I'm grateful for the way you're always here for me.'

Madge gave her an affectionate squeeze. 'I know that, lovey.

And I'm glad I've been here for you when yer've needed me, and I hope I always will be.'

A thought struck Dee then. 'You know, if any of Mam's old clients ask you to take them on, don't hesitate. I'm sure if anyone else had to have them, Mam would have wanted it to be you. And I know you could do with the income from them.'

Madge wasn't quite so sure Della would have shown her such benevolence, considering how selfish she had been. But Dee was right, she needed all the income she could get at the moment, though it wasn't quite the time to be thinking of such matters. She gave Dee another affectionate squeeze. 'If any approach me I'll consider it, lovey, but let's see Del given a proper send off before we start thinking about things like that.'

Dee's face suddenly filled with horror. She forced herself to sit up out of Madge's embrace.

'What is it?' Madge demanded, worried.

'Me mam's funeral . . .'

'Oh, me darlin', don't worry about that. I'll help you arrange it.'

'But that's just it . . . I can't pay for it! I've no money of my own and we've nothing here to sell that'd make enough to cover it. Mam'll be buried in a pauper's grave,' she cried in alarm. 'Oh, I couldn't bear that for her, Aunty Madge. What on earth am I going to do?'

Madge stared at her. She was still so shocked by Della's sudden death, trying to come to terms with the loss of her friend and to support Dee at the same time, any thought of how the money was going to be found to bury Della hadn't entered her head.

'Was there anything in her purse to go towards it?' she asked hopefully.

Dee looked across at Della's handbag to the side of the armchair. 'I don't know,' she whispered. 'I can't bring myself to look inside. It feels wrong for me to be going through her private stuff.' She looked expectantly at Madge. 'Would you . . .'

''Course I will, lovey,' she cut in, patting Dee's arm reassuringly. After checking through it, she said, 'But for a handful of loose change, there's no money in her handbag.'

Dee looked perplexed. 'Mam told me she'd made good money from her last client, and as far as I know she never had the chance to spend any of it.'

'Oh, well, maybe she put it safe in her bedroom before she went out that night.'

Dee smiled at her. ''Course, that's what she would have done.' Again she looked expectantly at Madge.

'I'll go and have a look for you.' It was a good ten minutes before she returned to take her seat next to Dee on the sofa, her face looking perturbed. 'Well, yer mam never was the tidiest of people. It was like looking for a needle in a haystack, thinking where she might have put any savings, but sorry, lovey, apart from the odd copper on her dressing table, there's no other money I could find. Mind you, I'm not surprised. Del always did spend what she made, and age didn't seem to improve that trait in her.'

'But what happened to the money she made from her last punter? It must have been a few pounds, she was with him two days and nights. She never spent any of it, to my knowledge. She said he paid for her new coat and shoes.'

Madge saw the worry return to Dee's face, and her own thoughts raced frantically to find a solution. Suddenly, and thankfully, an idea sparked inside her. 'Listen, lovey, I have to pop out. Just a bit of business I need to take care of. You'll be all right for a while, won't you?'

'Of course I'll be all right, Aunty Madge. I understand you need to go to work. I appreciate the time you've spent with me already.'

'I'm coming back,' Madge assured her. 'I'm not leaving you on your own until I'm happy you're all right. I don't know how long I'll be, but I'll try to get back as fast as I can.' She worried that Dee would sit brooding while she was away. She needed something to occupy her, something to concentrate her mind on so she hadn't so much time to dwell on her mother's death and her own inability to pay for the funeral.

The last thing Madge felt like doing was eating but she asked, 'Look, I know it's a bit of a cheek, but I'm starving. While I'm gone, would you see what you can rustle up for me?'

Dee looked at her blankly. The last thing she felt like doing was cooking, she just wanted to sit and nurse her devastation. But for Madge she would make the effort. 'Yes, of course I will.'

Madge patted her hand. 'Good gel.'

After she had hurried off, Dee got up and began mechanically to prepare a meal.

Madge returned two hours later to the smell of faggots heating up in the oven and the sight of a pan of potatoes on the boil. There was a roaring fire, too, and the coal bucket was full on the hearth. Dee was wrapping potato peelings in newspaper to burn later on the fire.

'Sorry I was so long, lovey,' Madge said, plonking her handbag down on the draining board. Unclipping it, she pulled out a heavy object and put that down on the board beside the bag.

Wiping her hands on a cloth, Dee stared blankly at a pint beer mug stuffed to overflowing with coins of all denominations and several paper notes.

'It's yer mam's funeral money,' Madge told her.

Dee gasped. 'What?'

'Everyone willingly chipped in. They were all glad to help give Della a good send off.'

She was lying, but with the best of intentions. When she had done her rounds of the pubs and streets where Della was well known, most people she had accosted had scoffed when told her reason for collecting, saying in no uncertain terms that they had better things to spend their money on and wouldn't lose any sleep should Della be buried in a packing case at the bottom of a garden, so long as it wasn't theirs. Madge had then pointed out that they might not be mourning Della's death but she had a daughter who was, and that daughter hadn't the means to bury her mother. People might not have been fond of Della but they were of Dee. When it was put to them like that, most readily chipped in with as much as they could spare. The landlord of the Hind grudgingly gave five pounds when Madge reminded him that Della may have given him more than one reason to throw her out of his pub, but over the years she had brought him good custom through her own liking for a drink and the countless clients she had brought in with her. Madge had made it her business also to obtain everyone's promise – for as much as it was worth – that they would attend the funeral and wake afterwards, for Dee's sake. She had been most surprised by the generosity of the landlord of the Admiral Beatty, who not only put money into the funeral pot but also said he'd lay on a few sandwiches for the wake afterwards at no cost.

Dee was speechless. When she finally found her voice it was choked with emotion. Tears brimming in her eyes, she uttered, 'Oh, Aunty Madge! I didn't think many people would be sorry about Mam going, but this proves me wrong. They are sorry, aren't they?'

She broke down then. Wrapped tightly in Madge's arms, Dee sobbed for the loss of the woman who had given birth to her. Madge, too, shed tears for the loss of a friend. Whether Della actually deserved such heartfelt mourning was another matter.

CHAPTER EIGHT

Early on Monday afternoon Dee returned from an interview with Samuel Potter, owner of the local funeral parlour. Whether he was aware of her mother's occupation or not, he had dealt with Dee as he would any other grieving customer, with patience and the utmost respect. He used his expertise to arrange the best funeral he could that the collection money would cover. Despite Mr Potter's courteous attitude towards her and Madge's stalwart support, Dee still found the whole experience extremely distressing. Having never discussed such an event with her mother, she had no idea of her wishes. In fact, Dee was all too aware that Della had been a non-believer, vocally announcing the fact on many occasions. Her own funeral would be the first time she had ever been inside a church and in view of that Dee had insisted the service be a short one, the presiding clergyman instructed not to dwell on the Almighty welcoming back a lamb into his fold. She was pretty sure her mother wouldn't have stood for any of that pretence.

Although not liking to be leaving Dee on her own again, Madge had excused herself for a short while after the trip to the undertaker. She had a regular client she needed to attend to or risk the loss of some precious income. Before she left she made Dee promise to keep herself busy during her absence, so Madge knew she wouldn't be sitting brooding.

True to her word, Dee tackled the housework, albeit mechanically. She was in the process of browning some mince for their evening meal when an unexpected thudding on the front door made her jump. So far only Winnie Watson and Nell Baker had taken it upon themselves to call in and express their condolences. Although she had appreciated their effort, she was aware that both of them had arrangements with Della for rental of a room in which to entertain her regular clients. They knew Madge was keeping Dee company for the time being and were clearly hoping she would jump at the chance to fill the gap. These two desperate widow women were heavily reliant on the income this arrangement brought them. Madge, though, had given both of them short shrift, outraged they hadn't had the grace to wait until Della was at least buried before touting around to replace the revenue her death had lost them.

Thinking that her caller was another of these types, Dee went to answer the door. She was taken aback to see two men standing on the doorstep, and positively shocked when she was rudely pushed aside and they both made their way down the passage into the back room as if they owned the place. Bewildered as to who they were, and extremely angered by their rudeness and audacity, Dee hurriedly shut the door and rushed after them.

Arriving in the back room, she found one man had made himself comfortable in her mother's armchair while the other was poking around nosily. Both of them were well dressed in expensive-looking camel overcoats, and smartly suited underneath. The seated man was around five foot ten, slim of build, with his dark hair cut neatly short and meticulously groomed. He was good-looking, in fact, almost alarmingly so. The standing man was at least six foot three, his bulk seeming to fill the small room and intimidate Dee. His features were arranged in a way she knew her mother would have bluntly described as 'like an old man's backside', his ugliness not helped by his broken nose and a deep puckered scar running from the corner of his right eye to the side of his mouth.

When she arrived in the room, the standing brute turned to stare at her menacingly. The seated man smiled charmingly.

'Something smells good,' he observed.

'Look, who are you and what are you doing here?' Dee demanded.

He dusted an imaginary speck off his lapel before saying, 'I heard Della Kirby was dead?'

Dee swallowed hard at this reminder. 'She had an accident.' These two men were definitely not the sort to have been clients of her mother's and she wondered in what other capacity they were acquainted with her. 'Well, I assume you'd like details of her funeral. It's . . .'

The brute sneered at her and in an insulted manner cut in, 'Do we look the sort who'd be seen dead at the funeral of a slapper like Della Kirby?'

While Dee stared in shock, the seated man said sharply, 'I'll handle this, Ronnie.' Then he looked enquiringly at Dee. 'You are?' he asked.

'Her daughter. Look, if you haven't come to pay your respects, why are you here?'

He seemed put out by this. 'Her daughter! So Della had a daughter, did she? She kept that quiet. Inside or out?' he demanded.

'Sorry?'

He snapped in irritation, 'Don't play thick with me. Beat, brothel or hotels?'

'Oh! None of those. I don't follow my mother's line at all. I do shop work.'

The man she now knew as Ronnie made to step towards her, but the other man stopped him by putting up his hand. Grinning sardonically at Dee, he said, 'You expect me to believe that, considering what your mother was?'

'You can believe what you like, I've told you the truth,' she snapped.

He gave her a look designed to leave her in no doubt that he meant what he was about to say. 'Well, if I find out you're lying, you'll find yourself in serious trouble. Now, we've come here to collect the money Del owes us.'

This news came as a shock. Her mother had never borrowed in her life, to Dee's knowledge. Like her own mother before her, Della had held the belief that owing anyone anything in any guise made you beholden to them, and no Kirby ever willingly allowed themselves to fall under an obligation. Dee had not inherited many of the Kirby traits or their views on life, but she was with them on this. 'For what? she asked suspiciously.

'For a service we provided.'

Dee pulled a bemused face. 'Service! What sort of service?'

'Insurance.'

She frowned. 'Insurance for what?'

'Against any harm coming to her. The streets aren't safe any more.'

Dee gave an ironic laugh. 'My mother could take care of herself. In truth, people needed to take out insurance against harm from her! I can't see her ever taking up your offer.'

'But that's just it, our services weren't optional. Now, debts don't die with a debtor, so it passes to you to settle up what she owed us. Two hundred pounds.'

Dee was astounded. 'What! That's a fortune. Expensive, your insurance.'

'It is when you don't pay up weekly. Interest is added. Della was warned she'd land herself in serious debt by refusing to pay up, but she ignored our warning.'

Dee reared back her head and eyed the man in defiance. 'Well, why should my mother have paid for something she didn't want or need? And whatever you think she owed you, I couldn't find a fraction of that even if did feel obliged to settle – which I don't. I've no intention of paying, as my mother obviously hadn't.' She looked over at the brute of a man poking through the items on the sideboard and, despite her anger at his audacity, said matter-of-factly, 'You're wasting your time if you're looking for anything of value.'

He gave a snort. 'I can see that! Nothing but crap here,' he said to the other man. 'I think I already got . . .'

He was silenced by a warning glare and the order, 'I *said*, I'll handle this, Ronnie.'

These men were meant to be intimidating, and yes, they were to a degree. But throughout her life Dee had faced a far more intimidating force and stood firm against it – her mother. She stared at the seated man. 'If there's nothing else, I'd appreciate you both leaving my house now.'

He looked at her for several long moments before he stood up. 'Have it your own way.' He came towards her then, leaned over and whispered in her ear, 'A debt is a debt. We'll see ourselves out.'

Dee stared after them. It was quite apparent to her that these men were the sort who preyed on vulnerable people to finance their own lives, but they had been mistaken to think her mother would fall for their tricks or that Dee would either. She had enough of a struggle on her hands, keeping herself on the wages she earned, let alone helping to fund someone else's lifestyle. A memory stirred unexpectedly then, a vision of the night Della had been making a spectacle of herself in the Admiral Beatty and Madge and Dee had dragged her away before she ended up spending the night in jail. After her mother and Madge had exchanged their angry words, Madge had announced she needed to get back to work or she feared she would not be able to pay the men their dues that week. Dee had wondered afterwards what men she'd been referring to. Now she knew. But Madge could hardly afford to keep herself on what she earned, let alone hand over a percentage every week. There were some wicked people in the world, preying on the vulnerable, and Dee was proud of her mother for standing up to two men of the sort who'd just left her house. Dee just thanked goodness the way she earned her own living didn't bring her into contact with people like that.

Then she gave a gasp of horror as a terrible thought struck her. She was supposed to have started her new job today, and with all she'd had on her mind had completely forgotten about it. Her eyes flew to the clock on the mantel. It was approaching three. By now her new employers had probably given up on her. But she needed that job. Her only hope was that her excuse for not showing up would be accepted and the position held open for her until after her mother's funeral.

Thinking of nothing else now, she grabbed her coat and handbag and rushed out.

Mrs Stafford didn't look too pleased to see her. 'Well, I'd given up on you I'm afraid, Miss Kirby,' she said sternly. 'I have to say, you came across at your interview as the conscientious sort. I was proved very wrong there, wasn't I?'

Having run all the way, a breathless Dee blurted out, 'Oh, Mrs Stafford, you weren't wrong about me, honestly. You see ...' She paused, swallowing hard before adding, 'My mother died on Saturday and ... well ... I will be honest and say I forgot I was starting here today, until a little while ago. I came straight here to put things right as soon as I remembered.'

The cross expression on Mrs Stafford's face had gone, to be replaced by one of deep sympathy. 'Oh, my dear, I'm so sorry to hear about your loss. No wonder you forgot, with everything else you must have on your mind.'

'So will you give me another chance?' Dee tentatively asked. 'The funeral is on Wednesday. I could start on Thursday, if you'll still have me?'

Mrs Stafford smiled kindly at her. 'In the circumstances, yes, I'm prepared to let you do that. We'll look forward to seeing you on Thursday morning at eight-thirty sharp.'

In the street, Dee let out a huge sigh of relief. On top of everything else she was dealing with, thank goodness money coming in wasn't going to be a problem. She knew, though, that without her mother's contribution she was going to have to tighten her belt considerably. For now the details of how escaped her but she would put her mind to it after the funeral was over. As she turned in the direction of home, she jumped when a hand unexpectedly clamped her arm and she was pulled to a halt.

'Oh, Dee, I'm so glad I've bumped into you,' a familiar voice said.

She was surprised to see Susan Johnson's pleasant plump face, and even more surprised that the girl really did look glad to see her. But after her experience at Cleanrite, and knowing Susan was aware of her background, she wasn't quite sure how to respond. 'Susan ...'

'Look, Dee,' the younger woman interjected, 'I was so sorry to hear you'd been sacked.'

She stared in surprise. 'Were you?'

'I was, really. I thought it was wrong of them to treat you like they did. It's not your fault what yer mam does.'

'You really mean that, Susan?'

'Yes, I do. I've left too.'

'Left Cleanrite! But why?'

'Well, if they could treat you like that because of your mother, I wasn't sticking around to find out how I'd be treated if they found out about me.'

Dee frowned at her, confused. 'Found out what, Susan?'

'About my dad.'

'Your dad? What about him?'

'That he's black.'

Dee stared at her. 'Eh?'

The other girl grinned. 'I know, yer can't tell, can yer, looking at me? I take after me mam's side. My brother takes after them both. He's sort of coffee-coloured and he's had to put up with all sorts, as you can imagine, but thankfully he's the type to stick two fingers up at the lot of 'em and not let it bother him. But you can see why I kept all this quiet, can't you?'

Dee nodded. 'Only too well. Same reason I did about my mother.'

Susan gave an aggrieved sigh, a pained expression on her face. 'I hate being secretive about me dad. He can't help what colour he was born and shouldn't be treated rotten for it. Neither should we, his family. He was an American soldier, one of the first lot that came over here to set things up for the rest who followed during the war. When me mam's family found out she was seeing him there was bloody hell to play, and you can imagine what it was like for her when she got pregnant with me. After the war ended he came back, and against her family's wishes they got married. He settled here, and thankfully me mam's family eventually came round and accepted him. I can't say that was true of others, though, and neither me mam nor me dad has had it easy, but they stuck by each other and they're ever so happy together. He's lovely, my dad, really handsome, the most gentle, kind-hearted man you could ever meet in your life. He works

99

as a conductor for the Midland Red. It really upsets me when people at his work call him "nigger" and "sambo" or "golliwog". All credit to him, though, he doesn't let it get to him. Just laughs and says they're all jealous because he doesn't have to sit in the sun for hours to get some colour in his cheeks, like they all have to. He's funny my dad is.

'Whenever I was asked about me family, I knew if I was truthful I risked being cast out 'cos people look down on women who go with black men, let alone being the daughter of one. School was awful for me. I never had any friends, not because the kids didn't want to be but because their parents wouldn't let them. It was as if they were worried their kids would catch some dreadful disease if they were allowed to mix with me.

'No one was more glad than I was when I left school to go to work because none of the people there knew about me dad or that I was a half-caste, as long as I was careful. You can see now why I never really talked much about me family or asked me friends back to mine. And you can guess the trouble I've had with boyfriends when they found out about me dad's colour, but thankfully my Owen loves me enough not to care. His family thought I was the best thing ever to happen to him until they found out me secret. Then they turned on me and threatened to disown him, but Owen stood up to them and called them small-minded. He said to go ahead and not have anything to do with him if they were worried what other people would think of them for having a half-caste as a daughter-in-law. Thankfully, his family came round eventually and we all get on fine now.

'Anyway, Dee, I never got a chance to speak to you as you'd already left Cleanrite when I was told what had happened, but I still want to be your friend, if you'll have me. I like you. I don't care what yer mother is, honest.'

Dee couldn't believe she had finally met someone who had suffered from similar prejudice throughout her life, all because of others' inability to live and let live. She smiled at Susan in delight. ''Course I'll have you as my friend. I'd be honoured. I like you too. At least we can be ourselves with each other, can't we? Nothing to hide, eh?'

'Oh, the relief,' Susan said. She looked keenly at Dee then. 'So what are you doing tonight or tomorrow? Sometime soon anyway. You could come around to mine. I'd love to introduce you to me family.'

'I'd love to come and meet them too, and soon, but . . .' Dee's face twisted then. 'Well, you see, my mother died on Saturday and . . .'

Before she could say another word Susan was offering her sympathy. 'Oh, Dee, I'm so sorry. I can imagine how you must feel, losing your mother. I'd be devastated if I lost mine. Can't imagine life without her. Look, we'll make arrangements to meet up when . . . well, yer know, afterwards. I've just landed meself a job in the shoe department at Lea's. Just come out the interview. I start on Monday. When you feel like it, come in pretending to be a customer and I'll pretend to serve you. We can make definite plans for something then.'

Dee was looking at her in astonishment. 'Well, would you believe, I've just landed myself a job at Lea's too? In the baby department. I start on Thursday.'

'Really! Oh, that's just great. We'll definitely see each other then.' A look of sympathy on her face again, and patting Dee's arm affectionately, Susan said, 'I'll be thinking about you.'

Dee smiled wanly. 'Thanks, Susan, I appreciate that.'

They said their goodbyes and went their separate ways.

As soon as Dee walked through the back door, Madge pounced on her. 'Where have yer been, lovey? I got here a few minutes ago and found you gone. The dinner's half-prepared so you obviously left in a hurry . . . well, I was worried sick.'

'I should have left you a note, Aunty Madge, and I'm sorry for not, but you see . . .' Dee proceeded to tell her, finishing off with, 'How stupid of me to forget I was starting a new job today.'

'Oh, fair dos, Dee. It's not as if you've not had more pressing matters on your mind. Anyway, it's turned out all right. That new boss of yours sounds a nice woman, and the staff too from what you've told me. A whole new start for you, eh?' Madge looked at her thoughtfully. 'Look, I don't mean to speak ill of the dead, but now yer mam's gone . . .'

'I know what you're going to say, Aunty Madge,' Dee cut in. 'I could move to another area, town even, and make a new start.'

'Well, yes, that's exactly what I was going to suggest. As long as you kept in touch with me, mind, just to let me know you was faring okay.'

'But don't you see, Aunty Madge? Wherever I went there'd always be the risk of bumping into one of Mam's old clients who'd see the resemblance and cause me problems. Look what happened with Kevin's dad. And that new client Mam picked up was from out of town, she said. How do I know for sure I'll never meet someone who'd take the chance to cause some mischief? Anyway, I bumped into one of the girls I palled around with at Cleanrite today and she told me she's had similar problems as her dad's black. I felt sorry for her. I know what she's been through. But it was so good finally to find someone who's had to put up with the sort of prejudice I have. If Susan can deal with it, so can I. I have so far, haven't I?'

Dee paused, looked around and gave a sigh. 'My main worry now is how I'm going to keep this place on without Mam's money. I shall have to move somewhere cheaper, I suppose.' Then an idea struck her like a thunderbolt. It was a good one, the perfect solution, all she could hope was that Madge thought likewise. 'Aunty Madge, would you consider moving in with me?'

The older woman looked stunned by her offer. 'Would I consider . . . Oh, Dee, you really mean that?'

She nodded vigorously. 'I most certainly do.'

'Oh, but I'd love to. Just the thought of leaving that miserable room . . . Not that I'm complaining about Phoebe Gibbs, I've been grateful enough to have a roof over me head. Only she does have some disgusting habits which I've had to learn to turn a blind eye to. But if I lived here with you, Dee, well, I can't tell you how much happier I'd be within meself.' Then Madge stressed, 'I'd pull me weight, you know that. Not like yer mam, expecting you to skivvy for her. Not that I mean to speak ill of the dead, but you know what I mean.'

Dee smiled at her. 'Move in when you like.'

'I'd move in right this minute but it doesn't seem right to do such a thing until after the funeral. I'll give you a hand clearing out Del's room for you to move into, if you'd like me to, Dee?'

She smiled gratefully. 'I'd like that very much, but I'm happy in my own room. If it's all right with you, I'd like you to have Mam's.'

'Well, if yer sure, lovey. But should you change yer mind, then I'm happy to do a swap, you just let me know.'

How lucky Dee felt to have someone like Madge to turn to. She felt she could never repay her fully for the unconditional support she had shown in the past. At least now she'd have a comfortable home, and Dee would have her companionship. It couldn't have worked out better.

CHAPTER NINE

Dee was slowly sipping her drink.
'You all right?' Madge asked her, then quickly added,
'Well, I suppose that's a stupid question. You have just buried
your mother.'

Studying the contents of the glass she was holding, Dee sighed.
'I feel guilty, if you must know.'

Madge frowned at her. 'What on earth have you got to feel
guilty for?'

'Well, it's just that when we were at the graveside and the
vicar was saying his bit, all I could think of was how long it
must have taken the poor gravedigger to dig the hole.'

Madge patted her arm. 'That's understandable, ducky. No one
likes to be thinking of what's going inside that hole, do they?
Especially when it's someone close to them. Anyway, I can't say
it didn't cross my mind how long it must have taken the poor
sod in weather like this. I wondered how he'd managed it too.
He looked ninety if he was a day to me. Did you see him, squatting by a big oak tree smoking a fag, waiting for us to go so he
could get on with it? Wanted to get home for his dinner, I
suppose. Anyway, as services go, it wasn't a bad one. Not too
Godly or too long either.'

A flashily dressed woman went tottering by on impossibly
high stilettos. Well on the way to getting drunk, judging by the
way she was swaying, she turned to Dee and said in a slurred
voice, 'Great send off, gel. Del would have loved it. Can't lie
and say we was exactly bosom buddies, but she was good for a
laugh was old Del – when she was in a good mood, that is. She
caused a few rumpuses in here when she was in a bad one and

they were a bloody laugh too, I can tell yer! No one could cause a rumpus like Del. No, siree.' Raising a near-empty glass of beer, she gave a toast: 'Here's to Del!' Then she tossed back the contents and stumbled over to join a group of other revellers at the bar.

Madge was smiling. 'Maisie's right. If yer mam was here now she'd be having herself a whale of a time. Actually, she'd more than likely have got herself chucked out by now.'

Dee smiled wanly. 'Yes, more than likely. I hope somehow she knows that everyone rallied round for her.'

Madge hoped that Dee never discovered that most of the mourners had been pressured into attending for her sake. Plus, of course, the lure of the free spread. 'Sure you don't want anything stronger to drink?' she asked.

'I don't really want this,' Dee responded, looking at the nearly full glass of lemonade and lime she was holding. She turned her head then to have a look out of the window, glad to see that night had fallen as it meant she had been here long enough to make her excuses and leave. The other mourners might be in the party spirit and set to make a night of it, but she certainly wasn't. 'It won't look bad if I go home, will it?' she asked.

Madge patted her hand reassuringly. 'Not at all, me darlin'. You've stayed longer than I thought you would. I'll come with you.'

'Oh, I don't expect you to. You stay and enjoy yourself.'

'I'm hardly enjoying meself, lovey. The way she was with me, especially these last years, people might think I'd be glad to be shot of Del, but that's far from the truth. Like you, I'm missing her.' Madge's eyes glazed over. 'I remember the first time she ever brought me into this pub. I'd never been in one before so you can imagine . . .' She stopped her flow and patted Dee's hand. 'I'll tell you about it later because, if it's agreeable to you, I'd like to spend the rest of the night sitting by the fire, reminiscing about her. If you want me to stay with you again tonight, I'm happy to do so.'

'I thought you would be, that's why I never even mentioned it. Look, why don't you fetch your stuff and move in properly now?' Dee suggested.

A look of pure delight appeared on Madge's face. 'You want me to move in permanently, right now? Well, I must admit, I'm all packed up and ready. Not that I had much to pack. But if you're sure, I don't need another telling, lovey.'

Dee smiled at her warmly. 'I'm sure.'

Outside they parted, Madge to collect her belongings from her lodgings, Dee to make her own way home. It was a bitter night with a cutting wind. She would be glad to be back. Her intention was to have the fire roaring as a welcome for Madge to her new home.

It was pitch dark in the yard. The jetty gas lamp that usually illuminated it had been broken by kids a while ago and the Council hadn't got round to fixing it yet. Dee had to inch her way tentatively over the uneven cobbles, fearing at every step she'd trip over a protruding one and cause herself damage. With great relief she reached the back door. As she pushed her key into the lock she was taken aback when the door creaked open under her touch. She stood staring at it. She knew the last thing she had done on leaving the house that morning with Madge for the funeral was to check it was locked. Or had she . . . She couldn't have if it was open now. She had obviously been in more of a state than she had thought, but it wasn't really surprising in view of where she had been heading.

Inside the dark kitchen she was feeling along the window sill for the box of matches when a sudden sound from the back room froze her rigid.

She wasn't alone. She hadn't left the back door unlocked. Someone had broken in. She had come home and disturbed a burglar. Though her emotions were swinging between fear and outrage, part of her wanted to laugh too and tell whoever it was that if he thought there were rich pickings to be had in the Kirby household he was badly mistaken.

Arming herself with the first thing that came to hand, which happened to be an empty milk bottle, and with her heart hammering painfully in her breast, she called out: 'Who's . . . who's there?'

A dark shape suddenly filled the kitchen doorway. Before she could react in any way whatsoever, it had lunged at her. She felt a blow to her temple, and heard the sound of the milk bottle shattering on the floor. Then she passed into oblivion.

CHAPTER TEN

Earlier that morning, Calum Jackson gave a violent shiver as an Arctic blast of wind hit him as he set foot in the outside world. What a welcome after a year detained at Her Majesty's pleasure, he thought ruefully as he looked up at the dark clouds above. It was going to rain any minute or else snow, it certainly felt cold enough to Calum.

'See you soon, Jackson. I'll be waiting for you,' the burly, hard-faced prison officer escorting him out commented nastily.

'Then you'll wait in vain. You'll never see me inside again,' Calum shot back at him.

The man gave a sardonic laugh. 'That's what they all say. Like I said, see you soon.' Tapping the truncheon hanging from his belt and with a wicked glint sparking in his eyes, he reiterated, 'I'll be waiting for you.'

Calum glared darkly at the man as he disappeared behind the heavy door. Out of all the unsavoury sorts he'd been mixing with during his stay inside the castle-like walls of Leicester Prison, that man was the most brutal and terrifying. Calum wasn't by any means a violent man, had to be extremely provoked ever to raise his fists, but although he'd meant every word he'd said about never again spending time inside that place, he did rather hope he encountered that particular prison officer just once more, so he could repay the man for all the unwarranted beatings he'd received during his stay. Give the brute a taste of his own medicine.

Pulling the collar of his coat up around his neck, he slung his haversack of belongings over his shoulder and made off, wanting to be far away from this dreadful place as quickly as he could. He was stopped in his tracks by a voice calling out to him.

'Oi, Cal! Over here.'

He knew that voice well. He should do, it belonged to his father. Turning back, Cal saw Harry Jackson, a broad grin on his weather-beaten face. As usual he was sporting a couple of days' growth of beard. 'Come on, son, hurry up. I'm freezing me nuts off here,' he called jovially.

A heavily built man of medium height, Harry was leaning against a car, a dark blue Ford Zodiac, fairly new-looking. As he went to join him, Calum said, 'I take it you've *borrowed* this, Dad?'

Harry slapped him hard on the shoulder. 'Come on, jump in, yer mam's got yer favourite dinner on the stove – stew and dumplings. Vic and Garry are waiting at home to welcome yer back, and they've got a few crates in so it's a party we're having later. I don't need to tell yer that yer mam's beside herself to have all her family around her again, just like it should be.'

Calum inwardly groaned. If he got into this car he risked landing straight back where he'd come from, with his father for company. What was he thinking of anyway, turning up to collect his son from prison in a stolen car? 'Look, Dad, don't take offence but I fancy a walk. Why don't you leave the car here and we'll walk back together?'

'Walk, in this weather, when we have transport? Are you mad, son?' he exclaimed, looking at Calum as though he'd suggested they jump together off a railway bridge in front of a speeding train. 'I went to a lot of trouble to make sure I took you home in style. Well, I have to admit, I've always had a hankering to drive one of these. This looked like the ideal opportunity so I purposely sought one out. Now, get in, fer Christ's sake.'

While Calum stood here arguing the toss with his father they risked attracting unwanted attention. Sighing, he hurried round the passenger side, pulled open the door and eased his lithe six-foot frame on to the soft leather seat.

As soon as the car drew to a halt outside their council house on the New Parks Estate, roughly three miles from the city centre, the large figure of Fran Jackson came hurrying down the path, flabby arms outstretched in greeting. She was shouting hysterically. 'Oh, me baby's home! Hurry up and get out of the car, our Cal, and give yer mam a hug.' Her somewhat embarrassed youngest son was enveloped in her bear-like embrace. With tears of happiness streaming down her face, Fran blubbered, 'Welcome home, son. Welcome home.' Then she pulled away from him to fix him with her eyes. 'Why wouldn't yer let me visit yer?' she scolded. 'It ain't like I'm a stranger to prison visiting, is it? Yer dad and brothers have been in and out the place like yoyos in the past.'

And she'd tasted life inside herself for shop-lifting in her younger days. But, regardless, she was still his mother, and Calum hadn't felt comfortable about her mixing with types who made his own family look saint-like in comparison, not for his sake.

Before he could respond his brothers were on him, both slapping his back, their pleasure at having the younger back in the fold very apparent.

'I'll just get rid of the car. Be back before you've dished up,' Harry Jackson was informing his wife.

'Yeah, well, make sure you are. I don't want our Cal's welcome home dinner spoiling, not after all the trouble I've gone to to do his favourite,' Fran warned him. As her two older boys went to check the car over before their father took it back to somewhere it would be easily found by its rightful owner, she took hold of Calum's arm and started propelling him up the path. 'Come on, let's get you settled in.'

Inside the house he noticed several new items of furniture had been added since he'd been here last. There was a new brown leather Chesterfield and armchairs that were expensive-looking; deep-pile fitted carpet in the living room; and new curtains – quality velvet not cheaper Draylon. The Jackson family business was thriving, it seemed.

'While I mash the spuds and make the gravy, why don't you go up and unpack yer stuff?' his mother said to him. 'Yer old bed's all freshly made. Our Garry was a bit miffed about having to share his room again with you after having it to himself since yer left home, but I expect you can understand that. I asked him to clear a couple of drawers in the chest to make room for you. He'd better have or I'll give him a thick ear, for all his age.'

Calum looked at her uncomfortably. It seemed they all assumed he was moving back in, but that wasn't his plan and he wasn't looking forward to telling them. He didn't want to spoil the mood over dinner; it could wait until afterwards. 'I could do with a cuppa, Mam,' he said to change the subject.

She smiled at him. ''Course you could. Bet yer gasping for a decent brew after prison cat piss. One coming up.'

A while later they were all seated around the dining table, tucking in.

Victor Jackson, Calum's eldest brother by three years at twenty-eight years old, was as tall as him and as ruggedly handsome. He had a string of women to his credit, along with a waiting list, all champing at the bit for the chance to be the one to get him up the aisle. Possessing a love 'em and leave 'em attitude, Victor took full advantage of this to bed his willing victims. Now he was saying to Fran, 'You've surpassed yerself, Mother. No one makes stew and dumps like you do. That right, Cal?'

He looked fondly at his mother, who was looking coyly proud at her eldest son's praise. 'No, they certainly don't,' Cal agreed.

Shovelling food down him like there was no tomorrow, a dribble of gravy running down his chin, Garry was the middle brother. Eighteen months older than Calum, he wasn't quite as tall or as good-looking as the other two but, regardless, still had an impressive list of past conquests and plenty more lined up for the foreseeable future. Through a mouthful of food he said, 'Well, little brother, after yer long holiday inside, I hope yer ready for some graft. We could sorely do with you back on board. We're in the middle of a roofing job just now, and with you along we can finish it quicker and get our money.' He grinned. 'Poor woman thought she'd a few loose tiles needing sorting until I convinced her she needed a complete new roof. We're doing it for her now, using her old roof tiles which we took off, carted away then took back after giving them a swill over with the hosepipe. We told her they looked weathered 'cos they'd been stacked in a builder's yard. Some folks are such suckers, thank God!'

'It was me that convinced her she needed her whole roof replacing,' Vic corrected him.

Garry glared. 'Bloody well wasn't, it was *me*. She was humming and haw-ing over whether she could afford it until I stepped in with me charm.'

'That's enough from you two,' ordered their mother. 'This is Cal's welcome home day, I don't want it spoiling by a punch up.'

Both his brothers looked suitably ashamed and muttered, 'Sorry, Mam.'

Harry raised a glass of beer in the air. 'To our Cal's return!'

Apart from Calum, the rest of them raised their glasses and clinked them together.

As he heaped more mashed potato on his plate, Harry said to Cal, 'There's a small job you could tackle this af'noon while we three get on with finishing off that roof. I know you need time to learn the operation but the job I have in mind for you is n'ote a three year old couldn't manage, so you'll be fine. It's . . .'

'Yer not expecting the lad to start work today, surely?' his wife cut in, looking appalled. 'At least give him some time to settle back in, for Christ's sake.'

Harry looked ashamed. 'Oh . . . .er . . . I suppose tomorrow is soon enough.'

'With four of us at it, we could be finished with that roof by tomorrow night, then Cal could help me start digging out the foundations on that old chap's drive, ready for the tarmac. You and Vic can get cracking on repointing that gable wall over on Braunstone Lane,' said Garry. 'If you remember, the old boy whose drive we're doing told us not to go on a Thursday 'cos that's the day he goes to his daughter's. He won't be around then to keep his beady eye on what we're actually doing. So long as the end result looks good enough for us to get our money and be off, that's what it's all about, ain't it?'

Cal pressed his lips together tight. That old man had no idea he was about to be fleeced out of his hard-earned money, the same as all the other people his father and brothers persuaded to let them carry jobs out. The top quality work promised by Handyman's – whose logo was, *'No job too big or small, very reasonable rates'* – allegedly using the best materials, was anything but. Neither Harry, Victor nor Garry had served their apprenticeship nor had they any certified qualifications between them. Harry's father, Harry Senior, had picked up his limited knowhow via a variety of labouring jobs for building and joinery firms before going out on his own. He'd passed on his scant knowledge to his son, and Harry did likewise to Victor and Garry. All their materials were second-rate, bought on the cheap from various questionable contacts. But by the time this was discovered by the unsuspecting members of the public they'd conned into employing Handyman's, they would be untraceable as the business address on their letterhead given out was bogus.

'I saw Paddy Flattery this morning, on me way to collect our Cal. He told me the Council are repairing the roads not far from that old boy's address. Handy for us. For his usual backhander, soon as we're ready Paddy'll make sure the equipment's left accessible for us to borrow and have back before it's missed,' Harry told Garry.

'Most of the slabs on the old boy's drive are in good condition. After a clean-up we can store them in the lock up, ready for use on another job. We can charge them out as reconditioned, or if we're lucky even pass them off as new,' Vic informed him.

Harry eyed Vic and Garry proudly. 'I taught you all the tricks of the trade, didn't I? Like my old man taught me. Yer granddad would have been proud of you two, God rest him.' He looked at Cal then. 'With your quick brain you'll soon pick it all up, and then I'll have three sons to be proud of.'

'With my cut of this week's profit I'm gonna put a down payment on a set of wheels. Summat like you collected our Cal in, Dad. I'm irresistible to women as it is but in a swanky car . . .' Winking at the rest of them, Victor left the sentence unfinished, leaving it to their imagination.

'I'm decking meself out in a suit I've had my eye on in John Cheatle's, and a pair of new winkle-pickers. Then, with what's left, I'm planning a night down the dogs with Vanda,' Garry bragged.

'Can we afford that new washing machine for me now? The twin tub I saw advertised in me *Woman's Realm*?' Fran asked her husband.

'We just might. And I tek it you'll be wanting the posh pinny the model in that magazine was wearing too,' he said back to her, tongue in cheek.

As Cal listened to them talk about how they were all going to spend their cut, he felt sick to his stomach. He loved his family dearly but did not approve one iota of the way they went about earning their living. No matter which angle he viewed it from, to him it was all wrong. Trouble was, they didn't see any harm in it; in fact, saw him as the one with the problem for not choosing to be part of it.

Cal stared fixedly at his father. 'You're assuming a lot, Dad.'

Harry looked back at him, non-plussed. 'Eh?'

'That my time inside has changed me and now I'm willing to join you in the family firm.'

'Well, you are, ain't you?'

Cal shook his head. 'No. You know I don't agree with the way you go about things. And I won't change my mind.'

'I told yer it wouldn't work, Dad,' put in Garry.

'What wouldn't work?' Cal asked him.

'N'ote,' cut in Harry. 'Garry is talking out his arse, as usual.'

But they all had an aura of guilt about them that was not lost on Cal. Laying down his cutlery, he demanded, 'Yes, he did mean something by it, and I want to know what?'

'Put him out of his misery and tell him, let's get it over with,' piped up Vic. 'Yer know what Cal's like when he gets the bit between his teeth. He won't give up.'

'Yeah, well, he wouldn't have got the bit between his teeth if you'd given proper thought to what you was about to say before opening yer big gob!' Harry shouted angrily at Garry.

'Shut up, all of you!' Fran erupted. She took a deep breath before announcing to Calum, 'It was me they did it for.'

'Did what?' he asked, frowning quizzically.

'Got you . . .' Then she blurted, 'Got you banged up, that's what.'

He felt stunned. 'What?'

'Look, son, yer mam was beside herself with worry about yer.' His father was talking now. 'Living in that pokey bed-sitter, working all hours for a pittance in those dead-end jobs yer've had. Never any money to speak of to look after yerself properly, and you'd never take anything off us to help you out. Sooner starve than do that, wouldn't yer, yer stubborn cuss? In fact, we was all worried about yer, not just yer mam. Well, we tried everything we could to make you come to your senses about living here where you belong and joining us in the family business. Finally we'd no choice but to take drastic action.'

Cal was frowning at them quizzically. 'What drastic action?' Then the truth hit him like a sledgehammer and he slapped his hand to his forehead, marvelling at his own stupidity. Memories arose of that evening just over a year ago when the police had paid a visit to his bed-sitter after a tip off by an anonymous caller that he was in possession of stolen property. Not having any idea that a canvas bag full of items from a very recent burglary was hidden behind his shabby second-hand sofa, he had welcomed the officers inside and given them permission to search his abode. Two weeks later, Judge Sebastian Featherstone, on learning Calum was a member of the very same Jackson family who regularly came before him, didn't believe his claim to be innocent or that this was his first offence. He'd presumed this young man was just extremely clever not to have been caught by the law before, and heaped on him the longest jail term for the offence he could.

Calum had never been able to fathom just how that bag of someone's else's property had come to be behind his sofa. The revelation that it was his own family who'd done it utterly astounded him.

He fixed his eyes on his father in disbelief. '*You* were behind me spending a year in that hell hole, just in the hope it'd get me to change my mind, come back home to live and join you in the firm?' he asked incredulously.

Harry squirmed uncomfortably in his seat. 'Well . . . when we came up with that plan, we thought you'd only get a couple of months, being's it was yer first offence. We was shocked summat wicked when that bastard Featherstone sentenced yer.'

Calum was still gazing at them all in disbelief. 'I can't believe you did this to me.'

'Only 'cos we love yer and want the best for yer, son,' said Fran.

'If you wanted the best for me, you'd allow me to have a mind of my own and live my life the way I want to, not the way you think I should,' he shot at her.

'How can you be sane, living the way you do, when you could have what we have?' said Vic, looking mystified. 'You've got a screw loose, must have.'

'I reckon someone did a swap with another baby when yer back was turned, Mam, and that's why Cal ain't n'ote like any of us,' put in Garry.

'That's enough, you two,' said Harry. 'Look, Cal, whether you like it or not you have no choice now but to come home and work with us. Yer going to find it nigh on impossible to get set on with any other firm now you've a prison record. That's why most old lags don't become reformed characters after a spell inside – they can't get legitimate jobs. I know yer angry at what we did, but given time, when you see how it feels to have money in yer pocket like our Vic and Garry, enough to look after a family of your own when you decide to settle down, you'll be thanking us for making you see sense.'

Calum gave a heavy sigh. 'Why can't any of you just accept that I don't think the same way as you do? Have you any idea what my life's been like as part of this family, torn between the fact that I love you all but deeply ashamed of the way money comes into this house? I had hardly any friends when I was young because of the other parents forbidding their kids to have anything to do with the Jackson family, and I've lost count of the number of good jobs I've lost because someone spotted a mug shot of either my dad or my brothers in the *Mercury* when you each got sent down. Well, we all look alike and with the same name . . . the upshot was I got asked to leave as they all thought, like father, like son. Brother like brother. As for girl-friends . . . well, any decent ones ran a mile when they found out I belonged to a family of convicted villains. Thanks to you all, I've finally got a criminal record myself.' Cal pleaded with them now. 'Once and for all, will you leave me be to build a life for myself, and I'll leave you to get on with yours?'

'Well, if our Cal wants to turn his back on making himself a good living and live like a pauper instead then let him get on with it, I say,' Vic declared.

'His loss,' agreed Garry.

'I suppose we've no choice,' muttered Harry.

Cal looked mortally relieved. 'At last that's settled!' He pushed away his plate and got up. 'That was great, Mam. Now, I'm sorry, but I have to rush off to see a man about a job.'

Harry looked surprised. 'Yer've got an interview for a job straight out of nick? Doing what?'

'Washing cars.'

'Bloody washing cars!' scoffed Vic. 'Call that a job?'

Calum flashed him a sad look. 'You might see it as beneath you, but at least it pays an honest wage. I'll be staying in a hostel until I can afford a place of my own. The prison social worker sorted it all out for me.'

His mother was looking at him searchingly. 'I wish I could understand yer, son. We all wish we could understand yer. We've tried, but we just don't. There's always a runt in every litter so they say, and you're it for us.' Her face screwed up in thought. 'I wonder if it's 'cos I was in labour such a long time with you, unlike the short time I took with yer brothers? You was born with the cord tight around yer neck and the doctor did say at the time he was worried you might have been starved of oxygen . . . There seemed no evidence of it when you was tiny, but I did begin to wonder when you showed signs of being different as you grew older. It might explain how yer got that kink in your nature, lack of oxygen to yer brain when you was born.'

Calum smiled inwardly to himself. Just because he didn't show any criminal tendencies his family believed he wasn't right in the head.

'Once I'm settled, Mam, I'll come and visit you.'

Fran smiled at him. 'You know where we live.'

Swarthy-looking Maurice Dilks, the forty-five-year-old proprietor of Dilks Quality Car Sales, was looking Calum over suspiciously. Dilks was small and wiry, his curly hair slicked back with hair cream, pencil moustache neatly groomed. He was clothed in a smart grey-checked suit and loud tie with a red rose in his button hole.

'Well, I'm not at all happy about employing an ex-criminal,' he was saying. 'I've expensive cars in this showroom. Very tempting for someone with your tendencies, I'd guess. You were in for theft, weren't you? So Miss Lambert told me anyway. The silly cow's into good works, isn't she? Nothing better to do with her time, unlike us lot who have to work. If it was up to me, I wouldn't have your sort anywhere near my premises but the trouble is, Valerie Lambert's father is rich. He owns Lambert's Medical Supplies, my best customer, and if I want him to keep coming to me for his own Daimler and the fleet of Morris Oxfords he annually purchases, it seems I have to keep his daughter happy. I'm being blackmailed, no less, into taking you on.

'Right, well, this job is for a valet . . . car-washer to you. We usually have thirty vehicles on the premises at any one time and they're washed and polished daily. After a test run also they're thoroughly cleaned, outside and in. I expect a top-class job, mind. Not a speck of dirt or a smear on the chrome, got that? Then all the cars that come out of the workshop after repair ready to be returned to the customers are thoroughly valeted too.

'You don't approach the customers for any reason. You're invisible to them, in fact. If any of the staff here need any errands doing, you're the man. Hours are seven-thirty until I say you're finished, with a half-hour for lunch. You don't set foot in the showroom for any reason. At the back of the workshop there's an old lean-to. It's full of rubbish at the moment. First job for you is to clear it out, then you can use it to keep your belongings in and store the equipment for your job. You'll take your lunch there too. Pay is two pound a week gross. Start tomorrow. I'll dock your wages if you're a minute late.'

He made to walk away but Calum stalled him. 'Just a minute, Mr Dilks.'

He turned to look back at Calum impassively. 'Was there something you didn't understand, Jackson?'

'Oh, I understand perfectly, Mr Dilks. I am quite an intelligent man. Just because I've come out of prison and there are few opportunities for the likes of me, you feel you're at liberty to treat me like dirt and use me as your lackey for half the pay you'd be offering anyone else. I think you've probably gathered by now that I won't be taking up your offer.'

Calum made to walk away then but stopped, adding, 'By the way, for all her la-di-dah ways, I personally found Miss Lambert a thoroughly decent woman, very understanding and far from being the silly rich do-gooder you're making her out to be. She appreciates we all sometimes make mistakes and deserve another chance.'

Calum flashed a look around the showroom filled with expensive gleaming saloons and sports models. Several salesmen were waiting eagerly to pounce on customers as soon as they walked through the door, ready to persuade them that without one of Dilks' cars their lives weren't complete.

'It's my guess that if the law, and especially the taxman, were to take an interest in your business, all sorts of underhand practices might be uncovered.' At the sight of the colour draining from Maurice Dilks' face, Calum knew he had hit a nerve there. As a parting shot, even though he would never cross paths with Valerie Lambert again, he added, 'I'll let Miss Lambert know just why I turned down the job when I see her next.'

With that he turned and marched purposefully away, leaving Maurice Dilks staring after him.

Outside in the street, Calum gave a despondent sigh. Valerie Lambert had led him to believe that Maurice Dilks was a decent sort who believed like herself in giving people a second chance. But then, he would hardly have presented himself in his true colours to the daughter of his most valued customer. But that job had been Calum's only lead so what did he do now? He had just about enough in his pocket for some cheap shelter and food for a week at most. Going back cap in hand to his family was not an option. His only other avenue was to slog through the streets, trying everywhere in the hope that some liberal-minded employer would take a chance on him.

At just before four o'clock, and at least ten approaches later, a worried expression had settled on Calum's face. He was well aware that his quest for work wasn't going to be easy but he hadn't quite been prepared for the callous reception he'd received. They all seemed interested in him at first, but once he'd come clean to them about his recent whereabouts their attitude completely changed. Either they looked at him as if he was carrying a deadly plague or they behaved as if stunned by his audacity in thinking they'd even consider employing an ex-con. Either way he had the door slammed in his face. His hope that an employer somewhere must possess enough compassion to give him a chance was beginning to fade. But Calum wasn't the sort to give up easily. He wouldn't do that until he'd exhausted every employer in Leicester. If he still wasn't successful, then the only option left was to leave the town of his birth and try his luck in another.

He was on the busy thoroughfare of Uppingham Road, passing a café whose large glass windows were misted with condensation. The need for refreshment and a place to rest for a few minutes before continuing with his quest made him enter.

He was met by a queue of at least ten people, all seemingly in a state of high irritation at having to wait to place their order with the harassed-looking woman serving behind the counter.

One of the queuing customers shouted to her, 'Oi, get a move on, Doris. I just want a sandwich to take out. At the rate you're going, the bread'll be stale.'

She flashed the heckler an angry glare. 'I'm doing me flipping best. Just wait yer turn like the rest of 'em.'

'Where's Bernie? Why ain't he giving you a hand during this rush?' another piped up.

'Don't know where he's got to,' Doris shot back, blaspheming under her breath as a cup she was filling overspilled and a pool of tea swamped her preparation area, soaked up by the bread she was in the process of spreading. Banging down the teapot, she threw the ruined bread into the bin under the counter, grabbed a cloth and started mopping up. 'Now look what yer made me do. BERNIE!' she yelled. Getting no response she went over to the hatchway in the wall to the side of her and stuck her head through it. She pulled back, turning round to face the throng of customers, looking puzzled. 'He musta gone off with them two men that came in to see him a while ago. One was a right big old bruiser. Long time since I saw such an ugly mug. Reminded me of a grizzly bear, he did. Anyway, Bernie might have told me he was going out. Just 'cos he's the owner of the place, he thinks he can do what he bleddy well likes,' she fumed. Then she made her way into the kitchen through a door at the end of the counter. Seconds later she came back, announcing loudly, 'If any of you lot want hot stuff yer outta luck 'til Bernie gets back. I can't do that as well as be out front so I've turned the gas off under the pans for the time being.'

At this announcement mumbles of displeasure were heard from the queue.

'Just pour us a cuppa, will yer, Doris? Me throat thinks there's a drought on,' called out another fraught customer.

Her face screwed up in defiance. 'Right, that's it,' she said, untying her apron and slapping it down on the worktop. 'I've had enough of this. You lot can help yerselves 'cos I'm off home. That'll teach Bernie a lesson he won't forget, gallivanting off without a word and leaving me to manage on me own!'

Grabbing her handbag from under the counter, she went to the end, swept aside a pile of dirty crockery then flung up the flap. She marched through, letting the flap bang down behind her, snatched her coat off a set of wall pegs and left the customers to it.

They all stood looking blankly at each other for a moment before one of them, a thick-set man wearing a shabby donkey jacket and work trousers covered in brick dust and globs of hardened cement, announced in a thick Irish brogue, 'Well, she said to help ourselves.' He began barging his way through the throng towards the flap in the counter.

The look on all their faces read, Food for free! Not often a chance like this comes along. All but Calum surged forward to follow the Irishman behind the counter and serve themselves. Shouts of, '*Get out the way, I was here before you! Watch where yer going, yer clumsy clot!*' angrily erupted.

As Calum watched the scene being played out before him, his mind was whirling. Already a woman who had been in the queue was slumped on a chair, nursing a bruised foot. If someone didn't get the situation under control quickly he feared more serious damage would result. As well as the fact that when the absentee owner returned, he'd find his profits severely affected.

Without further ado he barged his own way through the crowd, managing to reach the front just as the Irish builder, counter flap in hand, was making his way through. Shoving by the stunned man and banging the flap shut behind him, Calum threw his haversack of belongings down, stripped off his coat, then stood at the counter, smiling at the crowd.

'Now, who's first?' he shouted above the mayhem.

'Who are yous?' the Irishman demanded.

'The Cavalry, that's who,' he answered, still smiling. 'Now, come on, who's first?'

During his time inside Calum had never once thought he'd have reason to be grateful for some of the things he'd been ordered to do, one of them being a stint in the prison kitchen. Now, though, he realised that without that experience he would never have acquired the knack of quickly satisfying the requirements of a hungry mob. A short time later he had poured several cups of tea from a freshly brewed pot, the boiling water obtained from a large metal urn, along with cups of milky coffee. He'd prepared several sandwiches, and cut slices of cake off the slabs of Madeira, currant and mixed fruit kept in a glass case on the counter top, hoping his portion size was neither over-generous nor under but with a strong feeling he would have been told by the customer if the latter was the case.

At last the original queue was all satisfied and had either left with their purchases or were sitting at tables to enjoy their refreshments. Calum now found he was serving a steady stream of new arrivals.

Before he knew it the last customer was leaving the premises and it was with a sense of shock that he looked at the clock on the wall and saw it was six. How quickly the last couple of hours had flown by, and to his surprise he realised he had enjoyed what he had done. Even if he should have been directing his attention towards urgent matters of his own. It was too late now to resume his search for work but he really ought to set about securing himself a bed for the night in a local hostel before all of them were taken by people like himself, with no permanent address.

He hadn't felt it right to use the till so all the money he had taken during his stint lay in a pile to one side of it for the owner to find. He could look to Doris for an explanation. Calum collected his coat and bag and made to leave. It was then that the state of the café hit him. The tables were still littered with used crockery and the behind the counter area left much to be desired. He gave a sigh. His conscience wouldn't allow him to depart leaving such chaos behind. Another half an hour or so while he straightened the place up shouldn't put paid to his getting a room for the night – or he hoped not, at any rate. He had never had cause to sleep out in the open and didn't at all fancy it, especially not in this weather. He only hoped his benev-olent act of today towards the mysterious cafe-owner wasn't going to result in hardship for himself.

Setting to, the Formica table tops were soon cleared of crockery and wiped clean, chairs placed on top ready for the floor to be mopped over once he'd tackled the washing up, next the mayhem at the back of the counter – his own contribution to it quite substantial – and then he tackled the kitchen which the owner seemed to have abandoned in the middle of cooking fried eggs. They had congealed in a huge frying pan along with a large tray containing cold sausages, bacon and black pudding, as well as saucepans of tinned tomatoes and beans. A basket of half-cooked but now stone cold chips sat by the fat fryer, and in the oven were a dozen or so sorry-looking chicken and steak and kidney pies, which would all have been cremated by now if Doris hadn't turned the gas off. The problem that had taken the owner away must indeed have been extremely urgent for him to have left in such a hurry, without informing his staff. Natural curiosity made Calum wonder what it could have been, but he supposed he would never find out now. It didn't look like the owner would return before he left himself and, besides, he owed Calum no explanation.

Then suddenly a worrying thought struck him. If the owner did come back while he was still here, would he believe that Calum had had no intention of departing empty-handed? Finding a stranger in his café, he might not believe the story of why he was here, which when all was said and done was highly improbable. He might call the police and very soon Calum's criminal record would come to light, then it would be assumed that his good intentions were in fact the very opposite: to line his own pockets. This concern spurred him on to finish up and go.

Finally all that remained for him to do was to empty the huge plastic bucket of the day's rubbish into the main bin which he assumed was out in the yard, then his conscience could allow him to take his leave.

Night having fallen, it was dark in the yard and Calum had to stand by the back door for a moment to accustom his eyes before what looked like dustbins materialised a few feet away from him. Mindful of the slippery cobbles, he gingerly made his way over to a row of them lining the large outhouse wall. He lifted the lid of one of them, tipping in the contents of the bucket, then replaced the lid. As he turned to make his way back inside, a faint moaning sound reached his ears. It appeared to have come from the side of the outbuilding. Then he almost leapt out of his skin when a cat jumped off the outbuilding roof, followed closely by another in hot pursuit. Both shrieking loudly, they shot past him across the rest of the yard then up and over the boundary wall, dropping down into the alley at the back. Trying to still his hammering heart from the shock the feuding cats had given him, he made to set off back inside when yet again he heard a groaning noise, the sort given by someone in pain. It was definitely human, and definitely seemed to have come from around the corner of the outbuilding.

Very tentatively, he made his way to the end of the building and poked his head around. To Calum's shock he saw the outline of a man slumped against the wall, seemingly in a state of disorientation. Calum hurried over to drop down beside the man, looking at him worriedly. The side of his face that was visible was caked in dried blood. His immediate thought was that this man had been attacked. Simultaneously it struck him that, judging by the butcher-style stained apron the man was sporting, this must be the elusive Bernie.

He gave a soft groan again. Placing a hand gently on the man's arm to alert him of his presence, Calum said. 'I'm going to get you some help. A doctor. You've had a bump of some kind.'

'No . . . no doctor, I'm fine,' came the laboured response. 'Just need some help getting back inside.'

'If you're sure, mate. Do you think you can sit forward a bit so I can slide my arm around the back of you, help you up?'

'I think so.'

The man he was trying to help was no lightweight. Although not exactly a weakling himself, nevertheless it took a lot of effort of Calum's part of help him back inside the premises. Finally having seated him on a chair at one of the café tables, nursing his head in his hands, Calum went behind the counter to make him a mug of tea.

With a steaming mug on the table before him, Calum said, 'Are you sure you don't want me to fetch a doctor to look at you?'

Bernie shook his head. 'No, I'm fine, honest. Flaming headache, though. There's a packet of Aspro somewhere amongst the stuff on the back shelf behind the counter. Oh, and a box of Elastoplast too. I'd be obliged if you could get them for me.'

Calum was still of the opinion he needed professional medical treatment, but who was he to argue with the man?

The tablets taken, along with half the mug of tea, dried blood wiped away and wound covered by a thick smear of antiseptic cream and plasters, Calum judged that the corpulent, completely bald man was looking decidedly better than when he'd first found him.

'I need to thank you for coming to me rescue,' he said. 'No telling how long I'd have been out there if you hadn't found me.' He looked at the stranger quizzically then. 'Er . . . just how did you come to find me, as a matter of interest?'

'Well . . . it's a bit of a long story. My name is Calum Jackson, by the way,' he said, holding out his hand in greeting.

His hand was accepted and shaken. 'Bernard Stubbs. People call me Bernie. I own this place. So how did you come to find me then?'

Calum took a breath. 'Well . . . it was like this. I came into your café for a cuppa and the woman behind the counter was in a tizzy, trying to deal with a long queue. Thinking you'd gone off somewhere on a jolly and not told her, she decided to go home and leave the customers to it. I could see the beginnings of a free-for-all so stepped into the breach, so to speak. The money I took is all by the side of the till, by the way. I hope I haven't lost you any customers with the food I dished up. Hope I haven't poisoned any either,' he added jocularly. 'Anyway, I didn't get any complaints, everyone seemed to go away happy.'

Bernie was looking at him, staggered. 'Doris walked out and left the customers to help themselves? I can't believe the woman did that! If it wasn't for you doing yer Good Samaritan act, I could have found my café stripped bare and an empty till! She deserves sacking for what she did, and it's not like she's always polite to the customers either. But, trouble is, I've only just taken her on after I caught the bloke before her with his fingers in the till when he thought me back was turned. Getting Doris wasn't easy. Not many people want to work in my sort of café, they prefer more genteel tea shops with customers who leave tips.

Anyway, thanks . . . thanks very much for stepping in when Doris walked out.'

'Well, it was the least I could do. Are you going to report the attack on you to the police?' Calum asked. 'You were attacked, weren't you, judging by that wound on the side of your head? Someone gave you a good thump, by the looks of it. When I first came in one of the customers asked the woman serving behind the counter where you were and she said she thought you'd gone off with two men who'd come in to see you a bit earlier. One of them was a big man, she said . . . "a big old bruiser" to use her very words. Was it him who did this to you?'

'Eh? Oh, no, I wasn't attacked, no need for the police,' Bernie vehemently insisted. 'I . . . er . . . went outside for a blow of fresh air as it was hot in the kitchen, and to have a fag. I must have slipped on the cobbles and hit my head when I fell. It's all a bit hazy, but I know that's what happened.'

Calum knew instinctively that the man was not being truthful with him, but after all it was none of his business why he was choosing to lie. 'Well, if you're okay now, I really ought to be making tracks.'

'Before you go, you must let me pay you for your time. It's the least I can do.'

'I wouldn't dream of it. Glad I was on hand to be of help.'

'Well, next time you come in, whatever you have is on me. Me breakfasts are the best you'll get in Leicester, if I say so meself.'

If he didn't secure paid work soon, Calum feared he'd be desperate enough to take up that offer. He smiled. 'Deal.'

Bernie rose awkwardly. 'I'll see you out so I can lock up behind you.' As he accompanied Calum to the door, he took in his surroundings. 'The place looks spotless. I know only too well what a mess it gets into after a day's trading. I can't believe you stayed on after the customers had all gone just to clean up the place. I wish I could find someone like you to come and work for me.'

Calum saw an opportunity presenting itself, one he wasn't about to let slip through his fingers. 'Well, if you do find your-self wanting staff, I'd appreciate you considering me.'

At the door now, Bernie stared at him, astonished. 'What? You'd take a job here, if I offered it to you? But you come across to me as the sort of man who'd already have a perfectly good job.'

'Then looks are deceiving. I would accept a job here if you offered it to me, most definitely I would.' Then Calum's face clouded over as a thought occurred to him. 'Well, that is, if you still felt you wanted to offer it to me when I've told you about my background.' He paused before adding, 'I've just come out of prison. Served a year for theft. I suppose you wouldn't believe me if I said I was innocent?'

Fully expecting Bernie to show him the door, Calum was surprised to be asked, 'Leicester Prison you've just come out of, was it?'

'Yes, that's right.'

'Did you meet a guard in there called Wilson?'

Calum stared warily at him, wondering where this conversation was leading. 'Er . . . yes, I did.'

To Calum's shock, Bernie wrenched aside his apron to pull up the stained tee-shirt underneath, baring his huge gut to display an ugly-looking scar. 'That bastard Wilson did this to me as a warning. Wanted to show me who was boss when I wouldn't hand over some packets of fags a mate had brought in for me. He wanted to sell them on to the highest bidder or give them to one of the top-dog prisoners he was sucking up to at the time. He got me alone in my cell, jabbed a fork into me and twisted it around. Then he convinced the hierarchy I'd done it meself, to get some leisure time in the hospital wing.'

Calum was gawking at him now. 'You've been inside too?'

'Come and sit down again,' Bernie requested, heading back to the table they had just vacated.

Seated now, Bernie put his hand in his apron pocket and pulled out a packet of Senior Service. Opening the packet, he offered it to Calum. He accepted and, once both cigarettes were lit, Bernie said, 'Until five years ago I was no stranger to prison life. In and out on a regular basis, I was, mostly for petty theft and burglary. Every time I was back inside I promised meself that when I got out I'd go straight, but I was soon back to me old tricks when I couldn't get a job. And even if I did, the pay was bad because employers had me over a barrel with my record so I was forced to supplement it somehow. But the last time I was inside, Wilson did his fork trick on me and it put the frighteners on me big time, I ain't ashamed to admit it. That pig could have killed me. It's one thing having to constantly watch yer back with the dangerous looneys yer banged up with, but having to contend with crooked screws as well . . .

'Anyway, five years ago there I was, forty-five, family having disowned me years ago, no wife or kids 'cos I hadn't been long enough out of prison to get meself a permanent relationship. And besides, it takes a special type of woman to want to tie herself to my sort. It's not like I've got Gary Cooper's looks, is it? I'd hardly a penny to me name for all me years of effort, so I made a decision. I'd do one last burglary. Me swan song, I called it. Make enough from it to set me up. I wouldn't go about it in my usual gung-ho way, but carefully plan it all beforehand.

'Me efforts paid off and it all went like a breeze. The upshot is, I was able to finance this place. Crime doesn't pay, they say, and mostly it doesn't, but that particular crime certainly paid off for me. I've been straight ever since. There's summat to be said for not jumping a mile when yer front door knocker goes, always thinking it's the coppers coming to arrest you. I got put away twice for summat I hadn't done, like you said happened to you, was made a scapegoat by the coppers who wanted a quick capture. Because of me past history, the judge believed them. How did you get banged up? Just happened to be in the wrong place at the wrong time, did yer, and the judge wouldn't believe yer story?'

Calum sighed. 'Not quite. This is going to sound cock-eyed but I was set up by some people who felt they had a good reason for what they were doing. Only they hadn't.'

Bernie pursed his lips. 'Sounds very intriguing, but you obviously want to keep the whys and wherefores to yerself and I ain't a man to pry unless I'm invited to do so. Right, young man, still interested in a job here, now yer know yer boss is an ex-con?'

'I'd jump at it, yes,' Calum eagerly responded. 'I can't give you any references and I'll have to ask if you'll take me on trust?'

Bernie gave a bellow of a laugh. 'You ask me that, after what you've done for me tonight? Four pound a week suit yer? And any tips you get are yours to pocket, but don't bank on hardly any as the types we get in here can't afford to leave much.'

Four pounds a week wouldn't fund a family but it was enough to keep him and double what Dilks had been going to pay him. 'Sounds fair to me.'

'Then can you start tomorrow?'

'I'd be happy to.'

'Good, then I can give Doris her marching orders, which is no less than she deserves. We start at six, to cater for the early workers, and finish at six too. Four on Saturdays. Are yer lodgings local? Be handy if they are.'

'Er . . . no. I'm in the process of looking, but now I've a job in these parts I'll be beginning around here.'

'Oh, I take it you're living in a hostel at the moment? I should have guessed by the haversack. Carried the very same sort meself on many occasions. All me worldly possessions, such as they were, were in it when I first came out.

'Look, one good turn deserves another, in my book. I live in the flat upstairs. You can save yer hostel money tonight by kipping on my sofa. I'll throw in a hot meal into the bargain. There's a couple of liberal-minded old dears within walking distance who rent out rooms, basic but clean and reasonable, so when we get a lull in the morning you can pop round to have a word. I'm sure one of them will have a vacancy. With a recommendation from me, they'll take you in. Mind you, don't let on to any of them about my background. No one round here has any idea, and I'd like to keep it that way.'

'Your secret is more than safe with me, Bernie.'

'Yours with me too. Well, I think our new arrangement calls for a toast. I've a drop of malt upstairs, if yer fancy joining me?'

Much later that night, appetite well taken care of by the meal of boiled potatoes, faggots and mushy peas Bernie had put before him, mellowed from the glass or two . . . or maybe three, he'd lost count . . . of malt, Calum lay on the comfortable sofa, snug under the pile of blankets Bernie had provided him with. This morning when he had walked through the prison gates his prospects had seemed bleak. Now someone else's misfortune, namely Bernie's accident – although Calum still wasn't convinced the injuries the man had sustained were accidental – had indeed turned into good fortune for himself. Calum knew he was being given a chance to put his family connections behind him, and not for one moment was he going to let this opportunity pass him by.

CHAPTER ELEVEN

As Calum slipped into a blissful sleep, a short distance away Dee's head felt like a million hammers were beating rhythmically inside it. The drumming sensation brought her out of oblivion. Groaning softly, she forced open her eyes, blinking hard to focus, and was extremely confused to find she wasn't at home in her own bed but on a strange one in an unfamiliar room.

But whose room was it? And how did she get here?

She struggled to sit upright. Once perched on the edge of the bed, she looked around her. The room was plainly decorated, in need of redecoration in truth. Along with the iron-framed single bed whose lumpy mattress she was sitting on, there was an ancient-looking chest-of-drawers, and in an alcove by the chimney breast an old-fashioned sink. From the view of the sky through the eaves window this was an attic room. But whose room was it, and how did she get here?

The last thing she remembered was . . . yes, that was right! She had left the wake and been on her way home to make it welcoming for Madge who had returned to her lodgings to collect her belongings. It was all coming back to her now. She'd arrived home to find the back door open, though she felt sure she'd locked it before leaving for her mother's funeral. In the kitchen she'd been about to light the mantle when she'd heard a sound. She had come home to disturb a thief raiding the house! Then she'd felt a terrible pain at the side of her head, and that was where her memory ended.

But why had the burglar brought her back here? It didn't make sense.

Well, whoever they were, and whatever they wanted with her, she wasn't going to allow them to keep her here against her will. Not without putting up a fight.

Getting off the bed, she went over to the door, gave the knob a turn and pulled. It was stuck fast. Locked. She was locked in. Without further ado, and despite her pounding head, she banged her fists on the door and yelled out, 'WHOEVER YOU ARE, LET ME OUT!' Then she pressed her ear to the door and listened. She could hear nothing so repeated her actions and once again pressed her ear to the door. She heard the sound of footsteps on the stairs outside. Heart hammering, she leapt some distance away from the door and stared at it in panic as she waited with bated breath to discover the identity of her abductor. A key was inserted and she saw the knob turn. Then the door opened and a man stepped inside.

Smiling charmingly at her, he said, 'Glad to see there doesn't seem to be any harm done. My brother can get carried away at times. He wasn't supposed to bring you back unconscious, just bring you back, but that's my brother for you.'

A bulky man then filled the doorway. 'Need a hand with her, Lennie?'

Leonard Monks flashed his brother a disparaging look before responding sardonically, 'I think our guest has had enough of your handiwork for one day. She could do with a cup of tea. Go and make her one.'

Ronald Monks's brutish features screwed up in disappointment. His special expertise wouldn't be required in this instance it seemed. 'I ain't a tea boy, Len,' he grumbled.

'Quite soon now you'll never have to make one for yourself or anyone else again, will you? Call this your swan song. So go on, off you go,' Leonard prompted him.

Ronnie disappeared and his brother turned back to find Dee glaring furiously at him.

'Why have you brought me here and locked me in this room?' she demanded.

Still smiling charmingly, he nodded towards the bed, saying evenly, 'Sit down and all your questions will be answered.'

'I'm quite happy standing, thank you. Now . . .'

She was cut off by a very menacing command. 'I said, sit down.'

She gulped, fear filling her suddenly. The huge man who had just left revealed himself for the thug he was by his appearance, but this much slighter man, immaculately dressed and with a disarming smile, who gave the impression he was either a bank clerk or a posh salesman . . . Dee was in no doubt that he was the more dangerous of the two and that she'd be a fool to antagonise him. Common sense told her to hear him out, agree to whatever he was after and make her escape, hopefully in one piece. She did have some idea what it concerned.

Obediently going over to the bed, she perched on the edge of it. Looking him in the eye she said, 'I know I refused to pay you what you felt my mother owed when you paid a visit on me, but I've thought better of it now and . . .'

'Well, I'm glad you're seeing sense,' he interjected.

'So if we can agree on how much I can afford to give you each week, until it's settled up, then I'll be off.'

While Dee sat waiting for his answer, he walked slowly across to the window, gazed out for a moment, then turned back to face her. 'I'm afraid paying off your mother's debt weekly isn't an option. I've come up with something that will suit me and my brother far better.'

Dee looked surprised. 'But how do you expect me to pay it off then?'

'By working it off.'

'But in what way do . . .' She froze mid-sentence as just how he expected her to pay him occurred to her. Jumping up off the bed, she shouted, 'By giving you sex, that's what you mean, isn't it? Well, you can think again because . . .'

He leapt towards her, forcefully pushing her back down on the bed. His face ugly with contempt for her, he jeered, 'I wouldn't lay a finger on the likes of you, you slut! And neither would my brother. You might not have prostituted yourself like your mother did but a prostitute bore you, so to me that makes you a piece of scum like your mother was.'

135

A look of pure madness seemed to glint in his eyes then as he blurted out, 'My father made my own mother's life hell with his filthy whores! Spent most of his wages from his factory job on them, leaving his own family to virtually starve and to clothe ourselves in cast-offs donated by people who felt sorry for us. My mother suffered years of humiliation from what she knew he was doing behind her back. Everyone in the neighbourhood knew too.

'When my father finally ran off to set up home with one of his floozies, God knows where as we never heard from him again, she sank into a deep depression, started to drink, and one night she couldn't bear any more and took her own life. Me and Ronnie came down one morning to go to work in the dead-end factory jobs we both had then, to find our mother hanging from a beam in the kitchen in the rented hovel where we lived. We'd no choice but to bury her in a pauper's grave.

'So you see, if it was up to me, I'd have all whores who entice men with sex stripped naked and flogged in public, then thrown in a pit to rot! But then, had I been able to do that, I wouldn't have been able to put into practice the idea I came up with later for how my brother and I could make a good living for ourselves on the backs of the very women who'd ruined our lives. Justice, wouldn't you say? First thing we did, though, when we got a good wad, was to give our mother a decent burial.'

The look of madness vanished as quickly as it had appeared and he returned to his normal charming self. 'I thought long and hard about how you're going to pay off your mother's debt to us before I came up with an ingenious solution. You'll become our live-in housekeeper.'

Astonished, Dee uttered, 'Housekeeper?'

'That's what I said. Cook, cleaner and bottle-washer. And you'd better do a better job than the slovenly old bitch you're replacing. Well, let's put it this way, if you don't come up to scratch, we'll make damn' sure you learn.'

She was still staring at him. 'But how long do you plan to make me do this for?'

Lennie emphasised, 'Until I say the debt is clear.' Then he

paused and looked at her, a smug smile playing around his lips. 'I know exactly what's going through that mind of yours: that we can't keep you here against your will or stop you going to the police if you see or overhear anything you think they might be interested in. Not that we're careless about what we leave around or speak of. But you will stay here until I say otherwise, of your own free will, and you won't even think of going to the police for any reason.' He paused for a split second before adding, 'Remember what happened to your mother.'

She frowned in bewilderment. 'What happened to my mother?' Then it hit her like a thunderbolt. 'You're . . . you're saying it wasn't an accident my mother had? That you killed her?'

Ronnie lumbered into the room then, carrying a cup of tea. 'I just roughed the old trollop up a bit, to show her who was boss. What happened to her after that was n'ote to do with me.' He was thrusting the cup of tea at Dee. 'Are you going to take this or what?'

She was staring at him in blind rage. 'You roughed her up enough to cause her to fall and knock herself unconscious. That makes you responsible for her death,' she spat accusingly. 'You're nothing but a murderer. You evil . . .'

The blow to her face sent her upper half reeling back to hit her head hard against the wall. Simultaneously a crash rang out when her attacker dropped the cup of tea he was holding. Dee was then grabbed by the scruff of her neck and yanked forward. With his face pushed into hers so close his breath was hot on her cheek, the sour odour assailing her nostrils, Ronnie hissed at her, 'See this, you slut?' With his free hand he was pointing at some healing scratches on his face. '*She* did that to me when she clawed me with her nails. Stupid cow should have just handed over the fiver she had in her bag instead of trying to stop me taking it. Then she'd still be alive now.'

'That's enough, Ronnie,' his brother ordered. 'Ronnie, I said, that's enough. We want her fit and well enough to look after us, not to have to bury her alongside her mother.'

Reluctantly he let go of Dee and righted himself. 'I was just telling her what's what, Lennie.'

'I'm sure she got the message. You can leave us now.'

Sniffing disdainfully, Ronnie departed.

Lennie looked back at a frozen-faced Dee. 'Now and again we have to let people know we mean business. Because she wouldn't play ball, Del was made an example of. So now you know what you're up against with us, and that only a fool would cross us. You might still be thinking you can escape to another town where we won't find you. Well, that's your choice, if you want to spend the rest of your life looking over your shoulder. You'll never know whether we're on to you, but I'll just remind you now that you have a friend called Madge you'll be leaving behind. I know Madge. She's one of the contributors towards our very good standard of living. Be a shame to lose that contribution, but the ball's in your court.'

Dee's eyes were darting wildly. 'You're . . . you're threatening to harm her if I don't do what you say?'

'I wouldn't get far in my line of work by just making idle threats. You don't agree to my terms in any way, then I'll make sure Ronnie is let loose on that filthy whore you call a friend. If it ends up for her like it ended for Del, it won't be me or Ronnie losing sleep. Now, do you agree to my terms or not?'

She despised the two men who had brought about her mother's death, just because Del had not given in to their demands and stood by her principles. Now they'd added a threat towards Madge if Dee didn't comply with their wishes. She wasn't a violent person by nature, but these men's crimes made her want to commit murder herself. She couldn't believe the Monks brothers were expecting her to work for them in such close proximity now that she knew they were responsible for Della's death. But Dee loved Madge dearly, couldn't bear the thought of anything happening to her, and knew she had no choice but to agree to these terms, for her friend's sake.

'You're not giving me much choice, are you?' she said finally.

'No, not really, not if you value your friend's safety. Well, I expect you'll be wanting to collect your things to be ready to start work first thing tomorrow. Don't be long. When you come back, I want to go over your duties with you so you're quite

clear what's expected of you and there are no misunderstand-
ings.' He flashed a look at the smashed cup and saucer and the
splattered puddle of tea on the floor. 'You'll find all you need
to clear that up with in the scullery downstairs.' With a look of
amusement on his face, he added, 'Cleaning it will be your initi-
ation into your new role, won't it?'

CHAPTER TWELVE

Madge pounced on her as soon as she walked through the back door, her relief at Dee's return most apparent.

'Oh, there you are! I've been frantic. I couldn't think what had happened when I found the back door wide open, the place in darkness, and a smashed milk bottle on the floor. I went to the pub to see if you'd gone back there for some reason, but no one had seen you. I took a tour around but couldn't find any trace of you at all. I was just about to go to the police station in case you'd been involved in an accident on the way back from the pub. They wouldn't bother to come and inform me, yer know how the coppers treat the likes of us. So, where have you been, lovey?'

Dee couldn't meet her eyes. 'Oh . . . well . . . when I came back . . . I . . . well, I thought I'd be all right but I just couldn't bring myself to come in here alone, so I went for a walk.'

A look of shame filled Madge's face then. 'Oh, lovey, I should have come back with you and left getting me belongings until tomorrow. How thoughtless of me. Forgive me, Dee, please?'

'Oh, Aunty Madge, there's nothing to forgive,' she insisted. 'I should have left you a note telling you what I was doing. It was I who was thoughtless.'

'Well, you weren't thinking straight after what you'd been through today. How did the milk bottle get smashed, though?'

Dee still couldn't meet her eyes. 'Oh, I knocked it off the draining board when I was searching for some matches to light the mantle, before I decided to go for a walk.'

'Oh, well, that explains it. I must say, when I came in and found the place like I did, my first thought was we'd had burglars.

141

I thought you'd gone off to fetch the police, but then when I got the lights on and saw nothing missing, I knew that wasn't the case. Oh, I'm so relieved to have you back home safe and sound. Er . . . just a minute, is that a bruise on yer face? How did you get that?'

Dee's hand flew to her cheek. 'Oh . . . I . . . walked into the door when I first came in. It was that dark, I couldn't see where I was going.'

'I must admit, I nearly went all me length in the yard when I first came back 'cos I couldn't see where I was going either. Blasted kids, breaking that street light. They think it's funny doing things like that and don't give a thought to what danger their bit of fun can cause others. Well, you need to put some witch hazel on it, me darlin', help bring the bruise out and heal it quicker. Anyway, get yer coat off and go and sit by the fire for a warm while I make you a cuppa.'

'Er . . . I'm not stopping, Aunty Madge.'

At her announcement Madge looked dumbstruck. Finally she said, 'What do yer mean, you ain't stopping?'

Dee hated the thought of telling Madge the concoction of lies she was about to. The only saving grace was that she was doing it purely for the sake of Madge herself. She took a deep breath and blurted out, 'I've got myself a job. As live-in housekeeper for an old gent. I met him while I was out walking. We got talking and he mentioned he was looking for one. He said he liked the look of me and asked me if I was interested. Took me back to his house. It's nice, Aunty Madge. Real posh.' And without a thought she told her, 'It's off Uppingham Road, at the top end. His wife died recently and he's been struggling ever since to look after himself.'

'But you've got a job with Lea's. You're supposed to start tomorrow,' Madge reminded her.

She'd forgotten about that but felt sure they wouldn't have any trouble filling the vacancy her non-show would create. Then she was reminded of Susan and the friendship she had hoped to have with her. Well, that wouldn't happen now, or not at least until the Monks brothers saw fit to release her. She hoped that

142

in the meantime Susan didn't think badly of her for not getting in touch. 'Yes, I know, but this one suits me better.'

'Really!' Madge exclaimed, bewildered. 'Clearing up other people's muck against working in a shop? You're worth better than skivvying for others, Dee. Look, are you sure . . .'

'I'm sure,' she cut in resolutely. 'I've never been surer of anything. As I said, he's a nice old gent and I shall enjoy looking after him. You've no need to worry, Aunty Madge, you can stay here. You can get someone in to help pay the bills. Someone like Elsie perhaps, or I'm sure one of the other women would jump at the chance to live here with you instead of those grotty rooms they have.'

Madge was reeling from this sudden turn of events. 'Oh, well, yes, I suppose,' she uttered. Then she eyed Dee closely. 'But if this job doesn't work out for any reason, this is always your home, Dee, and don't you forget that.'

Dee wanted to tell her that hopefully it wouldn't be long before her mother's debt to the Monks brothers was deemed settled. Then she and Madge could carry on where they'd left off.

There were tears in Madge's eyes. 'Well, I can't say this hasn't knocked the stuffing out of me. I was looking forward to sharing this house with you. You know how fond I am of you, Dee, and I ain't half going to miss you. But if this is what yer want then I'm happy for you, really happy, believe me. This is a chance for you to make a fresh start for yourself. But you warn that old gent that he'd better be good to you or else he'll have me to deal with. You'll keep in touch with me, won't you?'

Dee threw herself at Madge and hugged her fiercely. 'Oh, yes, 'course I will. I'll come and see you as often as I can.'

Madge would dearly have liked to satisfy herself that Dee was indeed in good hands in her new job by paying a visit but was very aware someone like herself turning up there wouldn't do Dee's credibility any good. Returning her embrace, Madge murmured, 'You'd better.'

CHAPTER THIRTEEN

The large, three-storey, double-bay-fronted Victorian redbrick house on a tree-lined street off the affluent end of the busy Uppingham Road required a lot of effort to keep clean and tidy, especially as the owners took blatant liberties now they had blackmailed themselves the services of a full-time, live-in housekeeper.

The house itself was very expensively furnished, it being obvious the Monks brothers were out to impress on any visitors that they were men of taste. It was Dee's opinion, though, that they had in fact created the opposite impression as the house was filled with an assortment of mismatched furniture, the soft furnishings too flamboyant with their loud colours clashing badly. She strongly suspected any guests of the Monks brothers with a morsel of refinement would not fail to see the owners for what they in truth were: working-class types who'd come into money and had delusions of grandeur.

At Dee's disposal, though, were all the latest household gadgets, including a Hoover Supermatic washing machine, vacuum cleaner, large Frigidaire with ice compartment, and an Electrolux cooker. For that she was grateful as she dreaded to think how she'd manage all that was expected of her without these labour-saving machines.

Despite their efforts to be perceived by the outside world as men of standing, fortunately for Dee the Monkses' taste in food reflected their lower-class upbringing. So far she had received no complaints about the meals she had prepared them using basic home cooking, but dreaded the day they would drop on her the fact that she was to provide food for a dinner party as she wouldn't have a clue where to start.

It seemed to Dee that the brothers viewed their home as their private castle as, since she had been here, other than tradesmen there had been no visitors so any business dealings were obviously conducted elsewhere. She assumed both men had women friends. Well, Leonard at least who, regardless of how he earned his living, was a very attractive man, the sort women threw themselves at. And although Ronald was in truth ugly, he did have plenty of cash in his pocket and that in itself was enough to make him attractive to the types who viewed wealth and what it bought as being far above looks. Regardless of how many women each of them had in tow, they didn't entertain at home.

It horrified Dee to realise that the house itself, everything in it and the cost of maintaining it – right down to the ten shillings a week given to her for her own incidental expenses – had been obtained from people like Madge and her own mother, hard-working types who didn't deserve to be preyed upon by the likes of the Monkses. It was said that crime didn't pay, but it certainly seemed to as far as the Monks brothers were concerned.

One thing puzzled Dee, though. Even if the brothers were exploiting every prostitute operating in Leicester, not that she knew exactly how many that was, she didn't think it would bring in enough to cover their ostentatious lifestyle. She wondered what else they were involved in that would account for the shortfall.

It was almost a month now since she'd come to work for them and she'd hated every second of it. She had to stick it out, though, for Madge's sake.

Lennie sauntered into the drawing room where she was busy cleaning. He ran his hand over the top of the baby grand piano – which neither of the brothers could actually play – and said sarcastically, 'Oh, dear, I've just smeared the top of this. You'll have to polish it all over again, won't you?'

Dee jumped at the sound of his voice and spun round to face him, forcing down the urge to tell him that she hadn't polished the piano yet today. She knew better than that, however. Men like Leonard Monks had to feel they were top dog at all times.

If they thought their status was in danger of slipping they would act violently to reinforce it. Smiling sweetly she said, 'You'll be back at your usual time of six for dinner this evening, Mr Monks?'

'Have I informed you any different?' he shot back at her.

Dee took a deep breath, smoothing her hands down over the old-fashioned maid's outfit she was made to wear while on duty around the house. 'I'm sorry if you felt I was being imperti-nent, Mr Monks, I didn't intend to be.'

He looked pleased. 'Servants should always know their place. Glad to see you know yours in this house.'

What a nerve he had, calling her a servant when by birth he was no better than she was.

'Have you collected my dress suit from the cleaners like I told you? I need it tonight,' he was saying now.

'I plan to do it this afternoon when I'm out doing the shop-ping, Mr Monks.' Despite the fact that Leonard demanded a receipt for every penny she spent so he could check she wasn't fleecing him over the housekeeping, shopping was the only part of the job Dee enjoyed and she took her time over it. It afforded her some time away from this house and the people who owned it.

'Don't forget.' His tone was warning. 'Where's my brother?' he demanded then.

'I'm not sure, Mr Monks.'

'Find him. Tell him I'm ready to leave and to hurry up, we've a busy day ahead.'

Busy collecting their ill-gotten gains from women they terrorised, Dee thought. Seething inside, she hurried off to do his bidding.

After she'd checked all the downstairs rooms, there was still no sign of Ronald. The only other place he could be was in his bedroom. Tapping on the door, Dee called out, 'Mr Monks? Mr Leonard told me to tell you he's ready to leave.'

She waited for some verbal response to this and jumped when instead the door opened and Ronald stood before her in a state of undress. He was not an attractive man at the best of times but like this was positively revolting to Dee, dressed only in his underpants and an undone shirt, displaying thick tree-trunk hairy legs and a huge protruding belly.

'I hurt my hand last night and can't get my shirt buttons done up. You do them,' he ordered her, walking back inside his room.

She wanted to inform him that the duties of a housekeeper didn't include those of a personal dresser, but mindful this could lead to her being on the receiving end of his fists, she held her tongue. Someone obviously had been the previous night to cause this injury to his hand. She took a deep breath in an effort to force down a feeling of utter revulsion at the task she was about to perform.

While she did it, she was very aware he was staring at her and his close scrutiny was unnerving. She had never fastened a set of buttons so quickly in her life, desperate to be away from such an intimate situation, with Ronnie Monks of all people.

Buttons fastened, she made to leave but he wasn't finished with her yet.

'Cufflinks,' he commanded. 'On the dresser.'

She went over to collect them. They were heavy, obviously solid gold, and encrusted with diamonds. It sickened her to think just how the money to purchase them had been obtained.

That afternoon as Dee was doing the household shopping, inside the Uppingham Road Café Bernie was taking advantage of a lull in business to have a mug of tea, a cigarette and a read of that morning's *Daily Sketch* which a customer had left behind. The newspaper had obviously been perused by more than one customer as several pages had dried baked beans on them and splashes of egg yolk.

The clanging of the bell announced a customer's arrival. Bernie automatically lifted his eyes to greet them. The customer was elderly Sybil Brown who treated herself once a week to a cup of coffee and slice of Madeira after her visit to the local library.

'How goes it, Mrs B?' he called across to her.

'Oh, can't grumble, ta, Bernie,' she said, putting her pile of borrowed books down on a vacant table before going across to the counter to place her order.

'Mr B all right, is he?'

She pulled a face. 'Now there I *can* grumble, Bernie, but I don't want to ruin my afternoon out by talking about that miserable bugger.'

Calum, who had been taking advantage of the lull in trade to clear up behind the counter, ready for the next onslaught, dropped what he was doing as soon as Sybil entered. He came out from behind the counter and went over to pull out a chair for her.

'You take the weight off your legs, Mrs Brown, and let me take your order for you,' he said.

'While yer at it, could yer get another mug of tea for me, Cal?' a man sitting nearby, studying the racing pages, called over to him.

'Be my pleasure, Frank,' Calum politely responded.

Looking on, Bernie smiled to himself. The circumstances leading to Calum Jackson's arrival hadn't been pleasant for Bernie, but regardless he was grateful. If he'd been beaten up any other time, Calum and he might never have met. The man was indeed proving more than handy to Bernie. He took a keen interest in how the place was run in order to assist in every way he could. The customers liked him, especially the older women who all had a twinkle in their eye for him, and Bernie couldn't fail to notice the steadily increasing number of factory women from nearby coming in for their morning cob orders or to sit and take lunch, purely in the hope of catching Calum's eye. As a result his profits were up nicely. As far as Bernie was aware, Calum hadn't so far taken advantage of any of the invitations extended to him, shrugging them all off politely. Bernie did wonder why he was shying away, especially since several of the women who had blatantly let it be known they wouldn't say no to Calum's company were stunningly attractive. He obviously had his reasons, though.

Calum seemed to have settled in well in his lodgings with Audrey Fry, a sixty-two-year-old homely war widow who supplemented her part-time cleaning job by taking in a lodger in her spare bedroom. Her home was shabby but clean and comfortable, a two-up, two-down flat-fronted terrace house several streets away. Bernie knew she fussed over Calum like she had her own son before he'd left home to marry his childhood sweetheart, and from what Calum had said he was more than happy with their arrangement.

Bernie's only concern was that the day would come when Calum wanted to move on to a job affording him better prospects than working in a café could. Bernie just hoped, though, that that time was later rather than sooner as a replacement for him would be hard to find.

'Watch it, Cal,' he called across now jocularly. 'Mrs B'll be expecting the personal service every time she comes in.'

Calum grinned back at him. 'Happy to oblige when I can.' Returning his attention to Sybil Brown, who was now comfortably seated, he said to her, 'Usual, Mrs B? Cuppa and a slice of Madeira?' He leaned over and whispered, 'If the boss isn't looking, I'll cut it extra thick for you.'

She stared at him thoughtfully for a moment. 'I think I'll be a little devil today and have a scone instead. Plenty of butter, lovey. In fact, I'll be a big devil and have two.'

Calum laughed. 'Coming up!'

Outside in the street, carrying two heavy brown carriers of groceries, Dee was looking up and down. She felt sure the new dry cleaning company that Leonard Monks had instructed her to take his dress suit to was around here somewhere, but she couldn't find it. A man was approaching. She waylaid him.

'Excuse me, sorry to bother you, but can you tell me where the dry cleaner's is round here, please?'

The shabbily dressed man gave her a withering look. 'Ducky, do I look the kinda bloke that teks his stuff to the cleaner's?'

Then he continued on his way, leaving Dee feeling stupid for approaching his sort with her request. She looked around for the sort of person who probably did use that service, but could see nobody suitable. She was standing by a flower shop. Its owner would surely be able to help her? She entered the shop to find a couple of customers already waiting for attention and a woman she assumed to be the proprietor engaged in arranging

150

a bouquet for another customer she was serving. Dee left the shop. Several doors down was a café. Maybe she'd have better luck there.

Moments later Calum became aware that someone had approached the counter. He lifted his head from buttering Sybil Brown's scones to acknowledge their presence and his eyes met those of a very pretty young woman. For a split second it was as if time stood still for him, everything else around him faded away and all he was aware of was this woman's face.

Dee meanwhile was beginning to feel slightly uneasy at the way the man behind the counter stood looking at her. He was staring in a frozen sort of way that had her wondering if she'd suddenly sprouted a huge spot on her nose. The fact that he was very good-looking with the most arresting blue eyes she had ever seen in a man, and with exactly the kind of build that attracted her, didn't escape her, though.

Calum was now feeling a bit embarrassed about the way he had reacted. 'Er . . . sorry, I won't keep you a minute,' he blustered. 'If you . . . er . . . want to take a seat, I'll come over and take your order. Save you waiting here.'

Dee smiled politely at him. 'I haven't come in for anything to eat or drink. I just wondered if you knew where the dry cleaner's is around here?'

He didn't, having no need for such a place himself, so looked across to Bernie for help and was taken aback to see his boss already looking in his direction, an amused expression on his face.

'Next to the Co-op, down the road just past the chip shop,' he piped up before Calum could ask. It was obvious he'd been eavesdropping.

Dee turned and smiled over at Bernie. 'Thank you. I've already walked past it, stupid of me.'

'Thinking of yer boyfriend?' he said to her, grinning.

'Er . . . no, I haven't got one.'

He winked at her. 'You surprise me, a pretty woman like you. Well, I'm free if yer fancy a night on the town?'

Dee chuckled. 'I'll bear that in mind. Thank you for pointing me in the right direction.'

'My pleasure, lovey. Sure we can't tempt you to something before yer go?'

It was a very appealing offer but she'd already wasted any free time she'd had in her search for the elusive dry cleaner's. Now she needed to get back to make a start on preparing the evening meal. She didn't wish to be on the receiving end of any reprisals if she was late putting it on the table. 'I need to get on. Maybe another day.'

'We'll look forward to seeing you,' Bernie said sincerely.

Before she retraced her steps Dee flashed a look at Calum. 'Sorry to have disturbed you.'

As she shut the café door behind her, Bernie folded up the newspaper he had been reading, stubbed the butt of his cigarette out in the ashtray and went to join Calum behind the counter.

'She was pretty,' he casually commented as he handed a plate to Calum for him to put Sybil Brown's scones on.

'Mmm,' mouthed Calum, now in the process of pouring out the old lady's cup of coffee.

'She certainly tickled your fancy. First time I've seen a woman have such an effect on you since you've been working for me. You tickled hers too.'

Calum gave Bernie his full attention then. 'What! She was in here barely a minute, how do you make all that out?'

'I ain't blind, son. Look me in the eye and tell me I'm wrong about you fancying her?'

Calum stared at him a moment. 'Oh, okay, so maybe I did.'

'Well, why didn't you ask her out then? She didn't have a boyfriend, she said.'

'She's more than likely married.'

'No, she wasn't.'

'How do you know?'

'Wasn't wearing a ring. So next time she comes in, are you going to ask her out then?' Bernie urged him.

'No,' Calum said bluntly.

'Whyever not? Yer not shy with the women, are yer, Cal? You haven't given me that impression when yer've been bantering with the factory gels.'

He sighed. 'Because there's no point in asking her out, Bernie. Even if she did agree to have a night out with me, once she finds out I'm an ex-con she'll run a mile, like all the decent women I've been out with in the past did once they found out my family were no strangers to prison.'

Bernie gave a disdainful tut. 'Just 'cos those women didn't want n'ote to do with yer, it don't mean to say she'll be the same. Listen, lad, I'm only suggesting a night out, not a proposal of marriage. You don't need to tell her about yer background unless things look set to get serious between yer, and you won't know if there's any chance of *that* unless you ask her out, will yer? You could do with a bit of female company. The only social life you have that I know of is either a drink down the pub with me, or the evenings in you spend in yer landlady's company.'

'I rather enjoy Mrs Fry's company. Yours too for that matter.' Calum saw the look Bernie was giving him, knew the man wasn't going to stop his badgering until he got his way, and sighed. 'All right, my past doesn't need to come out unless I see things getting serious between us. I'll consider asking her out the next time she comes in, if I get the opportunity. But on one condition.'

'Oh, what's that?'

'That you concentrate on finding a woman to settle down with yourself.'

'Easier said than done at my age and with my looks. I'm not exactly film star material, am I? And let's not forget the string of criminal convictions I have to my name. Take a pretty special lady to turn a blind eye to all of that,' said Bernie. In fact, he doubted anyone that special existed. But despite the fact he'd resigned himself to dying a lonely bachelor, he was generous-natured enough to want for Calum what he had given up hoping for himself.

CHAPTER FOURTEEN

It was a week later when Dee found herself in the vicinity of the Uppingham Road Café again after paying another visit to the dry cleaner's to drop in several suits for the Monks brothers whose weekly dry cleaning bill far exceeded the amount she and her mother had paid out for food to cover them a month. Dee felt it was an unnecessary extravagance on their part too as the suits hadn't looked to be in need of any attention, but then it saved her the job of sprucing them up and was also an excuse for her to be out of the house, a place she hated.

As if she hadn't enough to deal with already, since that morning Ronnie had commandeered her services to aid him dressing he had started to take a personal interest in her. It was becoming increasingly apparent to her that deep down Ronald Monk did not share his brother's views on associating with prostitutes or anyone connected with them. She had a terrible foreboding that it was only a matter of time before he found a way to proposition her behind his brother's back. She hadn't a clue how she would handle the situation as neither of the brothers was the sort to take no for an answer. She just thanked the Almighty her room in the attic had a lock on the door so he couldn't sneak into her room at night and force himself on her while his brother was asleep.

Dee had never had cause before to regret the presence of Madge in her life, but now she did. The Monks brothers would never have had the hold over her they did had it not been for her love for the older woman.

A visit to Madge was long overdue and something Dee had been putting off. Madge knew her so well that putting on an act that she was deliriously happy in her new job would be an ordeal. The last thing she wanted was for Madge to get any inkling that all was not right and for this whole sorry mess to come to light. She had no doubt her friend would be mortified to discover what Dee had agreed to do for her sake. She'd probably demand that the girl should immediately leave the Monks brothers' employment, and then both of them would have no choice but to go on the run. Though in many ways life on the run, compared to how she was living now, sounded like bliss to Dee. She couldn't have that for Madge, though. Soon she would have to visit her friend or else Madge would come looking for her, and as Leicester wasn't the size of Birmingham it was only a matter of time before her secret was revealed.

She was so intent on her thoughts she didn't hear the voice addressing her until the second time it did.

She spun round to see a portly, balding man wearing a heavily food-stained white apron over denim jeans and black tee-shirt, leaning in a shop doorway smoking a cigarette. He was grinning at her. 'Weather's improving at long last, glad to say. Anyway, you looked miles away, ducky, like the weight of the world was on yer shoulders. I can't for the life of me think what could be that bad it would put a scowl on that pretty face of yours.'

Dee recognised him as the man who had kindly pointed her in the direction of the dry cleaner's the week before when she'd gone into his café. 'Was I scowling? Oh, dear, I had no idea. Yes, it is getting a little warmer, thank goodness,' she responded, smiling at him. 'And thank you again for helping me out with directions last week.' Then she made to continue on her way.

Bernie, though, was not about to let this opportunity for Calum pass him by, not when he had witnessed the attraction that had flared between them last week. Besides, he rather liked the thought of playing Cupid, and if those two did end up together he liked the idea that it was him they'd have to thank for it. 'So you're going to break yer promise to me, are yer? I didn't think you looked the type to break promises but obviously I was mistaken.'

Dee looked at him, puzzled. 'Sorry? What promise?'

'To have a cuppa and a piece of cake when you were next passing my café.'

Dee couldn't exactly remember making such a promise, and she did have other things to do. There was a pile of ironing waiting for her, and she had the evening meal to prepare, but now that she had established a routine all her other regular chores were up to date so in truth she could spare a few minutes for herself. She liked the thought of spending time amongst friendly faces, bringing a bit of light relief into her otherwise cheerless life. And if she had indeed led this nice man to believe she'd accepted his invitation, then she should honour it. 'Lead the way,' she said, smiling.

The roles were reversed from the last time Dee was in the café. Taking advantage of a quiet period, Calum was sitting at a table, reading the paper over a mug of tea and a cigarette. The outer door opening had registered with him, but thinking it was just Bernie returning after a few minutes outside, Calum did not break off from what he was doing. He did not notice Dee's arrival until he heard the scrape of a chair being pulled out opposite his and Bernie saying, 'Sit yerself down, gel, and Cal can keep you company while I get you a cuppa. What type of cake do you fancy? No Madeira left today, but I've currant and mixed fruit or there's a selection of smaller ones. Eccles are my favourite. I can eat three of them at a time, as you can see,' he said, chuckling as he patted his large stomach.

Calum raised his head and was startled to come face to face with the pretty young woman who had caught his attention when last she'd visited the café. He'd made a deal with Bernie to ask her out on a date the next time she came in, he remembered.

Dee meanwhile was feeling uncomfortable at being foisted off on the café-owner's assistant who wasn't being given any choice in the matter. Not that she didn't find him attractive. 'Er . . . an Eccles cake will be fine, thank you,' she said to Bernie.

'Coming up then.' Before he shot off to attend to Dee's requirements, with a meaningful look on his face he said to

Calum, 'Introduce yerself to our new customer then, Cal, and let her know we're a friendly lot in here. Otherwise she won't come back.'

He was well aware just what Bernie's game was, and although there was no malice whatsoever in what he had done, Calum was nevertheless annoyed with Bernie for putting himself and this young woman in a compromising situation. He felt very uncomfortable, and what was worse he was sure that she did too. Not that he didn't want her company. There was certainly something about her . . .

Dee flashed him an embarrassed smile. 'Look, I don't want to disturb your break . . .'

'No, you're not,' he insisted, folding the newspaper and shoving it aside. 'There wasn't any interesting reading in it today anyway.' He held out his hand to her in greeting. 'Calum Jackson . . . Cal. Pleased to meet you.'

She leaned over to shake it. 'Diane Kirby. Dee. I'm pleased to meet you too.'

There were several seconds of awkwardness while each of them sought something interesting to say.

It was Calum who found his voice first. 'Nice-looking dress suit,' he commented, nodding at the garment in the dry cleaning cover which Dee had laid carefully over the back of a chair before she sat down.

'Er . . . yes, it is,' she said vaguely. The last thing she wanted was to talk about the people she worked for.

'Your husband's, is it? Going out somewhere nice together, a posh do or something?'

'Oh, no, I'm not married. I've just collected the suit as . . . er . . . a favour.'

He was relieved by her answer. Bernie's assumption that she wasn't married because she wasn't wearing a ring could have been mistaken. 'So . . . er . . . lived around here long?'

'No, not long. You?' she asked him back.

'Me neither. I got this job kind of by accident so I moved round here to be closer. I'm glad I did because I like it round here. The people are friendly.'

Not all of them, she thought. 'Yes, they seem to be. Like you, I moved around here with my job.'

'What job is that?' he asked keenly, wanting to know more about her.

'I'm a housekeeper. For ... er ... an old gent. He's very nice.' Dee hated telling lies but she didn't know if Calum or his boss had heard of the Monkses and what they stood for. It wouldn't look good for her if they had. They probably wouldn't speak to her again.

Calum looked surprised. 'Oh, really? I always imagined middle-aged spinsters did that sort of job, not someone your age.' He wanted to add 'and as pretty' but thought better of it.

'Have you always worked in cafés?' she asked.

'No. I ... well, the job I had before this one was in engineering. I just fancied a change.'

There was another awkward silence while they both sought for something else to say.

'Thank ...' they both said together.

'You first,' said Calum in gentlemanly fashion.

'I'm sure what you were going to say was far more interesting.'

He looked doubtful. 'Well ... I was just going to say, thank goodness spring seems to be on its way at long last, that's all.'

Dee laughed. 'Exactly what I was going to say too.'

Bernie came over then with a cup of tea and plate containing two Eccles cakes. He placed these before Dee, then pulled out a chair and sat down next to her, giving her his full attention.

'I didn't quite catch your name,' he said. 'I'm Bernie. Or Bernard Caruso Stubbs to give you me full title.' He flashed a warning glance at Calum. 'And before you say 'ote, me mother had a crush on the famous opera singer when she was expecting me.' Then he returned his attention to Dee and bluntly asked her, 'So what do you do with yerself of an evening if you haven't got a boyfriend teking you out? You did say you hadn't got one, last time we spoke.'

Calum cringed. He had an awful feeling he knew where Bernie was heading with this line of conversation. 'I think I smell something burning in the kitchen,' he put in.

Bernie stared at him blankly. 'Well, there's no gas on under anything, I turned it all off before I took a breather outside, and I can't smell 'ote so it must be your imagination.' He turned back to Dee. 'You were telling me what you get up to of an evening?'

She gave a shrug, knowing that what she was about to say wouldn't exactly make her appear interesting in Calum's eyes . . . 'Er . . . well . . . not much really.'

'Cal doesn't get up to much either,' Bernie said encouragingly. 'Do you, Cal?' Before he could respond Bernie was off again. 'Cal's not long moved in round here so doesn't really know that many people well . . . 'cept me, of course, and his landlady. And she's old enough to be his gran.' Bernie acted as though he'd suddenly had a brainwave. 'Why don't you two young things get together for a night out? Better than both sitting round at home twiddling yer thumbs, don't yer think?' He fixed his eyes on Calum, looking to him to take the lead.

Dee felt mortified at the compromising situation the café-owner had put her in. She had no doubt, looking at Calum's face, that he wasn't very happy either.

'Well, Cal?' Bernie prompted him.

Just then the shop bell announced the arrival of a customer. Before Calum could respond to it, Bernie jumped up, saying, 'You and Dee are making arrangements for yer evening out, I'll see to this customer.'

After he had gone Calum looked at her in embarrassment. 'Look, I must apologise for my boss, I don't know what the hell has got into him.' Then he realised he could be giving Dee the impression that the last thing he wanted was to spend time in her company, when in truth he felt exactly the opposite. 'Of course, if you did fancy going out somewhere then . . . well, I'd be very happy to take you, really I would.'

She stared at him blankly. Despite his boss's engineering of this situation, Calum did genuinely seem to want to take her out. A night out with a man any woman in her right mind would want to spend time with, including herself, would give her something to look forward to. It would be much better than spending what time she wasn't ministering to the Monks brothers alone in her room reading. Trouble was, though, time to herself had never been discussed and she didn't know whether the brothers felt she should have any. But then, they were out every evening from about seven-thirty, except Sundays, and by the way they dressed they were either attending to business or socialising – sometimes both. They never usually returned until the early hours of the morning, so how would they even know she'd gone out during their absence, if she was back before they were?

She smiled warmly at Calum. 'I'd love to, then.'

His delight at her response was unfeigned. 'Great,' he enthused. 'We'll do whatever you fancy.'

'Oh, I'm happy with whatever you choose. I'll leave it to you.'

'We could go for a drink first, then to the Troc for the dancing. Is eight o'clock all right for you? And would you like me to come and call for you or meet you somewhere?'

His coming to the Monkses' house was out of the question, for obvious reasons. 'I'll meet you outside here, and eight is fine.'

Just then a customer approaching the counter spotted Calum and detoured towards him. 'Hi, Cal.' He looked at Dee then back to Cal, with a look on his face which said, I approve of your choice of company. 'I'll just interrupt you long enough to say my goodbyes,' he said.

'Your goodbyes, Don?' Calum queried.

'Leicester's not for me, mate. Not that it's a bad place by any means, and the folk here are nice enough, but I'm an Oldham lad. Only came to this town when I were put on short time there. But I miss my family and friends so I'm off back up to Oldham. The old mill's running at full capacity again, and taking on. The fact I worked for them before will stand me in good stead.'

'Well, it's been nice knowing you, Don, and best of luck,' Calum said sincerely.

'Thanks, mate.' He flashed a look at Dee then back to Calum, saying jocularly, 'You don't look like you need any, lad.'

As Don went off to place his order with Bernie, Calum returned his attention to Dee and couldn't help but notice the thoughtful expression on her face. He assumed he knew what was going through her mind and said, 'Look, Dee, I'll understand if you've changed your mind about going out with me.' Though he hoped she hadn't.

Dee wasn't listening to him, though, her thoughts fixed firmly elsewhere. That customer announcing to Calum he was leaving Leicester in order to return to his home town had given her an idea for escaping her own situation. If she could somehow persuade Madge to make up her differences with her family and move back home with them, the Monks brothers could no longer hold the threat of harming her over Dee. With Madge back in the bosom of her family, Dee could then escape to another town, change her name, do everything in her power in fact to make herself untraceable. Should the brothers decide she was worth spending the time and trouble of coming after she would doubtless suffer the consequences, but at least she'd be happy in the knowledge that Madge was safe from them, because no matter what they did to her she would never divulge her friend's whereabouts. The fact that she would be making her escape virtually penniless was not really a consideration. She had her legs to carry her, and was prepared to do the most menial of jobs to buy food. She'd sleep rough if necessary. Anything so as to be free of the Monkses, that was all that mattered to her.

She could hurry double-quick through her chores tomorrow then travel across to see Madge in the afternoon – praying she wasn't out entertaining any of her clients as that meant repeating the visit until Dee did catch her in – then during their catch-up chat she'd slip in her suggestion of making things up with her family, and just hope Madge took the bait and acted upon it.

Dee realised Calum was looking at her expectantly, as if he was waiting for an answer to a question. 'I'm sorry, did you ask me something? I didn't hear you.'

'I just said, I'll understand if you've had second thoughts about us going out?'

In fact, she'd need a distraction during the worrying wait for the outcome of the meeting with Madge, and a night out with this handsome man would be just the ticket. 'Oh, no, not at all. There is just one thing, though.'

'Oh?'

'Well, we've made arrangements for what time to meet and where but not what night?'

Calum laughed. 'Tomorrow suit you?'

Dee smiled. 'Suits me fine.'

Calum noticed then the café was starting to get busy. 'Would you excuse me, I need to get back to work?'

'Oh, yes, of course I will.' Dee scraped back her chair and rose to her feet, saying, 'I really must be off anyway.' She wanted to be on her own so she could plan the best way to approach Madge with her suggestion. Then she noticed the full cup of tea and plate of cakes, realised she hadn't paid for them and went across to the counter, arriving just ahead of Calum. 'How much do I owe you?' she asked Bernie.

'Compliments of the house being's it's yer first time with us. Besides, I can hardly charge yer for summat you ain't eaten, can I?' He gave her a mischievous wink. 'Looking forward too much to yer night out with our Cal, are yer, to be thinking of eating?'

Dee just smiled at him. Calum appeared beside her, and before she departed she said to him, 'I'll see you at eight tomorrow night.'

Once she was out of earshot, he glared furiously at Bernie. 'What on earth got into you? You gave her no choice but to go out with me, and me no choice but to ask her, so I've no idea whether she really wants to or not.'

Bernie flapped his hand. 'Oh, 'course she does. Dee doesn't come across to me as the sort who'd go along with anything because she was afraid to say no. It was obvious to me you were both pussy-footing around, I just helped you cut to the chase, that's all. There was a danger you'd both be pensioners before 'ote got going between you, left to your own devices. Instead of having a go at me, you should be thanking me for lending a helping hand.' Then, with a twinkle in his eye, he added jocularly, 'Just remember my contribution to your relationship in the wedding speeches. Now come on, we've customers to take care of.'

Calum said nothing to this and Bernie bustled off to the kitchen to see to Don's order of pie and mushy peas. He had a valid point as without his intervention there was a strong possibility Cal would still be secretly admiring Dee, with no prospect of a date with her. But as for a wedding . . . well, there remained the fact that he was an ex-con which Dee was not aware of. It was debatable whether matters between them would progress much further than a couple of nights out.

Minutes later the café door opened and a huge man entered, accompanied by a smaller arrogant-looking one. Both of them were expensively dressed. Calum had seen these men before. They usually came in around about this time every week. If Bernie was out front, the three of them would disappear out the back together then minutes later the men would return and leave the premises. Today, with Bernie in the kitchen, without a word to Calum the men made their way straight through to the back. Minutes later they returned, swaggering their way through the tables to leave the premises.

Calum did not like the look of those men in any way whatsoever. He was of the opinion that the unsightly scar running down the side of the thuggish-looking one's face could only have been caused by a knife. He assumed they were old friends of Bernie's from his criminal days, though he did say he'd turned his back on all criminal activity five years ago. What puzzled Calum, though, was the fact that the meetings between these men and his boss only lasted a couple of minutes at the most. After witnessing several weeks of this behaviour, he was beginning to wonder if Bernie had been truthful about his claim to be on the straight and narrow. It didn't look like it, associating with that type. But in what way? Calum couldn't fathom that due to the shortness of the time they spent together. Still, it wasn't his place to question what his employer did privately, so long as it didn't affect Calum himself in any way. And he had more important things to occupy his mind – such as the forthcoming date with Dee.

*   *   *

Seconds before six o'clock that evening, Dee was just about to tap on the study door to inform the brothers that the evening meal was ready when the door opened and Leonard Monks appeared. Before she could tell him her reason for being there, he shot at her, 'You eavesdropping?'

'No, Mr Monks,' she insisted. 'I just came to tell you dinner is ready.'

He grabbed her by her chin, squeezing tightly, and hissed at her, 'You'd better not be.'

Just then Ronnie came out of the study. 'What's going on?'

'Just checking our housekeeper hadn't got her ear to the door,' Lennie told him, his hand still clamped painfully around Dee's face.

'Oh, I'm sure she hadn't, Len,' Ronnie urged him. 'Come on, leave her alone. You're hurting her.'

Lennie released his grip on Dee to look at his brother quizzically. 'Why are you sticking up for her?' His eyes narrowed darkly. 'You haven't got a soft spot for our housekeeper by any chance, have you, Ron?'

'No, no, Len. Don't be daft,' Ronnie insisted. He flashed Dee a derogatory glance and snarled, 'She's just a fucking slut like the ones that took our dad away. Come on, let's have dinner, I'm starving. And we don't want to be late for our night down the dogs, do we?'

As the brothers made their way into the dining room, Dee decided she'd been right. Ronnie was taking a less than healthy interest in her and it was only a matter of time before he made advances in no uncertain terms. He had just come to her defence, there was no doubting that. The thought of having to submit to Ronnie out of fear made her feel sick to her stomach, but the probable consequences of his elder brother ever discovering such a liaison terrified her witless.

Oh, Madge, please be at home tomorrow and take me up on the idea of moving back to be with your family, she silently prayed. Otherwise she could see herself becoming what she had fought against all her life. But whereas prostitutes were paid for their services, she would be giving hers to Ronald Monk for free.

CHAPTER FIFTEEN

Early the next afternoon Madge launched herself at Dee, hugging her fiercely as soon as she opened the back door and recognised her caller.

'Oh, me darlin',' she cried out in delight. 'I've been so worried about you. I haven't heard or seen hide nor hair of you since yer walked out of here over a month ago. I was beginning to worry you wasn't ever going to come back and see me. But yer here now and I can sleep better at nights again.' Releasing Dee she urged, 'Come on in . . . not that you need an invitation, this is your home, yer know that, Dee. But get yer coat off and I'll put the kettle on and then we can have a proper catch up. I'm dying to hear all about this job of yours and the new life yer've made for yerself.'

Stepping inside the kitchen, Dee swallowed down the lump that had formed in her throat when she found herself back on familiar territory, particularly now she knew her mother's death had been no accident.

What she was experiencing did not escape the astute Madge. Putting her arm around the younger woman's shoulders and giving her a reassuring squeeze, she asked her softly, 'You all right, lovey?'

Dee flashed her a wan smile. 'I'm fine.' Then she sighed. 'For a moment I expected Mam to come charging in from the back room, having a go at me for something or other she wasn't happy about. I don't miss her having a go at me, or clearing up the mess she always left behind her, but I miss *her*, Aunty Madge.'

She smiled her understanding. 'If it's any consolation I have those experiences all the time, expecting Del suddenly to appear,

167

demanding to know what I'm doing living here.' A sorrowful expression flashed across her face, one that was far more attractive and softer-looking when scrubbed clean of the thick layer of make-up she wore while working. 'It's still hard to accept she's not longer with us, ain't it?' she uttered. 'She was a larger-than-life character, was our Del.'

Still would be if those mindless thugs I'm being forced to work for hadn't cut short her life, Dee thought. 'Mmm,' she mouthed. She planted a smile on her face. 'This is the first chance I've had to come and see you, and I was worried you might be out working.'

'Well, aren't I glad you picked today because I've nothing on until I go out on me beat tonight. So until then, I'm all yours.'

Taking off her coat, Dee asked, 'How are things with you, Aunty Madge?'

She was filling the kettle with water from the large single brass tap protruding over the antiquated pot sink. 'Fair to middling, ta, lovey. Nothing exciting has happened to me since the last time I saw yer. Before you ask, no, I didn't tout after any of yer mam's old clients. Not that I couldn't have done with their custom, but I didn't feel it right to as Del was me friend.

'I must apologise for the state of this place. I took yer advice and asked Elsie to move in with me, telling her it'd only be temporary like if you decided to come back. Well, I thought yer mam was an untidy bugger who expected everyone else to fetch and carry for her, but Elsie takes the cake! If I'd known what she was like to live with, I'd have thought twice about asking her to share with me. Still, she pays her way which is what's important so I can keep this place on, and I've got to say it's a damn' sight better living here than in my old lodgings. Elsie's out at the moment so we've the place to ourselves.'

Having now put the kettle on the stove and lit the gas beneath it, she turned round to appraise Dee. 'Oh, it's so lovely to see yer, ducky. Done me the power of good, the sight of you has. So come on, hang yer coat up, sit down and tell me all.'

After hooking her coat on the peg on the back door, Dee began to gather crockery by way of helping Madge, but also so as not to have to look her in the eye as she told the pack of lies she was about to. She vehemently hoped the older woman didn't see through them. 'My job's great,' she enthused. 'The old gent is really nice. I've made lots of friends. I feel really settled, Aunty Madge.'

While she waited for the kettle to boil, Madge pulled a chair out at the table and sat down, smiling at Dee. 'I'm so glad to hear that.' Then she looked guilty. 'Well, that's not exactly the truth, lovey. I have to say, deep down I was hoping to hear different, that you'd not settled and was after coming back. But that was selfish on my part. Anyway, tell me more about your employer.'

'Such as what?' Dee asked.

'Well, such as what he did for a job before he retired. You know I care about you like you was me own, I just want to know a bit more about him, that's all.'

So consumed was she with not missing a chance to bring up the real reason for her visit, Dee hadn't thought to concoct a history for her fictitious employer. Madge had caught her on the hop. 'Oh, er . . .' Then she gave the first occupation she thought of. 'Bank manager.'

Madge looked impressed. 'Bank manager, eh? Well, your employer's obviously done well for himself, to be able to afford a housekeeper in his dotage. What's yer room like? I bet it's lovely. Got matching counterpane and curtains and a view from the window, that sort of room?'

'Oh, yes, it's really pretty,' Dee lied. 'Looks out on to the garden.' Her room did, in fact, but she had to stand on a chair and crane her neck to see that far down from the attic.

'Garden, eh?' Madge said wistfully, thinking of the one she had always hoped to have surrounding her cottage in the country. 'Big one, I should imagine. Got a gardener to look after it, I suppose?'

A miserable old bugger of a sixty year old who came in once a week to tend to it and didn't even try to pass the time of day with Dee when she went out to take him a cup of tea. But then, she didn't know whether or not his services had been obtained in a similar fashion to hers by the Monkses. 'Yes, nice bloke,' she said shortly.

'Well, I have to say, you sound like yer've landed on yer feet.' Then more to herself than to Dee, remembering how the girl had met her new employer and how she herself had first met Dee's mother, Madge added, 'It's amazing how a chance meeting with someone can change the course of yer life. Yes, amazing indeed.' The kettle started singing then and she got up to pour the water over the leaves in the pot. 'Oh, I've got a packet of arrowroot biscuits somewhere.'

Her stomach already turning somersaults over the conversation to come, the last thing Dee felt like was eating. 'Don't bother for me, Aunty Madge. I'm fine with just the tea, thank you.'

On her way to the larder Madge did an about turn and sat back down again. 'Well, I expect yer used to far more fancy biscuits than plain arrowroot now. Anyway, knowing Elsie she's probably scoffed them all. We go halves on the food but, by God, she makes doubly sure she gets what she calls her half when in truth it's more like three-quarters.' Pouring out the tea, she pushed Dee's cup before her and said, 'Get that down yer before it goes cold.' Picking up her own cup and nursing it between her hands, she asked, 'So what are yer new friends like?'

'Oh, er . . . very nice.'

'How did you meet them?'

'In a café. You know how it is? You get talking and one thing leads to another. I'm going out with one of them tonight, in fact.'

The older woman's eyes lit up. 'Oh! Man or woman?'

'Man actually. He's taking me for a drink first then dancing afterwards.'

'Oh, Dee, I am pleased for you. It seems you certainly did the right thing accepting that job. I'll keep my fingers crossed yer night out with this man is the beginning of something special for you, and it doesn't turn out like all yer other relationships with chaps in the past. You above anyone else I know deserve some happiness in love.

'Just a bit of advice. You've no need to tell him what yer

mother was. It's not like he'll ever have to meet her or see for himself what she did. And if anyone should remark on your likeness to a woman they knew who worked the streets, just tell 'em they're mistaken and stick to yer guns. Promise me yer won't let the past hinder yer any more, Dee?'

If Madge knew how much the past was hindering her right now she'd be horrified. 'I'll do my best not to.' As she sipped her tea, Dee looked at Madge through her lashes. This was the ideal time to raise the subject she had come to broach. She replaced her cup in its saucer and took a deep breath. 'Aunty Madge . . . well, now you know I'm happily settled, I'd be even happier if I knew you were too.'

Madge looked at her strangely. 'Oh, lovey, I'm as settled as I could ever hope to be. My life is what it is and I have no choice but to get on with it.'

'So you've given up on your dreams of retiring to a cottage in the country?'

Madge gave a snort. 'It's a case of having to. Pie in the sky that dream was. You know fine well I haven't the money even to rent that cottage, let alone buy it.'

'Yes, but what about your . . .' Dee took a deep breath before she added '. . . family, Aunty Madge?'

Madge looked quite taken aback by this unexpected reference to them. 'What about them?' she asked shortly.

'You've never talked about them to me, and from a couple of things you've said in the past, I assume there's some sort of rift between you?'

'Mmm, you could say that,' Madge said shortly.

'Don't you miss them?' Dee asked bluntly.

Madge gave a heavy sigh. ''Course I do.' Then she looked at Dee. 'Why all this interest in my family?'

'Well, as I said, now I'm happily settled, I just want the same for you.' She looked intently at the older woman. 'I know life is no picnic for you, and you said yourself the night you came to sit with me when Kevin had broken up with me that you're not getting any younger. And in your line of work it's not like it's going to get any better, is it, only more of a struggle.

You know how much I care for you, Aunty Madge. I know I don't have any idea what caused the trouble between you and your family, but if you made up your differences . . . well, it was just a thought I had, then you could leave all this behind and return to live with them again. Your family don't have to know how you've been earning your living since you last saw them, do they? You could make up a story to cover yourself. You could find work, Aunty Madge, serving in a shop or something similar, and be able to afford the rent on a little place for your-self. I could come to visit you there.'

Madge sighed. She couldn't say the thought of doing what Dee suggested didn't appeal. Having herself a job where she knew each week what wage she would be getting to live on, instead of the constant day-to-day worry of what she got depending entirely on how many clients she managed to secure herself, and not having to hand over a portion of her earnings to two threatening thugs, sounded like pure heaven to Madge. And a place to live in that had a view over greenery, not the sooty walls of other houses. And a space she didn't have to share with inconsiderate people like Elsie . . . yes, it sounded absolute paradise. And the thought of being part of a family again, involved in their lives, and they in hers . . . that she would give anything for.

'I have to say, I'd like nothing more than to make amends with me family, Dee. But what if they thought that what you'd done was so bad they'd never forgive yer?' Madge put to her.

'What you'd done . . . Oh!' Dee thought Madge such a lovely person it hadn't occurred to her that any problem between her family and herself could have been Madge's fault. She racked her brains for something Madge could have done that was so bad her family deemed it unforgivable. Getting herself pregnant out of wedlock was the obvious answer. But then, Madge had no children so it couldn't have been that . . . The only other really bad thing she could think of was that Madge had killed someone. But she would have served a lengthy prison sentence for such a crime, and as Madge had met her mother when they were both fifteen and they had a long history together, she clearly hadn't been in prison.

'I can't believe you would do anything so bad it was completely unforgivable, Aunty Madge,' Dee said resolutely. 'And, anyway, how do you know that by now they haven't forgiven you for what you did, if you haven't been back to find out? What if they've been trying to trace you all these years to make amends because . . . well, because they don't see whatever it is that caused all the trouble between you as being that bad anymore?'

Madge turned her head to stare thoughtfully out of the kitchen window at the depressing back yard outside. She wasn't seeing the soot-blackened bricks of the outhouse and crumbling boundary wall beyond, she was seeing a vision of her family as she had last seen them on the day they had thrown her out twenty-five years ago.

Her mother at thirty-three, looking ten years older from years of constant worry, feeding and clothing her growing family on the meagre wage her husband brought home each week. Her father at thirty-four looking nearer fifty from his sixteen-hour-days spent labouring for a local farmer, a hard taskmaster who demanded his money's worth. Her parents had always conducted their lives in accordance with the teachings of their religion and tried to guide their children to be honest, upright members of society, but regardless both of them had been warm and loving, their humble home a haven for their family.

Then she pictured her sister Colleen, a year younger than herself at fourteen, already showing signs of the beauty she would become. She was outgoing, a born actress, and full of her dreams of a career on the stage, although it was everyone else's opinion that Colleen's aspirations were just a young girl's fantasy and as soon as she left school it was the local dairy where she would be working, to end up married to a local boy with a horde of children of her own and probably become aged before her time like her mother was. Next was her brother Fergal. At twelve he was tall, gangly, full of cheek, always up to something he shouldn't be, and never a week went by without a visit from the village constable and a clip around the ear for Fergal. At ten and a half there was Dougal, slight of build and studious-looking, his nose permanently in a book. At school they called him The

Professor. Last came Evelyn, the baby at six. 'Little Evie' they had affectionately called her, and she had been her mother's helper, hardly ever seen without a happy smile on her chubby face.

What had become of them all during the intervening years? Had her father's work prospects improved, and along with them her mother's lot? Had her sister Colleen fulfilled her ambition to go on the stage against the odds? Had Fergal grown up and matured, to leave his scalliwag days behind and become a pillar of society? And what of Dougal and Evelyn?

But above all, had the priest's violation of Madge herself come to light? Had her family discovered she'd been telling the truth all along about who had fathered her child and come to regret their expulsion of her? What if they hadn't, and he was still dominating everyone in the village? Well, maybe it was high time, now that she was older and wiser, she faced that monster, brought him to task verbally for what he had done to her, let him see she knew him for the vile creature he was. Then, having faced her demon, she'd finally be able to put the memories of his despicable action and the result of it in the back of her mind and live the life she was meant to live, not the one that had resulted from his violation of her. Armed with the fictitious background she had invented for herself, would her return indeed result in a family reunion and a chance for Madge to turn her back on what others perceived as a depraved life, in exchange for one where she was welcomed into people's homes and looked on with respect? Might she even find herself a man who'd take her as his wife? Dee was right, she would never know any of this unless she went back to the place of her birth to find out. Yes, it was certainly something to think about.

She gave Dee's arm an affectionate pat. 'It's wonderful for me to know you care about me enough to want my happiness, Dee. I shall give your suggestion serious thought.'

Her face lit up. 'You will? Oh, that's great, Aunty Madge. When are you going to go and see them? The sooner the better,' she urged.

'Dee, I said I'd give it serious thought.'

Thought was no good, Dee needed action. 'But what do you need to think about? Before you realise it another year will have passed, then another, and by the time you get around to going to see them, it might be too late. No one lives forever, do they?' she implored. 'If anything happened to your parents while you were spending time thinking about this, then you'd have lost the chance to make your final peace with them.'

Madge gave her a quizzical look. 'Dee, the way you're pushing me to do this it's like it's a matter of life and death to you. Is there something going on you're not telling me about?'

Dee froze. How she wished she could tell Madge that if she herself put a foot wrong in the eyes of the Monks brothers it *could* well be a matter of life or death for her friend. 'No, 'course there isn't,' she insisted.

Madge sighed. 'Oh, lovey, I'd do anything for you, yer know that, but this . . . well, I really do need to think about it some more.'

Dee's heart sank. She knew Madge was frightened she could be facing rejection from her family, but how could anyone reject such a kind and caring woman? Her family would be bound to see those qualities in her as soon as they met up again, and want . . . no, demand . . . her back in their lives. Dee knew Madge well enough to know that once she had her firm promise to do something, then Madge would honour it, no matter what. Getting that promise was proving far more difficult than Dee had envisaged. It seemed to her the only way she was going to prevail was to resort to emotional blackmail. Taking a deep breath she said, 'I lied, Aunty Madge. I'm not really as happy as I'm making out because . . . well, I feel guilty.'

'Guilty?' Madge asked, looking bemused. 'Whatever for?'

'Having a good future to look forward to.'

'And why should you feel guilty for that?'

'Because you haven't, and I know I won't be completely happy within myself until your situation is better. I won't, Aunty Madge,' Dee said with conviction.

Tears of emotion glistened in Madge's eyes. She knew Dee cared about her, but had never before realised just how much.

She couldn't live with herself, knowing she was responsible for standing in the way of Dee's happiness. 'Oh, lovey, if I do agree to do what yer asking me, and it still doesn't work out the way you think it will, you do promise me you'll give up worrying about me and just get on with your life?'

'Oh, don't be silly, Aunty Madge. Of course it's all going to work out,' Dee said resolutely.

Madge sighed. 'All right, if it means so much to you, I'll go . . .' She paused, wondering if Dee had any idea what it was taking for her to commit herself to this. 'Tomorrow.' As soon as she'd committed herself she regretted it, but it was too late. She had.

Dee wanted to jump for joy finally to have gained Madge's agreement. Instead she said evenly, 'I can't imagine your family not being over the moon to see you again.'

Madge hoped she was right.

Dee finished her tea and rose to go. 'I'd better be off. I'll be back the day after next to help you start packing for your move,' she informed Madge. And then she herself could escape from her employers.

Dee's automatic belief that she would receive a warm welcome back from her family was beginning to rub off on Madge. She smiled. 'I'll look forward to seeing you then. Maybe we'll both have good news for each other, eh? You'll have had a good night out with your new fella and both of you'll be wanting to see each other again. And my visit to see my family will have gone like you're predicting.'

Madge waved her off at the back door and watched until Dee had disappeared out of the gate into the jetty. Then the enormity of what she'd promised sank in and her stomach began to churn with trepidation. She suddenly knew how unarmed Roman slaves must have felt, being turfed into dens of ravenous lions. A desperate urge to rush after Dee and tell her she had changed her mind swamped Madge. Had she made her promise to anyone else she would have done it and not cared what they thought of her, but she had made that promise to Dee and whatever she faced tomorrow she would have to suffer the consequences.

Then a glaring fact registered within her. One thing was for certain: she couldn't turn up at her family home looking as she did now or any hope of a reconciliation would be doomed before it started. They'd need only one glance at her to see what she had become since they threw her out. Better pretend to them she was a woman who had not done that well for herself financially but was nevertheless virtuous.

A rummage through her wardrobe was called for to dig out her most conservative attire. Hopefully she could cobble a presentable outfit together, but if not a trip to the second-hand shop was called for. Then on to the chemist's for dye to change her hair from the henna-red men found attractive to a more fitting colour. And shoes . . . She couldn't turn up in her shabby stilettos. And that mottled fur coat was definitely a giveaway.

This transformation was going to cost her money she hadn't got spare so she'd need to be out sharp tonight. As it was, she'd have to borrow from the rent to fund her shopping trip this afternoon. And if tonight she needed to use all the tricks of the trade she'd learned off Della, even against her principles, down to luring clients off other prostitutes, she would do it, give what she was about to do every chance of success, for the future well-being of the very dear daughter of her deceased friend.

CHAPTER SIXTEEN

Dee was so convinced that Madge's family were going to welcome her back with open arms, she didn't experience the usual sense of dread when she let herself back into the Monkses' house a short while later and began to prepare the evening meal. She hoped that this was one of the last she would be making for them. Pity she wouldn't have the satisfaction of telling them so herself.

Thoughts of her evening out with Calum had been overridden by the need to get Madge to do her bidding. Now she had achieved that, Dee was able to concentrate her thoughts on the night ahead. As she washed the dinner dishes she was mentally going through her wardrobe, deciding what to wear and wishing she had the means at her disposal to buy something new. Out of a ten-shilling-a-week allowance that was out of the question. Whatever she decided upon, though, she wouldn't have much time to ready herself. The brothers seemed to be creatures of habit and usually left the house by seven-thirty in the evening to go off to wherever it was they went. She was meeting Calum at eight outside the café which was a good ten-minute walk away, so as soon as the brothers left she needed to get a move on. Like all women she wanted to look her best on a date.

The chores for the evening done, it was on Dee's mind to make use of the time while she waited for the men to leave by checking the pantry, making a list of the household requirements she needed to shop for the next day. Suddenly she had an overwhelming sensation that she was being watched. She spun around, gasping in shock to see Ronald, dressed for the off, leaning against the kitchen door, staring at her with a predatory look in his eye.

179

He wanted her.

Dee stared back at him, her heartbeat pounding in her ears. The time had come for him to make his move on her and dread filled her. She was no match for him, had nothing within her immediate reach to use as a weapon of self-defence, so she stood looking fixedly at him, fearing the worst. They both heard footsteps descending the stairs then, and with a look in his eyes that said to Dee *One day soon*, Ronnie turned away and lumbered off down the hallway to join his brother. It was apparent to Dee that he was not about to let Lennie catch him with her. For now she was safe, but Dee was well aware that a man's lust for a woman could drive him to commit murder in extreme cases. Should Ronnie's desire for her become all-consuming, his brother's obvious domination of him and their pact never to associate themselves physically with females connected in any way to prostitution would be forgotten.

Dee planned to be well away by then.

From her position in the kitchen she was able to hear most of what Lennie was saying to Ronnie as they joined forces in the hallway. It was something about a couple of bits of business they had to attend to first, then they were off to a casino as he was feeling lucky tonight.

While listening to Lennie relate his plans for the evening, Dee experienced her normal fury at the way they used their ill-gotten gains so frivolously. How she so wished she could find a way to put a stop to their callous money-making scams and win justice for her dead mother; for the suffering she knew they had brought to others too, in order to get their way. But as matters stood it was all she could do to find a way to get free from them herself.

When the door shut behind them Dee shot upstairs to her room to make herself as presentable as she could in less than twenty minutes. She didn't want to keep Calum waiting.

Under normal circumstances she would have been extremely nervous over a first date with a good-looking man, but as matters stood she was not really treating this evening as a first date or harbouring any hope of its leading to further ones. Even if Calum showed signs of wanting more she didn't plan to be around long enough to build relationship between them.

As she arrived at her destination, though, and saw what an obvious effort he had made to look smartly fashionable for her in jeans and black tee-shirt under a hip-length black leather jacket, and his evident delight at spotting her, a wave of remorse surged through her. He could be hoping for far more from this evening than she was. Maybe she should not have agreed to spend it with him in the first place.

In fact, Calum had not been daring to hope for very much, too conscious of Dee's probable reaction to his family connections. Regardless, he meant to enjoy his time with her. But then he spotted her approaching and saw just how attractive she was. Underneath her open coat she was wearing a full-skirted emerald green and white skirt with several stiff net petticoats beneath, and a fitted sleeveless white blouse with its collar turned up around the back of her neck. A black belt accentuated her waist, and she wore low-heeled pointed black court shoes. Her dark hair was fashionably backcombed and flicked out at the ends just short of her slender shoulders. Despite the fact he still knew little about her personally, he was already regretting the fact that she might not want to see him after he'd told her what he must about himself.

'I haven't kept you waiting, have I?' Dee asked as she came up to join him.

He smiled down at her, trying not to look too deeply into her eyes. 'Only a couple of minutes but I won't hold that against you,' he replied jocularly.

She laughed and said, 'Shall we go then?'

As soon as Calum had guided Dee through the doors of the Humberstone public house, he realised he'd know better next time than to ask Bernie's advice about a decent pub within easy distance. He'd planned to take Dee in for a quiet drink so they could become better acquainted before they set off for the Trocadero to dance. This place was heaving and deafeningly noisy.

As he pushed his way ahead of Dee to the bar he felt a hand

grab his shoulder and heard a loud voice that was very familiar to him say, 'These are on me, Cal, so what are you and Dee having?'

Cal turned, looking surprised. 'You didn't say you'd be in here tonight, Bernie. And you told me this place was quiet.'

'Well, it usually is. But I forgot there was a darts match on tonight, and you never enquired if I planned to be here when you asked me about a good pub to take Dee to.' Then he spotted her behind Cal and grinned broadly. 'Hello, me darlin'. You do look nice,' he said admiringly, then jocularly added, 'Pity I'm not a few years younger or I'd be fighting Cal for you. While we get the drinks in, why don't you make yer way over to that corner over there? I've saved a couple of seats for you.' He pointed to a table.

As soon as Dee was out of earshot, Bernie said to Calum, 'Rather good of me, don't yer think?'

Calum frowned at him, puzzled. 'What was?'

'Giving up a night by the telly to get you two off to a good start. I've made sure I'm on hand to keep the conversation flowing between yer both. I know what it's like when yer first take a gel out, how nerves can get the better of yer. Suddenly yer can't find 'ote of interest to say and come out with a load of codswallop instead, then you feel really stupid, and the woman thinks yer stupid too and gives you short shrift. Well, I'm on hand to make sure *that* don't happen with you two tonight. You can thank me later. You'd better get the drinks while I get meself over to Dee before she thinks we've abandoned her.' He slapped a handful of coins into Cal's hand. 'Make mine a pint of best.'

Whether Calum welcomed Bernie's intrusion or not, he had no wish to upset him so had no choice but to accept his presence. He just hoped Dee wouldn't have any objection to Bernie joining them in the pub.

When Cal arrived to join them with the tray of drinks which had taken an age to obtain from the harassed bar staff, he was relieved to see that Dee didn't seem to have any objection to Bernie's presence. She was laughing at something he was telling her about the antics of the customers in his café, and what he had done by way of retaliation.

'You really purposely put a mouldy sausage on a customer's plate, to stop him coming in again?' Dee spluttered with mirth.

Bernie was sitting back in his seat, hands clasped over his large belly as if holding court. 'Well, it weren't quite mouldy as such, but definitely off enough to give him a dose of summat nasty. The bloke was a pain in the arse. Oh, pardon me language, lovey, but he was. I knew what his game was. After freebees, wasn't he? Thought if he complained about the grub I dished up loud enough for everyone to hear, I'd give it him for nothing or at a discount just to shut him up. Well, his tricks might work in other establishments but not mine. Anyway me sausage trick must have worked because after that he never darkened my door again. Then there was the time . . . Oh, there you are, Cal,' he said, spotting Calum and standing up to take the tray of drinks off him.

Calum had only just sat down on the seat next to Dee when a man of about Bernie's age approached the table, carrying a pack of cards. 'Fancy a hand of rummy?' he said to Bernie.

'Yeah, why not?' he responded. Then, without asking Calum or Dee whether they wanted to play or not, added, 'Let's see what these youngsters are made of, eh, Kenny?'

'I've never played rummy before,' Dee told him.

'Don't worry, lovey. Cal will run through the rudiments with yer. But in fairness to yer, we'll play a couple of friendlies first before we put our cash on the table.' He saw the look on Dee's face then. 'Don't look so worried, we only play for a penny a round, yer won't break yer bank. Cal, shift up to make room for Kenny.'

Several rounds of drinks later, Bernie looked at Dee, astonished. 'For someone who said she ain't never played rummy before, that's the third hand in a row you've won. I'll be bankrupt at this rate.'

Mellowed from her four halves of cider and relaxed in the very amiable company she found herself in – especially Calum's – her dire life outside these walls was temporarily forgotten. Dee laughed as she collected more winnings to add to her growing pile. 'Well, I have Calum to thank for putting me straight on how to play before we started, so really he deserves half my winnings.'

He inwardly glowed at her compliment. During the time he had spent in her company this evening he had been able to observe Dee closely and he liked her easygoing nature; her readiness to laugh even at Kenny's lame attempts to outdo Bernie's hilarious jokes; the warmth of her. Bernie and Kenny were practically eating out of her hand. As for Calum himself, despite his resolve not to until he'd received her reaction to his family background, he knew he was falling for her.

'Well, shall we see how good you are at darts, now the match is over and the board is free?' asked Bernie.

'Well, I'm game,' said Kenny.

Before either Calum or Dee could voice their agreement, Bernie had grabbed Dee's arm and was guiding her over to the board, leaving Calum to follow with their drinks and find them a closer table, while Kenny went off to the bar to collect sets of darts.

A couple more rounds later, Bernie said to Dee in a slurred voice as she sat back down after her turn, 'I think we ought to call it a day with the darts. You nearly took that bloke's eye out with the last one you threw.'

'I'd better be making tracks. I told the wife I'd take back chips and she's probably given up by now,' said Kenny to them all.

Bernie looked at him in disappointment. 'Ah, not off so early, are yer, mate? I thought we could have a game of dominoes next. I don't know about you lot but I'm really enjoying meself. Great night . . . really great.' He gave Dee's knee a friendly pat. 'We'll have to make this a regular thing.'

Just then the clanging of a loud bell startled her.

'What they ringing that bell for? Is there a fire?' slurred Bernie, looking over towards the bar.

'It's last orders, yer drunken clot,' Kenny slurred back.

Bernie looked stunned. 'It never is! How time flies when yer enjoying yerself.' He put his hand in his pocket and pulled out a handful of change which he slapped on the table in front of Calum. 'Go and get 'em in before we miss out. You'll stay and have the last one with us, won't yer, Kenny? Chip shop is still open for another hour yet.' Before he could respond Bernie added, 'Go on then, Cal, off yer go.'

Half an hour later, having said their goodbyes to Kenny who'd rushed off to buy his wife's peace offering before the place closed for the night, Dee and Calum were supporting a very drunken Bernie between them, guiding him back towards his flat above the café.

'It's very good of you both to be seeing me home,' he was slurring. 'Why ain't you two as pissed as I am? You had as much as I did.'

'We didn't have as much as you did,' Calum told him. 'You were having two to our one with your whisky chasers.'

'You shouldn't let me drink whisky, it makes me really drunk.'

'Now you tell us,' came Calum's dry response.

'Oops-a-daisy!' giggled Bernie as he stumbled over his own feet and was only stopped from falling over by the fact that Dee and Calum each had an arm of his hooked through theirs. 'How many whiskies did I have then?' he asked.

'At least seven,' Calum told him.

'Oh, I never!' Bernie groaned. 'I'm in for a thick head tomorrow. Looks like you'll be in charge, Cal.'

'Well, you enjoyed yourself, Bernie, that's the main thing,' Dee told him.

'Oh, I did,' he affirmed. 'Best night out I've had for a while, and great company. What about you?' he asked, seeing two of her as he turned his head to look at Dee. 'By God, you're both pretty. Ain't they pretty, Cal?'

He wondered if Bernie had any idea how much he was embarrassing him in front of Dee. He doubted it very much, the state Bernie was in, but Cal would be sure to tell him when he had sobered up. 'Yes,' he muttered, trying to catch Dee's eye by way of apology for his boss's behaviour, but Bernie was swaying so much he kept blocking his view.

Bernie then abruptly stood still as a thought occurred to him. 'You two was going dancing, wasn't you? Why did you change your minds?'

'Oh, we were enjoying ourselves so much in your company, we forgot,' said Dee diplomatically.

'Ah, what a lovely thing to say. Wasn't that a lovely thing to say?' Bernie mumbled to Calum as they resumed their journey. 'She's a nice girl, don't let her get away.' Then to Dee, 'And you, young lady, don't let this man get away. He's a good lad is Calum.' Then to Calum again, 'You could take her dancing next time you see her, to make up for not taking her tonight.' Then to Dee again, 'You'd like to go dancing with Calum, wouldn't yer? Yes, 'course yer would.' Then to Calum, 'Well, ask the gel then, Cal, or she'll be thinking yer don't want to see her again.'

Calum was wishing the ground would open up and swallow him. He glanced behind Bernie's back to catch Dee's eye. Thankfully he did this time. 'I apologise for Bernie,' he mouthed.

'I heard that,' Bernie erupted, and glared at Calum, demanding, 'Why are you apologising for me?' Then with a look of innocence on his face, he asked, 'What have I done?' Before they could answer he suggested, 'Friday.'

'Friday?' Calum queried.

'Yeah, Friday. Good night for going dancing is Friday. Oh, that's tomorrow, ain't it? See, I ain't that drunk I don't know what day it is today. Got a nice frock?' he asked Dee.

'Er . . . yes.'

'Good. If Cal's too shy to ask you, I'll have to do it for him. He'll see you same time, same place he met you tonight, only tomorrow. Ah, thank God we're home.' Then he grabbed Dee unexpectedly by the shoulders and asked, 'Are you able to find yer own way from here, lovey?'

'Yes, of course I am.'

'Good, 'cos me legs have suddenly decided to give up on me and I need Cal to help me up the stairs.'

Calum grabbed Bernie by his shoulders, frogmarched him across to the doorway leading to his flat above the café, and ordered, 'Don't move.' Then he came back over to Dee, to look at her in remorse. 'Look, I apologise for Bernie again.' He paused, knowing that before he asked her what he was about to he really ought to tell her his secret, let her know what she was letting herself in for. He ought to give her the opportunity to decide whether she wanted to continue seeing him, but Bernie's shenanigans weren't allowing him the chance to do it properly. Hopefully she would agree to what he was about to propose and then he'd find the right time and place to divulge what he must.

He took a deep breath. 'I really enjoyed myself tonight, and I was going to ask you out again before Bernie got in before me. Would you like to go dancing with me tomorrow night – if tonight hasn't put you off me?'

Most men would be furious at another for sabotaging their evening but Calum seemed to be taking Bernie's hi-jack in his stride. Some woman in the future was going to be very lucky to land him. Dee was only sad that it wasn't going to be her. She would have liked nothing more than to accept his offer to take her out again, but the fact was that by tomorrow night, having seen Madge packed and off to rejoin her family safely out of harm's way, she could be shoving her belongings into a suitcase and making ready for her own escape. Knowing what she did, it wouldn't be fair of her to make arrangements with Calum that she couldn't keep.

She opened her mouth to decline his offer but was stopped in her tracks by a loud, 'Oh, bloody hell!'

They both turned to see Bernie sprawled on the pavement, rubbing his head.

Very obviously suppressing laughter, Dee said to Calum, 'You'd better see to him.'

Stifling mirth himself, he nodded. 'Yes, I'd better, before he makes a bigger spectacle of himself.' He turned to fix Dee with his eyes. 'So . . . about tomorrow?'

'Calum, give us a hand up, will yer?' Bernie shouted across.

'Hang on a minute, Bernie, I'm coming,' he called back. 'Dee?' he urged.

Bernie's state of intoxication wasn't going to give her a proper chance to explain to Calum why she was declining another date with him. And a night out tomorrow would be better than sitting alone in her room. It would also be her last night in Leicester and she didn't know when, if ever, she'd be returning so she might as well have some fond memories to look back on.

Dee smiled. 'I'll see you same time, same place, tomorrow night.'

CHAPTER SEVENTEEN

At just before twelve o'clock the next day, a smartly dressed mature woman alighted from the train at Earl Shilton. Outwardly she looked self-assured and in control, but inside she was in complete turmoil.

A porter in his late-fifties passed by pushing a handcart piled high with deliveries taken off the train. He stopped and said politely to her, 'Can I be of assistance, madam, only you look lost?'

Madge wasn't used to non-clients addressing her cordially. She looked at him in shock for a moment, waiting for the usual tirade of abuse, before she remembered she wasn't Madge the prostitute today but Madge the upstanding woman.

She smiled politely back. 'I was just getting me bearings. Long time since I've been on this station. Over twenty-five years, in fact. I used to help me dad herd cattle on board when they were going off to market.'

The man smiled warmly at her. 'Oh, a local lass then. Just a visit or are you moving back to Shilton?'

'Just a visit today, but hopefully I could be moving back, if things go well.'

'Well, yer won't find much altered since you went away. Slow to adapt to change is Shilton. Lots of houses still waiting for electricity and most people still journey around in horse and cart, except for a few wealthy types who have a motor car. And we do have a proper cinema now instead of the makeshift effort in the village hall with the travelling projectionist we used to have in your day.'

Madge remembered it well. When they could afford the couple

of pennies entrance fee, her mother would pack her, her brothers and sisters off to watch what was on offer, provided she felt it suitable viewing for her children. Her brothers had loved the Westerns best, acting out scenes as they appeared on screen, using their fingers as guns, shouting 'bang-bang'. Colleen and she had loved Flash Gordon best, swooning over the very handsome Buster Crabbe who had played him, booing loudly, even openly crying, when his adversaries maimed him in any way. They'd both drooled over the leads in the romantic films too. Evie . . . well, she just sat sucking her thumb through everything on offer.

'Oh, we've a proper dance hall too,' the porter was saying to her now. 'Grand place it is. Bands come from all over to play. The local ballroom team are in the county finals and it's being held there this year. Anyway, you'll excuse me, won't yer? I'd better get this lot where they're supposed to go or I'll have the station master after me. Hope yer trip goes the way yer want it to.' He tipped his forelock. 'Good day.'

He went on his way, leaving Madge looking after him. She couldn't remember the last time she'd had such a pleasant exchange with a stranger. A man walked by then and, after looking at her admiringly, lifted his trilby respectfully as he too continued on his way, then a woman with a child in her arms wished her good afternoon as she got on the train Madge had just left.

Oh, I could get used to this, she thought. Hopefully her family were going to give her the chance.

Giving her newly dyed mid-brown hair a pat to ascertain it was tidy after her journey, she took out the compact from her handbag to retouch her lips with the subtle pink shade she had purchased from the chemist along with the hair dye the previous day. She put it away, then after taking several deep breaths in an effort to calm her jangling nerves, she walked purposefully out of the station.

The porter was not entirely accurate in his statement that Madge would not find much changed in the village of her birth. As she walked down the main street towards the outskirts where a row of five cottages stood, the middle one being her family home, Madge noticed that Sidney Brown's general store was no longer the only shop supplying the villagers' needs as several more had now joined it. Where old Granny Fisher had once lived there was now a haberdasher's, a notice in the window announcing the owners needed an assistant, and Fred Mason's house was a proper hairdresser's. There was also a butcher's shop, and where the blacksmith used to ply his trade stood a garage. There was also a post office.

Fortunately for Madge, her journey did not take her past the church, so she was spared any possibility of coming face to face with the priest.

The cottage where she had been born and spent her youth had not changed outwardly at all. As she stood before it, steeling herself for what lay ahead, it appeared as shabby as it had always done, the woodwork on the ill-fitting window-frames and doors still seemed in dire need of a lick of paint, and the walls needed repointing where time had eroded the masonry. Obviously the landlord, the local squire who resided in a mansion between here and the larger town of Hinckley, was still as lax as he'd always been over getting around to repairwork on the numerous cottages he owned locally. Despite spring having barely made its mark, the long front gardens leading up to the cottages still looked as well kept by the residents as they had always been. Come summer they would bloom abundantly, as they always had done. Madge wondered if the residents still supplemented their income by gathering bunches of those assorted blooms to sell to passers-by, the same as they did with the extra vegetables they produced in their back gardens, or if this practice had died out in these changing times.

The upstairs windows in her family home were ajar so at least she knew her mother was in. In the process of cooking her father's dinner, Madge assumed. Then she wondered if she would be invited to join them? Well, that she wouldn't find out unless she got on with what she'd come to do.

She made to unlatch the small garden gate and suddenly her hands started shaking as the enormity of what she was about to face hit her. What was she thinking of, turning up out of the blue after twenty years of estrangement? She should have given her mother some warning that she was coming, instead of risking giving her a heart attack. Better to have written a letter to her and seen what kind of response that got before she ventured a meeting.

Madge about turned and began hurrying back the way she had come, only to stop abruptly as a vision of Dee swam before her. She had made a firm promise to her, couldn't face letting her down. How could she ever expect Dee to have faith in her again if she did? Madge about turned again and retraced her steps.

She walked purposefully up the cobbled path and rapped on the front door. As she heard the click of the knob the breath seemed to leave her body. Time stood still for her as she prepared herself to come face to face with the woman who'd once rejoiced at her birth, only to reject her fifteen years later.

The bent old woman who greeted her was not her mother. Madge did recognise her, though. This was Cissie Smalley from next-door. She must be visiting and been asked to answer the door.

Cissie peered questioningly at her through rheumy eyes. 'Yes?'

Madge took a deep breath. In a voice that sounded far more assured than she felt, she said, 'I've come to see Clodagh Feeny.'

Cissie looked taken aback for a moment before she responded, 'Well, yer twenty-odd years too late for that, ducky.'

Madge gasped. 'She's dead?'

'Well, she wasn't at Christmas. She sounded in fine fettle from the card I got from her.'

Madge's face fell in disappointment. 'Oh! Does that mean the Feenys don't live around here any more?'

'Not since 1937, me duck. Clo just couldn't settle here any longer after . . . well, they decided to return to Ireland as it wasn't working out for them here.' She looked at Madge closely. 'Who's asking for her anyway?' Before Madge could respond she said, 'You look familiar. Do I know you?'

Madge took a breath before nodding. 'Yes . . . you do, Mrs

Smalley.' She wasn't sure what sort of reception she was going to receive from the old woman. As her mother's closest friend in Shilton she would know the reason for Madge's expulsion. 'I'm . . . well, I'm Magdalene, Mrs Smalley. Magdalene Feeny. I'm called Madge now.'

The woman gawped in shock. 'Never!' she exclaimed. 'Well, blow me!' She peered closely at Madge. ''Course, I can see it now. Yer the spit of yer mam. She was a handsome woman too. Oh, ducky, they didn't know what to think had happened to you. High and low they looked for yer, everywhere they could think. Yer mam and dad were desperate to put things right with you when they found out what a terrible mistake they'd made, not believing you about the father of the baby you was carrying. Terrible business, that, just terrible. Who'd have believed a man of the cloth . . .' She grabbed Madge's arm. 'Come on in, gel. I've got a letter for you somewhere. Before she left, Clo made me promise that if ever you should show up, I was to make sure you got it. I have to say, I'd given up hoping for that long ago so I'll have to make a search for it.'

Still stunned by learning what she'd hoped to, that her parents had somehow discovered the truth, Madge willingly allowed herself to be herded inside and followed Cissie's instructions to make a pot of tea for them while she went off to search for the letter left in her safekeeping.

It felt strange, almost like being an intruder, to find herself back in the kitchen where she had spent so many happy hours during her childhood. She made tea with water boiled from a blackened kettle hanging over the small range, just like she used to do at her mother's request.

The pot of tea was almost at stewing point before the old lady finally shuffled back into the living room and eased herself into the ancient rocker opposite her late husband's horsehair-stuffed chair. Madge sat there waiting impatiently.

Cissie looked apologetically at her guest and unfolded her hand, holding out something for Madge to view. 'Sorry, lovey, looks like the mice took a fancy to it.'

Madge gazed in mortal disappointment at the chewed remains

in Cissie's hand that were just recognisable as once having been a letter. She said the only thing she could say in the circumstances. 'These things happen, don't they?' Then she looked at the old lady expectantly. 'Do you know what it said?'

Cissie shook her head. 'God's honour, I never read it. That was your private letter from yer mam.'

'You can tell me what happened after I left here, though, can't you, Mrs Smalley?'

Cissie leaned over to throw the scraps of the letter into the fire. 'I can that. Pour the tea while I collect me memories.'

Then she relaxed back in her rocker, cradling a cup of tea between her gnarled hands. 'Just how I like it, nice and strong. Clo used to mash a good cuppa. She said her Irish hand gave it the magic touch. I used to love listening to that twang of hers, and the laughs she gave me with some of her sayings! Mind you, sometimes I couldn't understand her and had to ask her to repeat herself, especially when she got excited.

'I have to admit, I wasn't best pleased when I found out I'd be living next-door to an Irish family, when I first moved in. That was just before you were born. Neither of us had kids then. I was just married, and your folks had not long come over from Ireland in the hope of a better life here than they had back home. But it weren't long before I realised I could have been landed with a lot worse neighbours than the Feenys. Your mam was the first to welcome me here on the day we moved in. Brought me in some of her own dad's poteen they'd brought over with them for us to have a drop in our tea, and I provided a slice each of my own mam's special fruit cake, and that sealed our friendship. Afterwards we shared many a drop of poteen yer own dad used to brew up, using his father-in-law's recipe, through our ups and downs living next-door to each other nearly twenty years. I still miss yer mam. Grand woman, just grand.

'She was a grafter, I'll give her that, and so was yer dad. How Clo managed to care for you all on what Seamus brought home, I'll never know. My late husband's factory job paid much better than Seamus's did, and I only had two kids, unlike yer mam and dad who had five. My Archie used time and again to try and persuade Seamus to take a job alongside him, but yer dad flatly refused even to consider it. He loved the land, you see, couldn't bear the thought of working inside all day, more pay or not. Clo wasn't the sort to nag her man either as it was her opinion that his happiness came above wealth.

'The only thing me and Clo never agreed on was religion. Well, I'm not religious, you see, and I could never get me head round how strictly they abided by the teachings of their Church, treating the priest like he was the be all and end all. Oh, it was an honour indeed when he paid them a visit. I know many a time Clo mashed up for that man with the last leaves she had until next pay day.' Her aged face screwed up grimly. 'She'd have thrown that bleddy tea in his face if she'd known what he was cleverly hiding under that priest's garb of his.'

She paused and took a sip of her tea. 'Anyway, lovey, you want to know what happened after yer left here. But first, I know you must be thinking the worst of yer mam and dad for what they did to you so I must try and help you understand, then maybe you'll think more kindly of them. They were absolutely distraught when they found out your condition. You were such a sensible girl, never given them a minute's trouble in yer life before that. Clo felt it was her and yer dad's responsibility to make sure the lad involved did right by yer. Well, at first you wouldn't tell them, would you, who it was so when you came out with the story about it being the priest, you can imagine how they couldn't believe it. Father O'Flannagan was such a respected member of the community. Even I thought him above reproach, and me an atheist.

'Well, Clo and Seamus were in a dilemma. You was their daughter and they loved you, but it seemed to them you was prepared to wreck an innocent man's life just for the sake of shielding your seducer. When you wouldn't budge about it being the priest, they felt they had no choice but to believe they'd got a bad 'un on their hands in you, that you wasn't the lovely girl they thought but had a kink in yer nature. They couldn't see any other way out of it but to ask you to leave and make yer own way in the world.

'It was horrible that night. I could hear it all through the walls. You pleading with yer mam and dad to believe yer; them pleading with you to stop hiding the identity of the real father and trying to put the blame on an innocent man. And then after they'd finally shown you the door, listening to yer mam crying her eyes out all night. Clo was broken up inside, but to her credit she put on a brave face and told everyone, including yer brothers and sisters, that you'd gone off to seek a better life for yerself elsewhere. Only I knew the truth of why you had gone, and I was made to promise to keep me own counsel.

'Do you think you could throw another log on the fire, Magdalene dear, as it's getting a bit chilly in here?'

Madge was experiencing a mixture of emotions as she relived the past and Cissie's request took a moment to register with her.

'Oh, yes, 'course.'

She got up to squat down before the hearth, taking a log from a stack by the side and placing it in the centre of the dying embers. Then she gave the fire a poke to help ignite the wood. It crackled and hissed, small flames licking around it. Madge retook her seat then, desperate to hear more. She went to urge the old lady to continue and to her disappointment noticed Cissie appeared to have dozed off. Her head was cocked to one side, her mouth gaping, a trickle of saliva was running down her chin. Madge stared at her, unsure what to do, but Cissie's eyes suddenly opened. Wiping the saliva off her chin with the back of her hand, she immediately picked up her narrative from where she'd left off.

'Well, it was a few weeks after you'd gone, maybe a couple of months but no longer, that young Carol Heaps . . . you must remember her, she was the school teacher at the primary? Used to alternate with Herbert Greaves playing the organ for the services . . . well, it was her turn for choir practice that night. When she got home afterwards she realised she'd left her music books behind. She could have got them the next time she was in church but she taught piano in her spare time and needed the music for a pupil of hers the next day, so she went back to fetch it. She found the main door locked and thought she was too late, that the priest must have gone back to the Presbytery. She was just about to go home herself when it struck her that Father O'Flannagan might still be in the vestry. So she went around the side of the church to check. Sure enough, there was a light on. She'd caught him after all. When she went inside . . . well, I can't imagine how the poor woman felt, coming face to face with what she did. The priest was abusing a young girl. Carol was the very prim and proper sort, the kind who I'm sure wouldn't let a chap even kiss her unless she'd an engagement ring on her finger. Terrible trouble she had afterwards speaking to the police about what she'd come across. Quite traumatised she was, and went off to live with her aunt somewhere and never came back here.

'Anyway, Dan Hinkle came across Carol in a right old state, crumpled up by a gravestone as he was cutting through on his way to the pub. All he could get out of her was, "*In the vestry, in the vestry.*" Well, he wasn't sure what to think but left her to get himself to the vestry and find out what on earth had caused Carol to be in the state she was. There he found Father O'Flannagan, stone dead by now, hanging from a rafter. He'd used the sash from his robes. Coward, he was. Couldn't face the public retaliation for the disgusting crimes he'd carried out, using the protection of his position. He'd chosen the easy way out.'

Madge was staring at Cissie, appalled. It was in that vestry he'd forced himself on her, telling her it was God's work she was doing, that their Saviour would be pleased with her, saving her a special place in Heaven next to Him when she died. But at the moment her thoughts weren't for herself and what she'd suffered through his vileness, but for the child he'd abused after her. 'What about the young girl Carol Heaps caught him with earlier? Where was she while he hanged himself?'

Cissie shook her head. 'She watched him, didn't she? Not only had he defiled that young child, he showed her no compassion whatsoever when he knew the game was up and killed himself in front of her, like he'd forgotten she was even there, like she didn't matter. Dan found her standing by the cupboard where the Communion wine and such like was kept. Frozen like a corpse she was, her dress around her waist, no knickers on, just staring wildly up at that . . . that . . . animal. As far as I know the poor gel never uttered a word after that. She ended up in the mental home, and is still there to my knowledge.

'You can imagine yer mam's and dad's reaction when this all came to light. They were beside themselves for branding you a liar and casting you out. They immediately set about trying to find you, desperate to put things right. They didn't tell anyone what Father O'Flannagan had done to you, and it wasn't because they were frightened of what people would think of them for not believing you, but because they meant to bring you back home and help you raise the baby. They felt it would be bad enough people thinking you were a hussy for getting yerself pregnant out of marriage, but for them to know you'd been . . . well, raped by a man of the Church, and then the poor baby be forced to live with that stigma, too . . . well, they felt that was far worse than you being branded a harlot.' She realised Madge was crying now. 'Oh, lovey, it must have been tough on you all these years, thinking yer parents were still believing the worst of yer?'

'Yes,' she uttered. 'Yes, it was.'

'Well, at least you know different now. You need a drop of something to help you with all this shock.' Cissie struggled up and headed off into the kitchen, returning moments later with a drop of rum at the bottom of a dusty-looking bottle. She poured it all into Madge's now tepid tea. 'Drink that, it'll do yer good,' she ordered.

The way she was feeling, Madge would have preferred it neat, but regardless she picked up her cup and knocked it back. 'Thanks, Mrs Smalley,' she croaked.

The old lady eased herself back into her rocker, then leaned forward and looked at her enquiringly. 'What made you come back after all these years?' Then, before Madge could respond, she said, 'Well, that's a daft question. Takes a lot of courage to face yer accusers and it's hardest of all when it's family, the people who are supposed to love you and believe in you. And all these years you must have been worried sick you'd be risking the same treatment again should the truth not have been discovered. It's taken you all this time to pluck up yer courage, hasn't it? Your baby will be twenty . . . what . . . four now, won't it? Boy or girl, did you have?'

'Oh, er . . . I don't know what it would have been. You see, I . . . well, I lost it not long after I left here.'

Cissie looked genuinely grieved to hear it. 'Oh, my dear, I am sorry. Well, maybe it was for the best, in the circumstances. Maybe there is a God up there after all who was looking after you. Bringing up a kiddie on yer own, and you hardly more than a baby yourself, without any help from yer family . . . well, I wouldn't wish that on any gel, and more especially when it wasn't their fault they got in the family way.'

Madge took a handkerchief from out of her handbag. She wiped her eyes and blew her nose. 'Have my family done all right for themselves in Ireland, Mrs Smalley?' she asked, returning the handkerchief to her handbag and clicking it shut.

'Seem to have from the letters yer mam's wrote me over the years. In my view, better than they would have done staying here, and yer dad continuing to work for that miserable Seth Warren. He got work straight away on a farm in Ireland and he's head cowman now. Your sister Colleen works for the Irish Broadcasting Company in Dublin. She's doing very well for herself apparently. Never married but never short of a fella either, according to yer mam, and the fellas are all the well set up sort. Fergal and his wife Grainne run the pub in the village where they all live now. They have three youngsters, and don't ask me their names 'cos I can't remember them off pat. Dougal . . . now what is it he does? Can't remember exactly but he works for a brewery. Ah, and last of all, little Evie. What a lovely girl she was. Always popping around, asking if she could help me. Mind you, not so little now according to yer mam. She's shot up to be five foot ten and is a big-built girl. She runs the dairy for the farmer yer dad works for now his own wife has took a back seat, and after a few non-starter relationships Evie's courting their son who's a widower with a young boy. There's talk of marriage.'

Madge smiled. 'It's good to know they're all well and happy.'

'I tell yer what'll mek them even more happy, lovey, and that's a letter from you. I've got yer mam and dad's address, I'll get it for you before yer leave. Anyway, I want to know what's been happening to you meantime?'

Madge wondered what the old lady would say if she told her the truth. 'Oh, not much to tell really, just like everyone else, making ends meet,' she said vaguely.

'Where have you been living?'

'Leicester.'

'Your mam and dad wondered if you'd gone there as it's the nearest big city. They spent all the hours they could for weeks by the clock tower there, their eyes peeled for you, but they never saw a glimpse. They put adverts in the local paper along with a photo of you, hoping someone might recognise you, but nothing came of that either. Eventually they gave up and hoped you'd come back of your own free will, then after four years they gave up hoping for that too. Living here was just a constant reminder of it all, so it was decided they'd go back to Ireland. Your mam left the letter in my safekeeping so if you did show up, you'd know where they were. Anyway, married, are you? Children?'

Madge shook her head. 'Never found anyone who'd put up with me,' she joked.

Cissie flapped one gnarled hand. 'Ah, get away with yer. Fine-looking woman like you.' Then she looked at Madge meaningfully. 'Oh, or is it that what that dreadful man did to you soured you for others?'

'Just never found anyone I wanted to commit myself to, that's all,' she replied lightly.

'So what have yer being doing job-wise?' the old lady asked her keenly.

Lying wasn't a trait Madge was born with but over the years it had become second nature to her through her job. She'd quickly learned that the more you grossly exaggerated men's prowess to them, the more likely you were to receive a hefty tip. 'Shop work, that kind of thing, and at the moment I'm a housekeeper for an old gent,' she said, pinching Dee's job for herself.

'Your mam will be so relieved to learn that what happened to you, as bad as it was, didn't blight your life. She was so worried . . . well, that you'd not be able to find proper work with a baby in tow and have to resort to earning a living for you and the baby by . . . well, I'm sure you know what I'm getting at?'

Madge looked away, wondering how Cissie would react if she told her she'd resorted to just that, and at one time had made a substantial amount from it. She wanted to change the subject. 'I take it you moved in here after my family left, Mrs Smalley?'

She nodded. 'This house was in better shape than mine at the time so me and my family moved in, and a family called the Rogers moved in to ours. She wasn't a bad sort was Tess Rogers, but I didn't get on with her as well as I did with Clo. Tess and her husband are both dead and one of their daughters and her husband live there now. Six kids they've got, a noisy lot of buggers and into stuff that would make what your Fergal used to get up to seem really childish. But I can't complain 'cos Clive, that's the husband, keeps me garden up for me and makes sure I've plenty of wood in winter to keep me fire going, and Tess's daughter pops in at least once a day to see if I want 'ote, espe- cially as I can't get to the shops as easily as I used to since I had a fall and broke me leg last year. Me own family don't live nearby, you see. You remember my Harold? Well, he's in Birmingham, on the production line for Leyland, and makes good money. Lena, well, she lives with her husband the other side of Hinckley in Atherstone. He's a solicitor's clerk.'

Madge picked up her handbag then. 'If you'll get me mam and dad's address in Ireland I'd be obliged, Mrs Smalley, then I'd better be off. There's a train just after five and I really should be on it.'

'Oh, aren't you going to stay and have some tea with me?'

Madge would have liked that very much but she had to get back and at least try and do some business tonight, to help towards the costs of today.

At the station the porter who had chatted to her when she arrived had just showed a woman to the waiting room to await her train. He spotted Madge arriving and went over to her.

'I take it it's the five-twelve to Leicester you'll be catching, it was the Leicester train you arrived on, only it's running nine minutes late due to cattle on the tracks. The refreshment room is still open if you fancy a cuppa while you wait.'

She smiled at him. 'Thank you, I just might.'

'Enjoy your visit back to Shilton?'

'Let's put it this way, I learned what I was hoping to.'

'Well, that's good then, isn't it?'

'Yes, it is.'

'So, still considering moving back?'

She stared at him thoughtfully. Just because her family were no longer living here it didn't mean to say she couldn't begin a new life for herself in Shilton, did it? Dee's plea for her to make a better future for herself than the one she was facing now had struck home. The visit here had given Madge a taste of what life could be like for her, the kind of life she had believed was closed to her forever because of what she had become after leaving home. But now she was seeing matters differently. She had so enjoyed spending a day as this Madge, the one who was treated with respect and looked at admiringly, in such a contrast to the Madge she was yesterday and would turn into again as soon as she got home and readied herself for work tonight. She had no desire to turn herself back into the old Madge again, doing a job she'd never, ever have considered had a priest not looked in her direction the wrong way. She wanted to stay new Madge forever. And why shouldn't she? All she had to do was save enough money to rent a place for herself here and live on while she found a job. She felt sure she could get herself one now she had transformed her appearance, and armed with the fictitious but plausible background she had created for herself, and that Cissie Smalley seemed readily to accept, why wouldn't prospective employers accept her?

She would have to return to being the old Madge meantime, but just for a short time, while she got some money together to fund the beginning of her new future. It was a small sacrifice she was more than prepared to face for the rewards it would bring her.

'Yes, I am, as a matter of fact. Might be a few months' time, though, before I get everything sorted out, but I'm definitely coming back to live here.'

'Well, when you do, if you fancy a drink, most Fridays I'm in the bar of the Station Hotel.'

Madge smiled. 'I might look you up then.' Might even manage to get myself a job behind the bar there, she thought. There were people who frowned on women who worked behind bars, but nowhere near as hard as they did at prostitutes. She could live with that.

Madge was happy in the knowledge that although her visit hadn't quite turned out the way Dee had prophesied, due to her parents' return to Ireland, Madge's way of life was nevertheless going to change for the better. So now Dee could stop worrying and concentrate on her own life instead.

CHAPTER EIGHTEEN

Lennie Monks, not the nicest person at the best of times but especially first thing, had come down in a bad mood that morning and been even more vile than usual to Dee, complaining bitterly about the breakfast she had put before him, moaning that his eggs weren't exactly as he'd wanted, even though she had paid great attention to making sure they were exactly as he liked them. He literally threw the lot of them all over her, demanding she cook him another complete breakfast, and get it right this time. Then he'd had a go at her for the standard of her cleaning, saying he'd found dust behind the ornate French clock on the mantelpiece in the drawing room, when she knew he was lying because she made it her business not to leave a speck in order to avoid such complaints from him. Also according to him, she hadn't hung the working suit he'd worn yesterday squarely on the hanger after he'd changed out of it. Finally he threatened that if she didn't up her standards to what he felt was acceptable then a visit to Madge was on the cards. Ronnie would leave her out of action for a day or so with not a clue what she had done to deserve it.

He'd only seemed to be satisfied when Dee had begged him to give her another chance to prove her worth to him, and assured him she would pay far more attention to her work in future. She was mortally thankful that her submissive behaviour seemed to satisfy his massive ego, and he and Ronnie departed then to attend to that day's business.

As she washed their shirts and underwear, handling them at arm's length, she wondered if the dried blood she had come across on the shirt Ronnie had worn the previous day had had anything to do with his brother's bad mood that morning. Maybe one of their victims had decided to retaliate. She hoped that was the case as it was about time they got a taste of their own medicine. Regardless, it was what Madge was facing today that was uppermost in Dee's mind as she went about her work after the brothers had left.

In her mind's eye Dee visualised the wonderful reunion that was about to take place between Madge and her family. She had no doubt that her friend would be extremely nervous when she knocked on the door of her family home after all these years, but as soon as her family realised who their caller was, Dee saw them all falling into each other's arms and tears of happiness being shed at the return of a lost daughter and sister. Surely Madge would be welcomed back into the fold? Dee couldn't wait to hear all about it when she went over to see her tomorrow.

Her greatest fear now was that something untoward would happen to delay her next visit to Madge. If the brothers were not able to leave the house as they usually did, for whatever reason, then she would not be at liberty to slip away. Normally their well-being was of no consequence to her, but when they arrived home that evening, money bag bulging with the collections they had made that day, she was mortally glad to see them both looking fit and well. There didn't seem to be anything wrong that would stop her visiting Madge the following day.

Despite all that was occupying her mind she hadn't forgotten her date with Calum that evening, was in fact looking forward to it as she really liked the man. Hopefully for the few hours she was with him, she'd be able to take her thoughts off her own problems and enjoy his company.

As it had the previous evening, Calum's face lit up like a beacon when Dee joined him, albeit she was fifteen minutes late as Ronnie had delayed his and Lennie's usual departure time from the house by mislaying his wallet. It had eventually been found down the back of his dressing table, having obviously slipped there when he had carelessly thrown it down while changing out of his day clothes, leaving his discarded garments on the floor for Dee to pick up after him. It was she who found it, but not before Lennie had pinned her by the throat up against the kitchen wall, threatening her with serious bodily harm should the wallet not turn up. There had been no apology when it had been recovered. Instead they had slammed out of the house like it was all her fault they were late departing, and Dee then shot up to her room to get herself ready. To her dismay she found it in complete chaos, all the drawers in her dresser pulled out, her carefully folded belongings tossed around like rubbish, her bedding piled on the floor and mattress upended during Ronnie's futile search for his wallet.

'You look nice,' Calum said to her admiringly now.

Dee didn't feel it. She had only had time to pull on a sleeveless black fitted shift dress, apply a smidgen of make-up, and give her hair a quick brush.

'Thank you,' she reponded lightly. 'So do you.' He did too. He was wearing a fashionable light blue suit, the single-breasted jacket hugging his lithe upper body, the tapered legs of the trousers emphasising his physique. A dark blue shirt contrasted perfectly with the suit and a narrow maroon tie finished it off. Both suit and shirt were obviously new and chosen with care to suit the wearer.

Calum was relieved she thought so as he'd spent his wages today on his new outfit, appealing to Bernie's good nature to allow him to go off and shop for it in town during their normal afternoon lull. On his return he'd again had to appeal to Bernie's good nature for a sub off next week's wages to fund tonight.

'Shall we go then?' said Calum now, catching hold of Dee's hand. 'I thought we'd go straight to the Troc. They've a bar we can have a drink in, and the place doesn't start filling up until after nine-thirty so we should be able to hear ourselves speak until then.' If they went to the pub first they could risk a repetition of the previous evening if Bernie happened to be there, and Calum wanted Dee all to himself tonight.

'Sounds good to me,' she said, falling into step beside him. Then added, with a mischievous look in her eyes, 'Isn't Bernie joining us tonight?'

'No, he damned well isn't,' Calum blurted out. Then realised this could sound as if he'd deeply resented Bernie's intrusion last night, when in fact he'd accepted it with good grace. Bernie was good company, and Calum had found his drunken antics very funny. His boss had paid the price today for his over-indulgence, spending most of his time nursing a hangover in the office next to the kitchen, telling Calum he had paperwork to catch up on, but actually sleeping. Calum had managed the lunchtime rush himself, only disturbing Bernie when he absolutely had to.

He was glad he'd been kept on his toes all day as it had kept his mind off his date with Dee tonight. He liked her a lot, more than he'd liked any woman in the past, and he was highly nervous about her reaction when he came clean with her about his background.

'I didn't mean I don't want Bernie to come out with us again, but if you want the truth, Dee . . .' he looked down at her and flashed a smile '. . . well, I wanted to spend the evening alone with you.'

She liked the thought that he wanted her to himself. Despite trying hard not to let this man get under her skin, she hadn't succeeded. She knew she could really get to like him, and felt grieved that due to forces beyond her control she would be denied the chance. She wanted to tell him that although she had enjoyed Bernie's company last night, had found him a very friendly man, she too was glad he wasn't joining them again tonight. But that could be giving Calum false hope that this evening was a prelude to many more like it, and in fact Dee wasn't going to be around any longer. 'Does this dance hall we're going to get busy?' she said, to change the subject.

'I haven't been to it personally, but from what I've heard it can get absolutely packed, especially on a Friday. They have good bands on, apparently.'

'Great. I love dancing,' Dee enthused.

'So do I,' Calum told her, smiling. 'I might be a bit rusty though as . . . er . . . I haven't been out for a while. You'll have to excuse me if I've two left feet to begin with. I've not had the right partner to take dancing before you came along.' There was so much he wanted to ask her in his thirst to know more about her, but the last thing he wanted was to sound as if he was interrogating her, so casually he asked, 'Your old gentleman all right, is he?'

She frowned quizzically as Calum stopped her at the kerb in order to check for traffic before they crossed. 'What old gent?'

He flashed her an equally quizzical look back. 'The one you work for?' he reminded her as he protectively placed his hand around her back to guide her across the road.

His gesture did not escape Dee. Such a show of respect would never have entered the head of the sort of men she had been out with before. She liked it. It made her feel the man she was with cared about her safety. But how stupid of her not to remember her own lies! 'Oh, that old gent. Yes, he's fine, thank you.' Then she heard Calum exclaim, 'Oh!' and looked at him enquiringly. 'Anything wrong?'

'Oh, no, not wrong exactly. But it looks like we're not the only ones going early to the Troc tonight.' Which meant an end to his hopes for a quiet drink and the chance to start getting to know Dee better before the dancing started and the noise level peaked.

She looked towards the dance hall which was now in view and saw at least forty people of around their own age group milling around the entrance, all seemingly looking forward to the evening ahead. 'Well, that's good, isn't it? A queue this early means there must be a decent band on, so we're in for a good night.' The excitement of the crowd rubbed off on Dee then and she tugged at his hand. 'Come on, let's hurry up and join them.'

After depositing her coat and leaving Calum waiting for her in the foyer, she went off to the ladies' room to check her appearance. All the other women arriving ahead of her seemed to have had the same idea. The room was packed with females of all shapes and sizes, jostling for a space before the row of mirrors over the wash basins, backcombing hair and spraying it with clouds of strong-smelling sticky lacquer, touching up make-up, adjusting clothes. Finally it was Dee's turn and she thought her reflection looked a bit wan. Beside the other girls whose efforts to look their best tonight had obviously taken hours, her own looked as hurried as it had been. In her haste to be out she hadn't remembered to bring her own hairbrush or lacquer so there was nothing she could do with her hair unless . . . She glanced around her for a friendly face and spotted what she thought was one, patiently waiting her turn for the mirror. She was about Dee's own age and wearing a bright yellow and white spotted sleeveless dress with a low neckline. Her dark hair was cut to mid-neck-length and backcombed to form a mushroom shape around the white Alice band she wore.

Smiling at her, Dee said, 'Excuse me, but like an idiot I've forgotten my hairbrush and lacquer so . . .'

'. . . you want to borrow mine?' the young woman finished off for her. ''Course yer can. I'd have had a dicky fit if I'd arrived here and found I'd forgotten mine. But on one condition – that you let me squeeze in beside you. The others, especially me fella, will be thinking I've fell down the lavvy or summat if I don't get back to them soon.' As she squeezed in beside Dee she introduced herself. 'Me name's Joy.'

'Dee,' she reciprocated, smiling gratefully as she took the hairbrush Joy handed her and began to attempt to transform her hair style from one that was more suitable for a hurried trip down the shops than a night out dancing.

'You here with your friends or a fella?' Joy made conversation as she retouched her lipstick.

'A male friend,' Dee told her. 'He's not really my boyfriend, we've only been out once before.'

'That's enough to class a fella as a boyfriend, in my book. I've been seeing mine nearly a month now and I class *that* as serious. Another month and I'll be accidentally taking him past the jewellery shops, pointing out rings. Are you two on your own or is there a crowd of yer?'

Dee had now backcombed her hair to give it body and was in the process of smoothing it over. 'Just the two of us.'

'Well, in that case, you can join us, if yer like? Not much fun coming dancing on yer own.'

'Oh, that's very nice of you . . .' Dee was just about to add she would ask Calum whether he wanted to join Joy's crowd or not, when the girl interrupted her.

'Good, that's settled then. You ready?'

Dee had made the best effort with her hair she could under the circumstances and felt it did look better than it had a couple of minutes ago. After giving it a coating of lacquer, she handed back Joy her belongings. 'I appreciate the loan of those. Right, I'm as ready as I'll ever be.'

Back in the foyer, Calum immediately noticed Dee had changed her hair style. 'You've done something different with your hair. It's looks nice,' he said approvingly. Then added as an afterthought, 'Not that it didn't before.'

She was touched that he'd noticed and smiled appreciatively. 'Thank you.'

Joy was by her side then. 'We're off for a drink first. This your fella?' she asked, looking at Calum. 'I'm Joy,' she said to him. 'My boyfriend is that one over there.' She proudly pointed to a tall, skinny man with a pitted complexion who was mingling within a group of other males and females. 'His name's Jason. I'll introduce you to him and the others in the bar.' She then made her way over to rejoin her boyfriend and the crowd they had come with, obviously expecting Calum and Dee to follow her.

Dee glanced apologetically at Calum, who was looking enquiringly at her. 'I . . . er . . . hope you don't mind, but I met Joy in the ladies' and we got talking. She asked us to join her and her friends when I told her we were here on our own. She took it for granted we would.'

She could tell by his expression that he did very much mind but graciously he said, 'Then we'd better not disappoint her.'

Joy introduced them to a friendly bunch who readily welcomed two new members to their circle. They all came from different parts of town, and knew each other through their various workplaces and relationships. They usually all got together at least once a week to go dancing at the various halls Leicester boasted, and this week it was the turn of the Trocadero. Over their first drinks, introductions and pleasant banter were exchanged. Despite her desperate need to flee the area, once again Dee felt a sense of disappointment that circumstances were dictating her departure. Besides Calum, she'd met some nice people tonight. She felt she and Joy, in particular, could have got on really well given time.

The band had just finished their own version of the Teddy Bears' hit 'To Know Him is to Love Him', which several couples had been smooching to. As soon as the first chords of Buddy Holly's 'It's So Easy to Fall in Love' were struck, women grabbed their partners for the first rock and roll of the evening. Within the blink of an eye the floor was filled with gyrating couples.

Tapping her foot to the music, desperate to be on the floor amongst the others, Dee willed Calum to ask her to dance. She was rewarded when he touched her arm and offered, 'Shall we?'

Her response was to grab his hand and rush him on to the floor.

After a couple of false starts they soon fell into timed step, dancing the jive as though they had practised for many hours together perfecting their technique. Several dances later, both of them panting breathlessly as they clapped at the end of Danny and the Juniors' 'At the Hop', a laughing Dee shouted above the noise, 'I thought you said you were rusty?'

Calum grinned at the compliment. He had worried that his enforced absence would make him clumsy, and was mortally relieved to discover that dancing was like riding a bike: once learned, never forgotten.

Joy arrived to join them, dragging Jason along with her. 'You two should go in for the competitions. Win hands down, you would. How did you both learn to dance like that?' she demanded.

Dee smiled at memories of Madge and her painstaking attempts to put the girl through her paces when Dee had begged her for help. They were both well aware it was no use her turning to Della for support in this as her answer would have been that she had better things to spend her time on.

'My Aunt Madge taught me,' said Dee.

'She a dance teacher?' Joy asked. 'She's gotta be, to have taught you so well.'

'Er . . . no, not exactly.' Not wanting to pursue this line of conversation, Dee grabbed Calum's hand again. 'Come on, they're playing "Yakety Yak" by the Coasters. I love this one.'

He feigned a groan of protest but willingly allowed Dee to lead him back on to the floor again. In the past he'd never been short of dancing partners, in fact there had been times when girls had fought to dance with him, but for Calum none of them compared with his partner of tonight. He and Dee seemed to fit together like pieces from a jigsaw. As the evening passed he became more and more confident that tonight was the start of something meaningful between them.

As Calum twirled her around, Dee was intent on savouring every second of her time with him, always aware that it was marching on and would soon come to an end. She didn't want it to, was in fact deeply resentful of the fact that others' actions were forcing her to turn her back on a man who could have turned out to be the love of her life. She knew that Calum liked her, that fact was glaringly obvious, and knew too it was more than likely he was going to ask to see her again. She only hoped that when she explained there would be no further nights like this for them, he would not be too upset.

She was surprised when Calum abruptly stopped dancing and pulled her towards him protectively.

'What's wrong?'

He leaned over to speak against her ear, so she could hear him above the loud music. 'Hopefully, nothing. It's just I noticed the potential for a fight developing over there.' He indicated with a nod of his head the other side of the dance floor. He could tell Dee was bemused as all she could see were colourfully dressed couples swirling around them, but with the advantage of his height he could see over the top of most people's head. 'A couple were dancing and another bloke just barged in and broke them up, taking the girl as a partner for himself. She doesn't look too happy about it and the chap she's with is even less happy,' he explained.

Calum recognised the man who had taken it upon himself to commandeer the woman as the arrogant-looking sort who, along with a thuggish sidekick, paid a visit to Bernie once a week. He hadn't liked the look of them then, and liked the look of them even less after witnessing what he just had. It was then that he spotted the arrogant man's usual companion over by the edge of the dance floor. He had the woman's original partner restrained against a pillar, ugly face shoved into his, and it was obvious to Calum that it wasn't a friendly chat they were having.

Just then, through the dancers, Dee momentarily caught sight of the dancing couple Calum was referring to and froze in horror. It was Leonard Monks who'd grabbed himself an unwilling partner. And if Leonard were here then so would Ronnie be, as the pair were never separated, to her knowledge.

Satisfied that this incident didn't look set to turn into a free-for-all, Calum made to release his protective hold on Dee and for them to resume dancing when he noticed the horrified expression on her face. 'Whatever is the matter?' he asked, worried. She didn't appear to hear him. 'Dee, what on earth is it?'

Panic was flooding her. This was the last place she had expected the likes of the Monks brothers to come on a Friday evening. She'd thought they both felt themselves to be above such working-class venues. She'd thought she'd be safe here. But what if the brothers saw her, their personal skivvy, enjoying herself in the same way they had decided to? Leonard especially could take it as a personal insult that the person who charred for them, whom he viewed as the lowest of the low, had the audacity to be seen at the same place as he did. The reprisals that might be dished out to her should they discover her presence didn't bear thinking about. But it wasn't her own safety that worried Dee most, it was Calum's. He had already proved to her he was the sort who would automatically come to her rescue should the need arise. She couldn't put him at risk from these murdering villains she was forced to work for.

'Oh, it's just . . . I've noticed the time and I have to go,' she said urgently.

Calum looked hugely disappointed. 'What, now? But it's only just half-past ten.'

Frightened one of the brothers would spot her, she turned

abruptly and hurried off the dance floor in the opposite direction. A stunned Calum stared after her for a moment before
rushing to catch her up. He caught her arm, pulling her to a
halt. 'Dee, why the sudden rush to go?'

She flashed a worried look around to make certain she could
see no sign of the brothers before she answered. 'I should have
told you at the beginning of the evening that I needed to be
home before eleven. My old gent likes to lock up before he goes
to bed. You know what the elderly are like.'

Her hurried glance around, and the look on her face while
she did so, convinced Calum this wasn't the whole truth. He
flashed a quick look round himself but couldn't see anyone
watching them. He looked at Dee and smiled. 'Okay. We'll go
and tell the others we're off, else they'll wonder what's happened
to us.'

That could mean an encounter with the Monkses which she
wasn't prepared to risk. 'Oh, er, could you do that while I fetch
my coat?' Dee urged. 'I really do need to be off.'

She was definitely acting as if she was desperate to get away
from the place. Or was it from him? 'Are you sure nothing is the
matter, Dee? Have I done something to upset you?' Calum asked.

'No, of course not,' she reassured him. 'Like I said, I don't
want to be late getting home as I told my old gent I'd be back
well before eleven and I don't want him worrying about me. I'll
go and fetch my coat, see you back in the foyer,' she said, shooting
off in the direction of the cloakroom.

It took several minutes for Calum to locate Joy and Jason
who had left the dance floor where he'd last seen them and
returned to their table to take a breather before they started
dancing again. They seemed disappointed their new friends were
leaving so early, but appreciated Dee's need to get home due to
her job. They said they hoped to see him and Dee here again
sometime soon. Calum said he hoped so too. Making his way
into the foyer, at first he couldn't see any sign of Dee and thought
she had already left without him, a fact which both puzzled and
upset him. Then he caught sight of the edge of her coat poking
out from behind a pillar and sighed in relief.

He went across to join her. Before he could greet her, she grabbed his arm and frog-marched him through the entrance doors, an action that once again fuelled his belief that for some unknown reason she was desperate to be away from here. Outside in the street she seemed to relax a little and slowed her pace. 'Oh, fresh air,' she said lightly. 'Is was very hot in there. I thought I'd faint if I didn't get outside quick.' She knew Calum must be wondering why she seemed so keen to be out of the place, and hoped her excuse was convincing.

'Yes, it was hot,' he agreed, smiling down at her. 'Which way then?

'Sorry?'

'To your home? I don't know where you live, do I?'

'Oh, it's a couple of streets down that way. Not far. I can see myself home from here.'

'Not likely! I wouldn't sleep, wondering if you'd got home all right.' He grabbed her hand. 'Come on.'

They fell silently into step with one another. As they walked Calum was rehearsing in his mind how to approach asking her out again. Feeling she had a good idea what he was thinking, Dee was trying to work out how best to let him down gently.

They arrived at the corner of the street where the Monkses lived. Dee stopped walking and let go of his hand. She found it difficult to look Calum in the eye because she really did not want to say this. 'It's been a lovely evening, Calum,' she said breezily. 'I've really enjoyed myself. Thank you for taking me.'

He was looking at her as if he never wanted to let her out of his sight. 'It was my pleasure, Dee,' he said meaningfully. The time had come for him to bare his soul to her. He took a deep breath to steady his nerves. 'Look . . . er . . .'

She knew what was coming and didn't feel it would be right to put him through all the agony of asking her out again. 'I ought to tell . . .'

He pressed one finger to her lips to silence her. 'No, please let me finish while I've got the courage to tell you what I have to.' And before he could procrastinate further he blurted out: 'Dee, you obviously know I want to ask you out again, but before I do in fairness to you there's something I need to tell you about myself.' He looked at her apprehensively. 'I want things to become more serious between us – I've never wanted that so much before, believe me. You're a very special woman, Dee. I'm really hoping you feel the same way about me, and I hope . . . I really hope . . . that what I have to tell you won't put you off seeing me again.' He paused for a moment, eyeing her anxiously before continuing. 'I . . . well . . . I've just come out of prison.'

She stared at him in disbelief, wondering if she had heard him right. 'Did you say, prison?'

'Oh, Dee, you're shocked . . .'

'No, not in the way you think. It's just, I can't imagine you doing anything that would warrant a prison sentence. What were you in for?'

'Theft.' Calum looked at her imploringly. 'I'm glad you think I'm not the sort of person to do anything like that because, you see, I didn't do what I was accused of. I was set up.'

'Set up?' She couldn't for the life of her think why someone should have such a grudge against him as to want to see him in jail. 'Who'd want to set you up?'

'My . . . family.'

'What!' she gasped. 'What on earth did you do to them, to make them do that?'

'It's what I didn't do, Dee. You see, my parents aren't the normal sorts who raise their children to be law-abiding citizens. They're quite the opposite, in fact. Of the opinion that if you're not committing a crime, it's a crime – if you follow me? They don't see anything wrong in what they do. To them, it's just making a living. They're not the gangster sort by any stretch of the imagination. Petty thieving, burglaries, car break-ins, that sort of thing. You certainly don't leave any valuables lying around if my family are in the vicinity. Although, according to them, they've gone legit now.' He laughed uneasily. 'They don't see anything wrong with fleecing people by convincing them they need far more building work doing than is really necessary. They give a big quote then make a shoddy job of it, but by the time the customers have found out my family are long gone, and the customer's money along with them.

'They think I'm an oddball, have some sort of brain disorder, because I won't go along with what they do. They've tried all sorts over the years to get me to join the family firm, but I've always managed to resist. As a last resort they thought a stretch in prison would do the trick. I can't imagine why they would think it, but that's the way they are. Anyway we've all finally reached an agreement that we'll live and let live.' He looked at her, hard. 'They're my family, Dee, and I do love them even though I believe that what they do is wrong. I know it's a lot to ask you to continue seeing me now, but I'm really hoping you will?'

'Coming from a family of thieves isn't as bad as coming from a family of prostitutes, is it?' she responded matter-of-factly.

He was gawping at her in astonishment, her answer not at all what he'd been expecting.

'You're not the only one with skeletons in your cupboard, Calum. My gran made her living by selling her body. So did my mother until just a few weeks ago when she . . . died. She tried everything to get me to follow on in the family tradition, but it wasn't for me. It was always a bone of contention between us. I still loved her, though. She was my mam, earning her living the best way she knew how, just like my gran before her. People don't frown on stealing for a living as harshly as they do on prostitution. I should know, I've been on the receiving end often enough. So the question is not whether I would consider turning a blind eye to the way your family make their money, Calum, but whether you can ignore the way mine did?'

He grabbed her in his arms then and swung her round. Putting her down at last, he proclaimed, 'Oh, Dee, Dee! It doesn't matter what our folks do or did. It's you I'm interested in, not them. I can't believe I've finally found someone who understands what it's like to grow up being treated like a leper because of their family, while at the same time loving them because they *are* family. You will see me again, won't you?' he implored.

Her face puckered in distress. 'I can't see you again, I'm sorry,

Calum. I won't be around. I'm going away.' It was the hardest thing she'd ever had to say and she loathed the Monkses for making her say it, but she had to or put Calum as much at risk as Madge was.

'What do you mean, you're going away? Why? Why are you?'

'I've got a job in another town. The one I've got now isn't for me after all.'

Calum was flabbergasted. He couldn't believe he'd finally found a woman who looked set to be the love of his life, and now she was about to slip through his fingers because of a job in another town. 'I'm . . . well, I'm sorry to hear your job hasn't worked out. But surely you don't have to move away to find work, there's plenty here in Leicester for someone like you?'

Dee couldn't look at him and instead cast her eyes down. 'I can't let them down now. They're expecting me to start on Monday. I'm leaving here tomorrow to travel there and get settled in.' She didn't know how much longer she could keep up this act of seeming to be more interested in her new job than she was in a future with Calum. Also she worried that he'd ask her where she was going so that he could write or possibly visit, and she hadn't a clue yet. Just any big town far enough away that there was no threat of the Monkses ever coming across her. Before he could say anything further, Dee reached up and pecked his cheek. ''Bye, Calum,' she said shortly, then turned and ran off.

As she approached the house, despite her own wretchedness at what she'd just done, a thought struck Dee. She'd just delivered Calum a dreadful blow. He might come after her in an attempt to talk her out of leaving tomorrow, possibly want her new address so he could write and visit, and then it would all get really complicated. Meantime, should the Monkses return, not only would Calum see her for the liar she was, the Monkses might not take kindly to finding a stranger on their doorstep. They weren't exactly the sort to politely ask someone to leave. Immediately she diverted her route to cross the road and entered the garden of the house opposite where she waited, safely hidden from view by the high privet hedge, until she felt sure Calum would have gone home. Eventually, poking her head around the hedge and seeing no sign of him, she ran across the road and entered the Monkses' residence.

What Dee did not realise, though, was that her news had so devastated Calum he still stood rooted to the spot where she'd left him, obscured from her view by the shadows.

He thought he was seeing things when he saw her emerge from the gateway she had not long since entered and dart across the road to enter the house opposite. He made to call out to her but she'd already disappeared inside.

As a bereft Calum slowly made his way back to his lodgings, upstairs in her sparse cheerless attic room an equally subdued Dee was taking off her clothes as she readied herself for bed. She could barely hold back tears at the terrible sense of loss she was experiencing, but knew it was no good dwelling on what might have been with Calum. At least she had had the privilege of meeting him and knowing there was at least one man who had liked her enough not to care what her mother had done for a living. Whether she would ever meet his like again she did not know. Men like him were rare.

CHAPTER NINETEEN

The next morning, just before ten-thirty, Dee was starting to panic. On previous Saturdays the Monkses had left the house later than they did on weekdays, but certainly before this time, and she was starting to worry that for some reason they weren't leaving the house at all today. She didn't know what she would do then. She couldn't make her own escape until she had seen Madge and ascertained that she would soon be safe within the bosom of her family. If Dee couldn't go and see her today, then tomorrow was out of the question. Sunday was the worst day of the week for Dee, pure purgatory, as the brothers did not go out at all but lazed around, expecting her to jump at every click of their fingers while producing a perfectly cooked full breakfast, a roast with all the trimmings promptly at one o'clock, and full tea at seven, in between all the drinks and snacks they demanded. Sunday was supposed to be a day of rest, which it was for the Monks brothers, but never for her.

Leonard had demanded a cup of coffee. Having made it, Dee was transporting it to the lounge where he and Ronnie were literally lounging. As she approached the door she heard Ronnie saying, 'I thought we told Corrigan we'd pay him a visit at ten?'

Leonard's response was snappy. 'After the time we've been in this game, haven't you learned anything? The secret is to make 'em sweat. He should be nice and nervous by about twelve. I'll teach him to stand against us . . . and this ain't the first time. Obviously the last warning we gave him didn't teach him enough of a lesson. Bring the piece with you. Let's see how brave he is when he's threatened with that.'

They were going out! Music to Dee's ears, but regardless she felt mortally sorry for the man Corrigan who was going to be on the receiving end of their wrath today. It was a pity she couldn't warn him.

Then she heard Ronnie laugh. 'Be glad to. The only decent thing our dad did for us was to leave behind that old Kraut pistol he sneaked home from the war. If we hadn't found that gun in the attic . . .'

'I found it,' Leonard corrected him.

'Well, if you hadn't found it, when we was clearing out to move into a better place after we started making money from our . . . your idea of fleecing prossies, then we'd not've been able to branch out into bigger things, and had the money to move into this place and live the way we do. That gun gives us the edge, don't it? I mean, even the most bolshie of women cave in after a good thumping, but some men ain't easily frightened. A gun shoved in their face, though . . . well, it's enough to sway 'em then.' Ronnie gave a laugh. 'I wonder what they'd say if they realised it wasn't loaded as we've no ammo for it?'

Outside the door Dee seethed to think of the depths to which these two were prepared to descend in order to frighten people into parting with their money.

'Anyway, I hope our business this morning don't take long, 'cos I'm looking forward to our afternoon down the dogs,' Ronnie responded.

Leonard gave a sardonic laugh. 'That snivelling little runt Corrigan will take one look down the barrel and hand over his dues. We'll be in and out of his poxy chemist's in five seconds flat. Straight after we've that little bit of business we need to deal with at the florist's. That shouldn't take more than ten minutes so we'll be at the races by two, plenty of cash in our pockets. Now where's that slut got to with my coffee? KIRBY!' he bellowed out. 'How long does it take to . . . ah, there you are,' he snapped at Dee as she entered the room. 'I was beginning to think you'd gone to bloody Brazil to collect the beans personally.'

She carefully placed the cup on the small table beside his chair. 'Sorry, Mr Monks, I was as quick as I could be.'

Dee was very aware that Ronnie was staring at her fixedly again and her skin crawled at the lurid thoughts she strongly suspected were going through his mind. What she would have given to inform him he wasn't going to get a chance, because she wasn't going to stay around.

'Not quick enough,' Leonard shot at her. 'Next time you take as long as that, I'll stick my boot up yer arse to get you moving.'

She fought an overwhelming urge to pick up the table lamp and smash it over his head for this abusive treatment. Smiling sweetly, she said, 'Can I get you anything else, Mr Monks?'

'Yeah. You can get out me sight.'

That was fine by Dee.

She almost skipped her way back to the kitchen. The brothers would soon be leaving the house, and be gone more than long enough for her to make her way over to see Madge and still be back in time to prepare their tea. Then later this evening, when they returned home, wouldn't they be in for a surprise?

Madge wasn't at home when Dee arrived, breathless from running in her urgent need to get there, but her housemate Elsie was.

'Hello, ducky,' the veteran prostitute greeted Dee as she opened the door to her, brassy red hair wound around large plastic rollers, face still showing traces of last evening's thick application of make-up. Her gaping threadbare candlewick dressing-gown revealed grubby underwear beneath. 'Madge said you was calling in today, and told me to tell yer if you arrived while she was out, to mash yerself a cuppa. She won't be long, just popped down the shops for some bits.'

For her move! So everything must have gone just as I predicted it would, Dee assumed excitedly. She was about to say to Elsie that she would go straight to Madge's room and start packing for her, to save her time, when she realised that Madge might not have told Elsie what was going on or indeed want her to be privy to the move. So instead she said, 'How are you, Elsie?' as she took off her coat.

The woman pulled a face and gave a shrug. 'Same as I always am, lovey. Hoping today will be the day I meet the man of me dreams who'll whisk me away from all this. Fat chance of that, though. We're good enough to bang up a back alley in the dark, me darlin', but not to be seen out in public with. How's it going with you? Madge told me about yer new job and how much you was loving it. Old gent you work for, ain't it?' A thought suddenly struck her and she eyed Dee keenly. 'Eh, he's not the sort that likes a bit of my sort of company, is he? If so, you could put a good word in for me . . . Oh, but I s'pose Madge has already got in before me if he's that sort. Anyway, I'd best get on as I've a regular at one.'

Dee was just pouring out the tea when Elsie came through the kitchen ready for the off. She turned to say her goodbyes. It was very apparent that she hadn't bothered to clean her face of the previous day's make-up, just retouched it, and Dee wondered too if Elsie had even bothered to wash. There was a strong whiff of body odour coming from her direction. One thing Dee knew about Madge was that she was meticulous over her personal hygiene, and for all her faults so had Della been. Dee wondered how her friend was coping, living with a sloven like Elsie. Having said her goodbyes to her, she made her way into the back room to wait for her friend's return and stopped abruptly on the threshold, staring at the state of the room beyond.

'That bloody woman is an utter disgrace.'

Dee spun around to see Madge come in behind her. 'Oh, I never heard you, Aunty Madge.'

She gave Dee a welcoming kiss. 'Good to see you, lovey.' Then she too stared at the chaos in the back room and gruffly said, 'I'm sorry you've had to arrive to this mess. It must be heartbreaking for you to see it like this, after the way you used to keep the place. You wouldn't believe I had a tidy round before I popped off to the shops half an hour ago. It's like a whirlwind just dropped a pile of rubbish while I've been gone. I never realised before she came to live with me just what a dirty cat Elsie is. She hardly washes, yer know, and only changes her underwear once a fortnight. She's the type that gives us prossies a bad name. Trouble is, I ain't got the heart to ask her to go if she don't buck up her ideas. She's a nice woman is old Elsie, the type that'd give you her last penny if your need was greater than hers. Anyway, when I leave to start me new life, she can live how she likes, can't she?'

Dee's face lit up. 'So yesterday went well?' she exclaimed.

Madge affectionately patted her arm. 'Lovey, the best thing you ever did was to persuade me to pay a visit to me family. It's made me see there is a better way of life for me than this one, which I hadn't thought possible. I owe you for that, Dee, I really do. Look, you pour me a cuppa and I'll clear a space on the table. Then at least we'll have some elbow room and can sit in comfort while I tell you all about it.'

Dee gladly did as Madge asked. As soon as they had shared a cup of tea together and Madge had relayed the happy events of yesterday, Dee would offer to help her pack. Hopefully she'd have time to wave her friend off on her new venture before she herself needed to be back. Later this evening she would be on the same platform, getting on a train herself, turning her back on the life she was living now.

A few minutes later, sitting next to Madge at the table, Dee demanded, 'Well, come on then, I'm dying to hear it all. Was it like I said? Did your family throw themselves on you when they opened the door to you? I bet they were so pleased to see you. I bet they're all so excited about you returning. I like your hair, by the way. The colour really suits you.'

Madge took a draw on her cigarette. 'Thank you. I like it too. I got a lot of admiring looks yesterday. Pity I've got to go back to me old colour and clothes, just for the time being while I get some money together to fund me new life. That's where I've just been, to collect a packet of dye from the chemist's before they shut for lunch, so I can do it this afternoon.'

Dee stared at her, puzzled. 'I don't understand. Haven't your parents offered you a place with them while you get a job and find yourself a new place to live?'

'Well, from what Cissie Smalley told me, I have good reason to believe they would have done. But, you see, I never saw me parents, lovey. They all moved back to Ireland about twenty years ago and are doing well there, according to Cissie. She was me mam's neighbour until they moved, then she and her family moved into our old house.

'You were right, lovey. Me parents forgave me a long time ago for what happened between us. If it wasn't for you persuading me to pay them a visit, I might never have found out and gone to me grave still believing they thought the worst of me. Cissie was left a letter from my mam to give me should I ever turn up, but unfortunately mice took a fancy to it. Still, I've got me family's addresses in Ireland and I'm going to write to them, once I've found the right words. Eventually I hope to get the money together to go and visit them. Might even move over to live back near them in time, who knows? One step at a time, eh?

'Oh, Dee, I can't tell you what it felt like to walk around in public with me head held high, not being looked at like I was a lump of dog muck by everyone except those wanting to do business with me. A bloke . . . a porter on the station he was . . . even asked me to look him up next time I'm there. Said he'd stand me a drink.' Madge grinned. 'I think he fancied me. Long time since a bloke has looked at me as a woman he'd like to get to know better, instead of wondering if he can afford the price I charge. I liked the new Madge I became yesterday and I'm not happy about having to go back to the old one the punters go for, but it's only a means to an end. I can't wait to turn me back on all this for good, Dee, the time can't come soon enough.' She looked at the girl quizzically then, not understanding why she had such a look of acute disappointment on her face. In fact, it was as if she'd just heard the end of the world was on them. 'You could look happier, Dee. I thought a new life was what you wanted for me?'

It was, but now, right this minute, not in . . . however long it took for Madge to gather the funds to move. How stupid not to have realised that Madge's parents might have moved away and not be around to offer their prodigal daughter shelter while she sorted herself out. The feeling of euphoria that her own time with the Monkses was at an end vanished, to be replaced with a sense of utter hopelessness. Now she was stuck where she was for the foreseeable future and didn't know how she was going to cope with another day of living under the brothers' regime, let alone weeks or months as Madge wasn't exactly coining it in.

'I am happy for you, 'course I am. So . . . er . . . how long do you think it will take you to get enough money together for your move?' Dee asked tentatively.

'I'll be as quick as I can, lovey. I should say twenty pounds should about cover it. It's hardly a fortune, is it, but it might as well be to me at the moment. I plan to cut back on me out-goings so I can put past as much as I can each week, but that's easier said than done because I don't exactly live a life of luxury, do I? Still, my mam used to have a saying, "If you take care of the pennies, the pounds will soon mount." Hopefully it won't take me longer than six months. I got a taste yesterday for what I could have, Dee, and I ain't gonna rest 'til I'm living that life permanently.' Madge smiled at the girl fondly. 'Again, me darlin', thank you so much for caring enough about me to want better for me, and giving me the kick up the jacksy I needed to see my way out of this rut.'

The world came crashing in around Dee then. Six more months of living as a slave to the loathsome Monkses didn't bear thinking about. And there were Ronnie's attentions towards her, too, that she felt sure wouldn't stay arm's length for much longer. As matters stood, though, she had no choice but to get on with it until Madge was in a financial position to make her move from here. So wretched was she feeling, Dee doubted she could manage to keep up her act of being happy and content for much longer. She picked up her handbag from the side of her chair. 'I'd better be off, they'll be wanting their tea.'

Madge's face fell. 'Oh, but yer've only just got here. You ain't told me how you got on with yer new fella the other night?'

'Oh, it was a nice night out but he didn't ask to see me again, said I wasn't his type. Better luck next time, eh?' She leaned over and kissed Madge on her cheek. 'I'll see you soon.'

After waving Dee off, Madge returned inside to set about

dyeing her hair back to its tarty shade before she went out on her beat tonight. It had been so good to see Dee today and to have it confirmed that the younger woman was still happy with the life she had working for her old gent. But she'd seemed a bit distracted, and Madge had gained the impression that Dee had been disappointed her move wasn't happening right this minute. But then, that impression must be wrong because why should it matter to Dee when her new future started, as long as it did? Then something else struck Madge. Dee had said something today that hadn't at the time registered as odd, but now it did. She felt sure it was said at just about the time Dee had announced she ought to leave. She had said . . . What had she said? Something about having to cook the tea . . . There was nothing odd in that. Oh, well, it would come back to her, and if it was still on her mind later then she would question Dee the next time she saw her.

To her credit, and out of fear that someone who knew her might see and report back to Madge, Dee managed to walk quite a distance away before she finally gave in to her devastation over today's news. In a deserted street, slouched against a crumbling wall, grief for her own plight that seemed to have no end in sight was released in a flood of bitter tears.

CHAPTER TWENTY

As Dee was giving way to her emotions, in the back room of a shop in Uppingham Road a woman held her head in her hands in despair.

Fifty-five-year-old Prudence Miller, a childless widow, had bought her small business with what her beloved husband had left her on his sudden death five years ago. Not a grand sum, but enough for her to fund a future for herself as she felt Anthony would have wanted her to do. Before she had married she had been an assistant in a florist's shop and the owner had encouraged her flair for arranging blooms, teaching her everything she needed to know about the care and arrangement of them. It had seemed common sense for Prue to resurrect those skills after her husband's death, now she no longer had his income to rely on.

The premises she chose for her new business had previously been a cobbler's shop. It had remained empty, gathering dust, and become home to an assortment of insects, rodents and vagrants since the previous occupant had retired ten years before. There'd been barely any interest in the property since, either rental or to buy. Fearing large repair bills should it remain empty for much longer, the owner was relieved to offload it on to Prue at the fair price she finally offered him. An added bonus was that the property came with a small flat above which Prue had planned to rent out for the extra income it would bring. Through sheer hard work and dedication, sometimes working twelve hours a day, Prue's Blooms, as she called it, had flourished.

During her five years in business here, she had rented out the flat four times. She'd trusted her instincts to pick honest, reliable tenants and up until today had had no reason to believe those instincts would ever fail her.

Her first tenant had been a very pleasant young bachelor who gave notice after a year as he was getting married and moving into a house with his new wife. Her second tenants were a shy young couple who had just got married. After two years they sadly admitted they were incompatible and went their separate ways. Her third was a very dear old lady who had sadly died two months ago. Prue had never actually met the present tenants, a trainee dental nurse and her shop assistant friend, as securing the rental for them had been handled by a man claiming to be the dental nurse's brother. He went by the name of Mr Brown, a very handsome, rather swarthy man in his early-thirties. He was extremely well dressed, though it was obvious he'd come from poor beginnings originally.

After convincing Prue to allow him to rent the flat on behalf of his sister and her friend and paying the required deposit, he had told her that the rent would be taken care of by himself, saying he would call by each week on a Friday to settle it.

The flat was accessed via a set of metal stairs that led from an alleyway at the back of the row of shops. As the owner, Prue had every right to pay impromptu visits on the property, to make sure the tenants were keeping it in order, but out of courtesy for her tenants' privacy she had not until yesterday actually exercised this right. She had only been driven to do so then because for the six weeks the latest tenants had been in residence, she had not received the rent she'd been promised and now was beginning to worry she would never see it.

Despite its being early-afternoon, the woman who'd answered the door to her was dressed in a very flimsy short negligee, a pair of heeled fluffy slippers on her feet. Her face was heavily made up and she was smoking a cigarette. She had looked expectant when she first opened the door, only to show disappointment when she saw her caller was a woman. Prue didn't need to ask her what her occupation was, it was already apparent to her, and she was incensed that her flat was being used for such purposes.

Looking daggers at the woman, she said stonily, 'I'm giving you twenty-four hours' notice to vacate these premises. I want you out by two o'clock tomorrow afternoon at the latest.'

The young woman merely laughed at her. 'We'll see what me brother says about that, deary.'

At her nonchalant manner Prue's hackles rose. 'I don't set much store by what your brother says. If indeed he actually is your brother. Regardless, he promised me faithfully he would take care of the rent. He hasn't honoured his promise and I have no reason to believe he ever will. He also lied to me about what you and your friend do for a living. You are definitely not a trainee dental nurse, and I doubt very much whether your friend is a shop assistant. I own this flat and I say who lives in it. I'm giving you both notice to quit. If you haven't left by two tomorrow afternoon, I shall have the police deal with you.'

Back in her shop Prue had needed a strong cup of tea with a drop of whisky in it to calm herself after that encounter. By the time she left for home at just after seven that night there'd been no sign of anyone packing up to leave the flat. She was worried witless that any of her neighbours might spot the obvious comings and goings she had been oblivious to herself due to the layout of the premises, and report her to the police for running a house of ill repute.

She hardly slept a wink that night, arriving for work the next morning looking haggard. The first thing she did was to go round the back and take a look up at the flat. All the curtains were drawn, as they were at the windows facing to the front of the street. It was difficult to tell whether anyone was home or not. She decided she would wait until her deadline of two o'clock and then let herself in with her own set of keys to check that they had indeed vacated. If not then she would immediately summon the police and ask for an eviction.

At just before twelve she was serving a customer with a wedding anniversary bouquet for his wife when the clanging of the shop bell announced a new arrival. She looked up to see Mr Brown had entered along with a huge thuggish-looking man. Before she could address them, to her astonishment Mr Brown turned the sign on the door from Open to Closed and the thuggish-looking man advanced on her customer, grabbing him by his shoulder and marching him to the door. He pushed the bewildered man outside, then Mr Brown shut the door and pressed down the snib.

Still holding her customer's bouquet aloft, Prue was left speechless by what she'd just witnessed.

While the heavy stood guard by the door, the man Prue knew as Mr Brown swaggered up to the counter. He stood right in front of her and said very quietly, 'A little bird tells me you've evicted my sister and her friend from the flat?'

Prue gulped. His tone may have been soft but it had a menacing edge to it. She felt suddenly very vulnerable. 'That's . . . that's right. I don't approve of what my property is being used for.'

'Oh, and just what is it being used for?'

'Well . . . for the purposes of prostitution.'

'Really! Well, I bet that's a nice little earner for you, taking a cut of their profits in exchange for letting them use your flat.'

Insulted that someone could accuse her of such a thing, Prue exclaimed, 'I certainly do not!'

'Well, you just try and convince the police of that. A "madam" I think they term people like you.'

'What! But I'll tell them I rented the flat to you and . . .'

'And I'll tell the police I've never clapped eyes on you before. You prove otherwise. And be in no doubt, the girls upstairs will swear blind it was you who approached them with a proposition they should use your flat as a base in exchange for a share of the profits. I trust you'll think again about pursuing any eviction then, shall I?' He took a keen glance around. 'Nice little business you've got yourself here. Seems to me you need protection. Well, you don't want to turn up one morning and find the place ransacked or burned to the ground, do you? You have to leave and go home at night, and these days you never know who's lurking in the shadows, do you? Some nasty people around. Five pounds a week is what we charge for our services.'

'Are you . . . are you threatening me if I don't pay up?'

'Not threatening, no. It's a promise. We'll take this week's dues now. I'll help myself, shall I?' He leaned over the counter and pressed the lever on the till. He extracted several paper notes adding up to five pounds, virtually all she had taken today, which he put in his pocket. 'We'll look forward to seeing you next Friday then, and every Friday after that. Best if you have the money ready. We're rather busy and I'm the sort who doesn't like to be kept waiting. Oh, and don't even think of selling up as a way to get out of this because one whiff that you are and we'll make sure the place is unsaleable, if you get my drift?'

With that he left her. As he turned the sign back from Closed to Open, the thuggish accomplice gave her a look that told her not to think of defying them or she would deeply regret it.

Prue put down her customer's bouquet on the counter and made her way through to the back room. There she sank down on a chair by her work table and cradled her head in her hands. She was an honest upright woman just trying to make a living for herself. Unwittingly she had allowed those men not only to land her in a situation that could see her with her reputation in ruins, but she had lost her rental income and was now being blackmailed for protection money too.

She could see no way out of this. She had no choice but to give in to their demands and pray it wasn't she herself who was brought to book for their way of lining their own pockets at the expense of others.

As Prue was trying to come to terms with the dreadful situation she found herself trapped in, another middle-aged woman was starting to worry. Homely Lorna Corrigan sat looking with concern at her husband, distractedly pushing food around his plate.

'Is there something wrong with the meal, Arthur?' she asked.

He eyed her blankly. 'Sorry? Did you say something, dear?'

She sighed. 'Oh, Arthur, what is the matter with you? You've not been yourself for . . . well, a couple of weeks now. You're tossing and turning at night, and hardly touching your food. You snapped at Julie when you came in for your dinner just now, and I know for a fact you weren't listening at all to Kenneth when he was reading his book to you last night. This isn't like you, Arthur. Not like you at all.'

He looked at both his children. Eleven-year-old Julie and nine-year-old Kenneth both stared back at him reproachfully, and a flood of guilt surged through him for letting his predicament affect his attitude to them.

But was it any wonder he wasn't his normal self? He'd worked hard to get where he was. His working-class parents hadn't found it at all easy to support him through university in order that he could gain his pharmacist's qualifications. Afterwards it had been one long hard struggle, trying to save what he could from his wages as an assistant and eventually head pharmacist in a hospital dispensary, in order to finance his dream of opening his own chemist's shop. During that time he'd met and married Lorna so he'd had her to support plus their two precious children when they'd appeared.

Making a success of his little business had not been easy when he was pitched against the larger establishments such as Boots and Timothy White's, but he had won a loyal band of customers by his friendly personal approach.

Then the two bully boys had come sniffing round, sounding him out as a 'contributor' to their funds. Five pounds a week they'd forced him to hand over, or he'd risk reprisals. People assumed that shop proprietors coined it in but they were wrong. His profit margins were tight, he was continually having to count every penny. He'd been working towards hiring an assistant to ease his workload, but now that was out of the question.

When the men had first approached him he had flatly refused to go along with their scheme. He'd been repaid by having his shop vandalised and had lost business as a result while it had been put to rights – thankfully the insurance company had agreed to stump up the cost. Stupidly, he had thought his stance against them had seen them off but they had returned this morning, entering through the back door and coming straight into his dispensary. While customers out front stood chatting amiably amongst themselves as they waited for their prescriptions to be filled, the big man pinned Arthur up against a wall and stuck the barrel of a gun in his face while the arrogant, dapper man quietly informed him that he would pay up, or not only would Arthur himself suffer, both physically and financially, but they would turn their attention to his family also.

The thought of any harm coming to his beloved family had been enough to sway Arthur.

Until those two bullies tired of their arrangement – and Arthur couldn't see that happening in the short term, as it was obviously proving very lucrative for them – he could see no way out of this situation.

Planting a smile on his face, he looked around at his family and said with forced brightness, 'There's a steam engine rally on Sunday in the Braunstone Park, I thought we could all go.'

While a tormented Arthur and his excited family were discussing their outing on Sunday, Bernie sat in his office catching up on some paperwork. He gave a fed-up sigh. It was all well and good going legit, not constantly wondering when the next collar would be, but it didn't come without its headaches.

Calum popped his head around the door. 'Want a coffee, Bernie?'

'Summat stronger would be preferable, help take the pain of this bookwork away. Bloody tax inspectors, wanting to know everything. The amount of your hard-earned cash they take is criminal.'

At least Bernie was declaring his earnings to the government, or a portion of them anyway, thought Calum. He knew for a fact that his own family weren't declaring any of theirs. It had been good seeing them when he had paid them a visit yesterday after finishing work, but as usual it had proved to be a mortally uncomfortable experience. Calum had to listen to them bragging about the amount of money they had made that week and how they planned to spend it, and also to their gibes over his own scant living as a café worker. He knew, though, that this state of affairs was something he'd always have to endure. The alternative was to turn his back completely on his family, and he couldn't do that. He might not see eye to eye with them on certain matters, but they were his family and he did love them.

'When I'm doing a job like this, it don't help neither looking at your miserable face,' Bernie continued, then looked remorseful. 'Ah, I'm sorry, lad, that was uncalled for. I know yer liked Dee a lot. Her going away knocked yer for six.'

Calum was feeling bereft at Dee's departure. She clearly hadn't felt the same way about him as there'd been no suggestion he should write or pay a visit to her in her new place. She had obviously not wanted to pursue a relationship with him in any way. He didn't want to prolong the misery by talking about her, just wanted to be allowed to get over it as quickly as he could. 'Did you want coffee or not?' he asked shortly.

Bernie smiled appreciatively. 'That'd be good, ta, Cal.'

After Calum had gone off to make his drink, Bernie sighed again. He felt a certain amount of responsibility for Calum's misery over the loss of Dee as he had been the one to push them both together in the first place. He'd felt so sure those two had a future together, but then how was he to know Dee wasn't going to be around long? In future he'd leave the matchmaking alone, he obviously wasn't any good at it.

After entering a figure in a column in his account book, he leaned over to open the small safe behind him. He intended to add the previous day's takings to those from the rest of the week and bank it all on Monday – after taking out the amount he did not declare to the taxman. Bernie sighed again. Besides the threat of the taxman, he was having to hand over five pounds a week to a couple of wide boys who'd been most insistent about it.

The threat of violence against his person did not frighten Bernie as he'd been on the receiving end of many a thumping from much harder types both inside and outside prison. When they'd first approached him offering . . . no, *telling* him he was now under their protection, and how much it was going to cost him each week . . . he had scoffed in their faces, telling them bluntly they did not frighten him. Using a string of expletives, he'd ordered them to go away and prey on other suckers with their so-called racket. For his bravado, he'd received a severe thrashing and been left semi-conscious in his own back yard. Thankfully for Bernie that was when Calum had found him or there was no telling what might have happened to him, the night being a bitter one.

The next time they had come in to collect their dues, they hadn't given him a chance to retaliate before the barrel of a pistol was shoved in his face and he was left in no doubt that, should he resist again, it would be used on him. Fists were one thing, guns another. Whether they really would use it, whether it was in fact loaded, he wasn't prepared to take the risk. He wasn't ready to die yet, and especially not at the hands of those two morons who, when all was said and done, were just a pair of bully boys.

He only wished he could think of a way to bring about their downfall. Bernie was well aware his wouldn't be the only business in these parts they were making money from, using the same tactics as they were on him. If he could maybe suss those others out and persuade them all to band together, present a united front to the police and let them deal with it, maybe they could get free. But even just getting people to admit they were under the protection of that pair, let alone persuade them to join with him in taking matters further, had proved a waste of time. When he broached the subject with his neighbours he had been given short shrift and asked to leave. It was obvious to Bernie that just the mention of the Monks brothers was enough to frighten his neighbours witless.

It seemed to Bernie he had no choice but to get on with it. Maybe there's be a miracle and the men's lives would be miraculously cut short, because that was the only way he could see himself getting free of them.

CHAPTER TWENTY-ONE

The Roaring Twenties was a private club that charged more for a yearly membership than a skilled factory worker could earn in three months. In a lavish twenties setting, attractive waitresses dressed as flappers, barmen sporting evening dress, and a fifteen-piece band, along with a variety of vocalists, both male and female, entertained guests. The meals provided for those who wished to eat were produced by a top-class chef, and like the extensive array of cocktails served, were extortionately expensive. But then the clientele the place attracted could afford to pay its prices. It was the in place at the moment, the one the city's elite frequented.

It was Leonard's favourite night club. It gave him such a buzz to socialise here with snooty types who would give him a wide berth if they learned the truth about his working-class background, and an even wider one if they knew how he obtained the large wad of cash he flashed in front of them.

Ronnie, though, hated the place, felt totally out of his depth there, and would have much preferred to be down the local pub, savouring a pint of best bitter and enjoying a game of darts.

A martini clasped in his bear-like paw, idly leaning his bulk against the bar, he was closely watching his brother lounging nearby on a comfortable couch, doing his best to seduce a jewel-bedecked, flame-haired woman to whom he'd taken a fancy.

Ronnie had always nursed mixed feelings for his elder brother. Half of him resented Leonard for being blessed with what Mother Nature had denied Ronnie himself: striking good looks, a manly physique, and the ability to charm into bed any woman he chose. The other half was in awe of him because without his brains they would still be labouring on the factory floor for a pittance.

At the moment, though, his resentment was taking precedence.

Leonard knew his brother wasn't comfortable in this sort of venue, yet he insisted Ronnie should accompany him here or to another such place every evening except Sunday when everywhere was shut. And Ronnie knew why. Despite Leonard's being the elder and much better-looking, basically he was a coward, terrified of the slightest physical harm, and even more terrified of anything spoiling his looks. He didn't feel safe if Ronnie wasn't beside him to act as his protector should the need arise, and over the years there had been many such occasions.

Leonard had always had a knack for getting on the wrong side of people through his arrogant manner but felt totally at liberty to act just as he liked, confident he'd Ronnie beside him to sort out anyone who took offence. Ronnie had the scars to prove this, and as if he hadn't been short-changed enough in the looks department, it was through his brother's conceitedness that he had acquired a disfiguring scar a few years ago. At a local dance, Leonard had set his sights on a woman he wanted and was blatantly eyeing her up. Trouble was, she was already with someone. The man she was with had had enough. With the end of a broken bottle coming in his direction, Leonard had darted behind Ronnie and the offending article slashed his face instead. Regardless of the excruciating pain this brought him, Ronnie reacted furiously and as a result the other man lost an eye.

Leonard shouldered no blame for the injury to his brother but instead homed in on the fact that the other man involved had fared far worse than Ronnie, in his opinion, which could only benefit his brother's growing reputation as a man not to cross.

Lennie and Ronnie had been in their mid-twenties at the time and it was only months after their mother's suicide. Previously Lennie had realised that women viewed his brother as unattractive, but now he was sporting a grotesque scar it was clear that Ronnie terrified them too. In truth, if ever a man deserved his nickname of 'Gorilla', Ronnie did. This fact, together with Leonard's own innate loathing for prostitutes, for what they had done to his family, planted the seeds of an idea in his mind. Within a matter of weeks he and Ronnie had terrorised into submission every prostitute who operated in their vicinity and were obtaining five shillings a week from each of them – which had subsequently risen to fifteen – all but for one hard-nosed brass who even Ronnie couldn't seem to intimidate, namely Della Kirby. She paid for that eventually, of course. In the meantime they were able to give up their dead-end factory jobs and concentrate instead on building their own far more lucrative protection racket.

Despite the fact that Lennie was firmly of the opinion that he was a controlling influence over his less intelligent brother, knew everything there was to know about him, had him believing he couldn't function without Lennie's guidance – when in truth they couldn't function one without the other – nevertheless Ronnie kept a dark secret that he never shared with his brother, one he knew Lennie wouldn't understand at all due to the events of the past. Ronnie took after his father in one respect: he craved the company of prostitutes. There was something exciting, forbidden, about them, and besides they were prepared to give him what other women weren't. Prostitutes weren't bothered about physical appearance, all they cared about was whether you had the means to pay for their services. Ronnie was aware that the girls who met his craving for sex were in fact contributing towards his means of paying for it, which only added to the overall satisfaction. Of course, all the girls involved were left in no doubt that they were never to breathe a word about this particular client of theirs or they knew exactly what would happen to them.

The only problem Ronnie faced was finding some time to himself so that he was free to pursue his lust. The only time Leonard did not expect him to be by his side was when he was off with a woman. So while he was occupied with his chosen female, believing his brother was patiently awaiting his return, Ronnie was usually off having just as much fun in secret.

Tonight, though, he didn't plan to go to his usual haunts to seek for a woman. Why should he when he had all he wanted waiting for him at home? He knew Dee would be far from willing to share her body with him, but that didn't bother Ronnie because the thought of taking what he wanted only added extra excitement. He'd lost count of the number of women he'd used and abused since he'd had the means to pay for their services, but since the arrival of the housekeeper it had become increasingly apparent to him that they were no longer enough for him. There was only one woman who would do for him now and he was fully aware of the reason why. Apart from the fact that he found Dee physically attractive, the knowledge that she hated him with vengeance proved the ultimate aphrodisiac. He had been managing to control his lust so far but now it had got to the stage where it was all-consuming and he was no longer prepared to deny himself. He meant to have Dee tonight, and as many nights thereafter as she served his purpose.

As he stood watching his brother work his magic on his chosen conquest, Ronnie was willing him to get on with it so that he could go too. He was relieved when he saw Leonard whisper something in the woman's ear then come across to join him.

'I'm disappearing for a couple of hours.'

Ronnie tried not to look eager. 'I'll be waiting here as usual, Lennie.'

Leonard glanced back at the woman who was busily checking her appearance in her compact mirror. 'I hope she's as good in the sack as she looks.'

'Take all the time you like finding out,' Ronnie encouraged him.

His brother slapped him on his broad shoulder. 'We'll call by Big Mo's place on the way home for fish and chips for you.'

Now Lennie was treating him like a mother would a child, bribing him with the promise of a treat if he was a good boy. It really irritated Ronnie. 'Great, Len,' he said, feigning childish excitement.

As soon as Lennie had left with his conquest, Ronnie downed the remains of his martini then called over to the barman, 'Oi, you, if my brother happens to come back before me, tell him I've had to pop home for summat and I'll be back soon.'

Perched on the deep sill of her attic window, Dee stared blindly out into a cloudy dark late-March sky. With no heating, this room was chilly and she pulled her dressing-gown tighter around her for warmth. She had never felt so isolated, so lonely, so absolutely desolate, in all her life. Before she'd fallen into the hands of the Monks brothers any troubles, however big or small, had always been shared with Madge. Because of the way she was threatened by this situation, though, turning to her now was out of the question. Dee realised she had no one else in whom she could confide a problem of this magnitude. Had she not been forced to come here and could instead have started her job at Lea's a friendship with Susan might possibly have developed to the stage where they became each other's trusted confidant, but she would never know now.

How deeply she regretted ending her relationship with Calum, regardless of the good reason she'd had for it. If she had not, even if she could not have told him everything now for fear of reprisals, at least she would still have his friendship to call upon. But as things stood it would not be fair on either of them.

A vision of him flashed before her and her heart lurched as she remembered how good it had felt to be in his arms, the tingling of her skin when his cheek had rested against hers while they were slow dancing, how much she had enjoyed just being with him. They were all telling signs that there was a strong possibility something special would have grown between them, given the chance. Despite how hard it had been for her, she had made it her business since the night of their parting not to go past the café, sometimes going well out of her way so as not to do so, but that didn't mean she didn't want to see him, just catch a glimpse of him to confirm he was all right. But thinking of what might have been between Calum and herself was only going to cause her unnecessary grief so she switched her thoughts back to Madge.

It was now coming up to a month since she had gone to visit

her friend, fired up by her belief that Madge's family visit would result in her immediate return to the fold. How wrong she had been!

No properly employed housekeeper would ever stand for what the Monkses expected Dee to do for them or tolerate the nasty manner in which they addressed her. Dee felt she had suffered their treatment of her for far too long. The only bright spot in her otherwise purgatorial existence was that she hadn't caught Ronnie leering at her quite so much recently, and hoped it meant someone else was occupying his thoughts now. She vehemently prayed it stayed that way until she was in a position to make her escape.

How was Madge's quest to obtain the money for her move going? Dee wondered for the umpteenth time. Her friend had seemed very determined to put all her efforts into getting together the amount she needed to make her move. Surely by now she had made some headway? Dee prayed nothing had befallen her since last she'd seen her to slow its progress or, worse, put a stop to it.

She gave a heavy sigh. All that lay between her own escape from here was the twenty pounds Madge needed. It wasn't that large a sum in the big scheme of things. If she could somehow obtain the amount Madge needed then all this would be over for both of them. But she had racked her brains continuously over the past four weeks and come up with nothing. Saving anything out of the ten shillings a week the Monkses allowed her was impossible as it barely covered the most basic personal necessities as it was. She was already worried about how she was going to find the money to buy herself some new shoes to replace the ones she had with holes in their soles. She had a strong suspicion that Leonard was waiting for her to approach him for money so he could add the amount to the debt she allegedly owed them, and that way she'd never settle it and be tied to them forever as their virtual slave. She knew there was no point in approaching any of her past acquaintances for help as the sort of people she had mixed with wouldn't have enough to bail her out.

The only people she knew who had money were the Monkses themselves, and it wasn't very likely they would advance her the amount she needed to make her escape from them!

Then a thought struck Dee and her heart began to thump wildly. She couldn't believe that a way out of her predicament had been staring her in the face all this time only she had been too wrapped up in her own misery to see it. It would mean resorting to stealing, something that was against her nature and made her feel uncomfortable, but how could what she was considering really be classed as theft if all she was doing was taking back the money the Monkses had stolen from Madge in the first place? Dee wasn't sure how much they fleeced her of each week or for how long it had been going on, but she felt sure the amount wouldn't fall far short of twenty pounds. She doubted they counted their ill-gotten gains every day and by the time they discovered some of it was missing, it would be too late to accuse Dee of taking it. She wouldn't be here.

She thought hard.

Both brothers kept a silver dish on their dressing table to hold loose change. She doubted the contents of the dishes added together would amount to more than a couple of pounds. The rest of their money was kept in their wallets, and usually those were kept on their person unless they were sleeping. To attempt to take money from their wallets while they slept would be insane. Dee gave a heavy sigh. This idea was looking like a dumb one after all. Then another thought struck her. Where in fact did they keep the bulk of the money they acquired through their blackmail?

Her brain whirled.

Judging by the fact that Leonard always put a small leather purse-type bag beside his place setting at the table every evening, the daily takings were kept in there. After the meal was over, he always took the bag upstairs with him to his bedroom when he went up to get changed. Some evenings she noticed he took the bag back out with him – and by the way he handled it she knew it was empty. On those evenings the brothers must be making their rounds of the prostitutes they hadn't caught up with during the day.

Dee doubted they banked any of their gains. People of their sort never trusted banks or any other official body in case suspicions were aroused as to how they were making the amounts they banked and awkward questions were asked. The less that was known, the better, was the code of people like the Monks brothers. So if they didn't use the facilities of a bank, it made sense to assume they must keep the takings somewhere on these premises, most probably somewhere in Leonard's bedroom.

Usually people who stored large amounts of money inside their home kept it in a safe but Dee had never come across one in his room, and as she was very thorough in her work, thought there probably wasn't one. But he must have somewhere he secreted the ill-gotten gains. It was just a question of finding it so she could take what she needed.

A surge of hope ran through her. It sounded so simple. She hoped it would be.

Adrenaline started to pump through her as she glanced over at her alarm clock on the floor by her bed. It read just after twelve. Definitely not the considerate sort, the brothers usually woke her up between two and three, when they returned from their nights of frivolity, by banging shut the front door, their heavy tread on the stairs, then again the banging of their bedroom doors. There was no reason for Dee to believe they wouldn't return at their usual time tonight, which meant she had at least a couple of hours clear to make her search for Leonard's hiding place. If she could find it, she would pay a visit to Madge tomorrow, hand over the money and tell Madge it was a bonus from her generous boss for her hard work. She'd insist she wanted Madge to have it then impress on her there was no need for further delay. She had been naive before to think that Madge could make her move overnight, but surely she could tie up any loose ends and be ready for the off by the end of the week? Hopefully by Saturday Dee would be away herself.

Without further ado, she eased herself off the window sill and darted across to unlock her door.

Although she knew no one was home, she crept down the stairs to the first-floor landing and made her way to Leonard's bedroom door. She stood still for a moment and listened before she opened it, fearing the brothers just might have returned home unusually early for some reason and she not have heard them. Apart from the distant hooting of an owl an eerie silence prevailed. Satisfied she was indeed alone, Dee turned the door knob and let herself in.

The house had four bedrooms and Leonard's was the master room at the front. Ronnie's, marginally smaller, looked out over the back garden. Two smaller unused rooms flanked the bathroom.

Everything about Ronnie's room was large and plain, like the man who inhabited it. His room held a huge dark oak wooden bed, a massive and very ugly-looking matching wardrobe, tallboy, six-drawer chest, and a dark oak-topped trouser press. The walls were covered in plain blue wallpaper and there were matching plain navy blue curtains. There were no pictures on the walls or ornaments on the mantel. He wasn't at all an orderly person. Dee was constantly tidying the top of his dressing table, and he lazily left his clothes where he dropped them for her to pick up, and never used the wastepaper bin. The neatly folded, washed and ironed clothes she put away in his chest-of-drawers and tallboy constantly needed to be refolded as he'd a habit of pulling everything out in his search for a particular garment.

In complete contrast, his brother's room was surprisingly tastefully furnished and decorated, startlingly so in fact, considering the elaborate furnishings and clashing colours of the rooms downstairs. A dado rail ran around the walls which were decorated in a dark shade of green wallpaper underneath, a pale olive above. All the woodwork was cream-painted. The curtains were of abstract design in shades of green, white and cream; the furniture was all in light mahogany. Leonard was basically a very neat person and his drawers were all kept pristine although he too left his clothes on the floor for Dee to sort through, wash or clean.

Now, leaving on the landing light to illuminate the bedroom, she made her way straight for the bed, crouched down and looked beneath it. As she already knew after cleaning thoroughly under it three times a week, there was nothing lurking beneath but she'd wanted to double check. Then she tried the wardrobe, moving aside the dozen or so tailor-made suits and two dozen white, blue or black shirts to check for anything container-like that might hold what she was seeking. But all the bottom of the wardrobe contained was Lennie's neatly lined up pairs of hand-made shoes in black or brown. There was nothing on top of the wardrobe. Next she tried the tallboy, opening each drawer, mindful not to disturb the neatly folded clothes inside for fear the fastidious Leonard would notice and suspect his room had been searched. She felt around for any kind of container she might not have noticed when putting his clothes away. All the drawers in the tallboy contained clothes and that was all. She did the same with the chest and found nothing but clothes until she came to the bottom drawer and under a couple of jumpers her hand touched something solid . . . wooden and box-like. Excitement ran through her. She must have found what she was looking for.

She pulled out the box and to her relief saw it hadn't a lock. Then it immediately struck her that if money were secreted inside it, it wouldn't be in the amounts she'd anticipated as this wasn't any deeper than a single-layer cigar box. But then, as long as it contained the amount she needed for Madge, that was all that mattered to Dee.

Down on her haunches, facing the open doorway so the light coming from the hallway could illuminate its contents, she opened the box. The expectant expression on her face vanished, to be replaced by one of disillusionment when she saw what the box contained. In her experience women usually kept family documents and items of importance in old handbags for safekeeping. Obviously Leonard kept all the Monkses' documentation along with a few special mementoes in this wooden box. Lying on top was a faded black and white photograph, with one half ripped off. The remaining piece showed a woman dressed in the clothes of the working class in the thirties. She was very pretty, smiling happily for the camera. It had to be a picture of the brothers' mother, and the torn-off part had once shown their errant father.

248

Sighing heavily, Dee closed the lid on the box and replaced it exactly as she had found it with clothes on top, shutting the drawer. She then got up and stood with hands on hips, staring thoughtfully around. She didn't know where else to search. There were no rooms leading off this one. The room was fully carpeted, all the edges and corners held tightly in place by carpet grippers so under the floorboards was out of the question. The walls in this room weren't thick enough for anything to be concealed behind the skirting boards. Her heart sank. She must have been wrong in her assumption that the hiding place was in here. But Lennie must be hiding their spare cash on this floor somewhere as he always brought the bag up with him. Well, she would just have to search through all the other rooms because she was bent on locating his hiding place.

She had been about half an hour in the room and deduced she still had time to make a search of Ronnie's room tonight before she risked them catching her at what she was doing, the consequences of which didn't bear thinking about.

She was just about to leave the room when her eyes flickered over the chest and to her horror she spotted the edge of one of Leonard's garments sticking out of the bottom drawer. Hurrying across, she bent down to pull open the drawer and tidy away the garment, which proved difficult because it had jammed. She knelt down to get more power and gave it a hard tug. Thankfully the drawer came free and she was able to push the whole garment back inside. Then she pushed the drawer shut. As Dee made to stand up, suddenly something about the drawer struck her as odd. Sitting back on her haunches, she frowned at it. It seemed a perfectly ordinary drawer but when she'd looked inside it had not held as much as the other four in the chest. But it should do . . . the front panel was the same size as the others.

Dee eased out the drawer, took out the garments then the box, and stared into the empty space inside. It was just a drawer, nothing odd about it at all, but regardless something was niggling away at her about it. Something wasn't right.

She peered closely at the bottom of the drawer. Light from

the landing didn't quite reach inside it, but she couldn't see any irregularities. She put her hand inside and felt around with her fingertips. On the right of the drawer, almost touching the side but far enough away for her to close two fingers around it, was a small raised knob. Gently she pulled it upwards. The wooden panel that was masquerading as the bottom of the drawer lifted up to reveal a hidden cavity beneath. Excitement raced through Dee. She had found what she been searching for! At the real bottom of the drawer were several tied bundles of banknotes in one- and five-pound denominations, and a bulky bag containing a large quantity of coinage. At a rough guess it was several thousand pounds she was looking at here. There was also a small A5-sized exercise book. Out of curiosity she went to pick it up to see what it contained when the sound of a car drawing up outside sent a chill of fear rushing through her.

Dropping the false bottom of the drawer back into place, she scrambled up and ran across to the window. Her worst fear was confirmed. It was the brothers' saloon. Sheer panic filled her as she saw the car door opening. With heart hammering she dashed back to the chest-of-drawers, squatting down to replace the box and the piles of clothes. She was just about to shut the drawer when to her horror she heard a key being inserted in the front door. Blind terror invading her, she shoved the drawer shut, scrambled up and shot from the room. As she clicked shut the door she turned in the direction of the attic stairs, intending to race back to her room before she was discovered. She sensed a presence and spun round to see Ronnie at the head of the hall stairs, staring at her.

'Oh, er . . . er . . . good . . . good evening, Mr Monks,' she stuttered, tightening her dressing-gown around her as her mind whirled frantically for a plausible excuse. 'I . . . I was just on my way to fetch a glass of water when I . . . er . . . heard a banging and thought Mr Monks had left his bedroom window open. I went in to check. He had so I shut it.'

At the moment her reason for being inside Lennie's room was not at all important to Ronnie, but his own reason for sneaking home without his brother's knowledge was. He had driven the car at breakneck speed in his urgent desire to get here, his lust for Dee steadily rising to fever pitch as he envisioned what lay in store for him. He lumbered down the landing to stand before her. Eyeing her hard, he said throatily, 'You being down here saves me coming up to fetch you.'

The way he was leering at her was sending alarm bells ringing for Dee. She shrank back several steps. 'To . . . fetch . . . me?' she queried. Then, with forced lightness, said, 'Oh, you wish me to make you a drink or something, Mr Monks? Yes, of course. Tea or coffee?'

She made to pass him but he blocked her way with his huge bulk. 'Neither. It's you I want.'

Next thing she knew he had grabbed her wrist with his right paw and was hauling her towards his bedroom.

'NO!' she screamed. 'LET ME G. . .'

The slap she received to her face was so forceful it sent her head crashing back against the wall. For a moment Dee saw double. Her legs buckled beneath her and she crumpled to the floor.

Ronnie stared down at her mockingly. Releasing his hold on her wrist, he snarled, 'Here will do fine for me.' In an instant he had dragged her away from the wall, pushed her flat down on the carpet and was standing over her, unzipping his trousers.

Despite being dazed from the blow, her desperate need to get away was still uppermost in Dee's mind. Pulling up her knees, she dug her heels into the carpet and began frantically to push herself backwards, to get out from under him. But before she had moved more than inches he dropped his full weight on top of her, immobilising her. His need for her desperate now, he was yanking at his zip in an attempt to get it undone. 'You hate me, don't you?' he asked her while silently cursing the zip which appeared to have stuck. 'I make you feel sick, don't I? Well, I'll let you into a secret . . . knowing that excites me. There's no escape from me,' he warned her. 'So you might as well lie back and enjoy it. This fucking zip!' he yelled, furiously yanking at it.

Seeing his attention was firmly fixed on the zip, Dee stiffened her fingers talon-like then reached up and clawed her nails down the side of his already scarred cheek. She drew blood. A river of it poured down his cheek. She screamed hysterically, 'Get off me, you bastard!'

Rearing back his head, he roared, 'You'll be sorry you did that.' Then he swung back his arm and smashed his fist into her face.

The pain of his attack exploded like a bomb in Dee's head. Her vision swam and she felt the blood pouring down her chin. Regardless, she wasn't about to give up without a fight and made to claw him again while still trying with all her might to wriggle her way out from under him.

He caught her wrist just before it made contact with his face again, gripping it so tightly she felt sure she'd hear the bone snap, and at the same time his zip freed itself and he cried out in triumph. He let go of her wrist and pulled down his trousers to expose himself, then raised himself just far enough to start wrenching up her nightclothes.

Clenching her fists, Dee frantically pummelled his chest. 'Is this how you get your kicks, by forcing yourself on defenceless women?' she screamed.

He was so consumed by what he was doing, he didn't appear to hear her.

She felt her strength ebbing and was fully aware that all her attempts to free herself from under this huge brute were pointless. Her situation was hopeless. Dropping her arms, she shut her eyes and waited for the inevitable. Then, to her astonishment, Ronnie abruptly stopped wrenching at her clothes and she felt his weight lift from her. She heard him hiss urgently, 'Get up, you bitch. I said, get up.'

Before she could open her eyes, she felt herself being yanked to her feet and thrown against the wall. Her eyes opened and she was stunned to see Ronnie frantically dressing himself. The next thing a voice was demanding, 'What the hell's going on here?' It was Leonard.

Ronnie hurried towards the top of the stairs to meet his

brother. 'You got my message then, that I'd popped back home? I . . . er . . . spilled a drink down me trousers so I came home to change. How come you're back anyway?'

Leonard had joined his brother on the landing now. 'That sort I was chatting up was no more than a high-class hooker,' he spat furiously. 'Well, she's the poorer for picking on me tonight as all the money she made before is in here,' he said, tapping his breast pocket. 'With no cash on her, I'd like to see how she intends paying for the room I took her to because I certainly didn't.'

He then reached up and grabbed Ronnie by the lapels, pushing his face into his. 'You shouldn't have left the club without me, Ron, you know I worry about you being on your own. What if you'd found yourself in a situation you couldn't cope with, and I wasn't there to protect you? You need me to take care of you, Ron. I left you safe in that bar. You should have stayed put there until I got back. Don't go off without me like that again, promise me?'

Ronnie was fully aware that it was in fact the other way round and Lennie was terrified of being caught in a situation he couldn't handle on his own. Regardless, he said, 'Yeah, okay, Len, I promise.'

Lennie released him. 'So what's going on here? And what's happened to your face?'

'Oh, that,' Ronnie said nonchalantly, wiping the blood from his fingers down the side of his trousers. 'I dunno.' He shrugged. 'Must have caught it on something. Anyway, I came home and caught her coming out your room, Len,' he said, pointing at Dee. 'I was just questioning her to find out what she was doing in there. She wasn't playing ball so I had to give her a thumping, as you see.'

'Good job I came home when I did then or she might have gone the same way as her mother,' Lennie said matter-of-factly. Then his face darkened murderously and he stepped over to Dee, still slumped by the wall, and thrust his face into hers. 'What were you doing in my room at this time of night, you slut?'

She lay staring up at him. 'I . . . I . . . was just shutting your window, Mr Monks. Honestly I was,' she pleaded. 'It was banging, you see. I tried to tell Mr Monks that but he wouldn't believe me.'

Leonard grabbed her by the scruff of the neck and pulled her up so her face was close to his. 'I don't believe you either, I never had my window open tonight so how could you have heard it banging? You was snooping, wasn't you? Find anything interesting, did you?'

Dee gulped, terrified. 'I wasn't snooping, honestly, Mr Monks. I wasn't looking for anything. Check my dressing-gown pockets, you won't find anything.'

He pushed her away from him, opened his bedroom door and disappeared inside.

Dee stared after him, panic-stricken. Dear God, she silently prayed. Please don't let him find any evidence I've been poking around. She felt a tap on her shoulder and spun round to see Ronnie grinning at her. He whispered meaningfully, 'There'll be other nights.'

Just then Leonard came back out and said grudgingly, 'Well, everything looks to be in order so I'll take your word for it this time. But in future, just to make sure, I'll be locking my door when I'm out. You can clean my room while I'm home. Now, get out of my sight.'

She didn't need telling twice. Kicking up her heels, she ran hell for leather to her room. Having locked the door behind her, Dee collapsed on her bed and cradled her head despairingly in her hands. Her face was throbbing excruciatingly, blood caking it from the wounds she had received at Ronnie's hands, but at the moment she couldn't think about that. Nor was she mindful of the narrow escape she'd just had from being raped by him. She was just desolate that the only avenue of escape from here she could see had been blocked, and with Leonard locking his bedroom door from now on it was closed to her for good. She had no choice but to bide her time while Madge saved the money to fund her own move.

Dee curled herself up on her bed in a foetal position, the tears starting to fall. Huge, fat, desperate tears soaked through her dressing-gown and nightdress. She wept until her tears ran dry and finally she slept.

CHAPTER TWENTY-TWO

Early that evening, Madge was willing the man she was with to hurry up and satisfy himself so she could get away from him. They were at the bottom of a narrow alley, between the bank and a solicitor's premises, off the London Road. Weeds grew there in abundance between cracks in the cobbles; discarded chip wrappers and newspaper lay rotting. It was almost pitch black and she was glad. It meant her punter couldn't see the revolted expression on her face.

About fifteen minutes ago, as she had been hurrying back to her patch after finishing with another punter, this character she was with now had approached her. It was very seldom she actually enjoyed being with a client, but she always did when she was with her previous one. Joe his name was, a very pleasant sixty year old, who for several years now had sought out Madge's company whenever he had saved enough to pay her to do for him what his wife had long ago called a halt to. He would take Madge up to his allotment shed where along with his array of gardening paraphernalia he kept an old but clean flock mattress, rolled up and covered in tarpaulin. He would always have with him a flask of tea and two arrowroot biscuits each for afterwards. While they finished this Joe would offload his woes on Madge, and she would patiently listen. He always gave her sixpence tip on top of her rate, telling her he wished it could be more and he looked forward to the next time he could seek out her company. Joe was always gentle with her, considerate, showing his appreciation for what she did for him, even though he was paying for it. She thought his wife very inconsiderate for denying her husband his pleasure when she wasn't suffering

257

any sort of disability that prevented her from doing so. Over the years, Madge had gleaned enough about Joe to know he was the kind of man who would be a good husband to his wife. She wondered if the woman realised that the world was full of others who would give anything to have a man like Joe, given the chance – including Madge herself.

As she was hurrying to return to her regular spot in the hope that he wasn't her last client of the night, she was thinking how much better her job would be if all her other punters treated her like he did.

She had nearly reached her destination when a rusting flat-backed lorry piled high with old electrical appliances and scrap metal drew up alongside her. Through the driver's-side window a gruff voice called curtly across to her, 'How much?'

In more lucrative times Madge would have considered she'd had a bad day if she returned home of a night with less than five pounds, but times had changed so much for her that she counted herself lucky these days if she made anything over fifteen shillings. Today had proved an unusually good one for her. She'd already made that amount, so her hopes soared to think she might actually make a pound today, even a little more if this man was a good tipper. That meant she'd be able to add several instead of a couple of shillings to her new life fund, which at the moment thanks to her severe cutbacks had reached the grand total of two pounds, seventeen shillings and sixpence.

Tottering over to the lorry in her worn-down stilettos, she looked up at the man, addressing her out of the window. She didn't like the look of him one little bit. He was dressed in grubby work clothes, his full greying beard and hair looking as though they hadn't seen a brush or a comb for years. If she wasn't so desperate for his money to add to her savings, she would have told him she was busy and continued on her way. 'Depends what you're after, love?' she said, smiling winningly at him.

'What do men usually want from your sort? A quick fuck,' he snapped back. 'If yer charge more than five bob you can forget it.'

This man definitely did not share Joe's sweet nature. In fact, very much the opposite. Five shillings was the rate she charged for what he was after, though. 'Five bob it is then,' Madge agreed.

He inclined his head towards the alley behind her. 'I'll meet yer down there.'

He had joined her seconds later and without another word slapped two half crowns into her hand. Before she'd had a chance to put it away in her purse, his trousers and underpants were pooled around his ankles and he was urgently pulling up her skirt. He was pumping away at her now, showing no consideration whatsoever, grunting pig-like. The revolting stench that was coming from him was making her stomach heave. It was no wonder this man sought sex from women like herself, he'd never get it through conventional approaches.

Then a sudden wave of disgust flooded through her. Disgust at herself for accepting his business. Even slovenly Elsie, who had been known to entertain vagrant types for a shilling when desperate, would have turned her nose up at the man Madge was with now. Was starting her new life really more important to her than her pride? She hadn't much to call her own in life, but she did have her standards.

Placing her hands flat on his shoulders, Madge gave him one almighty push away from her. Her actions were unexpected by him and caught him unawares. He thudded into the wall behind.

Despite its being too dark for her to see his face, Madge knew he'd be staring at her in shock.

'What the fuck . . .' he erupted.

'I'll tell you what the fuck,' she cut in, pulling her own clothes back into place. 'You stink worse than a sewer! Have you heard of soap and water, you filthy pig? No, not pig, that's an insult to them or any other animal 'cos at least they clean themselves. Despite what you may believe, us prostitutes have our pride, yer know.' She slapped one of the half crowns he'd given her back into his hand. 'Do us all a favour and use that down the slipper baths. If you hurry, you might still catch them open.'

With that she proudly lifted her chin and tottered off down the alley, leaving the man staring after her.

'A gin, please, Harry,' Madge told the landlord of the Admiral Beatty a short while later.

'Orange?' he asked her.

'No, neat. I need summat strong after the experience I've just had.'

'Oh, that bad, eh?' he said as he poured her drink out. Putting it on the counter before her and accepting payment, he said, 'Trouble from a client, I take it?' Unlike other landlords whose public houses the working girls frequented, Harry had a soft spot for all the street ladies who came into his place, as he appreciated they were only trying to make a living for themselves the best way they knew. Underneath their thick layers of Pan Stik, overdone eye make-up and gaudy cheap clothes, most of them were decent women. Unbeknown to Madge, he had always had a secret admiration for her. He thought her a very handsome woman and not at all hard-edged like most he knew in her line of work. Like her pal Della had been, in fact. A lonely widower for seven years now, if it had not been well known in this area how Madge earned her living, Harry would actually have asked her to accompany him on his night off, in the hope that something special might develop between them. 'He never hurt you, did he?' he asked her now with concern.

Madge picked up her glass and knocked back her drink, shuddering as the neat alcohol stung the back of her throat. She replaced the glass on the counter. 'Oh, it were nothing like that, Harry. In fact, if anyone was hurt it was him.' She laughed. 'His feelings! He smelled worse than bad drains at the height of summer, so I told him to use the money he was paying me to go and have a scrub.'

Harry chuckled. 'Good on you, gel. Want another?'

It sounded very tempting but due to the fact she had just given back half the proceeds to the punter and every penny was important to her, Madge said, 'I just came in for a quick one. I ought to be getting back out, ta, Harry.'

'Oh, it's as dead as a dodo in here tonight. Stay and keep me company while you have another one. On the house,' he said, picking up the bottle of gin and pouring another measure into her glass.

Madge smiled in appreciation. 'Thanks, Harry, that's really good of you.'

A man arrived at the bar then, dressed in a cheap suit and frayed shirt, a day's stubble on his chin. He flashed a look of disdain at Madge then said to Harry, 'I don't understand why you encourage the likes of her to drink in here. It lowers the tone of the place. Same as the rest of the trollops you serve.'

Madge had long ago grown used to comments like this, but it didn't mean to say they didn't cut her and make her feel she didn't belong. She didn't want to be responsible for losing Harry any customers though. 'I'll be off then,' she said to him diplomatically.

'You stay where you are and finish yer drink,' he ordered. Then he said to the man in question, 'There's plenty of other pubs in the area if you don't find the tone of my place agreeable to yer, Reg. Usual, is it, or are yer not staying?'

Reg snorted as he slapped his money down on the counter.

After he'd gone off, armed with his pint, to sit down at a table, Madge said to the landlord, 'Thanks for that, Harry.'

He was drying glasses. 'You've as much right to drink in my pub as he has, Madge. There's enough trouble in this world without people causing it unnecessarily, in my opinion. So, I heard you and Elsie are sharing Del's old place? What happened to her daughter? Don't know her name, she only came in here to coax her mother out of trouble, but from what I saw of her she seemed a nice young gel. Always amazed me, knowing Del as I did, how she came to raise such a lovely lass.' He looked at Madge meaningfully. 'You were about Del's only friend, weren't yer? I just wondered if the way her gel turned out has something to do with you.'

Madge smiled at the compliment. 'I tried to be there for her when she needed me.'

Harry looked at her enquiringly. 'Out of curiosity, is Del's gel . . . yer know?

Madge vehemently shook her head. 'Oh, no, Dee doesn't

follow after her mother in that way. She's a housekeeper for an old gent. Likes it a lot, so she told me the last time she came over to see me.'

Harry looked surprised. 'Housekeeper, eh? Usually middle-aged spinster types or widows do those kinda jobs. Not the sort of job for a young pretty gel like her, I wouldn't have said. Still, each to their own, I suppose. Big house, is it, that she works in? Usually people who can afford housekeepers have big houses.'

'Been invited over for tea yet then, Madge?' said a voice beside her.

Madge turned her head and saw Kathleen Chase had joined them. Or Kitty as she was known in the trade. She knew Kath was being sarcastic as women of their ilk didn't get invited for tea so ignored the comment. 'Hello, Kath. How's it going?'

'Oh, not so good, gel. Bit slow tonight. Only had one tickle and he was so pissed he couldn't get it up. I made sure he paid me, though. Half a mild, please, Harry. I've just come from the Hind and that place is about as lively as a cemetery at midnight, like this place is tonight,' she said, giving a miffed glance around at the near-empty room. 'After I've had me drink I'm off down the Cricketer's on Church Gate in town, to try me luck there. There's usually a few punters knocking around the clock tower at closing time too. What sorta night you had?' she asked Madge keenly.

She did not want to rub salt in Kath's wounds by telling her that her night had been a good one, and besides tomorrow their roles could be reserved and Kath fare well and she abysmally. It was the luck of the draw. 'Oh, about the same as yours,' Madge said lightly.

'Is Rosie Babcock still landlady at the Cricketer's?' Harry asked Kath.

She nodded. 'Far as I know. Why?'

'She was one of you, yer know.'

Both Kath and Madge gawped at him.

'What, Rosie was?' Kath gasped, shocked.

'Yeah, before she married Stan. She used to work the station on Great Central Street.'

'Well, she's kept that bloody quiet,' Kath snapped. 'Next time I see her looking down her nose at me, I shall remind her that she used to be just the same. Does her husband know?' she asked keenly.

'Oh, yes. He was one of her regulars.'

'Oh, shame,' said Kath, disappointed. 'I might have been able to blackmail her for a few quid to keep me gob shut.' Then she said to Madge, 'I wish I'd known you was looking for someone to share Del's old place with, I'd have jumped at the chance. Me and you could have had a right laugh together. Let me know if Elsie ever decides to leave, won't yer?'

Not likely, thought Madge. Elsie might be untidy and not that particular over her personal hygiene, but Kath was always cadging money off people and it was a devil to get it back from her. She also had a penchant for helping herself to other people's property and nothing was safe when she was around. Madge was clutching her handbag to her now as a safeguard against Kath's light fingers. 'Yeah, 'course I will,' she lied.

'Do you still see Del's gel?' Kath asked her then.

'When her job allows her to pop over I do, yes. Why?'

'Well, next time, can you do me a favour?'

''Course. What is it?'

Kath was fishing in her handbag. 'I borrowed half a crown off Del about five years back when I was going through a really rough patch. I caught her in one of her rare benevolent moods and I never did pay it back. I always meant to but I never seemed to have it spare,' she said, pulling out her purse. 'Well, I know it sounds daft but with her being dead it's been playing on my mind, in case she comes back to haunt me! I'm having enough of a run of bad luck at the moment without inviting more.'

Madge accepted the florin and the sixpenny piece that Kath gave her. It was her private opinion that the woman had actually helped herself to the money in question from Del, probably when she was drunk and hadn't seen her, and was only paying it back now because she was superstitious. 'I'll make sure Dee gets it as soon as I can,' Madge promised.

'If yer settling up debts, Kath, you've a six-bob tab behind this bar,' said Harry to her.

She chuckled. 'Yeah, well, when you're dead, I might think about settling it!' She gulped down her drink and pushed the empty glass towards him. 'Right, I'm off. Wish me luck, Madge.'

'Yes, 'course I do, Kath.' Madge then picked up her own glass and downed the contents, shuddering again as the neat alcohol stung the back of her throat. 'Oh, that's better. Those two gins have done me the power of good. 'I'd really better be off too. See yer soon, Harry.'

'Yeah, tarra, Madge.'

A short while later she was wishing she'd come up with Kath's idea of going to the Cricketer's to chance her luck as there was nothing more to be had on her own patch. Still, she'd had a decent night so she mustn't grumble, and her new life fund was certainly going to benefit. She dropped the end of her cigarette on the ground and stubbed it out with her shoe, then pulled herself away from the lamp-post she was leaning against, secured her handbag in the crook of her arm and set off for home.

As she journeyed along she slipped a hand inside the slit pocket of her shabby fur coat and her fingers felt the coins she had promised Kath she'd give to Dee the next time she saw her. When would that be? she thought. It was nearly four weeks since Dee had paid her a visit, and being very fond of the young woman, that felt like a lifetime to Madge. Despite missing her dreadfully, though, she sincerely hoped this meant Dee was busy getting on well with her new life and all the friends she was making. It would be good to see her, though. Let her know how Madge's plan was progressing.

She suddenly stopped pacing as a thought occurred to her. Dee's busy new life might be restricting her from paying a visit to Madge, but that didn't mean to say she herself couldn't go and pay a visit to Dee, did it? She had a good excuse for going, thanks to Kath, but a friend didn't need an excuse to go and visit another friend, did they? Presenting herself as she was now at Dee's workplace wouldn't do, but there was no reason why she shouldn't go looking like a respectable woman.

Madge really liked the thought of testing out her new look again. It was Saturday tomorrow, a good day for her to pay a visit as she had no clients during the day. Hopefully Dee's employer would see fit to give her a couple of hours off in the light of an unexpected visitor showing up, then they could spend some time together and have a good catch up. Of course, there was still the problem that she didn't actually know the address of Dee's new workplace, only the area it was in. Surely, though, with Dee being the friendly woman she was, someone would be able to point her in the right direction.

If she hurried home and tackled the time-consuming job of changing her hair colour tonight, that would mean she would have more time tomorrow to seek out Dee then spend some time with her before she needed to be back working her beat.

CHAPTER
TWENTY-THREE

Dee woke at six the next morning to the shrill of the alarm clock, feeling as if she'd been run over by a train. She hurt everywhere from the injuries she had sustained at Ronnie's hands. But it was inside she was suffering the most. She really hadn't thought her situation here could get any worse. How wrong she had been! It was bad enough before, dealing with the Monkses as their lackey, but now she was fully aware of Ronnie's intentions towards her, she felt she understood what being in hell must be like.

She painfully eased herself into a sitting position. Every movement she made was like a dozen red hot pokers being jabbed into her. Gingerly, she leaned down to pull up her handbag and rest it on her knees. Taking out her compact, she clicked it open and took a look at her face. It was so swollen she could hardly recognise herself, but much to her relief she didn't think she would suffer any permanent scarring. Then she checked her wrist where Ronnie had grabbed it. It was swollen too, and very bruised, but she didn't think it was broken. Although it was excruciating for her to do so, she could bend it backwards and forwards and wriggle her fingers. Her abdomen was very tender too where he'd rested all his weight on her to restrain her.

Tears pricked in Dee's eyes. If ever she'd needed the comfort of Madge's arms around her, her shoulder to cry on, it was today. She was desperate to go and pay her very dear friend a visit; desperate also to find out what progress she'd made towards acquiring the amount she needed to fund her new life, and then Dee might be able to see an end to this purgatory. But Madge was no fool, she would never accept that these injuries were accidental, so paying her a visit was out of the question until they healed.

If there was a good aspect to all this, it was the fact that Ronnie was terrified of his brother discovering he'd set his sights on Dee. One thing was certain, though; she was determined she wasn't going to make it easy for him to take what he wanted from her. In future, as soon as the brothers left the house of an evening, whatever tasks she hadn't completed, she would whizz through as quickly as she could and then come up to her room, lock herself in and then not come out for any reason whatsoever until morning. The fact that Ronnie would have great difficulty explaining to his brother why he had broken down her door was some safeguard. Plus she would buy a penknife to arm herself with when she went to the shops today for the weekend requirements, and would have no hesitation in using it to protect herself.

She glanced at the clock. It was coming up to six-fifteen. She had the boiler to fill and light so that the central heating warmed the house before they rose and the water was hot for them. That task was going to take her much longer today due to her injuries so she had better get a move on. Knowing the brothers as she did, she felt sure neither of them would excuse her for any lax performance of her work.

Leonard merely looked at her coldly when he came down in his silk dressing-gown and matching pyjamas for breakfast at just after nine. Dee was taking in a pot of coffee to the dining room in anticipation of his arrival.

As she hung back to allow him into the room before her, he commented on her bruised appearance, 'I trust you'll think twice before you pry around again, Kirby. I want Eggs Benedict for my breakfast today.'

Eggs Benedict! She hadn't a clue how they were cooked and knew he was aware of that too. And she'd laboured so hard the last hour, making sure that his usual sausage, bacon, black pudding, mushrooms, fried bread and eggs were done exactly as he usually demanded them. It was obvious to Dee he was doing this purely to assert his authority and remind her who was boss. It was also obvious to her he'd been reading up on what the affluent ate for breakfast, in his endeavours to become more like them. She deposited the coffee pot alongside the matching Queen Anne solid silver cream and sugar bowl. As quickly as her painful injuries allowed, she hurried back off to the kitchen, knowing he was watching her departure with a sly grin on his face.

Back in the kitchen she scoured her cookery book and thankfully found a recipe for the dish he was after. She had all the ingredients. Meticulously she followed the recipe and to her relief eventually produced something that looked like the picture in the book. When she took it through to the dining room, Ronnie had now joined his brother. She was determined not to give him the satisfaction of witnessing how terrified she was. After placing the plate of Eggs Benedict in front of Lennie she fixed her eyes on his brother and forced a smile. 'Eggs Benedict for you, Mr Monks, or your usual full English?'

He screwed up his face. 'Eggs what!' He looked at his brother's plate and pulled an even uglier face then glared at Dee. 'Me usual,' he snapped at her.

As she made her way back to the kitchen, she smiled to herself. She had scored a small victory. It was very apparent to her that Leonard was not enjoying his eggs at all prepared that way but he wouldn't say so for fear of looking foolish in her eyes, and Ronnie had certainly not liked the fact she hadn't shown any fear of him after what he'd done to her last night.

A while later the brothers had gone into the lounge, Leonard to read the morning newspaper, Ronnie to thumb through his car magazines. As it was Saturday they didn't leave so early as on weekdays to see to any business they had to attend to. As Dee was going into the dining room with an empty tray to start clearing away, what she heard Leonard saying to his brother stopped her in her tracks.

'Well, if the government's raising the prices of petrol and beer, I don't see why we shouldn't raise our rates too.'

'If you say so, Len,' Ronnie idly commented. It was obvious

he was more interested in the latest models of the cars he was studying in his magazine than anything his brother was saying.

'I think we'll put the women's rate up by five bob to a pound, and the shops and such like from five to six pounds.'

'If you say so, Len,' Ronnie idly commented again.

'And it's time we moved to a bigger place. This house is more in line with a bank manager's than men in our position now. I saw one advertised in the *Mercury* last week further towards Scaptoft way that's got six bedrooms and a tennis court out the back. The car means distance is no problem to us.'

'We don't play tennis, Len.'

'And we live on Tennis Court Drive where there ain't a tennis court to be seen, thicko. Same difference, ain't it? People judge you by what you've got.'

'Don't call me thicko, Len,' Ronnie said, hurt.

'Well, stop acting like one then.'

'Oh, Len, do you think we could maybe change the car while we're at it? I quite fancy the look of the latest Sunbeam Alpine.'

Lennie tutted. 'Those cars ain't built to take blokes the size of you!'

'Oh, no, s'pose not,' sighed Ronnie despondently. 'Well, what about a new Rover then?'

'Look, if it'll shut you up, we'll take a gander down a few showrooms this afternoon,' his brother snapped. 'First, though, we'll need to start getting a few more clients on our books. I think it's about time we flexed our muscles, started to expand the business.'

Dee heard Ronnie's knuckles crack. 'Well, I'm game for a bit of that. Things have got quite boring recently, everyone paying up without a squeak.'

Lennie laughed. 'Well, you might get a bit of fun when we deliver the news that we're raising our prices.'

'Oh, I do hope so, Len. It feels like a long time since I was giving someone a good thrashing. Last one was that chemist chap and he wasn't much of an opponent. Still, beats factory work, don't it?'

His brother laughed again. 'And far more lucrative! Anyway,

there's no time like the present to start expanding. We'll spread the good news to our clients about the raising of our rates on Monday. Meantime there's a new newsagent's opened up next to the dry cleaner's and a snooker room above the garage. Time we paid them a visit, methinks, to suss out whether they're the type to be easily persuaded. And we can start looking around for more flats like the florist's, so we can up that line of our operations too.'

Outside in the hallway Dee's blood was boiling. These two had no compunction whatsoever about the people they were bleeding dry. But far more worrying for her was that their decision to up their rates was going to affect Madge's ability to save towards her move. Her own situation was getting more intolerable on a daily basis. Dee didn't know how much more she could take.

The young assistant in one of the three bakery shops on Uppingham Road stood looking at Madge regretfully. 'I'm sure I know who yer talking about from yer description of her, sure she's a customer of ours, but I've no idea where she lives, sorry. You could try the chemist a couple of doors down,' she suggested. 'You said the person you're looking for works for an old gent somewhere around here? Well, old folks are always ailing with something, judging by my gran, maybe she goes there to have his prescriptions made up and they might keep his address on their files. Yes, love?' she said to the customer behind Madge.

A few minutes later she emerged from the pharmacy still none the wiser about Dee's address, although like the baker's assistant the pharmacist had been very helpful and she could see why Dee liked living around here. Madge looked up and down the street. Her years in Leicester had never given her cause to visit this area before and she hadn't had a clue before she arrived here today that the road was such a long busy thoroughfare. It could take her a whole day to visit all the retail outlets it offered. She'd been here two hours already and was still no closer to finding Dee.

The pavement was teeming with shoppers of all shapes and sizes. Any one of them could have the answer she was seeking.

'Excuse me?' Madge waylaid a passing young housewife, laden down with bags of groceries. 'I'm looking for a friend of mine, Diane Kirby. Do you happen to know her?'

The woman shook her head, 'No, sorry, love,' and she continued on her way.

Madge tried, again and again, but each time received the same response. Then she tried a bicycle shop and a haberdasher's, still with no luck. She was determined not to give up, though, as she meant to see Dee today. Had set her heart on it, in fact.

Two women standing behind her were greeting each other and their conversation was audible to Madge.

'Sorry I'm late, Gladys, but I got held up in the butcher's.'

'No probs, Queenie. I was late setting out today. The milkman was behind with his round and I didn't want to miss him as I needed to order extra for next week, with me sister coming to stop. Right, shall we go to the florist's first to decide on the wreath we want for Petulia's funeral, or have a cuppa?'

'Oh, cuppa, I think. Not like Petulia's going anywhere, is it?'

'Which café do you fancy, Queenie?'

'Oh, definitely Bernie's for me, Gladys. Roy uses cheap tea leaves and I like my tea strong, and he's mean with the fillings in his sandwiches. Besides, Bernie's is nearer and me sciatica is playing up something rotten today. I'm desperate for a sit down.'

A cuppa sounded good to Madge too. She was quite parched after all her fruitless searching. She followed the two women.

Bernie smiled a greeting at the three women who'd arrived before his counter. 'What can I do for you ladies? Three cuppas, is it?'

'Oh, I'm not with these two,' Madge told him. 'But I will have a cuppa, ta. That cake looks good too,' she said, eyeing up the slabs of mixed fruit, Madeira and currant in the glass container on the counter. She was hungry after leaving the house without any breakfast in her haste to be away.

He winked at her cheekily. 'Nearly as good as you.'

Madge blushed at his compliment, glad to have it confirmed

that her efforts with her appearance had paid off. It also didn't escape her notice that the two women she'd arrived with didn't like the fact that the portly, bald man behind the counter wasn't paying the same attention to them.

As if reading Madge's mind, he addressed the other two with, 'Right, my lovelies, as you got to the counter first, what's yer pleasure?' Then he said to Madge, 'If you take a seat, I'll bring your order over.'

A few minutes later he placed a cup of tea and a plate containing a generous chunk of each variety of slab cake before her, explaining, 'You didn't say which cake you preferred so I cut you off a bit of each. I'll just be charging you for one.'

Madge smiled appreciatively at him. 'Oh, ta very much.'

'Well, I'll leave you to enjoy it. If there's 'ote else I can get yer, just give us a shout.'

'Oh, you might be able to help me, as it happens. Or you might not as no one else I've asked yet has been able to. I'm looking for a friend, you see. Pretty girl, twenty-four, dark hair. Her name is Diane Kirby. She moved round here a few weeks ago, only stupid me has lost her address.'

Bernie was pulling a face and shaking his head. 'That name don't ring any bells with me, sorry, love. I get lots of girls of that description coming in here.'

Madge sighed. 'Oh, well, thanks anyway. There must be someone round here that knows of Dee. I'll just have to keep trying.'

'Dee, did you say?' Bernie asked. 'I know of a Dee. She's definitely dark and pretty and about the age you said. She moved away, though. Last week.'

Madge was staring at him. 'Moved away? Oh, no, we can't be talking about the same Dee. She would have told me if she was moving away.'

'Did she work for an old gent around here somewhere?'

Madge nodded.

'Then it's the same Dee we're talking about.'

'Oh! But I can't understand this. Dee would never move on without telling me. Er . . . do you know where this old boy lives so I can go and ask him if he's got a forwarding address for her?'

'I don't, sorry. Oh, but Calum might. Hang on a minute.' Bernie turned in the direction of the kitchen 'CAL!' he bellowed. 'Can yer come out here a minute?' Then he turned back to face Madge. 'Cal's my assistant, he's doing a stint in the kitchen. I'm training him up, see. He ain't doing too bad neither. Okay, Mrs Biddle, I'll get you another coffee in just two ticks,' he said to a customer behind Madge whose waving arm had finally caught his attention.

Calum arrived to join them, wiping his hands on his apron. 'You wanted me, Bernie?'

'You might be able to help this lady. She's looking for Dee.'

At the mention of her name Cal's smile vanished and a hurt expression crossed his face. 'Well, you know I can't help as I don't know where Dee's gone.'

'Yes, I know that, lad, but you can point the lady in the direction of where Dee worked so she can enquire there for a forwarding address. You walked her there after yer night out, didn't you?'

'Are you the young man Dee told me she was going out with on a date?' Madge asked him.

Calum nodded. 'Yes, that's right. We went out twice, in fact. I was hoping it was going to be more than that, but when I asked her out again Dee told me she wouldn't be around as she didn't like her job and had got herself another. She didn't tell me where. Anyway, I'm not quite sure of the name of the road she was living on but it's the one on the right before you cross the road over to the Troc.'

Madge looked non-plussed. 'What's the Troc?'

'Sorry, that's what all the locals call it. The Trocadero, to give it its full title. It's a dance hall. If you go out of here . . .'

'Just accompany the lady, Calum,' Bernie said to him. 'You're due a break anyway and we ain't that busy I can't cope.'

Cal smiled good-naturedly at Madge. 'I'd be happy to. If you'll just give me a minute, I'll take off my apron and put my jacket on.'

'It's very good of you to spare your staff for me,' Madge said to Bernie.

'It's my pleasure to help a lady in need.' He looked at her meaningfully. 'Besides, I'm hoping you might grace us with your presence again.'

Madge scraped back her chair and stood up. 'I might at that. Sorry I ain't got time to eat it but that cake does look good. How much do I owe you?' she said, opening her handbag to take out her purse.

Bernie placed his hand over hers to stop her. 'Settle up the next time you come in.'

Calum returned, dressed for outdoors. 'Be about fifteen minutes at the most, Bernie.'

CHAPTER
TWENTY-FOUR

As they began their journey Madge said to him, 'As a matter of interest, did you say that Dee told you she was leaving the night you took her dancing at this Troc place?'

'That's right, I did.'

Madge pulled a face. 'Odd. She came to see me around then and never mentioned about moving on to me at all. In fact, she told me how much she was loving her job and about all the new friends she'd made. And something else is niggling me . . . You said in the café just now that the night you took her dancing you asked to see her again. Only she told me you didn't ask, told her she wasn't your type.'

Calum looked taken aback. 'Dee told you *that*?'

'Definitely.'

'But that's not how it was at all! I did ask to see her again, and that's when she told me she had another job in another town. She was leaving the next day, she said, to start on the Monday.'

Madge looked grim. 'I'm getting an uneasy feeling. I've known Dee since she was born and we're good friends, close friends. In fact, I'm like a mother to her since her own passed on, and something isn't right here.'

After comparing his version of events with this woman's Calum had to agree with her. They continued the rest of the way in silence.

They turned the corner of Tennis Court Drive and walked a little way along it before Calum stopped and said, 'It's that one,' pointing to number thirty-three. Then a memory struck him and he added, 'Or, actually, it could be that one.' He was pointing at the house opposite now.

Madge was looking backwards and forwards, confused. 'Well, which was it then?'

'I didn't actually see Dee go in the first one. That night, we arrived where we're standing now and she said she'd be okay from there. She went into that garden first,' he said, pointing to it. 'Then, a couple of minutes later, I saw her come out by the garden gate, run across the road and go into the house opposite. I thought it was a strange thing for her to do at the time but she obviously had a reason for it.'

Madge heaved a thoughtful sigh. 'I can't think of one meself. Well, there's only one way to find out which house she did live in. I'll try the first one.' She smiled at Calum. 'Thanks for seeing me safely here. And thank your boss for me again, for letting you accompany me.'

'I will. Er...do you mind if I stick around? Only...well, if you do get Dee's address, I'd appreciate it if you'd give me it as I'd like to drop her a line. If she doesn't reply then...okay.'

Madge smiled at him in understanding.

An old man with a military bearing answered the door to them. Before Madge could say why she and Calum had called on him, he said, 'It's all piled around the back. I've left the side gate open. Please make sure you latch it firmly after you've finished. You'll excuse me, won't you, but I'm just listening to a programme on gardening.'

He made to shut the door but Madge stopped him with, 'We've not come about whatever it is you've piled up around the back.'

'Oh! You're not from the church, come to collect items for the jumble sale next week?'

'No. We're here to enquire after your old housekeeper. She's a friend of mine and she gave me the address of her new place only I've lost it. I was wondering if you had a forwarding address for her?'

He looked confused. 'But I've never had a housekeeper. I've got a daily, Mrs Harris, she's been with me and my wife for years.'

'I do apologise,' Madge said. 'The old gent my friend worked for must live in the house opposite. We knew it was either this one or that and happened to try yours first.'

'It's neither of them if it's an old gentleman you're looking for. Two young men in their thirties live in the house opposite.'

Madge frowned at him. 'Are you sure?'

He looked annoyed. 'There is nothing wrong with my eyesight, madam. There is a young girl living there who comes and goes, but what relationship she is to the two men I haven't a clue. They keep themselves very much to themselves. Can't say I like the look of the men either. Now, if you'll excuse me, I'm missing my programme.'

As they retraced their steps towards the gate, Madge said to Calum, 'Are you sure it was definitely this house you saw Dee going in first?'

'Positive. This house has a hedge at the front that she hid behind, and the one opposite has a lamp-post that lit her up when she ran across the road. That's how I knew it was her, otherwise I wouldn't have been able to tell. It was dark and I was a little way away at the time. But if two men live opposite, it can't be right.'

Madge pulled a face. 'This is all very strange. Dee definitely told me she worked for an old gent.'

'She told me that too.'

'But Dee's no liar. The old chap we've just spoken to has to be senile and got his wires crossed. Let's check for ourselves, shall we?'

They were just about to cross the road when the door of the house opposite opened and two men came out.

On recognising them, Madge gasped, grabbed Calum's arm to pull him to a halt, then stood with her face averted. Calum studied the men. A shorter, good-looking man was making his way to the front gate. The larger of the two suddenly stopped, patted his pocket, then said something to the other man. He turned around and made his way back into the house while the other looked on, seeming put out. Inserting a key in the front door, the large man shoved it open and bellowed out: 'Oi! I've

279

left me car keys on me dressing table. Go and fetch them – and hurry up!' A minute or so later he leaned inside, appearing to take something from someone in the hallway, then he turned away to walk down the path. The front door shut behind him. When he'd rejoined the waiting man, they both continued through the gate and proceeded to get into a car.

Ashen-faced now, Madge turned her back so she was not visible to the men. Calum was puzzled by her actions.

When she was certain the car had travelled some distance away, Madge raised her face to his. 'Oh, my God, please . . . please tell me that wasn't Dee I glimpsed at the door just now?' she begged him.

He gave a shrug. 'I couldn't see who came to the door, the big man was blocking my view. But you think it was Dee?'

'I'm not sure, I only caught a glimpse, but if it's not her then it's someone very similar. But it can't be! My Dee can't be tangled up with those two, she just can't . . .'

Calum looked quizzically at her. 'You know those men then?'

Madge nodded grimly. 'Oh, I know them all right.'

'So do I. Well, not personally, just by sight. They come in once a week to see my boss Bernie. Not exactly a friendly pair, I have to say, but who my boss chooses for his acquaintances is none of my business.'

Madge eyed him quizzically. 'Once a week they visit, you say? And stay . . . what? Just a couple of minutes?'

He nodded.

'Then, believe me, they aren't friends of his,' Madge said darkly.

Calum looked surprised for a moment then the penny dropped. 'You mean, they're . . .'

'I don't mean anything,' she cut in. If Bernie wanted his employee to know he was being fleeced by those two low-lifes who had just driven away, it was up to him to tell Calum. 'Come on, I need to make sure the woman I saw at the door just now wasn't Dee.' Then a memory struck her and she knew what had been niggling at her all along. As Dee was leaving her house last time she had said she had to get back as 'they' would be wanting their tea. A dreadful feeling of foreboding flooded through Madge. She only hoped she was proved wrong.

Several moments later three people stared at each other in shock.

It was Dee who found her voice first. Panic-stricken, she cried, 'Oh, my God, what are you both doing here?'

'Looks like it's a good job we are,' Madge returned, mortified by the sight of her injuries. 'Did those two bastards do this to you?' she demanded.

Dee gulped. 'No one did anything to me. I . . . I . . . fell down the stairs.'

Calum too was appalled by the state of Dee; at the thought of someone hurting this lovely woman before him. 'Don't treat us like idiots,' he exploded. 'Someone has given you a right pasting. Who's responsible? They won't do it again, believe me.'

Dee was physically quaking, terrified that the Monkses would come back for some reason and find Madge and Calum on their doorstep. She had no idea what they would do then. They could think she'd summoned help to escape their clutches while they were out. Both Madge and Calum could end up in the same state she was in now, or worse. She had to get rid of them. 'Look, you'll have to excuse me. I'm . . . I'm reading to my boss and he's waiting for me. I'll come and see you, Aunty Madge, soon, I promise. We'll have a good catch up then.'

'You're no more reading to an old gent or working for him than pigs fly, Dee! Stop this act right now,' Madge cried.

For a fleeting moment Dee looked ashamed that her lie had been detected but then the seriousness of the situation flooded back to her. 'Okay, so I lied to you. I knew you'd try and stop me working for two men and living with them as well, me being a young woman.'

'That's not the reason I would have tried to stop you working for those two had you been honest with me, Dee. They aren't good people, believe me. I know things about them you won't be aware of. Now, if you think I'm leaving you here at the mercy of the Monks brothers, then you've got another think coming. Go and pack your things, I'm taking you home with me,' ordered Madge.

Without thinking Dee blurted, 'I can't! I can't leave here until . . . until . . .' She realised what she was about to say and snapped her mouth shut.

'Can't leave here until what, Dee?'

'Nothing,' she insisted. 'What I meant to say was . . . I need this job and I'm not leaving until I'm ready to.'

'Dee, for God's sake, you can't need it that badly. They're bad men. How many times do I need to say it until you believe me?'

An urgent desire for them to leave was filling Dee, but also she desperately wanted to do Madge's bidding. How easy it would be to grab her hand and run away from here with her, but despite what her refusal was costing her she couldn't put Madge's life in jeopardy. 'No, they're not bad to me. They treat me fine,' Dee cried.

Madge looked astounded. 'Fine! Look at you, Dee, do you call that treating you fine?'

Calum spoke up then. 'Look, Dee, I don't know these men like your aunty does, and I only met her a short while ago, but she doesn't seem to me the sort to be lying just for the fun of it.'

Madge was shaking her head, astonished. 'What have they done to you, Dee? Look, please listen . . .'

'No, Aunty Madge, *you* listen to me. Just accept that I'm happy with my life the way it is. You've plans for your own, concentrate on those. Please, Aunty Madge, concentrate on getting the money saved so you can move away. Now, both of you, just go away and leave me alone!'

Before they could stop her, Dee had stepped back inside and shut the door on them.

They stood staring at it.

'I can't . . . I can't understand this,' Madge said in a puzzled way. 'That woman we saw just now wasn't the Dee I know. My Dee would never willingly work for those two . . . two . . . But that's it! She *can't* be working willingly. They've got to be holding her to it somehow. There can't be any other reason why she wouldn't come with us after what I just told her.' She gnawed her bottom lip anxiously. 'What possible hold could they have on her? What could she have done that they could use to keep her here? Dee's never hurt a fly in her life, to my knowledge.' Tears of distress pricked her eyes. 'And they're battering her too,' she said. She grabbed Calum's arm, squeezing it hard. 'I can't leave her here. We've got to force her to see sense and come with us. Drag her out of here, if we have to.'

She made to bang on the door but he caught her arm. 'I don't want to leave her here any more than you do. We could make her come with us, I could use my brute strength to do that, no problem, but if those men are as bad as you say we don't know how they'll react when they come home and find her gone. We could be putting her in danger by not thinking this through properly.'

'You saw the state she was in, she's in danger now,' Madge cried. Her face crumpled. 'Oh, God, what are we going to do?' she implored him. 'We've got to get her away from here. We've got to!'

Calum scraped his hand through his hair. 'Look, let's go back to Bernie's café and put our heads together. We'll work out a proper plan of action there. If we're basically going to kidnap her, we need a safe place to take her. Somewhere those two won't know about when they come looking for her. Maybe Bernie can help us there. I'm sure he'd let us hide her in his flat until we can make proper plans to get her safely away.' Calum grabbed Madge's arm. 'Come on,' he urged.

As Madge and Calum hurried off, inside the house Dee was sitting at the kitchen table with her head buried in her hands, quietly sobbing.

Bernie was relieved when Calum returned as the café was getting busy and he was finding it hard to cope on his own. He was even more pleased to see his assistant had brought back the woman he'd gone off with. It was a long time since one had taken Bernie's fancy and she'd certainly taken it. He smiled broadly at her in greeting as Calum sat her down at a vacant table, placed a hand on her shoulder and said something to her. It was only then that the fact she was crying registered with

Bernie. Leaving the customer he was in the middle of serving, he raised the counter flap and went to join Calum and Madge.

'What's wrong, Cal?' he demanded. 'Is it summat to do with Dee? Summat you found out about her at her last place of work?'

'Yes, it is.'

Bernie looked at the distressed Madge then back to Calum, his face worried. 'It's serious, ain't it? She's . . . not had an accident? Not dead or 'ote, is she?'

'No,' Calum insisted. 'But we think she's in serious trouble, Bernie.'

He looked shocked. 'Dee, in serious trouble? What kind of trouble?'

'Two bastards forcing her against her will to work for them, that kind of serious trouble,' Madge erupted, sniffing back tears. 'They've got to be doing it or why she insists on staying with them makes no sense. *And* they've beaten her up. You should see the state she's in! I'll swing for those monsters, so I will. If I could get hold of a gun, I'd have no hesitation in blasting them both to Kingdom Come.'

Bernie gawped at her. 'Eh? Er . . . just who are these blokes?'

Calum looked at him meaningfully. 'The same two who come in and see you once a week.'

He looked amazed for a moment before his round face darkened with anger. 'Why ain't I surprised it's those two we're talking about?' He pulled out a chair from beside Madge and sat down on it, looking at her earnestly. 'Don't worry, we'll get Dee away from them, you have my word.' Then he stood up again and said to Calum, 'Go up to my flat and fetch down me bottle of whisky. The lady certainly looks like she needs a good dollop and I think I do too, for that matter, after hearing this. I'll clear the café so we can sit down uninterrupted and decide what we're going to do.'

A while later, the café empty of all but the three of them, Bernie leaned back in his chair. He clasped his hands over his stomach and said, 'Well, that's settled then. When we go back, if there's no sign of the car we go in and fetch Dee out. If they've returned, we watch the house until we see them go out again and then we go in and make her come with us, kidnap her if necessary, and bring her back to my flat. What then?'

'What do you mean, what then?' Madge asked.

'Well, where do yer plan for her to go? She can't stay in Leicester, that's for sure. It ain't the size of Birmingham or London to hide away in. Sooner or later their paths would cross and . . .'

'I'll take her to Earl Shilton with me,' Madge cut in. 'I was planning to move there, I'll bring me plans forward. Only . . .'

'Only what?' Calum asked.

'Well, I ain't exactly got the money to fund it yet. I've just about got enough to cover the train fare for both of us and a couple of nights' lodging . . .'

'Well, I can help you there,' said Bernie. 'Call it a loan, you can pay me back later.'

'That's very good of you,' Madge said gratefully. 'I don't usually like being indebted to anyone, but in this case I've no hesitation. You can trust me to pay it back. So, we off then?' she urged, desperate to get Dee back.

Calum made to push back his chair but saw the thoughtful expression on Bernie's face and asked, 'Do you see any problem with our plan, Bernie?'

'No. So long as we make sure that pair are well away before we go in, I don't. I've been on the receiving end of that thug's punches and I wouldn't want to be again, not if I can avoid it. It's just, another thought crossed me mind. This might be the chance for us to really get the better of those two . . .'

'What do you mean?' queried Madge.

'What I mean is, we should put our heads together and come up with a plan for getting them out of everybody's hair, once and for all. Or at least for a very long time.' Bernie looked at her meaningfully. 'Yours and mine in particular.' He leaned over and patted Madge's hand. 'I ain't stupid. I take it they're doing to you what they are to me, and that's how you know this pair?'

She avoided his eyes and nodded.

'But how can we do that?' Calum asked.

'Short of murdering them, I can't see how we can do anything meself,' put in Madge.

Then Calum said thoughtfully, 'You two can't be the only people they're taking money off, judging by the house they live in and the car we saw them drive off in. Their clothes, too. So why don't we suss out all the others and persuade them to band together, go to the police and get them to deal with this?'

'That'll take time and we ain't got any,' snapped Madge.

'Madge is right,' agreed Bernie. 'We need to get Dee out of there today. Anyway, I've already tried what you suggested, Cal, but the ones I sussed out were all too scared of the repercussions if the police couldn't pin anything on them. I've no proof I'm being forced to hand over money weekly, see. The Monkses could tell the police it's a loan I'm paying back, and how could I prove it's not? I can't say as I blame the others for being scared either. It's no joke having a gun stuck up yer nose, with the threat to blow yer head off if yer don't do as yer told.

'It's a pity we don't know the time and place of their next extortion, then we could have the police lying in wait to witness it. The only way we could bring that about, though, is if they told us and they ain't likely to, are they?' His face suddenly lit up beacon-like. 'Oh!' he exclaimed.

'What?' Madge urged him.

'Have you thought of something?' Calum demanded.

Bernie looked smug. 'I might have. I just might at that.'

'Well?' said Madge.

'Yes, come on, Bernie, spit it out.'

'Just give me a minute to think this through and then I'll tell yer.'

Madge and Calum spent a very irritating few minutes until finally Bernie sat forward, rested his arms on the table and said, 'Oh, the nights I've lain awake, trying to fathom a suitable payback for that pair and never thought I'd come up with something like this. Pure justice, and no less than they deserve in my book.'

'Well, I'm all for justice for them two,' Madge said eagerly. Then added sharply, 'But that's only if we can do it today. I ain't

286

prepared to leave Dee in that house a minute longer than I have to. Come on, spill the beans.'

Bernie looked at them each in turn before he said, 'We're going to set them up.'

'Set them up? For what?' Calum asked.

'Armed robbery.'

Calum gawped. 'Have you gone mad, Bernie?'

'How on earth are we going to do that?' Madge exclaimed.

Bernie grinned. 'Easy. If they think there's money to be had, they'll come running, even if it's just from curiosity. We shove a note through their door with an offer that'll rouse their interest but say that to learn more they have to be here at eight o'clock on the dot. Nice and dark then, see. When they arrive they'll find the door's been broken open and they won't be able to resist taking a gander inside. It's only human nature. Basically we're all nosey. The place is in darkness but they'll see a light shining from my office. When they come in, they'll find a man bound, gagged and unconscious. Or it'll appear he's unconscious. A gun on my desk, the safe ajar with the key in the lock, and my week's takings visible inside. As soon as we see them arriving, we tip off the police that we suspect a burglary is taking place here – and Bob's yer uncle! Fifteen to twenty years for armed robbery.'

'Phew!' mouthed Calum. 'Sounds so simple. But just a couple of problems that strike me . . .'

'Yeah, me too,' said Madge.

'Fire away,' said Bernie.

'Where are we going to get a bound, gagged and unconscious man?' asked Calum.

'I was going to ask that,' agreed Madge.

'You're looking at him,' Bernie told them. 'Then I can watch the bastards meet their doom and be able to give you a blow-by-blow account, won't I?'

'Sooner you than me,' said Madge. 'You do realise what will happen if those two get an inkling you're faking, Bernie?'

'They won't get an inkling, I can assure you. I'll stop breathing if it means we can send that pair down.'

Madge still looked worried. 'They might be some things, Bernie, but those two ain't stupid . . . well, the big ugly one might not be the full shilling but the other certainly is. When Lennie looks back on it, he's bound to twig you was behind the set up, and when they get out of prison they'll come looking for you.'

'I'm well aware of that, Madge. If the price I have to pay is that I sell up and move away from here, then so be it.'

'But where are we supposed to get a gun from?' Calum asked him.

'I was going to ask that too,' said Madge, put out he'd stolen her thunder again.

Bernie looked smug. 'I know just where I can get one. From the very sods who stuck it in my face a few weeks back after I dared tell them to sling their hook.'

Calum was looking at him, both astounded and impressed. 'You mean, you're going to steal their own gun in order to entrap them?'

Bernie winked at him. 'You've got it, mate. With only their fingerprints on it. How will they explain away that?'

'How are you going to steal it off them?' Madge asked.

'A gun ain't the sort of thing you carry around unless you've reason to believe you might need it and I'm hoping that when I pay a visit to their house very shortly they ain't took it out with them today. Hopefully, they'll be back home when I go in and then I'll know it's on the premises. And if it is, I'll find it, believe me. No hiding place is safe from me. People put things in the most obvious places, you know.'

'So you haven't always been a café-owner, I take it, Bernie?' said Madge, looking at him knowingly. Her face clouded over then. 'I don't mean to doubt your abilities, but what if you can't find it?'

He leaned over and patted her hand. 'I know you want to go and get Dee out of there right this minute, we all do, but if we can pull this off, it'll be worth it. Then, wherever you two eventually land up, you won't be looking over yer shoulder all the time, wondering if those two are about to pounce. You have my promise, Madge, that one way or another Dee will be safely back with you in my flat tonight. Just give me the chance to get inside, see if I can find that gun. If not, we'll carry out the same plan but without it. It'll still mean they go away for robbery, just not for quite as long as we'd have liked, that's all. So, are we all agreed on going ahead with this?'

'I never thought I'd agree to do anything criminal, but in this case I'm game,' said Calum resolutely.

'Me too,' said Madge. 'I just wish I could be there to see their faces when the police arrive. Right, what's my part in all this?'

CHAPTER TWENTY-FIVE

'Oh, I'm so glad to see yer. Did you get it or not?' Madge demanded of Bernie as soon as he returned from his outing. She and Calum had been pacing the floor since he'd left them over an hour ago to tackle his mission, during which time their anxiety had reached fever pitch. 'You've been gone so long we was beginning to think . . . Well, anyway, yer back now. So?'

Conscious that both Madge and Calum were looking at him expectantly, with one gloved hand Bernie put down the canvas pouch containing the tools of his past trade and with the other pulled something out of his pocket, which he proudly displayed. 'Piece of cake,' he told them.

He wasn't being entirely honest as he'd had a couple of very scary moments. On arriving at the Monkses' abode, he'd noted that no car was parked outside so obviously the brothers weren't home. But that didn't mean to say no one else was. Discreetly, he'd checked through the windows for signs of Dee and had seen her through the kitchen one, putting away some shopping. As soon as he saw her go into the pantry, he had seized his chance to slip in through the back door and head upstairs. He was of the firm opinion, from his wealth of past experience, that people were creatures of habit and always kept precious items in their bedrooms. He had no reason to believe that the Monkses would be any different. It was just a case of finding which bedroom.

Upstairs several rooms faced him. To his annoyance the first one he tried was locked. Before he used his tools to open it, and mindful that time was precious, he decided to try the others first. The room next-door wasn't locked. Slipping inside and shutting the door behind him, he looked around. The room was obviously not occupied but that didn't mean to say the gun wasn't in here somewhere. He deftly began to search. All the drawers in the chest proved to be empty and so did the wardrobe. There were no secret hiding places he could find. What he sought was clearly not kept in here.

Flashing a look around to make sure nothing seemed amiss, he eased open the door to check the coast was clear and proceeded along the hallway. The next room was occupied and its owner was not a tidy person. A pile of clothes lay strewn on the floor, drawers in the chest were hanging out, clothes spilling from them, wardrobe doors thrown wide. The bed was unmade. He had his work cut out in here. He decided to try the chest-of-drawers first. He'd lost count of the number of times during his career as a burglar he'd found precious items in underwear drawers.

Just as he was making his way over to it the sound of footsteps on the stairs reached his ears. As a precaution, thankfully, as quick as lightning he dived under the bed just as the door opened and someone entered. As no one else was in the house it had to be Dee.

Bernie held his breath as he heard her moving around. It was obvious she was tidying up after the messy occupant. He just willed her to hurry up so he could get on with what he had come here for. He was also panic-stricken that she would have a reason to look under the bed and discover him, with no idea how he'd explain himself to her. Then, to his amazement, as he lay looking up at the bedsprings above his head he saw something lodged between it and the mattress, wrapped in what looked to him like a pair of underpants. His heart leapt. He knew he'd found what he'd come for and only just stopped himself from crying out, Eureka!

His excruciating wait lasted over fifteen minutes. Finally he heard the bedroom door click shut, announcing Dee's departure. Without further ado he scrambled out from his hiding place, lifted up the mattress and put the gun in his pocket. He was careful to smooth the rumpled covers of the bed back into place.

At the door he once again checked the coast was clear then slipped out. He had just crept to the head of the stairs to look down over the banister and make sure the hall below was clear when he heard a key being inserted into the front door. The two men he was out to bring to task for their crimes walked in.

'Shit!' Bernie hissed under his breath and stepped back to hide round the wall. Could they not have returned five minutes later?

He heard a voice call out commandingly, 'Coffee, in the lounge. Now.'

Bernie's temper rose at the way Dee was being addressed, but hopefully in just a matter of hours she would never have to face this sort of treatment again. Provided, that was, he could get out of here unobserved with his prize.

From his hiding place he heard the radio commentary on a football match which signalled to him that both men were now in the lounge. Gingerly, he stepped forward far enough to poke his head over the top of the banister and look down. The part of the hallway he was able to observe was empty. He spotted a coatstand just by the front door, holding garments. Tentatively, he took several steps down the stairs then poked his head around them to see Dee busy in the kitchen. He was glad that the door to the lounge was partly closed.

He tiptoed down the rest of the stairs and hid behind the coatstand. Carefully he parted the coats just enough to give him a view down the hall to the kitchen. Several minutes passed, his heart thumping madly meantime, until he saw Dee come out of the kitchen carrying a tray. He stopped himself from gasping in shock when he saw her injuries, fighting a strong compulsion to give those two low-lifes a taste of their own medicine right now. No wonder Madge and Calum were desperate to get Dee away from here.

As soon as he saw her disappear into the lounge, he came out from his hiding place and tiptoed to the door by which she'd just entered, peeking through the crack in the hinged side. Both men were lounging in armchairs with their back to the door, Dee busy offloading items from the tray on to a coffee table in front of them. Bernie continued on his way into the kitchen where he quietly let himself out the way he'd come in. He didn't let out a sigh of relief until he was well on his way down the road. Then a thought struck and he stopped abruptly to let out a groan. He'd forgotten to post his carefully prepared note through the letter-box.

'Shit!' he hissed under his breath for the second time in less than twenty minutes. His luck had held so far but he dare not chance it any further. He took a hurried glance around his surroundings. Three girls further down the street were playing French skipping. A young boy of about twelve was riding his bike in Bernie's direction. As he made to pass, Bernie signalled him to stop. 'How would you like to make a shilling?' he asked.

The boy looked warily at Bernie and in a very posh voice replied, 'Mother says I shouldn't talk to strangers.' He made to ride off but Bernie stalled him by standing in front of his bike. 'Good for yer mam, son. You never know these days who's about.' He wondered if that mother had any idea that two men of the sort she'd warned her son about were living on this very street. 'I'm not a stranger exactly. I'm yer mother's long-lost brother's uncle. Only we ain't met personally because . . . well, we just haven't. She won't mind you talking to me, honest. Tell her Uncle Bernard sends his love. Now put this note through that door of the house with the black car sitting out front, and I'll give you two bob. Have we got a deal?'

The boy looked thoughtfully at him for a second before snatching the note off Bernie with one hand and holding out his other for payment.

Bernie fished in his pocket and slapped a florin into his hand. 'Make sure you get the right house, son.' Then he watched as the lad rode off, and didn't continue on his way until he was certain the boy had completed the task.

'Did you see Dee?' Madge asked now.

Bernie nodded. 'The sooner we get her out of there, the better. Right, we've things to do.'

Back in the Monkses' abode, not sharing the same enthusiasm for football as his brother, Leonard was leaving the lounge to take the bath he'd ordered Dee to run for him. As he turned up the stairs he caught sight of something sticking through the letterbox and automatically went over to retrieve it. It was addressed to Mr Monks. Not stopping to consider whether it could in fact be personal mail for his brother, Leonard slit it open and took out the folded piece of paper inside. He frowned as he read it.

Interested in making an easy five hundred pounds? I know how but I can't do it alone. I'll be at the Uppingham Road Café at eight. A minute past and I'll know you're not interested.

It wasn't signed.

Lennie screwed up his face thoughtfully. Interested in making five hundred smackers easily? Of course he was. But he and his brother worked alone. This note intimated that whoever had sent it usually did too. A slow smile spread over his face. He and Ronnie would go along, find out the deal, then cut whoever it was out and take all the prize for themselves. Whistling to himself, Leonard went up to take his bath.

At a quarter to eight, inside his office, Bernie snapped at Calum, 'Not so tight, you'll cut off me circulation.'

'Well, you want this to look a proper job in case they check, don't you?' he snapped back.

'Will you get a move on?' Madge erupted. 'What if they happen to arrive early?'

'She's right, Cal,' Bernie anxiously agreed. Then he said to Madge, 'You should be on yer way to the Monkses' by now, to watch for when they leave. As soon as they do, you go in and get Dee.'

Madge grabbed her coat and started pulling it on.

'That's done,' said Calum to Bernie.

Arms secured tightly behind his back, Bernie checked the room. 'Right, key's in the safe and the door is open, showing what's inside. Gun's in view on me desk. Lock on the outside door is broken. Just make sure it's pulled to when you leave, you two. All lights except me lamp in here are to be off. Okay, all that remains is for you to give me a good one, Cal.'

Cal stared at him non-plussed. 'A good what?'

'Thump, wadda you think? I'm supposed to be unconscious and I need to show visible signs of why.'

Calum looked uncomfortable. Several times in the past the need had arisen for him to defend himself and he'd proved a worthy opponent. But he'd never been called upon to cause harm to someone he liked, no matter what the necessity. 'Oh, er . . . okay.' He clenched his fist, reared back his arm and bought it forward to punch Bernie on the chin.

Bernie gave a disdainful tut. 'That was no more than a tickle, Cal. You'll have to do better than that if I'm to look convincing. Yer've got to thump me hard enough to cause bruising at least.'

Having finished buttoning her coat, and extremely conscious that time was running out, Madge erupted, 'Oh, for God's sake, if you want a good job doing, you're best asking a woman.' Grabbing the lamp off the desk, with the heavy base aimed in Bernie's direction, she swung back her arm and with all the force she could summon, brought it down on his chin.

As he went down like a pack of cards collapsing, Madge put the lamp back on the desk while urging a startled Calum, 'Come on, let's get out of here!'

As Madge was making her way on foot towards the Monkses' residence and Calum was secreting himself in a shop doorway opposite the café, in order to hurry for the telephone box as soon as he saw the Monkses arrive, Lennie was issuing orders to his brother as he started the engine of their car. 'Remember, when we get there, we listen to what the man has to say. If there's any talking to be done, I do it, got that?'

'Who is this man?' Ronnie asked.

'I don't care so long as I get his plan to make this easy money.'

'What if he won't tell us, Lennie?'

He sighed. 'Then you do what you're good at and make him tell us. You did bring the gun, just in case we need to let him see we ain't the types to be messed with, like I told you?'

Ronnie gulped. He would have done if he could have found it. He felt positive he'd replaced it in its usual hiding place under the mattress after the last time he'd needed to take it out with them, but it hadn't been there when he had looked just before they left the house. A frenzied search of his room hadn't revealed it. He hadn't had time for a more thorough search as from downstairs Lennie had been shouting to him to hurry before they missed their appointment. That gun was a useful persuasive tool, had in fact played a big part in upping their income since they'd discovered it, and Lennie would see red if he found out it had been carelessly mislaid. Ronnie just prayed it wasn't required tonight and then his brother need never find out.

He realised Lennie was talking to him. 'Eh?' he said.

'Fucking hell, Ron, what's up with you?' Lennie snapped back. 'You're staring out the window like a village idiot. You're usually the first out of the house when we've something on like this. If we miss out on this chance to make some easy brass I shan't be happy, believe me. Now, get a move on.'

Ronnie revved the engine into life.

Back inside the house, totally unaware of the events happening around her, Dee was rushing around to complete her tasks so she could get to her room and barricade herself inside before she risked a repetition of last night.

Outside the café, Ronnie drew the car to a halt and he and Lennie got out.

'Place looks shut to me,' said Ronnie. He lumbered across and peered through the window. 'It's deserted but there's a light on through the back, Len.' He went over to the door. As his paw-like hand came into contact with the knob, the door swung open. He turned to look at Lennie who had now joined him. 'The man who wrote to you must be the café-owner. He's waiting in the back room for us, he's left the door open.'

Lennie looked thoughtful. If Ronnie was right then maybe this plan of the café-owner's was a bargaining tool for him to use by way of excusing himself from his weekly payments. He smirked. If that was the case then the café-owner had another think coming. Lennie would play him along, and once his plan became clear he would let him know that once a contributor to the Monkses' funds, always a contributor. 'Well, let's not keep him waiting,' he said.

Back at the house, Dee was just finishing off the drying up when the front door knocker was banged urgently. Tradesmen usually called during the day; never once since she had been here had anyone called at night. The door knocker pounded again and she heard a voice yell out, 'Dee, it's me, Madge. Open the door.'

Madge! She dropped her drying cloth and ran to open the door.

Before Dee could say anything, Madge had pushed past her and on into the hallway. She spun round to face her and ordered, 'Go up and pack your things. Now! Go on. We don't want to be here if the police turn up to search this place in case they think you're in league with them.'

Dee was gazing at her, mystified.

Madge grabbed hold of her shoulders. 'Listen, Dee, those two bastards are never going to hurt you again, you hear? They're going away for a very long time, believe me.'

Dee felt her legs buckle and her head start swimming. She couldn't believe what she was hearing. 'You . . . you mean that, Aunty Madge? You really mean that? The police have got something on them that will put them away for a very long time?'

'By now they should have.'

'Promise me this isn't just a lie to get me out of here while they're out, Aunty Madge?'

Madge looked her in the eye. 'I promise, Dee. You'll be able to walk the streets freely with no worry they're suddenly going to jump out on you. Now I'll tell you all the whys and wherefores when I get you safely back to Bernie's. Not forgetting I've plenty to ask you too.'

'Bernie's?' she queried. 'What's he got . . .'

'Dee, please, this isn't the time. Now, lead the way to your room and I'll give you a hand.'

In less than five minutes, case in hand, Dee was running back down the attic stairs with Madge behind her. She was just about to pass by Lennie's bedroom door when a thought struck her. She stopped abruptly, Madge almost colliding with her. Spinning round, Dee asked, 'This is definitely not a lie you're telling, to get me to leave?'

'Dee, for God's sake! How many times do you want me to promise you it's not?'

'Right, then I need a crowbar or something like that. There's a coal hammer in the shed, that'll do.'

It was Madge's turn to look stupefied. 'What! Whatever do you want something like that for?'

Dee grinned. 'You'll see.'

Entering the café, Ronnie went ahead of Lennie as he always did in situations that could potentially prove dangerous. As he arrived in the office he was surprised to see the café-owner seemingly unconscious at his desk. It was even more surprising to see on the desk what looked like his own pistol. Automatically he picked it up and began examining it.

Having heard no shouts or sounds of a scuffle and satisfied he was in no danger himself, Lennie arrived in the office then. He was taken aback to see Bernie apparently out for the count, but even more so to see his brother brandishing the pistol.

'What the hell did you knock him out for, Ronnie?' he demanded angrily 'And how the hell did you tie him up so quickly?'

'Eh? But I didn't. He was like that when I came in.' Ronnie was far more interested in what he was holding in his hand and still staring at it. This was definitely their pistol, but how on earth had it come to be here?

Lennie was just about to ask him why he was looking at the gun like a blithering idiot when to his own surprise he spotted the open safe, the lamplight from the desk illuminating a bundle of notes inside. His eyes lit up. Automatically he went across to it, bent down and picked up the bundle of notes. Then he looked at his brother, puzzled. 'There was no one else in here when you first came in?'

Still trying to figure out how their gun had come to be here, Ronnie stared at him blankly. 'Eh? Oh, no, I didn't see anyone.'

Lennie's face screwed up thoughtfully. 'Well, it looks to me like we've disturbed a burglary. But if that's so, where did the burglar go? There's no door in here, and if he'd come out to take the back way when he heard us come in, we'd have seen him. This don't bloody well make sense . . .' Then the awful truth struck him like a thunderbolt. 'Oh, fuck, Ronnie! We've been set . . .'

'I'd put the gun down, sir, if I was you.'

Both Lennie and Ronnie spun round to see two police constables and two plain-clothes men standing just inside the doorway.

Ronnie couldn't believe this was happening.

Lennie's eyes darted wildly and he blurted out, 'Er . . . look, officer, this isn't what you think.'

Detective Inspector Upton smiled at him. 'I've lost count of the number of times I've heard that one, sir.'

CHAPTER TWENTY-SIX

Hurrying past the café entrance on the way to Bernie's flat, Madge was relieved to see the place in total darkness and the door padlocked. She sincerely hoped this was a sign that their plan had gone well. Arriving at the door to the flat, she and Dee found it on the latch and let themselves inside. Madge discovered a scribbled note on the kitchen table from Calum, saying that their plan had gone as they'd hoped and that he'd taken Bernie to the hospital. They'd explain all when they got back. On reading it she was tremendously relieved they had achieved what they'd set out to do and couldn't wait to get a blow-by-blow account of exactly what had happened. But she was also worried witless as to why Bernie needed hospital treatment. She thrust the note into her pocket as she felt there was no point in worrying Dee unnecessarily about Bernie until she herself knew what the score was there. But she could deliver the other bit of news the note gave her.

'To put your mind at rest, those two are definitely safely under lock and key and won't be seeing outside any prison walls for a hell of a long time. Now, it looks like we've the place to ourselves for a bit as the boys have had to go out. We can talk in peace.'

'Boys?' Dee queried.

'Calum and Bernie.'

'Calum? He's been involved . . .'

Madge put up a warning hand. 'You'll get your chance to ask questions after I've put mine. I'm older than you. Now put down your bags and sit yourself at the table while I find out what Bernie has by way of something medicinal. I think we both need a large dose.'

Several moments later, both of them with a glass of whisky in front of them, Madge said, 'I'm waiting, Dee.'

She took a deep breath. 'I'd never voluntarily have worked for those . . . those . . . I can't even find the words to describe them, Aunty Madge. I hate them. I never knew what proper hatred was before I met them. They . . . oh, Aunty Madge, they're the reason my mother is dead.'

Madge's mouth fell open in shock. 'What do you mean? They killed Del?'

'As good as, from what they told me. She wouldn't meet their demands so they decided to take the money from her. She didn't fall over because she was drunk, like the police thought. It was Ronnie who hit her so hard she fell and knocked herself unconscious when she tried to stop him from taking her money off her. But they as good as killed her by leaving her lying in an alley in that bitter weather.'

'Oh, my God,' Madge gasped.

'Ronnie was waiting for me back home the night after Mam's funeral, when I went ahead while you fetched your stuff.' Dee didn't feel it necessary to tell Madge what he did to her to get her back to their house so they could inform her of their plans. The sight of the injuries she was suffering now had distressed Madge enough. 'He made me go with him to the house so Lennie could tell me about my new job, working for them. That was when Ronnie bragged to me about what he'd done to my mother. But there were no witnesses, of course, so it was my word against his if I went to the police. And, besides, Ronnie had an alibi – his brother. They told me all this so I was fully aware what they were capable of if I didn't do what I was told.'

'But . . . I can't understand why, if you knew what part they'd played in Del's death, you still worked for them?' Madge asked.

Dee took another deep breath before saying softly, 'Because they threatened me with what they would do to you if I didn't work off Mam's debt to them in the way they'd decided. I couldn't bear the thought of you coming to any harm so I had no choice but to go along with it.'

There were tears of distress in Madge's eyes. Her bottom lip trembling, she uttered, 'Oh, lovey, I knew you cared for me but I never realised you'd be prepared to suffer what those two dished out to you, for my sake.'

Dee laid her hand on top of Madge's, looking at her fondly. 'I'd do anything for you, Aunty Madge. You've always been there for me. In truth, you've always been far more of a mother to me than my own was. I couldn't bear the thought of any harm coming to you.'

'So that's why you were so desperate to get me to make up with my family? With me safely out of Leicester, you could make your escape from them, couldn't you?'

'That was the idea. Go as far away as possible, somewhere they'd never happen upon me.'

Madge heaved a sigh. 'So you were prepared to spend the rest of yer life in hiding from them, just to protect me?'

'As I said, I'd do anything for you. And you've proved you'd do anything for me by what you did tonight.'

Madge smiled. 'I had a little help with that. I don't know how I'll ever thank Bernie and Calum for the part they played in bringing you safely back to me.' Her face looked deeply saddened then as she asked, 'Why did they feel the need to give you such a thrashing, Dee?'

Again she couldn't bring herself to tell Madge the real reason for Ronnie's attack on her as it would distress her even more than she was already. 'I really did fall down the stairs,' she lied. Then she scraped her hands through her hair, sighing heavily, her face drawn. 'I can't believe this is all over. It's been a living nightmare. I was beginning to think I'd never get away, that they'd keep me skivvying for them forever. I can't tell you how much I missed you, Aunty Madge. I felt so lonely and isolated, not having you to turn to. It's made me appreciate you so much more.'

Madge swallowed back a lump in her throat. 'Oh, lovey, if it's any consolation, I felt like I'd lost half of meself, not having you around. If I'd had any inkling whatsoever what you were really going through . . . but then, you know what I would have done and that's why you never told me. Anyway, yer safe now, that's all that matters.'

Dee looked worried. 'Do you think Susan will still want to be my friend?'

'Susan? Oh, the young girl you used to work with at Cleanrite who's at Lea's now. Of course she will,' Madge said with conviction. 'Who wouldn't want to be your friend, Dee? From what you told me about her she sounded like a nice girl. I'm sure she'll be absolutely gobsmacked when she hears what happened to keep you from your new job.'

'I do hope so. She's the sort of friend I've always longed for, Aunty Madge.' Dee looked thoughtful. 'I suppose if the Monkses hadn't decided to make me their lackey to pay back what they felt my mam owed them, they'd still be at liberty, terrorising people into handing over money, so in a way this has all been worth it.'

'Mmm, well, I suppose that's one way of looking at it,' Madge mused. 'I expect there'll be a lot of people cheering when they read about this in the newspaper.'

'Yes, and won't it be just great to be able to give those people some of their money back, because we took all that cash from Lennie's drawer with us, along with the book containing all those names. That includes you, Aunty Madge, and Bernie too.'

'I couldn't think for the life of me why you demanded a crowbar in the middle of our escape. I must say, I couldn't believe my eyes when you showed me all that money in the false-bottomed drawer. Anyway, I can't say I couldn't do with my share of it back, and I'm sure Bernie won't say no to his either, or all the rest. What about you, Dee?'

She looked puzzled. 'What about me?'

'Well, you're due your share. I mean, I know Della wasn't paying them but you've worked for those two for weeks for virtually nothing. You're due your wages at least.'

'That money brought a lot of people into hardship, Aunty Madge, and I want no part of it,' Dee said resolutely. 'It's to be shared equally amongst all the people named in the book.'

'Well, I personally think you should have some, but if that's your decision then I must abide by it. Anyway, thank God you remembered about it before we left the house and the police found it. The Monkses would only have lied about how they got it. I'm sure Leonard wouldn't have been stuck for a plausible excuse,' Madge added ruefully. 'The police would have had no choice but to believe him and then it would all have been theirs to reclaim when they're finally released from prison.' She gave a satisfied grin. 'Well, now we know they'll come out without a penny, just as they deserve.'

'Not without a penny,' Dee told her. 'They still have the house, remember, so they've still profited from their crimes and there's nothing we can do about that.'

Madge grinned again. 'We might not be able to, but Mother Nature can most certainly help, along with a little assistance from homeless types once word spreads there's a vacant property going begging, owners not likely to materialise for a good few years. Lovey, by the time those two are released, that house will have fallen into rack and ruin and hardly be worth anything.'

Dee smiled too. 'That's good to know.' She eyed Madge eagerly. 'So, my turn to have my questions answered now.'

A few minutes later she gasped, 'You set them up for armed robbery!'

Madge laughed. 'That was Calum's and my reaction when Bernie told us of his plan.'

Just then the outer door was heard to open and seconds later Bernie came in followed by Calum.

'Now there's a sight for sore eyes,' Bernie said, smiling in delight to see Dee sitting at his table. He looked at Madge then. 'Talking of sore . . . Did yer have to whack me so hard? You knocked me clean out so I never got to see what actually happened. I only know 'cos of what the police told me when I came round. Those two sewer rats were already in handcuffs by then, being carted away while protesting their innocence. Mind you, at least I got to witness that. I had a hard job not to start laughing. God knows, they're guilty of worse than what the police just collared them for. I've made me statement, saying I've no idea who knocked me out and tied me up as I was busy doing me books. I heard a noise, got up to see what it was, and the next I knew a policeman was asking me how I was. The hospital thought I'd a broken jaw but it's not, thank God, it just bloody hurts,' he said, gingerly touching it. 'Anyway, any chance of a drop of my own whisky to dull the pain?'

Madge stared at him, mortified. 'Oh, I hope yer don't mind that I helped meself, but I was desperate for one? And I thought after what she'd been through, Dee could definitely do with some too. And I'm sorry about your jaw,' she added sincerely. 'I didn't mean to hit you so hard, but I was worried the Monkses would arrive before we was ready for them.' She jumped up from the table. 'I'll get you a glass.' She looked at Calum, standing by the kitchen door. 'What about you, love?'

'I'm fine, thank you, Madge. You just see to Bernie.' He walked over and sat himself down on the chair she had just vacated, fixing his eyes on Dee. 'I'm . . . er . . . well, I'm sorry I shouted at you at the door this morning, I was just so angry at what they'd done to you.'

She put her hand on his. 'First, I must thank you for what you did towards getting me out of there. But Calum, it's me that should be sorry for finishing our relationship like I did. I'm so sorry if I hurt you in any way. I didn't want to, really I didn't, but at the time I thought I wouldn't be around to carry on with it. I didn't lie to you about that. I thought I would be leaving the next day. You see . . .'

'Explanations can wait for now, Dee. What I need to know is, did you really mean you didn't want to finish with me?'

She nodded. 'Yes, I did.'

He eyed her hopefully. 'So there's a chance for us still?'

She nodded. 'As far as I'm concerned, there is. I'd like to think so. I felt . . . well, I felt we had the makings of something very special between us.'

'Oh, Dee, so did I. Look, I can't offer you much but I don't intend to be an assistant in a café forever . . .'

She pressed her fingers to his lips. 'I have even less to offer you. At least you have a job and somewhere to live. But we have ourselves to offer, haven't we?'

He threw his arms around her then and gathered her to him. His lips sought hers and they kissed long and deep.

Over on the other side of the room, watching Calum and Dee with keen interest while taking a sip of his whisky, Bernie said to Madge, 'Young love, eh?' Then he fixed his eyes on her. 'So has Dee told you yet how those two low-lifes blackmailed her into working for them?'

She nodded. 'They threatened to harm me if she didn't.'

'Those men don't belong to the human race,' he hissed. 'Dee really must care for you, to have gone along with it. I know I haven't known you long, but I can see why she would. You come across as a good woman, Madge. So . . . er . . . still off to Earl Shilton?'

She shrugged. 'I was planning to 'cos I'm fed up where I am. Can't wait to get out, in fact.' She looked at him coyly. 'But now those two are well and truly out of the way and I don't have to get Dee out of Leicester, I might reconsider me plans.'

Bernie cast a look in Dee's direction before looking back at Madge. 'Don't look to me like Dee will want to go far from here, and I wouldn't have thought you'd want to be too far from her so as to keep a motherly eye on her.' He said casually, 'Thought of moving round here?'

Madge shrugged again. 'Never crossed me mind. I could think about it, I suppose. It seems as good an area as any.' She looked coyly at him again. 'People seem nice enough.' She took a sip of her own drink before adding, 'I could have a look around, see if any jobs are going that'd suit me, take it from there.'

'Well, I know this area well, what sort of work would you be looking for?'

'Oh, barmaid, that sort of thing.'

'Well, actually, I know the landlords of a couple of pubs close by and could put in a good word for you. In fact, I know the Humberstone happens to be short of staff just now. The land-lord there would take you on at my recommendation. And . . . er . . . I suspect that Calum, being the man he is, won't be working for me that much longer so I'll have a vacancy here soon, if you'd be interested? There are always reasonable places to rent around here too.'

Her heart leapt. If Bernie could help her get fixed up with a job, then from this moment on she'd never have to return to being the old Madge again. 'Do yer think we could go and see the landlords now? Well, I mean, there's no time like the present, is there?' she urged.

'No, there isn't. I'd be glad to take you. Just let me finish me drink.' Then he looked at her enquiringly. 'So . . . if yer thinking of living around here, maybe me and you could get together for a night out soon. I could introduce you to a few people, help you settle in.'

'Mmm, yes, that would be nice.' Madge looked a bit bothered, though. She was aware that he liked her, had designs on her, and he seemed really nice, the sort of man she could get to like a lot. Just the type she'd always hoped might materialise for her, though she'd long ago stopped believing he ever would. She suddenly didn't think it would be right of her to let him become keen on her without knowing the truth about her occupation – well, hopefully, her former occupation now. And then it would be up to him whether he pursued matters or not, and she'd not have to live with the worry that one day it would all come to light somehow. A clean slate, so to speak. 'Bernie . . . look . . . before we go any further, there's something about my past you need to know.'

He pressed his fingers to her lips. 'Madge, no one gets to our age without having a past. If you have a big enough heart to forgive mine, and I know you know what that was, then I can certainly find it within meself to forgive yours, 'cos at the end of the day we all have to do what we have to do. I hope that makes sense to you, but I know what I mean.' He drained his glass and put it in the sink then placed both his hands on her shoulders and looked deep into her eyes. 'It's what we are right this minute that matters, ain't it? And what I see before me is a lovely woman. Not bad-looking either. A woman that'll suit me fine if she'll give me the chance to prove it to her.'

She took his hands off her shoulders and hooked one arm through his, smiling broadly up at him. 'You was taking me to the pub to see about a job, wasn't you?' She glanced back at Dee and Calum, still wrapped in each other's arms. 'We'll be back before they notice we've gone. Come on.'